CONFESSIONS OF A LAPDANCER

The author is living proof that variety is the spice of life! After a childhood in which her parents took scant interest in her love of dance and persuaded her, against her instincts, into a career in the City, she found an outlet for her natural performing flair in karaoke bars and night clubs. She is fascinated by the stripping industry and has befriended a number of women who work in it. Knowing that her career as a merchant banker is unlikely to reach the glass table top, let alone the glass ceiling, she decided to tell the story of maintaining two very different lifestyles. She firmly believes in keeping all options open . . .

ANONYMOUS

Confessions of a Lapdancer

AVON

AVON
A division of HarperCollins*Publishers*
77–85 Fulham Palace Road,
London W6 8JB

www.harpercollins.co.uk

This Paperback Edition 2012

1

ISBN-13: 978-0-00751-383-3

Printed and bound in Great Britain by
Clays Ltd, St Ives plc

MIX
Paper from
responsible sources
FSC® C007454

FSC™ is a non-profit international organisation established to promote
the responsible management of the world's forests. Products carrying the
FSC label are independently certified to assure consumers that they come
from forests that are managed to meet the social, economic and
ecological needs of present and future generations,
and other controlled sources.

Find out more about HarperCollins and the environment at
www.harpercollins.co.uk/green

With special thanks to Beverley Glick

Prologue

'No physical contact. No fraternising. No wandering about. No extras.' Jackie reviews the rules while Suzy sips champagne and I strip out of my business suit. 'We are wheels up in two hours, no exceptions. Once our limousine pulls clear of the security gates, we were never there.'

'Very James Bond,' I say, contorting to remove my bespoke silk suit. Thank God for tinted windows, or the commuters on Regent Street would be getting an eyeful.

'More like Pussy Galore,' Suzy retorts, refilling her glass with more bubbly.

I don't normally work Tuesdays but Jackie practically begged – and Jackie doesn't beg. I planned to pull an all-nighter at the office until I got her call on my mobile. Daryll expects my investment analysis with recommendations on his desk by Thursday morning. But I don't often get the chance to make £1,000 for a few hours' work.

I slipped out while the rest of the team went to reward themselves at the local Corney & Barrow. Daryll's got a big client and we are all working our balls off to develop a kick-ass portfolio. I'm the only one on

1

the team who doesn't even technically have balls, which makes life more difficult, but ultimately more interesting. It used to be that my job in the city paid the bills and my night job helped with extras – like Zeus, my stallion, and a stable in Sussex. But lately it feels like the other way around.

Jackie said our engagement is strictly black tie. That means no latex or vinyl or any other kinky fantasy shit. Suzy's best in the leather so I get to play the belle of the ball. Jackie unzips the garment bag. She's loaning me one of the Pearl's best gowns. I refuse to risk cum stains on the new Christian Dior strapless number I bought as a little bonus. I might as well give myself one since those tightwads at Sloane Brothers save the big bucks for the blokes.

I slip out of my bra and knickers: unsightly panty lines would spoil the flow of the crepe-backed satin. A few months ago I was a buttoned-up investment banker who barely exposed her wrists in public. Now I'm stark naked in the back of a limo sent by some European ambassador. Limos ooze sex. Long moving phalluses. Dark windows. Once I almost fucked the son of a sheikh in the back of a limo. I love fucking while in motion – cars, airplanes, motorcycles, double-decker buses. But that's on my private time. Tonight it's strictly cum dancing.

Jackie hands me a scarlet Vera Wang, with a plunging neckline and a side slit that almost meet. I wiggle into the gown.

'Have I ever told you what nice tits you have?' Suzy slurs.

'You're just buttering me up for some girl-on-girl action, you slut,' I say, and flick my lacy black thong at her.

'That's enough,' Jackie says, smoothing her long brown hair. She may be ten years my senior, but she's got a rock-hard ass and tits that would make any 16-year-old bloke stand to attention. 'We're almost there.'

She hands me my wig. I exchange my short black spiky locks for shoulder-length auburn curls and transform from Geraldine Carson, investment banker, into Ginger, high-class lap dancer.

I can only imagine what you're thinking, but please don't judge me. I'm just a modern woman trying to make her way in a man's world.

You think you're different; it's different.

Really?

Don't kid yourself; it's still a man's world. Men still make more money for the same work. Hold more management positions and own more property than women. But it doesn't mean they hold the power. Spend one night with me at the Pearl and I'll show you who's in control. You stand up in front of a few hundred sweaty men, whose cocks are so tense you can practically see their flies bursting, and tell me you don't feel powerful. That sexual tension is intoxicating.

And, to be honest, investment banking isn't all that different from lap dancing. It's all about knowing your client and developing the right package. Revealing and withholding. It's the same dance with a different audience.

Sometimes everyone walks away satisfied. Sometimes you get fucked and other times you do the fucking.

The ambassador's private secretary meets our limo at the back of the embassy. He opens the door and lowers his gaze. In my stilettos, I'm a full head taller than he is. He offers his hand and helps me across the gravel. He has an oily olive complexion and smells of garlic. He is used to being invisible. He ushers us in the back door through the kitchen and into the embassy's study. The staff has been dismissed early and the embassy is eerily quiet. He shows us into an oak-panelled study. I imagine two dignitaries exchanging state secrets over a civilised snifter of brandy – not two fit women lap dancing.

When the ambassador enters with his entourage, he sits in the leather wing-back chair Jackie has positioned in front of the Victorian desk. Everyone but his private secretary and his bodyguard exits. The bodyguard closes the velvet blue-fringed drapes and dims the lights. He positions himself by the only door, a solid wooden number built to withstand a military invasion. Jackie has a whispered conversation with the secretary. Are his rimless spectacles fogging up? She is reviewing the rules and, if I know Jackie, giving the arrogant prick a tantalising taste of what's to come. She's here to make sure her girls are treated properly – and to dance if the ambassador fancies a more experienced pussy.

While Suzy flips out her compact and puts the final touches on her Marilyn Monroe look – matte red lipstick, a beauty mark on her left cheek and a little eyeliner to create her trademark cat eyes – Jackie pulls me aside.

4

'Slight problem,' she says, giving me her sweetest smile and batting her eyes at the ambassador. I'm sure that's gotten her what she wants over the years. 'The ambassador doesn't like redheads.'

'So you dance,' I say, relaxing a little.

'He likes the look of you.' She pulls me closer; she's squeezing my arm.

'But I'm a redhead,' I say through clenched teeth and jerk my arm free. She knows I don't dance without the wig. I don't dance as Geri.

'God, Geri, do it for me, just this once. Don't be such a bloody ice princess and help a sister out.'

Now we're sisters? She thinks of herself as the designated fairy godmother for the dancers at the Pearl, but she's more like the prison matron.

'It's only for three foreigners – two of whom I'm not even sure speak English,' she pleads.

'For an extra two hundred,' I say, and loop a finger through one of my curls.

'You drive a hard bargain.' She smacks me on the ass.

Damn. She agreed too quickly which means I should have asked for more.

'You remind me of me,' she adds.

I don't know whether to be flattered or offended. I slip the wig off and hand it to her. I ruffle my short hair. Jackie plucks at a few strands on top and I smooth the sides. Suddenly I feel naked.

Suzy dances first. She's the better warm-up act and will most likely be stumbling drunk by the end of the evening. Jackie turns a blind eye because Suzy has danced at the Pearl for years. She's everyone's big sister and drunken aunt all mixed into one. But she knows how to keep her legs open and her mouth shut.

I lurk at the back of the room. I like to build an air of mystery. I finger the dusty volumes on the bookshelf. The ambassador watches Suzy's routine but he glances at me every so often. I look away and play the shy coquette. My show starts before I even take centre stage. Jackie has taught me well.

Suzy slinks off and drapes herself around the secretary who is responsible for keeping the champagne flowing. He shrugs her off, afraid, I'm sure, of her sweat staining his best suit. I nod at Jackie and Tina Turner blares from the Bose portable sound system – Jackie's most recent investment after her old boom box died at a high roller's boardroom party.

I start off slow and keep it simple. I stretch my legs and show him what he's paid for. I let him unzip me; that's about the closest he'll get to touching me for the rest of the night. Jackie cranks up the music and shifts to Joan Jett and the Blackhearts' 'I Hate Myself for Loving You'. After years of practice, Jackie knows how to read the mood of a room. She's taught me how to synchronise the music and my movement to ratchet up a client's sexual tension. Tease them. Draw them in and then push them away. Let their libido rise and fall. Make their pulses pound with the beat and their cocks beg for more.

One look at the ambassador's rosy cheeks and his sweaty brow and I know it's already working. I waste no time. I slink out of the gown and let it pool at my feet. I step one spiked fire-engine-red stiletto free and then the other. It's easy to let little moves like this wreck the illusion. Every movement must be fluid. Tripping over discarded clothes or a sticky zipper can lose the momentum you've painstakingly built.

I melt to the floor and crawl towards him. I claw the oriental carpet as I pull myself closer and closer. I can feel his body tense. He is already gripping the chair so tightly his knuckles are white. I pull myself upright and give him a good, long look at my hairless pussy. I slide one finger between my pussy lips and dip it inside me. The ambassador's not the only hot and horny one.

He uncrosses his legs and pins them together. There's the tell-tale sign – the cock rub, a quick adjustment when the strain gets too much. His eyelids are half closed as his whole world shrinks to the head of his penis. I straddle him, feeling my thigh muscles strain to hold my gyrating form inches from his dick.

He's gritting his teeth. His back involuntarily arches. I hover lower and brush his cock ever so slightly. He'll be wondering if he imagined it. He wants to grab my hips and ram his cock inside of me. He'd hand over the keys to the kingdom if I'd ask. He'd whisper state secrets and sell his youngest son right about now, if only I'd unzip his trousers and lower myself on to him.

Sometimes I try to make clients cum in their pants. I like watching how their faces contort with orgasm and then slowly morph into pink-cheeked embarrassment. But no party tricks tonight.

I turn it back a notch. I strut away. I cross my legs as if I'm about to spin around. I flick a quick look over my shoulder. I've still got him where I want him. He's squirming in his chair. I bend over slowly, running my hands down my sweaty legs, pausing at my ankles – the naughty schoolgirl begging to be spanked. He's leaning forward, willing my legs to part. He wants to see my soft glistening pussy.

Not yet. Be patient. I slide back to standing and strike a strong pose – legs wide, inviting. I twist around and wink then bend over again, this time exposing myself to him. He actually moans. A sly smile tugs at the corner of my mouth. I take my time swaying back and forth as I stand up again.

I turn to face him. I grip my thighs and drag my long, red nails along my lilywhite skin. I cup my breasts, not like most men do, not as if I'm grabbing a pint of beer. I hold them as if they are bubbles ready to pop with the lightest touch. I tense each nipple between my fingers and then draw them up towards my mouth. I flick my tongue over each nipple and eye him as if to say *you wish it was you*. But it's me. I'm catching each wave of pleasure that courses through my body. The ambassador's merely along for the ride.

The music rises and the beat quickens. I move faster, frantic. Now I'm an animal barely restrained. Sweat sprays from my body with every movement. The music shifts gears and everything but the bass falls away. On the final beat, I stop and pose. My chest rises and falls as I catch my breath.

For the finale, a little Def Leppard, 'Pour Some Sugar on Me'. I stride over to him, a model on a catwalk. His eyes are insistent and demanding. I hold his gaze. I tease his legs apart with the pointy toe of my shoe. I rest my foot on the chair with the toe of my shoe gently caressing his crotch. I lunge forward. I hold my breasts close to his face. I brush my nipples across his rough, dry lips. The tip of his tongue flicks my nipple as I pull away and I cross my arms tight across my chest. I bend over him slowly and lick my lips as if I might kiss him, but I snap away at the last minute. He groans and his eyes roll to the back of his head. My work here is done.

I freshen up in the toilet while Jackie collects the payment from his secretary and the bodyguard helps Suzy to the limo. I wonder if he will try to feel her up in her compromised state. I should go out there to make sure she's OK.

The gown is a bit wrinkled now, but otherwise I'm no worse for wear. Normally the wig and borrowed costumes make it easy to believe that this person isn't Geri Carson. Ginger really lives a parallel life. But now without the wig, my reflection in the bathroom mirror makes me uncomfortable. I've blurred the line.

There's a knock on the door. 'Coming,' I say, and laugh to myself.

When I open the door, the ambassador is looming large in the archway. He is handsome for a near senior citizen. I find his greying temples sexy. It's the round belly and the hairy knuckles that turn me off. I notice his gold wedding band and wonder where his respectable wife is. Is she upstairs sleeping? Will she have to satisfy the urges that I'd teased to the surface?

'I would like to take you to bed,' he says.

I smile. This is the tricky part. Turn them down yet still make them repeat customers.

'I will pay.'

I slip past him. I don't want to be trapped in the bathroom. 'What a very flattering offer, but I really can't.'

He catches up to me and pins me against the wall. His stomach keeps us a good few inches apart. 'I like you.'

'With all due respect,' I start, and quickly realise that the respect he is due is nil, 'you don't know me.'

'But I would like to,' he says, stroking my arms with his fleshy palms.

I shiver. 'Listen, Mr Ambassador, you can't afford me.' I side step free and walk away.

I pause. He did have a nice smile.

'Name your price.'

And with that I'm gone.

I race off to find Jackie but the study is empty. It's dark and looks like a library again. The books and leather seem to have absorbed the sexuality from earlier. I walk to the centre of the room and slowly spin around. I'd like to have a home like this some day, minus the lap dancers and toady private secretary.

That's when I notice it – a tiny red light blinking in one corner near the ceiling. A camera. Our entire performance was captured on film. I feel more exposed than I have ever been at the club.

I run out to the limo, losing one shoe like Cinderella on the way, but I'm too panicked to care. I grab Jackie by the collar and spin her around as she's ducking into the limo. 'You knew, didn't you?' I'm screaming at her. I push her against the car.

'What the hell?' Jackie shoves me off and looks around. 'What are you doing? Trying to wake the neighbours and blow our chance for a repeat performance?'

'A repeat performance? He simply has to press rewind and play any time he wants.' I'm poking my finger into the centre of her chest.

'What in the hell are you talking about?' She grabs me by the shoulders. 'And it better be good because no one talks to me like this.'

'They filmed us. The room is wired like a fucking movie set.' I kick off my other shoe.

'They *what*?' Her cheeks flush. She looks up at a light in a second-floor window, probably a bedroom, where the ambassador is already more than likely wanking off watching the video replay. 'I expressly told them no filming. Filming's extra.' She turns to me. 'I would never let them film without your permission.' She looks me in the eyes. 'You believe me, don't you?'

I want to but I shrug.

She grabs my stiletto and hurls it at the lit window. 'Bastards,' she screams. She takes off towards the embassy in time to see the bodyguard slam the door shut. I can hear the deadbolt clank. We aren't getting back in there tonight. 'I swear to you, Geri, we'll get that tape. No one fucks me about like this.'

Maybe I've spoken too soon. Maybe I'm in over my head. All I need is for that video to end up on YouTube and life as I know it is over. I can already see the headline:

11

Investment Banker by Day, Stripper by Night. I've worked too hard to climb the corporate ladder and tap that glass ceiling to see it wiped away by one stupid mistake.

How could I have let this happen?

Chapter One

Two months earlier

It was my first day back in the London office after a bumpy transatlantic flight and I didn't have the stomach for a fight. I crossed my fingers and hoped my guardian angel would get through the next twelve hours unscathed.

What annoyed me most was that I'd had no time to get the inside track on Sloane Brothers' latest golden boy, Luke Cotterill, apart from the fact that he had quickly established himself as a smart, smooth operator who worked hard and played even harder. Being on secondment in New York for six weeks had left me out of the loop, and out of the loop was not a place I liked to be.

However, there were some small mercies – the weak dollar had provided me with a new wardrobe of beautifully tailored trouser suits that I'd picked up at Saks Fifth Avenue, so it was with an extra swagger in my step and wearing black Armani that I approached the company's HQ that morning. Another bonus had been the amount of horny NY investment bankers, one of whom I ended up fucking on the walnut desk of his Wall Street office.

I was prepared to meet the new PA who had been recruited in my absence but there was no sign of her as I strode towards my glass box on the third floor. The fact that I'd recently been given my own office had ruffled some feathers on the team, but I'd insisted on it, given my seniority in Mergers and Acquisitions.

Most of the guys had their noses buried in the *FT* when I arrived but were suspiciously quiet. They didn't usually pass up the opportunity to make a fatuous remark. Then I noticed that my office door was open and a man with a shock of ruffled blond hair was sitting in my chair with his back to me.

'Can I help you?' I asked in my best clipped voice.

The chair swung round. 'Do I have to get up before you sit down?' the occupant replied.

I felt myself boiling up inside but betrayed nothing.

'Ah, Mr Cotterill I presume? Is that your way of greeting a senior colleague? How unusual . . .'

'The famous Miss Carson, if I'm not mistaken,' he replied without flinching. 'Thought I would form a one-man welcoming party and warm your seat, so to speak.'

'I usually have trespassers evicted but I'll let it pass on this occasion,' I told him, the false teasing note in my voice not fooling either one of us. 'Now if you don't mind, I have a lot of catching up to do.'

'I've heard a lot about you,' he continued, regardless. I look forward to working you . . . I mean working *with* you . . .'

'Look, Luke, I'm sure we will be having a briefing

session soon so please can you leave my office now so I can prepare for it?' I snapped.

'Ooh, I already love it when you're angry,' he said, grinning at me. 'I look forward to receiving further lashes of your tongue.'

'I don't want to get off on the wrong foot with you,' I told him. 'So I'd advise you to focus less on my tongue and more on keeping a civil tongue in your head.'

'No need to be so buttoned-up, Geri,' he said. 'You'll find out I'm a laid-back kind of guy really. I like to get laid back at my place . . .'

'Right, out of my office, now!' I ordered, still keeping that headmistress tone, like this was all *Carry On* and nothing to get worked up about, while tipping him forward out of my chair, 'and it's Geraldine to you.'

'You're no fun,' he said, reluctantly getting up and walking towards the door. 'I'm just having a little joke with you.'

'Well, Luke, I can share a good joke with the best of them,' I said. 'Let's just hope we share the same work ethic.'

'I'm not afraid to burn the midnight oil, Geri,' he said, ignoring my request to address me by my full name, 'as you will no doubt discover. See you later, Miss Sourpuss.'

And with that, Luke Cotterill moved his wise ass out of my space and back into his domain.

I closed the door behind him and felt like fumigating the place. I was rattled by his rudeness but I knew he wanted to provoke a reaction in me.

It didn't help that he was tall and lean as an Olympic rower, with the good looks to go with the physique.

15

And boy did he know it. He was clearly accustomed to women falling for his charms on a regular basis. This one was a dangerous beast, and I could not afford to give him the slightest ammunition.

Just as I was pondering how to deal with him, a young woman with long red hair came to sit down at the desk outside my office. So this was my new PA, Tania Peck.

I scrutinised her for a good few minutes. She had a great body, with legs up to her armpits and a ballet dancer's posture that thrust her boobs out in front of her like heat-seeking missiles.

Everything about her shrieked 'Look at me, boys!' and I guessed it had been Daryll Sidebottom's idea to hire her, probably to 'cheer up the office' or some such nonsense, but there was no point in arguing with the head of the investment team.

It pissed me off that she was flaunting herself in such an obvious way. I had the seemingly unpopular idea that hard work, intelligence and talent might actually get you places, so I had always been careful to cover myself up.

I felt like giving Tania a good talking-to but knew I'd be wasting my time. She was only 20, and she wouldn't listen to a 28-year-old like me.

My face was a studied mask of indifference when she stood up and walked into my office, proffering her hand.

'Miss Carson, it's really nice to meet you at last. I hope you had a fun stay in New York,' she said, speaking in an accent that was pure Sarf London, flashing a set of perfect white teeth.

'Yes, it was a valuable experience,' I told her, making eye contact but not accepting the handshake. 'And please, call me Geri.'

'OK, thanks Geri,' she replied sweetly, flicking her long, flowing red hair off her face. 'Give me a shout when you want to go through your correspondence.'

I nodded and closed my office door, making sure she realised I wanted a boundary between us. She was being too nice – a sure sign of a hidden agenda.

I sat down to check my emails and at the top of my inbox was a message from Ryan Buxton, the best-looking guy on the team and also my occasional fuck buddy.

Now please don't pre-judge me. The 'work hard, play hard' adage didn't really apply at Sloane Brothers. It was *all* work. My social life consisted of keeping up with college friends via facebook. I ate, breathed and dreamed the job. Had done for four years now. That was my world. Ryan was good for a no-strings shag when the fancy took me.

In the subject line were the words: *Watch out, there's a mole about!* I opened it up and read the contents:

Welcome back, Geri – see you've met your hot new PA! Don't be fooled by that cute exterior, she's a smart cookie. Guess who she's shagging? Only Luke Cotterill!

I rolled my eyes in disbelief. Tania probably thought it was a great career move; I thought it was career suicide.

In six short weeks, Luke had managed to put his alpha male stamp in every corner of the company like a dog marking its territory.

Luke had also sent me an email.

Guess you've heard the big horizontal merger has just gone through. Are we hot or what? Well, I am anyway!

Of course I knew about the deal; I'd been an integral part of the team that pulled it off for the company. I didn't dignify his email with a response and spent a few moments quietly observing Tania before calling her in.

'OK, here are a few ground rules,' I said. 'First, everything that passes between us in this office is confidential. Second, I expect you to show some initiative, but not to put anything into action unless I've approved it first. Understood?'

'Oh, of course, Geri. Deffo,' she replied, without a crack appearing in her smile.

Looking beyond Tania I could see that Luke was gathering some of the team around him.

I walked out into the main office to drop a document on a colleague's desk. As I did, Luke made sure I heard him inviting the guys – or 'the Brothers', as he insisted on calling them – out to celebrate the big merger deal. I wasn't having that, obviously, and went to have a quiet word with him.

'Luke, I don't care if the Sisters are not officially invited, I'm not missing out on this Brothers' party,' I said. 'I had as much to do with this deal as anyone else.'

'Ahh, it's Geri Boy,' he sneered, loudly enough so that half the office could hear him. 'She who wears the trousers and wants to be one of the lads.'

'As I said before, it's Geraldine to you,' I said, grinning at the other guys on the team. 'The first Jeroboam is on me, OK?'

'Ooh, that's a big bottle for a little lady,' laughed Luke, surrounded by giggling cronies. 'Will you need a man to help you with that?'

I bit my lip while trying to think of a decent comeback but thought better of it and marched purposefully back to my office. Tania was blocking the doorway. Was that a sympathetic smile or a smirk on her face? I couldn't be bothered to work it out.

'Tania, if you've got something to say, then say it.'

'Oh Geri, don't let them get to you,' she said. 'I'm coming tonight as well, we'll have some fun, you'll see.'

'Right, fine,' I said, incensed that Luke had invited her and not me. I'd only been out of the office for six weeks but I felt like I'd already lost my place in the team. 'You'd better be prepared to buy your round, though.' I immediately regretted that – there was no way a legal PA would be able to keep up with the spending.

I asked her to phone ahead to Corney & Barrow to make sure they were well stocked with Bollinger and Krug before the Sloane Brothers' wrecking crew arrived, and went back to work.

The rest of the day passed without much incident, with Luke postponing our briefing meeting, apparently in a gesture of kindness to let me properly recover from jet lag, but I guessed he was doing it as some kind of power play.

As the sun went down, I went to the ladies to prepare myself for the night ahead.

I'd always thought of myself as handsome rather than pretty and preferred short hair to long, but even I had to admit my spiky, jet-black cut – inspired by early

Siouxsie Sioux, I liked to think – was quite a strong statement.

I didn't wear much make-up at the office but for the evenings I liked to emphasise my pale skin and blue eyes by wearing deep crimson lipstick, black mascara and liquid eye liner.

I always wore my armour, though – a trusty black trouser suit worn with a polo neck or a shirt. Even wearing a skirt at work made guys like Luke think I was weak.

Tania came in.

'Geri, sorry to interrupt, but the guys are ready to leave and we don't want to be left behind, do we?' she said.

'OK, Tania, I'll be ready in a mo,' I told her.

After a good five minutes, I joined the male members of staff by the front entrance. Luke leered at Tania while I made eye contact with Ryan. He was a little too rugby club for my liking but served a purpose on the nights I felt horny.

At least Daryll was a man who knew his own mind. As our boss, he walked around the office with a proprietorial air that I found patronising, and he never attempted to curb the offensive locker-room banter indulged in by the guys, but I did respect his knowledge and experience.

'Daryll, how good of us to join you,' I said, cheekily.

'Very droll, Geraldine,' he replied in his deep, Leslie Phillips-esque drawl. 'I believe the first bottle will be on your account? And I trust I will not be seeing it on your expenses.'

'Of course not, Daryll,' I laughed. 'I wouldn't *dream*

of fleecing Sloane Brothers out of their hard-earned cash. Even though I've earned most of it for them.'

He smiled lasciviously.

'You have the cheek of the devil, young lady,' he winked, 'but I admire you for it.'

I winked back before exiting the office with Tania in tow, leaving the boys to make their own way to the bar.

Luke and his posse were right behind me though as I calmly strolled into Corney & Barrow and before I knew it he was reaching his long arm over me in an attempt to grab the neck of the £200 Jeroboam that Tania was holding, like an eager puppy, ready to please.

'No, Luke. This baby's mine,' I said firmly.

'So you like them big, do you, Geri Boy?' he taunted. 'Well, let's see whether you can make it shoot!'

Ryan, who had zero loyalty to me despite our 'relationship', laughed right on cue, leaving me to work on removing the cork. I wedged the bottle between my toned thighs and gradually worked it loose, hearing that reassuring pop as Tania was poised with a flute to catch any overspill.

'Oh, good show,' said Luke. 'Hardly a drop wasted!'

I ignored him, instructing Tania to fill the glasses as I tested my muscle strength by gradually tipping the bottle until it was empty.

'Wow, Geri, I'm impressed!' said Tania. 'Where did you get thighs like that?'

'I'm an experienced show jumper,' I replied, enjoying the look of surprise on her face.

'Really?' she said. 'How did you get into that?'

'Through Daryll, four years ago,' I told her. 'He's always

kept horses and he suggested I take lessons. Once I started, I found I had a natural talent for it. I'd recommend it to any woman – it exercises muscles you didn't know you had and gives you great posture.'

'Well, Geri – you are a dark horse, if you'll pardon the pun,' she giggled.

I laughed politely but inside I felt uncomfortable. I hoped she'd never find out that I only started working with horses in order to keep in with Daryll and advance my career.

'Geri, are you OK?' asked Tania, who could see I was drifting off.

'Yes, I'm fine,' I replied. 'Just thinking about Zeus, my gorgeous bay stallion.'

'What, you *own* a horse?' said Tania, her eyes widening.

'Yes, he's 16.2 hands, part thoroughbred, part warm blood,' I said. 'I keep him at a stable near my parents' house in Sussex.'

'God, that can't be cheap,' Tania remarked.

'No, but he's a beauty and worth every penny,' I said. 'Now, if you'll excuse me, I must go and talk to my boss.'

Tania gawped at me. *Jesus, Geraldine*, I thought to myself. *Don't forget, this girl is Luke Cotterill's piece of totty. Zip it . . .*

Aside from my flings with Ryan, I didn't like to mix business with pleasure too much.

Chapter Two

The celebration at Corney & Barrow proceeded in the usual fashion, with obscene amounts of champagne being bought and consumed and the boys becoming louder and more annoying with every bottle.

I managed to keep pace with them by sipping water each time I took a mouthful of fizz so I didn't get totally pissed. At least they couldn't accuse me of being a light-weight.

As the barman called last orders, Luke gathered the guys around him and called for silence.

'So, Brothers – the fun has only just begun!' he slurred. 'You're all coming with me to a sexy little place I know called the Pearl, where we'll get down to the *serious* business of celebrating.'

'What's the Pearl?' I asked Tania, thinking it was some after-hours drinking den.

'Oh, it's a lap-dancing club,' she replied, casually.

'Bloody typical,' I said. 'He's probably just trying to piss me off.'

Tania looked at me blankly and said, 'Oh, right. Well, actually it was my idea, not Luke's.'

Before I had a chance to find out how the hell Tania knew about a lap-dancing club, Luke had come over to pat her on the behind.

'Coming then, sweetheart?' he said to Tania, but looking directly at me. Under normal circumstances, I wouldn't have been caught dead in a strip club. I hated those sorts of places. They were nothing but exploitation. But I couldn't ignore the flagrant challenge in Luke's eyes.

'Oh no, Mr Cotterill, you're not getting away with this,' I said. 'You're not leaving me off the guest list.'

'You'll just spoil our fun, Geri Boy,' he said.

'I insist,' I said.

'Well, I guess my hot little babe here might need some company while I'm otherwise engaged,' he continued. 'But you'd better not spoil the party.'

Quite why Tania couldn't see that Luke was using her as arm candy, I had no idea, but there was no point in me tackling her about it as she probably would've thought I was jealous. Far from it.

How the fuck could Daryll condone all of this? But perhaps it wasn't a surprise. However urbane, he was a bit of an old lech himself. I felt he'd thrown me to the wolves by not preparing me for Luke's relentless barrage of snide comments but then I had to remember what he'd told me when I joined Sloane Brothers: 'If you want to play with the big boys, Geraldine, you have to beat them at their own game.' Was Daryll checking to see if I was capable of that?

I followed Tania and Luke out of the bar to be greeted by a white stretch limo. Luke had hired it to ferry the Brothers to the club, which I found utterly laughable.

'Want a ride in my pimp mobile?' he asked.

'I'll make my own way, thanks, Luke,' I laughed. 'If I'd wanted to look like a chav on a stag night I would have worn Burberry and plenty of bling.'

And with that I hopped straight into a black cab, most satisfied that I'd got one over on the arrogant bastard right in front of his boss. If Daryll wanted me and Luke to be at each other's throats, then he was getting just that.

By the time the Brothers' stretch had pulled up outside the Pearl, my taxi had already dropped me off and I had made friends with the club's two enormous doormen.

I watched in disgust as Luke fell out of the limo clutching a half-empty champagne glass and staggered towards the entrance to the Pearl dragging Tania behind him like a blow-up doll.

The two bouncers on the door blocked his path, while he stood waving a bunch of crumpled tenners in their faces.

I winked to let them know this was the party of pissed-up City boys I had the misfortune to be with, and handed one a crisp £50 note. And with that we were in.

'As you say, Luke, I always wear the trousers so put your money away,' I said. 'No need to bribe security. Use it to buy me some very expensive cocktails.'

'What about some very expensive cock, Miss Carson?' he shot back. A comment he would never have dared make sober or in the office. 'Although mine's out of your price range.'

Tania stood next to him toying nervously with her long, red hair.

'Hilarious,' I replied, moving through the club's entrance. 'Just get inside, I can't wait to see an animal in its natural habitat.'

The remainder of the investment team spilled out on to the pavement slightly the worse for wear. Even Daryll looked less dapper than usual, the handkerchief that matched his shirt sitting slightly askew in his jacket pocket.

Then Ryan Buxton came bounding towards me like an overgrown puppy, all ruddy cheeks and rugger-bugger enthusiasm.

'So, Geri, are you up for this?' Ryan asked.

'I'm not missing this one for the world,' I told him, avoiding the arm he was trying to put around me.

'I thought you hated places like this, though. You always tell me how sexist they are.'

'I'm not a big fan, no,' I told him, 'but I don't get to see the Brothers at play too often and I was as much a part of pulling off this merger as anyone else.'

'You're not wrong there, darling,' he said, nuzzling my neck while no one else was looking. 'Come in and join the fun, then.'

The interior of the club was surprisingly plush if clichéd in its style, with padded red and black leather booths, mirrored walls and mirror balls, with four or five dancing poles arranged on different levels, some with tables around them.

A petite brunette with enhanced breasts jiggling in her bikini brushed past me on her way to the stage and I flinched. What the hell was I doing in a lap-dancing club?

The things I did to advance my career . . .

Our bonuses were being announced the next day and my colleagues were discussing figures in voices loud enough for everyone to hear how loaded they were and how much more loaded they expected to be within twenty-four hours.

'How pathetic,' I said to Tania, who had momentarily been abandoned. 'It's all big cars, big bonuses and big dicks to them – except they probably have tiddlers!'

Tania laughed politely.

'Oh, I'm sure there's more to them than that, Geri. They must have some talent, after all.'

'I wouldn't bank on it, Tania,' I said. 'You haven't been my PA long enough to work that out yet.'

Tanya turned to smile at her man and I glimpsed a steeliness in her eyes.

Daryll beckoned us to join the Brothers at their large banquette.

Not long after we arrived, one of the club's dancers, a pretty girl with long, dark hair and olive skin who was dressed in a red spangled bra top and thong, approached our table and Luke beckoned her to one side.

'What's he up to?' I whispered in Tania's ear.

'Oh, he's just arranging to have a private dance.'

'Jesus, how can you sit by and let him do that? Do you have no self-respect?'

'It's not about that, Geri . . .'

I didn't want to hear any more.

'Excuse me, Daryll,' I announced. 'I can't sit here and watch this. I'm going to the bar.'

He nodded but Luke jumped up.

'What, you not man enough to hang around, Geri Boy? I knew you wouldn't last.'

Words seemed pointless so I gave him the finger and stalked off.

I went to sit on a stool at the bar and ordered a vodka and tonic. I picked out the wedge of lemon when it arrived and crushed it hard in my fist till the juice ran down my arm, wishing it was Luke's smug face.

'What did that lemon do to deserve that?' said the barman, offering me a napkin.

'Oh, nothing – I was just imagining it was someone's head,' I explained.

'Wouldn't want to get on the wrong side of you then, madam,' he grinned.

'I'm not that scary,' I said. 'Except when provoked by an idiot who thinks it's funny to call me a boy just because I wear trousers.'

'Take no notice. You look real smart to me.'

'Thanks . . . But I do feel a bit buttoned-up here and I'm supposed to be celebrating. Look at them,' I said, pointing to the Brothers. 'Allegedly the cream of investment banking. They didn't want me here being a killjoy but a strip joint is not exactly my idea of a fun night out.'

'Ah, we get a lot of City boys in here letting off steam,' he said. 'They're pretty harmless and they empty their wallets so we love 'em.'

'You try working with them, though. I wish I'd stayed in New York now.'

'Ah, I love the Big Apple,' he said. 'Worked the cocktail bars. How long were you there?'

'Six weeks, on secondment. Got back to London to find my boss had employed a Playboy bunny as my PA and she was going out with my nemesis.'

'Moral of story: don't turn your back for a minute. Want another vodka?'

'OK, go on,' I said, turning to check what the Brothers were up to. 'Can I ask you something?'

'Sure,' he said. 'Go ahead.'

'Do you think it's possible for a woman to be sexy if she never wears a skirt?'

'I love a good bottom in tight jeans. But, well, nothing like a good pair of legs.'

'I thought you might say that.' My knees haven't seen the light of day outside my bedroom since school sports day . . . I thought to myself.

But he'd already disappeared off to the other end of the bar to serve a rather irritated-looking little man and one of the dancers had mounted the adjacent podium to start her show. As I watched her spin and move expertly up and down the pole, I realised it was just as much about technique as sex appeal. These girls had to be seriously fit to do this stuff.

Then I glimpsed a tipsy but animated Tania chatting to a good-looking, dark-haired guy at the other end of the bar. As soon as she realised I'd seen her, she moved away and came up to join me.

'You don't look too happy,' she said, as if I was her best mate rather than her boss. I didn't know whether she was confident, over-friendly or just cocky.

'I just can't believe why anyone would want to spend any time in a place like this. It's for blokes too ugly or too dim to get a shag elsewhere. I don't think women should encourage it.'

'Lighten up,' said Tania. 'There's nothing wrong with using what God gave you.' She leant forward and gave a conspiratorial smile. 'I'll tell you something funny, Geri. I'm sure one of the reasons I got this job was because of my legs! I saw the way the personnel manager was looking at me so I played up to it. It's so easy to manipulate some guys.'

I stared at her in disbelief. 'Tania, why are you telling me this? I had to work damn hard to get where I am and to earn respect in this team and you come along and tell me I could have got there quicker by wearing a short skirt?'

'No, that's not what I meant . . .'

'Tania, please, just leave me alone.'

I left her at the bar and took refuge in the ladies' loo. Just like the women in the club, she flaunted herself effortlessly and that just wasn't my style. Tania Peck was a man's woman. I suppose my style could be summed up as look but don't touch.

She revealed; I concealed. It was as simple as that.

I couldn't delay my reappearance any longer, so took a deep breath and rejoined the party. My timing was poor. Luke was busy enjoying his lap dance, which he'd chosen to have in public rather than in the private booth.

It seemed to me he was getting into it a little too much as I could see him groping the dancer and it didn't take a genius to work out this was a breach of club rules.

Out of the corner of my eye I saw a couple of giant figures approaching, but before they could reach him,

Tania strode over, shooed away the dancer without a word and straddled Luke, fully clothed.

Her pneumatic frame came into its own, arching, twisting and circling over him as she ran her hands through his blond hair but moved out of reach every time he tried to grab her.

The security staff soon backed off as the mood lightened and the other guys started laughing and wolf-whistling.

But when she turned round to grind her bottom inches from his face, Luke ran his hands up under her skirt and grabbed both cheeks before slapping them.

'Bad baby,' he said. 'I'll tell you in future when I want you to dance for me. I don't want these guys getting an eyeful of what's mine.'

Tania ignored him and carried on gyrating until the end of the next track, to Luke's obvious discomfort. Then she dismounted and snatched the £50 note Luke had in his hand to place in the pro-dancer's garter.

'Thanks, Lukey baby,' she announced, 'that will pay for my cab home – alone!'

Luke's face was a picture and the Brothers were rolling in the aisles, which riled him no end. It was so good to see him being played by a girl.

'Bravo, Tania,' I clapped.

Luke saw me laughing and turned on me like a wounded beast. 'That turn you on, Geri Boy? Maybe you're more of a man than we thought!'

He clicked his fingers to summon one of the dancers – a pale honey-blonde wearing a tight red bikini top and short denim skirt.

'OK, I'll pay you £50 to do a private dance for my colleague here,' he said to her, pointing to me, 'and £50 more if you snog her afterwards, full tongues.'

'We don't kiss the customers, sir,' she replied. 'And we can't dance for a customer who doesn't give consent.'

'Jesus, you girls are no fun,' he said, his face dropping. 'How about you, Tania, why don't you dance for your boss? That would be a great way of getting to know each other, don't you think?'

'Leave Tania out of this,' I said, pulling Luke over to one side. 'I don't know if you're on some kind of bet to see how far you can wind me up, Luke, but you won't break me.'

'What makes you think I'm trying to break you? I'm just trying to have a little fun here. Women like you are all the same. You're so bloody obsessed with success that it turns you into hard-faced old boots.'

'I've had just about enough of your shit for one day,' I said. 'You've been on my case since the moment I met you and I will not tolerate you talking to me like this, especially in front of our boss.'

'Oh Christ, Carson,' he said. 'You don't get it, do you? If you can't stand the heat, get out of the kitchen. And by the way, I wouldn't fancy you if you were the last chick on the planet, you're so bloody uptight . . .'

'Fuck off, Cotterill, you know nothing about me, who I am or what I'm capable of. Just get out of my face.'

Daryll saw what was happening, from where he was standing with some of the Brothers, but did nothing. I could only conclude that Luke's juvenile behaviour had been condoned by the boys' club, as if they were putting me through some perverse kind of jousting competition to see who would be knocked off their horse first. It was all in a day's sport for them.

I had to do something that would completely floor Luke. What would wipe the smug smile off his face, short of punching him?

Suddenly I knew instinctively what to do. I strode over to Ryan, beckoning him with my index finger. He looked around, hesitating and waiting for their approval. However, he knew what side his bread – and his bed – was buttered on, so he followed me over to the dance area.

I slowly unbuckled my jacket, peeling it off and easing my black polo neck jumper over my head, revealing a skimpy black camisole over a black lace balconette bra.

Blinking under the harsh spotlight, I felt utterly exposed but I had to brazen it out. Luke had successfully upped the stakes and was standing with his arms crossed, waiting to see what I would do next. Would I stand or would I fall? There was no turning back now . . .

Chapter Three

It was time for me to put up or shut up so, in full view of my team, I bent over and unzipped my black spike-heeled boots, taking them off in as teasing a fashion as I could manage, dangling them in one hand before I let them drop to the floor.

Luke and Daryll seemed mesmerised by my breasts, as if they had convinced themselves I didn't actually have any. To be fair to them, I'd always tried my hardest to cover them up in the office.

Ryan, of course, had been allowed to enjoy them intimately on more than one occasion so he was looking very pleased with himself, as if he'd suddenly been promoted to leader of the pack.

I took a deep breath, kept my eyes on him as I carefully stepped backwards on to a podium and wrapped myself around the cold steel of the pole. First I slid my spine up and down, splaying my knees into a squatting position, before pulling myself up with my hands above my head, sashaying my hips side to side at the same time.

Remembering the dance I'd seen earlier, I hooked one leg around the pole and twisted around until I reached the floor. Just at that moment, 'Raspberry Beret', one of my favourite Prince tracks, started playing.

'Right,' I thought. 'I'll show you uptight.'

By this point I could see the bulge in Ryan's trousers, and the boys in the team whooping and cheering me on behind him.

I licked my lips as I swivelled around the pole, feeling damn grateful that I'd spent so much time on Zeus, not to mention the countless hours in the gym.

I was confident enough in my fitness and the strength of my biceps and thighs to try some of the more ambitious moves I'd seen that night, so I thought, here goes nothing, grabbed the pole at eye level and swung myself upside down, making a V-shape with my legs.

It required a lot of concentration to maintain a degree of gracefulness and sensuality; I had to make it look easy, even if it wasn't – but then I was used to doing that every day at the office.

When I looked up, Ryan was salivating and even Luke was looking vaguely impressed.

Adrenalin was pumping through my body, partly with the effort, partly with the sheer thrill of dancing in such an erotic way. I loved the feeling of power it gave me, especially seeing the effect I was having on Ryan and his idiotic pals.

Their eyes were filled with a mixture of admiration and sheer lust, which actually sent a bolt of electricity through me that seemed to heat me up and make my skin burn.

I carried on swivelling, spinning and arching my back to the music for a good five minutes and finished on an ambitious move. Bending forwards with my head near the bottom of the pole and my hands halfway up it, I levered my legs off the floor and up to the vertical, wrapping my legs around the pole and gripping with my ankles to pull myself up, grabbing the pole again with my hands and gently circling around with my legs pointed in opposite directions until I was back on the ground again.

I was operating in absolute fight-or-flight mode and would probably feel the pain later.

When I was back on my feet, I realised everyone in the bar had been watching me and not even the security guards who had been so keen to eject Luke earlier had tried to stop me.

Ryan was transfixed and the Brothers, along with the rest of the male clientele, gave me a standing ovation.

'Geri, you go girl, that's more like it!' one of the guys yelled, while Luke was pushed towards the back. I was drenched in sweat but every nerve ending in my body was tingling.

'Thanks, guys,' I said. 'I'm not making a speech, but suffice to say I had a ball.'

'Well, I think it's more that you've *got* balls, Geri,' said Tania. 'Bravo to you too.'

I wondered why they'd let a female customer get away with stripping off and using the club's equipment when I clocked a man in the top booth signalling to security to hang back. It was the same dark-haired guy that I saw Tania talking to at the bar earlier. I couldn't figure out how or why she knew him but I was so flushed with excitement I didn't care.

Gathering up my clothes, I waved to the boys and motioned to Ryan to accompany me.

I couldn't resist shooting Luke a triumphant look.

I put my top and boots back on and we hailed a taxi back to Ryan's apartment on the Isle of Dogs.

'Jesus, Geri, I mean . . . Jesus, that was fucking amazing . . . where the hell did you learn how to do that?' gasped Ryan, trying to conceal his erection.

'I guess I'm just a natural, sweetie,' I teased. 'You have to be damned athletic to pole dance and I'm practically an acrobat.'

'The guys from the office couldn't believe what they were seeing, especially Luke,' he said. 'That was just such a genius stroke to pull, but aren't you worried about what's going to happen when you go back to work tomorrow?'

'To be honest, Ryan, I couldn't give a flying fuck now,' I said. 'If women like Tania can flash their tits and still get a job, then why should I care about being one of the boys?'

'Good for you, Geri,' he said, grinning from ear to ear. 'I can't wait to find out what your new game is, babe!'

'Ryan, I'm not your babe or anyone else's,' I replied. 'Just shut up and come here.'

And with that I grabbed the back of his head and kissed him deep and hard, plunging my tongue into his mouth.

Our hands were all over each other as the taxi headed back to Ryan's place. I didn't give a shit about the driver getting an eyeful. After the club, I felt stripped of inhibitions. When the cab pulled up, I swung open the door and stood on the pavement with feet apart and arms crossed, waiting for him to pay.

I kept him at arm's length all the way up to his third-floor flat and waited until we were both safely inside before I told him what I wanted to do to him.

He tore off his jacket and was about to unbuckle his belt when I interrupted him.

'No, Ryan, I want you fully clothed,' I said in my best dominatrix voice, pushing him into the front room, which overlooked the river and Canary Wharf all lit up. 'Get that dining chair and put it in the middle of the floor.'

'Yes, mistress!' he laughed, but I could see he was slightly nervous.

'Right, sit down and stay down,' I said.

I went over to his iPod decking station and put on one of my favourite tracks from Massive Attack's *Mezzanine* album.

I took off the silk scarf I was wearing and used it to tie his hands behind his back, running my hands through his thick black hair before striding off to strip down to my thong and black lace bra, but this time putting back on the stiletto-heeled black leather ankle boots I'd had to discard while pole dancing.

Ryan looked terrified now, as if I was about to eat him alive.

'OK, are you ready, big boy?' I teased, before swinging my hips and easing them forward until I was straddling his lap. 'You can look but not touch, and I don't want to hear a peep out of you.'

I started grinding down as I straddled him, pushing my tired thigh muscles to their limit.

Grabbing the chair behind his head, I jiggled my breasts inches from his face and put my lips as close to his as I could without them touching.

He writhed beneath me, desperate to grab my flesh, his cock trying to burst out above his waistband.

I pulled away from him before turning round and bending over with one hand on each of my cheeks, swaying to and fro to the music and inching towards Ryan, who was quietly whimpering by now.

Backing closer to him, I dipped down as if to sit on his lap before reaching behind me and brushing my hand against his crotch.

Ryan was doing everything he could to contain himself while I was getting off on frustrating him. But after another five-minute bump and grind, I stopped. Part of me wished he would just say, 'I have to have you now,' pick me up, carry me into the bedroom and ravish me.

But no, he was happy to submit to me and I kind of resented the fact that he was so compliant.

Without warning, I pulled him up from the chair without untying his hands, dragged him into the bedroom and pushed him on to the duvet.

'OK, Ryan, your time has come,' I announced. 'I want cock and I want it now.'

'God, Geri, you're unbelievable . . . I've never been so turned on.'

'Shut up before I gag you,' I said, undoing his belt buckle and his fly in rapid succession. 'You do what I tell you and nothing else.'

Even as I spoke the words, I was daring him to argue back, to contradict me. In short, to have some backbone.

'Sure, whatever you say, babe – you're the boss.'

How I wished he'd be more of a man, put up a fight and make it more interesting for me but no, he was happy to let me do all the work.

'You know it's my fantasy to be dominated by a woman,' he said.

'Right, lie there, don't move, and let me do what I want.'

I pulled off his suit trousers with one tug, followed by his socks. His thick, seven-inch cock was already standing to attention through the front of his boxers, so I was immediately on my knees, teasing it with my tongue.

I licked each side like a lollipop, then flicked around the helmet, gently taking the tip into my mouth and sucking a little before working up and down the shaft with deep kisses. He tasted salty, like clean sea water.

I pulled off his boxers and took his length right down into the back of my throat, easing it in and out, fighting the urge to gag. It was my party trick and I knew he loved it.

'Mmmmmm, Geri, you give such fucking great head . . . careful, I might cum in your mouth . . .'

I withdrew. 'You most certainly will not.'

He looked like a naughty schoolboy, lying there in his shirt and loosened tie, naked from the waist down.

I peeled off my underwear and unlocked the clasp on my handbag, extracting a condom. Tearing open the wrapper with my teeth, I gently teased it on to Ryan's cock, keeping eye contact with him the whole time.

Sometimes I miss the texture of real cock inside me. But a girl's got to play safe.

Straddling him, I lowered myself on to his shaft, achingly slowly, until my bum was resting on his rock-hard thighs.

Maybe there is something to be said for rugby after all.

Rocking backwards and forwards and side to side, gripping his cock with my pelvic muscles, I waited until I found a rhythm that produced the most intense pleasure.

God, I loved being fucked – and I loved being in the driving seat while I was doing it. As I pumped him in and out of my pussy, my whole belly warmed and tingled as I allowed myself to start down the road to orgasm.

Our breathing came hard and heavy, every muscle taut. Sensing how he was getting too close – I wasn't ready yet, not nearly ready – I loosened my pelvic grip. Just a little, just enough. Give the boy a breather, hey? He moaned and thrashed around beneath me. And just as I started up again, ready to really get the momentum going this time, I heard a sharp intake of breath and the sudden spasm of his cock inside me. *Fuck!*

After a series of weakening thrusts, he rested his head against my breasts.

'Geri, sweetheart, I'm sorry. I tried to hold back . . . you know I can satisfy you. It won't take me long to recover, let's do it again . . .'

As we both lay there, panting, I just wished to God I could find a man who could control himself. And me. Handsome boys like Ryan were too easy for me to trample underfoot. He reached out to hug me, but I pushed him away.

'Not now, Ryan,' I said. 'I just want to sleep now.'

I was worn out, tired by the day, by the role play, by my life . . .

'Are you OK, Geri? What's wrong?' he asked.

'Nothing you can put right, Ryan,' I told him. 'You don't have to – you're not my boyfriend.'

'Yeah, I know, but that doesn't mean I don't care,' he said.

'Thanks, I appreciate that. But really, you can't help. Now, please, let me get some shut-eye . . .'

He kissed my forehead and rolled over. 'OK, sweetie. You are one hot woman, do you know that? Goodnight then.'

Ryan was a nice guy, and sweet enough when he was away from work and the influence of his buddies, but simply not man enough for me.

It had been an incredible night, the implications of which had not yet sunk in. I soon sunk into a fractured sleep, with images of the evening drifting in and out of strange dreams.

When Ryan's alarm went off early the next morning I hardly felt rested at all. I shunned his sleepy advances and quickly washed and dressed before he was even out of bed.

'See you at work,' I laughed, giving him a peck on the cheek.

With that I shut the door behind me and made my way down the stairs.

I was just lifting my arm to hail a cab on the main

road, when I thought to check in my beloved Prada handbag to make sure my purse was there. It wasn't. I knew I hadn't taken it out at Ryan's so I must have dropped it at the club. There was no way, after that exit, that I was going to go back and knock on Ryan's door, so I decided to bite the bullet and take the walk of shame home to Greenwich. Thank God my keys were in my pocket.

It gave me a chance to reflect. On the one hand I was proud of myself that I'd pulled off such a performance last night – but on the other I was concerned at the fallout I might experience at the office. Had I overstepped the mark? Would Luke make my life even more difficult now, or had my bravura performance shut him up for the time being?

After a quick shower and change of clothes, I headed straight to work. Before cancelling all my cards I called the Pearl, hoping against hope that my purse might have been handed in.

'Hi, my name's Geraldine Carson,' I told the woman who answered. 'I've reason to believe a black leather Prada wallet might have been handed in at the Pearl last night.'

'Oh yes, Miss Carson,' she said. 'Your business card was inside so we were going to call you later this morning anyway. And if you don't mind me saying, I enjoyed your show last night.'

'You saw me dance?' I asked, blushing. 'Well, thanks, I appreciate the compliment. I'll be in later to collect the purse.'

How funny that a girl who worked at a lap-dancing club – who was possibly a dancer herself – thought I'd done a good job!

I allowed myself a few moments of metaphorical back-slapping before getting my brain in gear for the day ahead. This wasn't any old day – this was Bonus Day.

Shit, I thought. I hope to God I get what I've budgeted for. If not, they'll be repossessing my home and I'll be shacking up at the stables.

That's the problem with working for an investment bank. Last night I was flashing £50 notes around like they were pound coins. And three months ago, I was overextending myself on a mortgage on a riverside apartment that was dependent on one hell of a bonus. Not to mention the fact that Zeus was a total drain on my finances, even if I couldn't bear to give him up. But, what the hell, I'd worked hard for it. And what's life without some risk? Until last night, it had been so long since I'd taken one, I'd forgotten what it felt like.

And with that, the focused, determined, ball-breaking version of Geraldine Carson with whom I was so familiar donned her armour and went into battle.

Chapter Four

I didn't like the look of pity on Tania's face when I walked into the office.

'Geri, Daryll asked to see you about ten minutes ago,' she said. 'I covered for you but I think you should go straight away.'

'Really, Tania? If I want your opinion, I'll ask for it,' I said, smiling sweetly.

I could feel myself losing my cool but had to hold it together for the meeting with Daryll. God knows what he was going to say about the incident at the Pearl.

He saw me approaching and smiled in that annoyingly paternal way of his. 'Geraldine, my dear. Do come in and sit down. Would you like a tea or coffee?'

'No thanks, Daryll. You'd better just say what you think of me,' I said, preparing myself for the worst.

'What I think of you?' he repeated. 'Let me tell you something, Geraldine. When I was a naïve young man on the dealing floor, there was such a thing as an initiation ceremony. My colleagues took me out to a strip club, where a lady of the night stripped me down to my underwear as she removed her own clothing. I was utterly humiliated and obviously the butt of my colleagues' jokes for some time.

'What you did at the club last night, my dear, was to turn the initiation on its head. Almost literally, when you did that extraordinary move on the pole. Geraldine, after all your time here, you finally initiated yourself into the Brothers. Well done,' he laughed.

For a moment I was speechless. I thought he had been about to tear strips off me.

'God, Daryll, I thought you were going to put me in detention, not give me a gold star,' I said. 'Trust me, it's not a ceremony I will be repeating.'

'Well, despite the entertainment, I'm pleased to hear it,' he continued. 'Now let's get back to business.'

'That sounds good to me,' I said.

'It's been a good year for the team, Geraldine, and you have been at the heart of it.' He handed me a sealed envelope. 'This is to say thank you for all your hard work.'

I opened it quickly, in silence. The letter inside confirmed that my bonus for the past year would be £20,000. *Oh shit.* I'd expected much more, counted on it in fact, but was determined not to show any sign of disappointment.

'Thanks, Daryll, that's great,' I lied, beaming so wide my cheeks hurt.

'My pleasure, Geraldine,' he said, moving towards the door. 'You're a great credit to Sloane Brothers. I'll see you later.'

As I made my way down the 'catwalk of doom' that took me through the open-plan part of the office past most of my colleagues, I felt several pairs of eyes boring into me for any clue as to what had just happened.

I kept gazing straight ahead and avoided any eye contact, passing Tania without a word and closing my office door.

Sitting down at my desk, I realised I had been clenching my right fist so hard that my nails had made heavy indentations on the palm of my hand.

I felt like punching a hole in the wall.

I'd taken a calculated risk in buying my house in Greenwich, borrowing over the odds and budgeting for a bigger salary top-up to comfortably afford my monthly repayments. Now I was in the shit, lumbered with a huge mortgage and a stallion I wasn't prepared to sacrifice.

My train of thought was interrupted by Tania knocking on my door.

'Geri, can I come in?' she asked.

'Um, just a minute,' I replied, quickly checking my make-up in a compact mirror. 'OK, what is it?'

'There's something you should know,' she said. 'There's an email going around that lists everyone's bonuses. The guys on the floor all know who's getting what. Did you receive it?'

I quickly scanned my inbox but couldn't see anything.

'Christ, Tania, how come you know more than me about what's going on?'

'I'm just telling you, Geri. I thought we were a team?'

'Yes, right . . . but bonuses are none of your business,' I told her. 'If you've got one of these emails can you please forward it to me now?'

'OK, Geri, no problem. I'll do that immediately. And . . . I'm sorry . . .'

I motioned for her to leave and close the door. A few seconds later, the email dropped into my inbox.

My heart was pounding as I opened it up and scanned the list of names. There was only one I cared about: Luke Cotterill. Next to it was the amount: £30,000.

His name came alphabetically just after mine, of course, so the difference was made even more painfully obvious. I'd been with the company for two years; he'd been there two months, yet he'd bagged £10,000 more.

My head felt as if it was about to explode. Luke bloody Cotterill had landed a bigger bonus than me, simply for having a dick, as far as I could make out. And my God, was he a prize dick. OK, the guy had the balls to play the market and had a good brain, but he had the inter-personal skills of a chimpanzee. Surely it would have been better to have me on-side?

This wasn't the worst of it, though. By the time I'd gone down the entire list it seemed as if every jerk in the office had received more than me.

A lone tear started to make its way down my face, blackened by Mac mascara. This time I'd been well and truly shafted by the boys' club, and there was nothing I could do about it.

I dabbed my face with a tissue and made myself presentable again, but who was I kidding? It didn't matter how hard I worked, how much money I brought in, I was never going to outgun the big swinging dicks. Short of having a penis transplant, it just wasn't going to happen.

I needed to get out of there. But I still had the morning to get through before I could attend to practical matters like going back to the Pearl to collect my wallet. At least I had an excuse for not joining them for lunch. For the rest of the morning, I barricaded myself in the office, even forbidding Tania to disturb me. Then on the stroke of noon, I opened the door to my office and strolled out, a huge fake smile plastered on my face.

'Tania, hold the fort, I'll be out for a couple of hours,' I announced.

'Oh, right, where are you off to, Geri?' she asked.

'I'll be on the mobile,' I said, knowing I was being rude, but not giving a shit.

If Luke Cotterill had so much as looked at me the wrong way as I left the building I might have done something I'd have regretted.

As I walked towards Canary Wharf Tube, I thought how I never wanted to go back to the office again.

Fuck 'em all, I thought. I might as well go and be a lap dancer and get screwed that way.

I jumped on the Jubilee Line to Green Park and walked the rest of the way to the club. At least I wouldn't have to be part of the lunchtime back-slapping that the Brothers would currently be indulging in at Ubon.

It was strange seeing the Pearl in the cold light of day, its neon sign switched off. Any semblance of glamour disappeared without the veiling mystery of the night. But as I descended those red-carpeted stairs into the womb of the club, it came back to me how liberated I had felt the night before.

'Hi,' I said, recognising the girl behind the desk as the one who had given Luke his lap dance. 'I'm Geraldine Carson. I'm here to collect my purse?'

'Oh yeah, I'll just ring Declan,' she said in a raw East End accent.

'Who's Declan?' I asked.

'Declan Meleady,' she said. 'He's the manager.'

'Right,' I replied, wondering if he was the dark-haired guy I'd spotted the night before, talking to Tania.

She disappeared for a moment, then returned with an odd smile on her face. 'If you just go in the club and wait at the bar, Declan will be with you in a minute,' she said.

As I perched myself on one of the high stools I surveyed the scene of my crime. Part of me wondered 'What the hell was I doing?' but there was also a tingle down my spine.

'Miss Carson?' said a voice behind me.

'Call me Geri,' I replied, turning round and blinking in the lights.

'Hi, I'm Declan Meleady,' he said in a sexy Irish voice, as I finally got a good look at the man who had given me unspoken permission to take over his club the night before.

He was even better close up: well-cut dark brown hair, with warm brown eyes and the sturdy build of a stable hand. He was wearing a very expensive suit, almost certainly Savile Row's finest, with a Ralph Lauren Polo shirt underneath.

'Here's your purse, Geri,' he said. 'I was going to contact you anyway.'

'Ah yes, it was you in the top booth last night, wasn't

it?' I said, drinking him in. 'I'm intrigued why you didn't set your Rottweilers on me – I was breaking the rules, after all.'

His eyes twinkled as he smiled softly at me. 'It's my job to make sure the customers are happy,' he said. 'And that means knowing when to send in the clowns and when to back off. I had a few regulars in last night and I could see they were enjoying your impromptu performance, so I allowed it to continue.'

'And did *you* enjoy my performance?' I asked, realising I was flirting with him.

'Indeed I did,' he replied. 'I was most impressed.'

'Wow, thanks,' I said. 'That was my first time.'

'But will it be your last?' he asked.

'I'm sure it will. I already have a very well-paid job,' I replied, opening my purse to check its contents.

It was only then that I realised the £500 worth of cash I'd taken out to pay for drinks at the club was missing.

'Oh shit,' I said, feeling a little panicked, 'I guess I shouldn't be surprised the money's been lifted but, Jesus, I could have done with every penny of that.'

'What happened to the very well-paid job, then?' he asked.

'Still have it, but it's perhaps not quite as well-paid as I'd like,' I explained. 'I have a high-maintenance mortgage and horse to support, you see.'

'Really?' He sat up more in his seat, and leaned forward a little. He smelled good; all musky and manly. 'I part-own a racehorse in Ireland myself.'

'Well then,' I said, warming to Declan even more, 'we must compare form some time.'

'I don't know how to ride,' confessed Declan. 'Well, not horses, anyway . . . I'm only in it for the investment.' *What a tease*, I thought.

I liked this man – he was alpha without being aggressive; smooth without being oily.

'So pay in the City is not all it's cracked up to be then?' he smiled in empathy.

'Well, it is for the boys,' I explained. 'But it seems the girls aren't always invited to the party.'

'I'd invite you to my party any time,' said Declan. 'If you were ever thinking of changing career, you could walk into a job here. Or shimmy, should I say.'

'Are you serious?' I asked.

'Let's say I was only half joking,' he said.

'OK, I'm curious now,' I smiled, enjoying the banter. 'How much could I earn, in theory?'

'Well, on average, between £400 and £500 a night,' he said. 'The big West End clubs pay more but then there's a list of rules and regulations as long as your arm. Here, it's more relaxed and there aren't so many girls on each shift, so you'll get more tips.'

My mental calculator was doing back flips – I worked out that if I were to do a shift every night from Wednesday to Saturday, 8pm to midnight, for six weeks, I could potentially clear £10k, which would keep Zeus in hay for the foreseeable future, and me with a roof over my head.

'God, that's tempting,' I said, recognising a good deal when I heard one. What was stopping me? Well, one very good reason. 'It's just a shame that I have an image to protect. After all, my real job would be down the pan if the guys saw me working down here.'

'That's not a problem,' said Declan. 'Mayfair's not our only branch. We have clubs all over.'

His voice was working its charms on me. The answers came slick and easy. Ten grand couldn't be sniffed at.

'So, hypothetically, if I were to take up the offer, could you guarantee that income?'

'Well, there are no cast-iron guarantees,' said Declan. 'But with your natural talents, I can't see there being a shortage of admirers.'

I paused for a moment to reflect as Declan moved behind the bar.

'Here, I'm sure you could do with this,' he said, pouring Sauvignon Blanc into a chilled glass.

'Thanks, you read my mind,' I said, taking a large sip. 'Look, you seem to be a straightforward kind of guy, Declan, unlike most of the shits I work with. Between you and me, I was expecting a bigger bonus at work and it didn't come through so I need the money. Fast. Plus I got such a kick out of dancing last night.'

'Not half as much of a kick as I did watching you,' he replied, and we both laughed.

This man had more charm in his little finger than all the guys in the office put together and I felt so relaxed in his company. But I had to be careful – after all, somehow he knew Tania, and I had yet to get to the bottom of that little conundrum.

'I'm glad you thought I had potential,' I said, pulling back a little. 'Perhaps you can help me develop it.'

'I'd be delighted to,' he replied.

'Listen, Declan, I really appreciate your confidence in my ability, but obviously I need to consider this really carefully,' I told him. 'I'd be risking my career if anyone found out that I was even speaking to you about this.'

'Sure, Geri, I understand,' he said. 'You take your time.'

'Thanks, Declan,' I said, offering my hand. His was big, warm and pleasantly rough.

He escorted me to the door, which was the most gentlemanly act I had been on the receiving end of for some time.

I floated back to the office, buoyed by Declan's flattery. He really was serious about the job offer, I knew that. But could I really hack it as a lap dancer?

There were a few puzzled faces at Sloane Brothers. Obviously they'd been expecting me to look crestfallen but I felt like I was coming back from a spa. Suddenly the world was full of options.

I closeted myself in my office and told Tania I wasn't to be disturbed. I needed to think clearly.

You must be out of your mind, Geraldine Carson. Why the hell would a woman like me, who has fought so hard to succeed in a man's world, go off and do the very thing that might unpick all her efforts?

I started to think about the consequences of being found out – what would happen at work, what would my poor parents think? This was a high-risk strategy, but isn't that what had got me up the career ladder in the first place?

I had to be honest with myself – the danger factor was the most attractive part of it. I'd always enjoyed chasing a deal, but ever since I discovered my natural talent for riding, I'd also become hooked on the visceral rush.

I'd experienced the same kind of gut-level thrill after

dancing at the Pearl, only this time the success of my performance was down to me and me alone. I was the thoroughbred, riding the pole, and it felt good. No, more than good – it felt great.

I had no worries about my physical abilities or showing off my body. Where the serious doubt kicked in was whether I could handle it mentally and emotionally. I imagined a scenario where I'd had a tough day at work and a customer got too familiar with me at the club. It could go one of two ways. Either I'd lose it and unleash a barrage of verbal abuse that might get me sacked, or burst into tears and run off stage.

I thought of Declan and his comforting presence, but he wouldn't always be there to make sure I was OK.

However, it would be a particularly delicious sort of revenge on Luke and the Brothers to earn money out of using my sexuality when they thought I had zero sex appeal.

I knew I would face moments of self-doubt but getting in touch with my inner sex goddess and parading her in public was too much of an adrenalin high to resist. I just had to be ultra-careful that my two worlds never collided . . .

My mind was already made up. I picked up the telephone.

'Declan? It's Geri Carson here. Can you speak?'

'I'm all yours.'

'OK, good. What the hell. Screw the Brothers, screw them all. If the offer's still there, I'm going to take it . . .'

Chapter Five

The morning sun streaming into my bedroom window helped me to jump out of bed on that crucial Saturday. In just a few hours, I would be taking my first steps towards becoming a professional lap dancer.

Declan had gotten down to business straight away. He told me there were no guarantees – I'd have to go through the training programme and audition like everyone else. I'd have to impress Jackie, who had been working at the Pearl for years, and if she thought I couldn't hack it, I'd be out.

That didn't frighten me – I was in good shape and wasn't afraid of hard physical work. Declan didn't seem to have any doubt I'd get through because he had already booked me in for a costume fitting at the suburban Pearl in north London, where I would be dancing.

I got up and switched on the TV to take my mind off the audition. I surfed the channels and found MTV and laughed out loud when the first video I saw was 'Lap Dancer' by NERD.

Maybe it was a sign that I'd found my calling.

I did a bit of a shimmy while I watched the lithe,

tanned, surgically-enhanced LA chicks on the video and tried to pick up a few tips before jumping in the shower and then slathering myself in cocoa butter to make my skin feel soft and gleaming.

I'd been told to turn up in shorts, a vest top and trackie bottoms – with a pair of high heels – hardly a glamorous combination, but I knew it would be quite a workout.

I rolled out my yoga mat and did a few sun salutations and recited my mantra: 'Geraldine, you have all the resources you need to succeed.'

I grabbed my gym bag, took a deep breath and shut the door behind me. Arriving in my BMW Z4 Roadster would only have aroused suspicion so I got the bus to the address Jackie had given me.

It turned out to be a nondescript-looking place in a grubby part of town. I rang the bell and someone buzzed me in. At the top of a short flight of claustrophobic stairs five other girls were sitting on plastic chairs outside a dance studio.

They all looked as apprehensive as I felt, so I clearly wasn't the only beginner. A couple smiled and nodded but didn't say anything. I wondered what had brought them to this point, whether they'd had an agonising choice to make.

I turned to the girl next to me. 'Hi,' I said. 'I'm Geri.'

'Hello. My name is Irena,' she said in halting English. 'I am from Poland.'

'Oh right, have you done this sort of thing before?'

'Yes, I have danced, yes, but not in club like this. This scary, no?'

60

'To be honest, I don't know yet. I'm waiting to find out . . .'

Ten minutes went by. And then fifteen. I didn't know what to do with myself. After all, fiddling with my BlackBerry or reading *The Economist* was out of the question.

I decided to repair some chips in my nail polish while I waited. The others watched me in silence. It didn't seem the done thing to strike up a conversation, so I kept quiet.

Before long, the familiar riff of Beyoncé's 'Crazy in Love' came wafting into the corridor and the studio door opened.

A ball-breaking brunette in her mid-thirties, with the ramrod posture of a classical dancer and a hard, good-looking face, strutted in. She was dressed in skinny jeans, knee-high boots and a hip-hugging, roll-neck grey sweater, which she whipped off to reveal a leotard beneath.

Ignoring us, she stood at the side of the room, stretching.

She had a natural presence and there was no doubting that she was top cat.

So this was Jackie.

Finally she turned to face us, hands on each slender hip. No matter how much horse-riding I did I could never dream of having a figure as svelte, yet still curvy, as hers.

'Ladies, welcome to the Pearl boot camp. I'm Jackie and I'm here to put you through your paces. Please strip down to your shorts and vests – no shoes at the moment, please – and take off any jewellery.'

I took the lead and wandered into the studio – a small space with polished wood floors and four metal poles placed at regular intervals.

'OK, when you're ready, please come and join me, standing in a circle,' said Jackie.

There were six of us, plus Jackie.

'Right, then,' she continued. 'Before we begin, I want to tell you a story. In the bad old days, you would all have been called strippers and you would have been paid by the owner of a strip joint to wiggle your ass and take your clothes off for a few dirty old men nursing cheap beer.

'You will be pleased to hear that we have progressed since those dark days. Now we have much more upmarket clubs that are professionally run, you will be called a pole dancer or a lap dancer and you will pay the club rent for the privilege of wiggling your ass. But the customers will be businessmen, guys on stag nights and, if you're lucky, celebrities, who will hopefully give you generous tips.

'If any of you survive this first session, I'll go into more detail about the various club rules. You'd better leave now if you have a problem about taking off all your clothes in public. If you're squeamish about men seeing your clit, then this is not the job for you.'

The sound of nervous laughter echoed around the room, and I felt my heart beat a bit faster as I realised what I was getting into, but I – like everyone else – stayed put.

'Good, that's the spirit, ladies,' said Jackie, smiling for the first time. 'Now, before we start moving, I'd like you all to introduce yourself to the group – your name, where you're from, and why you want to work at the Pearl.'

'You with the long dark hair, please start,' she said, pointing at the olive-skinned girl opposite me.

'Um, hello everybody, my name is Gabi and I'm from Brazil,' she said in a lilting accent. 'Back home I loved to dance the samba so I have good rhythm. I want to work at Pearl to earn money to pay for my study. I learn English and study law.'

'OK, thanks, Gabi – I'll be tapping you up for free legal advice,' laughed Jackie. 'Next, please.'

'Good afternoon. My name is Irena and I am from Poland.'

'Speak up,' said Jackie. 'There's no room for shyness in this business. Be loud and proud.'

'Oh, I am sorry,' said Irena, notching the volume up. 'Sorry, Poland. I want work at Pearl to pay my bills and also send money home to my parents. I also love to dance.'

'Thank you, Irena, no need to apologise,' said Jackie. 'But you need to toughen up. OK, next please.'

A long-limbed black girl with a great-looking Afro stepped up to the plate. 'Hi everybody, my name is Makani. My family is originally from Ghana but I was born in London. I want to dance at the Pearl in the evenings so that I can spend my days painting.'

'Thanks, Makani, good luck. Let's move on . . . OK, you with the spiky black hair,' said Jackie, pointing at me. 'What's your story?'

I had to think on my feet; there was no way I could tell the truth.

'Hi guys, I'm Geri,' I said. 'I'm from Surrey. I work as a temp secretary in the City but the pay's not great. I want to work at the Pearl so I can buy some Jimmy Choos!'

That broke the ice a little and everyone laughed, except Jackie.

'Well, Geri, I hope you're not the kind of girl who's a slave to her credit card. What makes you want to be a lap dancer?'

'I'm reasonably fit and I've been told I'm a sexy mover,' I answered. 'So I thought I'd try my hand at lap dancing because it beats working behind a bar.'

'Fair enough,' said Jackie, but I could see my joke hadn't gone down well with her.

The other girls said their piece and Jackie moved to the CD player and put on some relaxing music.

'OK ladies, listen up. Welcome to Jackie's Boot Camp. You don't do the talking here, you do the listening. If you screw around I won't ask you to drop and give me twenty, I'll just get some friends of mine to very politely escort you from the building. When I'm here, you take your orders from me. If I say "any questions" then you can ask questions, otherwise shut up and listen. If you need to pee do it in your own time.

'Now before we begin, everyone is always curious to know how we get into a business like this. Well, you've told me a little of your stories so I'll tell you a little of mine.'

Chapter Six

JACKIE'S STORY

I've always wanted to dance. When I was a girl I dreamed of being a ballerina. And yeah, yeah I'm sure you all dreamed that. But I was good. I auditioned at 15 and won a scholarship to the Royal Ballet. Surprised? Well don't be. There's more. My mother didn't want me to be a ballet dancer, she didn't think there was money in it. She wanted me to be a hairdresser. So I ran away from home when I was 16.

I studied at Barons Court for a year or so. The course was tough, but I could handle it. The reasons I left . . . well. Let's just say it involved a well-hung ballet teacher called Guy, a bottle of gin and the *Dirty Dancing* soundtrack. Guy and I woke up naked on a mat on the floor of studio two surrounded by twelve teenage ballerinas and a furious Madame. The teacher was fired and I was asked to not come back after the summer break.

I was gutted of course. But I had more immediate concerns than losing the love of my life. I had nowhere to live for a start. I couldn't go home. Mum wouldn't return my calls. I had no idea where my brothers were. My father was long gone and all my grandparents were either dead or senile. I was 17 and faced with a life of poverty and despair. Then I remembered my Aunty Linda. The only woman in our family who wouldn't judge me. She was a black sheep herself, you see. Aunty Linda ran a lapdancing club in Whitechapel.

Suffice to say my Aunty Linda made a better mum than my real one ever did. I came out the other end still alive but it could have been a lot worse. Plenty of homeless girls end up on the streets as hookers, thieves or both. I was still determined to make it as a dancer. I knew I had the talent, and I was young. I just needed a place to put down some roots while I sorted out my life.

When I was reasonably straight in the head Linda put me to work behind the bar, mixing drinks, keeping an eye on things. I took tips from the punters but wasn't allowed to dance. Aunty Linda wouldn't let me. I was desperate to do it though. I wanted to keep in practice for a start. Dancing takes a lot of strength and the best way to keep your muscles trim is to dance. It's not a coincidence that pole dancing has been taken over by the fitness clubs these days, though back then respectable women wouldn't be seen dead near a pole.

I've never been respectable and don't want to start. I didn't mind taking my clothes off. In Auntie Linda's the girls stripped down to nothing on stage and in the private rooms – Lord knows what else they got up to in there, but officially they weren't supposed to fuck the punters. I was proud of my body. There's not that much between a sheer pair of tights and a snatch open to the elements. I'd watch the other girls dance. Twisting, spinning, sliding up and down. Wrapping their beautiful bodies around the golden poles. I saw the boozy lads, or the quiet single men tucking notes into the g-strings or between a couple of pressed-together tits. I wanted it all.

I liked it there. I lived in a little flat above the club with one of the girls, a shy type called Melinda, or Marinda – I could never remember – and she was hardly ever there to talk to. I would sleep late, then make myself a coffee and look out the windows across the sea of chimney-pots and TV aerials that made up the East End skyline. I liked it behind the bar too. It felt safe. I was cut off from the action, the fights and the slaps when the punters got too fresh. I was immune from the drunken brawls that occasionally broke out. I watched it all, soaked it up, took it all in. I felt at home.

Linda didn't own the place, that was some shady guy called Col who we hardly ever saw. He had 'interests' all over London so left the day-to-day running to Linda.

The clients we had were a mixed bunch. This was the East End and there were office blocks nearby but we weren't close enough to the City to attract the really high rollers, though that was just as well for me. We all know how lairy they can get around bonus time. We got a lot of stag-dos, market vendors and even a few students from the college up the road. But the group I saw the most was Fat Desmond's crew, a gang of middling-violent gangsters. They were apparently 'associates' of Col's, which is why they were basically allowed free run of the place. They paid up, usually, but refused to tip, and often tried to cheat the girls. Linda had had to pay them out of her own pocket from time to time when they were left short by some crooked-nosed gangster.

Fat Desmond took a shine to me soon after I started working there and he was forever pestering Linda to let me dance for him. For once I was grateful for her refusals. I didn't want to dance for that fat slug. 'Her mother'd never forgive me,' she'd say. I shrugged at Desmond's raised eyebrows.

Now Desmond wasn't the only one of these gangsters who tried to make eye contact with me. There was another guy, Tony. He was good-looking, though a real rough diamond. He was the sort who'd terrify you half to death just by asking for a drink, then he'd smile, walk off and you'd find he'd left you wetter than the Little Mermaid.

Fat Desmond was in charge of this crew, but I could see Tony was hungry for power, and maybe for me too. I found him intriguing and exciting. I began to look forward to the gangsters' visits and found myself hoping Tony would make his move soon.

My friends were the dancers, I learnt a lot from observing and talking to them. I learnt about pole dancing and lap dancing of course, but more importantly I learnt about people, and how to make money from them. How to spot the difference between a mark, who you could fleece, and a customer that you should look after so he'd come back. My best friend was named Jen, though her stage name was Alicia. She was a beautiful African girl, with a lovely round bottom and a heavy lower lip that men never failed to try and kiss, only to have her turn her head away as they lunged.

I watched her, entranced, as she languidly swayed around the pole. Jen hardly seemed to do anything, but every angle, every pose, showed her assets off to their best advantage. Though undoubtedly attractive, she was far from the best-looking girl in the club, but she regularly pulled in more money than the others, however blonde and thin they were. She did it by picking her punters carefully and working them until they gave everything they were prepared to give, then leaving them wanting more, so they'd ask the bouncer on the way out when Alicia would be dancing again. Sometimes when watching her, I'd yearn to be up there, with her. I wanted to be her.

One night she showed me part of the magic that enabled her to extract so much money from the punters. She'd been entangled with a group of noisy suits all night. They'd been trying to get her to let them touch her and she'd been trying to get them individually into the back room where the real money was made. They were upping the stakes. '*I'll go into the room if you kiss my mate's knob in front of everyone. I'll pay you £25 if you let me touch your pussy.*' They were determined not to go back there, aiming to keep it all public, probably to cash in on some bet.

I was keeping half an eye on this as I stacked the dishwasher and eventually saw Jen look over at me and say something I couldn't hear. The boys looked over at me, interested, and I wondered with trepidation what she was suggesting. Then she walked over to me. She leaned across the bar and whispered, 'They think you're my girlfriend. Would you mind playing along? I'll give you a quarter of the tip I get.'

I nodded dumbly, thinking I should probably have asked for more, but too keen to see what she had in mind. Then she leaned further over the bar, grabbed hold of my top and pulled me over to her. Then we were kissing. That soft, inviting lower lip mashed into mine and I felt her tongue slip softly into my open mouth. The boys erupted into cheers and I felt Jen, no *Alicia*'s, hand inside my top, fondling my right breast.

Then she pulled away, but kept her huge brown eyes locked on mine for a few moments, a look of hunger on her face. She licked her teeth and walked back to the boys. She made a lot of tips that night and duly gave me a quarter of what she'd got from the suits.

What I'm saying, ladies, is in this business, you've got to roll with what comes your way. There's no room for prudishness here.

I found out more about the gang as time went on, including the fact that Fat Desmond was under suspicion of murder. Apparently his brother Mike had been found floating face-down in a canal. 'This ain't *EastEnders*,' Linda had said, 'and Mike's not ever coming back to Walford Square.'

'Why do the police think Desmond killed him?' I asked.

'Because he's as good as admitted it. They had a row over some bird and Des swore he'd kill him. Heard by a dozen punters in The Fox two weeks ago. Plenty of grasses around all too happy to put Fat Desmond away,' Linda replied. 'Too cocky for his own good, that Desmond, won't be long before someone knocks him off his perch. He won't go to jail though I reckon, he'll end up in the canal next to his brother.'

As she said this, I was watching Tony across the room. He was looking back at me. He smiled and winked, sending a thrill, or possibly a chill, down my spine.

One night it came to a head. The gangsters showed up late, just as we were about to close. It had been a long night and we'd had some trouble with a group of businessmen. One of the bouncers had a split lip from the fight that followed and was in a foul mood. The other one had already gone home. Desmond's crew came barging in, four of them, loud, half-drunk and triumphant. There had been some job go down that day and by the looks of it, they'd come away with whatever it was they were after and were in the mood to celebrate.

The bouncer tried to stop them and ended up on the floor, curled up and gasping for breath. He'd had a rotten night, I thought. As the gang made their way to their favourite table, Linda shrugged and asked a few of the girls to stay on, telling them they could waive their club fees for that night if they did.

I made my way over to the bouncer. Everyone called him Dublin, on account of his accent. God knows what his story was, he never told us anything about his background, but he'd certainly learned to fight somewhere, and the scars on his face showed it. He was a lovely bloke though, if you ignored the vicious beatings he gave to out-of-order punters from time to time. He loved the girls like an uncle and would do anything for them. I brought him a stiff drink and helped him back on to his feet. It always paid to keep the bouncer sweet.

Dublin thanked me and raised the glass to his lips to take a slug when a hand appeared from nowhere and slapped the drink to the ground.

'I think you should serve your customers before you serve the fucking heavies!' Desmond spat. 'Or we not good enough for you?'

He was drunk, and high on something perhaps. I was scared but didn't let him see. I stood straight-backed and looked him in the eye. 'What can I get you, sir?' I asked gently. Remember, ladies, the punter is always right. Especially when you know he has a switchblade in his boot.

'Get us a bottle of champagne. Bring a glass for yourself too.' I looked at Linda. I was allowed to accept drinks from the customers. Though not to dance, of course. She nodded, tonight was not the night to say no to Desmond. Dublin watched, eyes like gimlets, ready to take action should it come to it. I desperately hoped it wouldn't, as Dublin wouldn't have stood a chance against these four. I brought over the bottle and Desmond patted the banquette beside him. I sat down. Tony watched me from across the table, his face unreadable. I saw he had a cut over one eye. A big night for everyone.

Desmond poured five glasses, overfilling them and finishing the bottle, which he tossed over the back of the banquette. 'A toast,' he said, eyes fixed on mine. 'To getting what you want.'

'To getting what you want,' the gangsters chorused

while I mouthed the words. I knew too well that getting what you wanted wasn't always the best thing for you. I sipped the champagne and stared back at him coolly. He didn't seem to like the fact I wasn't simpering like some grateful, first-time hooker.

'Dance for me,' he said.

'I'm not a dancer,' I lied. Though, strangely, this time I wanted to do it. Not for him, but for myself, and maybe for Tony.

He laughed. 'Oh, I think you are, Jackie. I think you're quite the little ballerina.' He watched me react to this, champagne dripping off his double chin.

I gasped in shock, despite myself. How on earth did he know that? My eyes flicked over to Linda, who shook her head slightly, as bemused as I. Desmond had obviously been doing some research. Hardly anyone knew about my past. But why would he take the time?

'Now dance, Darcey-bloody-Bussell!' he roared. For the third time I looked at Linda who nodded.

I stood as someone put 'You Can Leave Your Hat On' on the stereo. The opening bars thumped out as I walked to the pole and I closed my eyes, feeling the music in my muscles. I stretched languorously as I leaned back from the pole, imagining I was in Guy's arms in the studio. As the music warmed up I spun and lifted a long leg up against the pole.

Then the chorus hit and I took off my top in one swift movement. There was a sharp intake of breath. No one had asked me to take off my clothes but to me it was all part of the act. I opened my eyes, and as I swivelled around the pole, humping it languidly, I saw Jen and one of the other girls – Amber – watching me, open-mouthed, that hungry look back on Jen's face. Linda was watching too, perhaps wondering if she should have let me dance before. Then the gangsters' table swung past my vision. Desmond's fat face leered at me, along with two of his minions, but Tony's attention was focused on his boss, a look of pure hatred on his face. Then as I flipped around and hung back off the pole, I saw Dublin, who winked at me. I smiled back. I was dancing. And it felt like I was floating on air.

The future was uncertain, the atmosphere in the place heavy and oppressive. Things were set to change, I knew that, but just at that moment, I felt free. I felt in control, and I felt as happy as I'd been since Guy and I'd been thrown out of the Royal Ballet.

It didn't last of course. Desmond summoned me over and asked me to give him a lap dance. I hesitated while he waved two fifties at me. Ultimately, it wasn't the money that persuaded me. I didn't doubt that he was the type of man to punch out at a woman if she didn't comply. I climbed on his lap as 'Danger Zone' from *Top Gun* started up. I loved dancing to this song and I knew exactly what to do. I'd watched Jen and the other girls do it often enough. I tried not to grind too hard on him but he kept shoving his pelvis up at me and eventually I just rode him, trying to think of something else, but feeling his dick jabbing into me. I pushed my tits up together and brushed them across his lips. I watched in thinly-disguised contempt as he drooled down his chin.

'In the back room,' he grunted.

I froze. Don't know why but I just hadn't expected this. What else was he going to ask me to do? Linda spoke up. 'No, she's not going back there. She's my niece, for Christ's sake.'

Desmond swivelled and shot her a sneering glance. 'She may be your niece, but she's also my employee. And I say she goes into the back room with me.'

Linda looked gobsmacked.

'Oh, didn't I mention?' he added, laughing now. 'I own this place now. Part of our little "business transaction" earlier involved the deeds of this place changing hands. Poor old Col won't be needing it anymore, not where he's going.' Desmond grabbed his drink in one hand, and my wrist in the other. He started to drag me off to the back room.

'She's not going,' Linda said firmly. Dublin stood and moved towards us. Desmond snapped his fingers and his two goons rose to their feet and moved towards Dublin menacingly. He stood firm. As the crooks came near, he unleashed a massive round-house kick that sent one of them sprawling and took the other completely by surprise, unsettling him and leaving an opening. Dublin punched him once, twice in the face and the goon staggered back. But by that stage the first one had recovered and leapt on Dublin, bringing him crashing to the sticky carpet. One of the girls screamed. Jen raced up and began trying to pull the thug off. But the second stepped up and backhanded her across the face, before kneeling down and punching Dublin repeatedly in the face as the other held him down.

'Stop!' a voice called out firmly. The goons stopped their punching and turned to look at the owner of the voice. Tony.

Desmond looked at him in surprise. 'No,' he said. 'Don't stop. Give him a good working over.'

But the goons hesitated. And Tony must have realised this was his opportunity. Tony walked over to Desmond, his eyes flicking over to me for just an instant, and said calmly, 'Let the lady go, Des.'

Des stared back in amazement. He hadn't seen this coming. 'Lady?' he sputtered. 'This ain't no lady. This . . .' But he never got to finish as he was suddenly lying on the floor with one of his own teeth in his windpipe, choking him. He coughed and turned a dark shade of purple. Tony merely walked up to him and kicked him hard in the solar plexus. The tooth shot out and rattled across a nearby table.

Tony made a signal to the goons, who seemed to have been expecting this. Maybe, like me, they were just waiting for Tony to make his move. They lifted the dazed Desmond, still struggling for breath, and hauled him out the back door.

'What's gonna happen to him?' I asked.

'You don't want to know,' Tony replied, rubbing his bruised knuckles. 'He wasn't a very nice man, but then again, neither am I.'

I eyed him up and smiled. 'You rescued this lady, you can't be all bad.'

He thought for a minute, wondering if I was flirting, then smiled, almost shyly. 'Look,' he said. 'I've got to chat to Linda for a bit. You gonna hang around?'

'I live here,' I said coolly, and walked away, swinging my behind. I could feel those piercing eyes watching me go.

I picked up my top and went back behind the bar, where I felt more comfortable. Maybe I shouldn't ever have stepped out from its protective embrace. I realised I was still shaking and poured myself a stiff drink. I got one for Jen and Amber too who wanted to know what Tony had said to me.

The goons came back, without Desmond, and joined in the chat with Linda and Tony, who I guessed was our new boss.

Later, Tony came over to speak to me. 'Are you OK?' he asked.

I shrugged. 'No broken bones, just a slightly bruised wrist.'

He gazed into my eyes, but I felt ready to meet that gaze. I had nothing to be ashamed of. Did I? What did he want from me?

'Let me buy you a drink,' he said. Now ladies, from the look of you, you've probably heard every chat-up line devised by man. Some of you look like most of them might have worked, too. But as far as I'm concerned, 'Let me buy you a drink,' is all it takes. It's simple, it's forceful without being creepy and it gets the message across.

You might think I should have grabbed that drink with two hands and without a second thought. I fancied him, and he had money. He could have rescued me, taken me away somewhere and installed me in a nice house somewhere, maybe Epping.

But I didn't. I stood and looked back into those eyes for a long time, thinking it over. I didn't mind the fact he was a gangster for myself, but I had other . . . concerns, shall we say?

'Trust me,' I told him. 'You wouldn't be interested in a girl like me.'

'I'll be the judge of that,' he said. But just then Linda asked me to help her with the till – it was forever sticking – and with a last, sad smile I left Tony standing in the middle of the bar and walked away.

And that's storytelling hour over, ladies. Now those of you who think you can handle the ride, in more ways than one, stick around and we'll audition you. Those of who ain't up to it: leave now.

Chapter Seven

Her story over, Jackie was suddenly back to business. 'Right, ladies, I want you warming up. Forward and side bends, please, then stretch out your quads and hamstrings. I don't want any injuries on your first day. Roll your shoulders and start doing some hip circles . . .'

Some of the girls seemed to be struggling even with the warm-up moves; they didn't have much chance of getting through the session if they weren't flexible.

'Now I want you doing some standing squats – it's important to have strong leg muscles for this work,' said Jackie, upping the tempo.

Shortly afterwards, she put on Beyoncé full blast and got us doing a high-intensity aerobic dance workout in front of the mirrors and didn't let us rest for a good fifteen minutes.

I was gasping for breath by the end of it.

Gabi and Makani had struggled to keep up with the steps but Irena, even though she looked skinny enough to snap in half, had managed to get through it.

'OK, ladies, take five, have a drink of water and join me at the poles when you're ready,' said Jackie. 'If that exhausted you, your fitness levels need to be improved. You need more stamina than that to get through a night shift at the Pearl.'

I thought I was coping pretty well thus far and was looking forward to doing some pole work.

'Gather round, ladies,' said Jackie, motioning us round the poles.

'As you can see, there are six of us and only four poles, so we'll do this in shifts. I will demonstrate some basic moves then three of you will follow. First, the wrap-around move. Wipe down the pole before you start, to give maximum grip.

'Stand at the back of the pole with your inside foot at the base. Using your strongest hand, grab the pole at head height, and keep your arm straight. Make sure your weight is hanging away from the pole.

'Keep your outside leg straight then swing it out and step round the pole, pivoting on your inside foot. Bend your knee slightly as you turn.

'Place your outside foot behind the other foot, transfer your weight to the foot at the back and hook the inside of your leg around the front of the pole, gripping it right behind your knee.

'Now practise arching backwards, slipping your hand down the pole so you can reach further back. Then straighten up and swing your leg back down.'

I quickly realised that, even though I'd put on a pretty convincing show at the Pearl that night, my technique left something to be desired. Jackie beck-oned for me to mount a pole, along with Gabi and Irena.

'Right, girls, I'll do it slowly at first, you follow me,' said Jackie.

We put on our heels and took up our positions at the back of each pole. I was doing fine until I started swinging around the pole. My hand slipped and I had to start again.

'Geri, move away from the pole,' ordered Jackie. 'Are you wearing any body lotion or oil?'

'Well, I put on some cocoa butter this morning.' I said, feeling sheepish.

'I thought I told you all, no lotions or potions on any part of your body while you're dancing, please,' said Jackie. 'It makes the pole slippery and hazardous. Go to the ladies, and wipe yourself down.'

I felt like the naughty girl who had been caught messing around at the back of the classroom. The other girls looked terrified. Jackie was turning out to be something of a Sergeant Major.

I sloped off to the toilets and did the best I could to remove the traces of cocoa butter with a paper towel, rubbing my skin red raw in the process.

I felt the same as when I first learned to ride and kept falling off my horse: small and foolish. But when I got back to the studio I tried again and this time the move came more easily.

Jackie then took us on to the fireman spin, back hook spin and then the more advanced cradle spin. The last one needed a lot of upper-body strength and some of the girls just couldn't hack it. Gabi had all but given up by this point, to the clear annoyance of Jackie.

'Gabi, I'm disappointed in you,' she said. 'I pictured

you dancing into the night at the Rio carnival, yet you give up half an hour into a pole-dancing lesson.'

'I'm sorry, Jackie,' she said. 'I'm not sure I'm strong enough to do this.'

'Is anyone else going to fall at the first fence?' demanded Jackie.

There were a few worried faces, but no one spoke.

'OK, let's carry on. And I want to see you smile and look sexy – and to do that you've got to feel comfortable in your body and trust that it won't let you down. I'm fast-tracking you here because you have to be ready to work as soon as possible. Let's have a go at an inversion . . .'

Gabi looked horrified and Makani shook her head, but Irena, of all people, seemed to take it in her stride.

I'd done this once myself without really knowing how to do it properly but I was worried it might have been beginner's luck.

I gave it my best shot and realised the key to the move was getting the right angle on the upward swing of the legs. It took a hell of a lot of effort, though, especially because of the pace at which we were going through the moves.

'OK, ladies, I don't want you falling on your heads,' said Jackie. 'Safety is paramount when you're doing this type of dancing. Let's take a break and I'll run you through a few rules and regulations about working at the Pearl – that is if you ever get that far.

'We do not employ girls who drink to excess or take banned substances. You need to be in full possession of your faculties at all times while you're dancing. Please make sure your partner doesn't have a problem with what you do at night – we don't want you missing shifts because of domestics.

'Here's the list of don'ts. Don't believe all the stories about how much girls are earning at other clubs, and don't boast about how much you earn either. Don't poke the payroll. Shagging members of staff at the club is a really bad idea and will end in tears – probably yours. Don't presume you'll be doing this for a few weeks or months. So many girls say that and then they come back again once they find their dream of being a rocket scientist comes to nothing. So take it seriously.

'Don't slag off the other girls. Try not to be bitch queens and get on with each other in the dressing room. Don't think you can rush out and buy designer clothes after two weeks. If you're making good money it's tempting to spoil yourself but it's better to save for that rainy day when you don't want to dance any more.

'Don't give customers free dances. Even if George Clooney walks in, he will have to pay like everyone else. But do respect the customers, even if you don't like them. If you go in there thinking every man who comes into a lapdancing club is a pervert it will reflect badly on you and the Pearl. OK, that's it for now. Any questions?'

'Yes,' said Makani. 'Is it possible just to do pole dancing at the Pearl and not lapdancing?'

'If you work for us you have to be prepared to do both and in any case, lap dances will earn you bigger tips,' explained Jackie. 'Once you've all cracked the fundamentals of pole dancing I'll teach you some key lapdancing moves.'

'Do we get to choose our own costumes?' asked Gabi.

'We like you to pick from our own range but your costume should suit the personality you want to project as a dancer,' said Jackie. 'It's up to you to create a look that will get you noticed. Now, if you have any more questions, ask me later. I'm going to demonstrate a series of moves and I want you to do your best to string them together into a routine.'

We watched in awe as Jackie swung up and down the pole with grace and ease, tossing back her long brown hair and throwing some amazingly sexy shapes.

The group burst into spontaneous applause when she finished.

I did my best to access my inner showgirl and managed to get through the routine only fluffing a couple of spins.

Poor Gabi was almost in tears now. She literally just couldn't get into the swing of it. Irena didn't say much but quietly got on with it and was looking pretty good.

When everyone had had their go, Jackie called us back into the circle to do some cool-down stretches.

'OK, everyone, relax now,' she said. 'Put on your track-suits and come and sit down. Now comes the tough part. I can only take on the girls I think can cope with this job, physically and mentally. Gabi, I think you already know this is not for you. And, Makani – you look beautiful, but I can't let you loose on a pole until you're more confident. The rest of you have the makings of decent dancers, but you'll have to work hard.'

She paused and looked me up and down.

'Geri, I'd just about put you top of the class, closely followed by Irena. As you know, you'll both be working in the Pearl here in north London. The others will go to the West End. Now, Geri and Irena, wait here and I'll get someone to show you downstairs so you can pick out your costumes for your first act.'

Irena and I looked at each other and smiled. I was chuffed to have got the nod from such a smart operator as Jackie. Jackie shot me a knowing look. Had she sussed me out or was she just testing me? I smiled and thanked her before leaving the studio, even more determined to make my plan work but knowing I had to watch my back . . .

Ten minutes later, a woman appeared through the connecting door and swept into the room. I'd have put her in her early thirties. Her flesh was soft rather than toned and she had milky-blue eyes and blonde hair. It was a very sexy, old-school glamour look with a definite nod in the direction of Marilyn Monroe.

'Ah, fresh blood!' she announced. 'Welcome, ladies, to what I hope will become your home from home. I'm Suzy.'

'Hi, Suzy,' I said. 'My name's Geri, pleased to meet you.'

'Well hi there, Geri, it's nice to hear an English voice around here. So who is this? Does she speak?'

Irena smiled sheepishly but didn't say a word.

'Yes, she does, but her English isn't great. She's from Poland,' I told Suzy.

'Well, I hope the kid can dance or she's screwed,' said Suzy with a grimace. 'Anyway, come this way and follow me into Aladdin's cave . . .'

Chapter Eight

She took us both down a spiral staircase into the base-
ment of the club where a range of shiny and spangled
costumes hung from a couple of free-standing rails. It
was a little low-rent for a businesswoman used to the
changing rooms at Prada.

'OK girls, pretend you're at TK Maxx,' said Suzy,
pointing a red nail at the racks. 'There's a lot of rubbish
here but if you look carefully you might find a diamond
in the dross. You'll have to hire it from us but the rates
are good.'

Despite her earlier reticence, Irena was the first to
start browsing. All the strip club clichés were here – the
peek-a-boo bikinis, front-zipping leather mini dresses,
metallic halter-neck tops, see-through bodysuits, French
maid outfits, mini school uniforms, nurses' uniforms,
sexy secretary get-ups and everything you'd need to
dress like a dominatrix.

Irena went straight for a cinch-waisted, sleeveless
leather dress with an in-built bustier with matching
elbow-length leather gloves and a Playboy bunny-style
white collar.

I was surprised. She didn't look the type to pull it off.

On first glance it looked as if there was nothing quite right for the image I wanted to project. I knew a shoulder-length wig was necessary – my initial thought was black, but I didn't want to look like Morticia Addams and it was too similar to my own hair colour. So, inspired by Tania's pre-Raphaelite locks, I decided my alter-ego would have red hair. But I didn't want to wear the usual stripper's tat.

'Suzy, do you have anything a little more unusual?' I asked. 'You know, something that doesn't get worn too often?'

'Geri, I'd recommend you go for the tried-and-tested. Don't be too ambitious on your first outing,' she advised.

'But none of this stuff is quite me,' I said. 'Isn't there anything that covers up a bit more flesh to start with? I always think that's far sexier.'

'Ah, I can see you're going to be the high-maintenance girl,' laughed Suzy. 'We have a special collection for picky ones like you.'

She opened a cupboard in the corner and pulled out a couple of outfits that looked far more substantial than the scanties on the racks.

One was a full-length gown with a side zip, but the other looked much more up my street. It looked like a normal man's business suit – pinstripe, of course – but it was held together by Velcro straps.

'I knew it,' said Suzy. 'You're going to go for the one that requires you to be Harry Houdini.'

'How does it work?' I asked, examining the outfit more closely.

'Give it a good tug at the right moment and hope to hell it actually comes off when you want it to,' she chuckled.

The jacket was normal but the trousers had a sort of tight waistcoat attached and the idea was if you pulled the Velcro, the whole thing would come off and reveal whatever was underneath.

'Oh, that's perfect,' I said. 'I love it. I don't care if it's labour-intensive, that's just what I was looking for.'

'Good luck, Geri,' said Suzy. 'Better girls than you have tried and failed to make this one work.'

'Don't worry, I'm incredibly persistent,' I told her.

'OK, it's all yours,' she said, 'but mind your stockings on the Velcro . . .'

'God yes, of course, I'll have to wear something underneath,' I said. 'I think I'll go with a four-suspender corset with fishnets so I don't have to worry about ladders.' I wanted to wear something that I felt sexy in; an outfit that I'd use to seduce a man in my bedroom.

'I think that will be the least of your worries, darling,' said Suzy, ominously.

As I was rifling through the racks trying to find a corset I liked, Irena had changed into her outfit and found a black wig to cover her blonde hair. She'd put on some heavy eye liner and red lipstick and brightened her deathly-pale face with some foundation and rouge.

'Wow, Irena,' I said. 'You look amazing. Like a completely different person, in fact – which is the idea, I guess.'

'Thank you, Geri,' she whispered. 'It is the only way I do this, if I turn myself into other. It is easier that way, you see.'

There was a sadness about her that I couldn't quite fathom. I didn't want to pry so I left her to paint her face a different picture.

It was time for me to get my glad rags on. I escaped to the ladies with a pair of borrowed fishnets, a black satin corset, a pair of black patent platforms and my Velcro-studded 'business suit'.

It was a bit of a faff to get all the Velcro done up properly but once it was all on, it looked pretty convincing. With the red wig and a bit more make-up, it would have been hard for my own mother to recognise me.

'Oh, suits you, madam,' joked Suzy when I emerged. 'Now see if you can rip it off.'

I stood in front of the mirror, tugged the 'ripcord' and nothing happened.

'I think you're doing it at the wrong angle, love,' said Suzy. 'Try pulling it straight down, it's not a parachute.'

I tried again and the whole outfit came away in my hands to reveal the corset and stockings underneath.

'Bravo!' said Suzy as Irena looked on, giggling behind her hand. 'Now all you need is a bowler hat and an umbrella!'

'No, I think that would be taking the City gent look a bit too far,' I laughed. If only Suzy knew . . .

'Right, Geri, and what's-your-name,' said Suzy, climbing the stairs, 'let me show you where you'll be working.'

I quickly put my costume back together as she guided us into the heart of the club.

'OK, we have a main stage here where the girls do their main routine for one or two songs on the pole,' she explained. 'Then over here we have horseshoe tables for up to ten gentlemen, with a pole in the centre. This is where you'd do your table dances. The bar is over there – and you will be expected to chat to customers and work the floor – and in the corner is the private dance booth, separated from the main club by that velvet curtain.

'Don't worry, the entire club is fitted with cameras that are constantly monitored by security staff so you will be completely safe.

'We have a strict "no touching" policy at the Pearl, so if a customer tries to feel you up, security will be down on him like a ton of bricks before the end of the chorus.'

'Has anyone tried it on with you, Suzy?' I asked.

'It happens to every dancer from time to time,' she told me. 'Early in my career a guy grabbed my clit when I was giving him a private dance. I resisted the urge to punch his lights out but suffice to say he never darkened our doors again.

'Remember, both of you – just because you're taking your clothes off doesn't mean you don't deserve respect.'

I liked Suzy. She was down-to-earth and had a great sense of humour without being too cynical. I thought she might be able to tell me a few home truths.

'Suzy, can I ask you about money?'

'Don't tell me, you've done a bit of research on Google and think you can earn two grand a night,' she replied.

'Well, not exactly, but I am a bit confused about how much I can expect to earn,' I told her. 'I spoke to Declan about it, but I think he was basing that on the Mayfair branch.'

'OK, honey, I'll try to give you the score, but it varies

from girl to girl,' she told me, brushing a platinum blonde hair off her shoulder. 'If you're good, you're in demand, you earn more, it's as simple as that. You pay us rent to dance in the form of a house fee, then it's up to you. Guys tip at a fixed rate per dance and anything else they want to give you over the top of that.

'You'll be expected to "tip out", which means you give a fixed percentage of what you've earned to share among the other people who work in the club – the DJ, the bar staff, the bouncers, and of course, the "house mother", Jackie.'

'So how am I going to earn £400 a night if I have to share my tips?' I asked.

'By getting private dances with high rollers, of course,' she said. 'This isn't Mayfair but you still get a lot of businessmen up here, and a lot of footballers who play for the north London clubs. If you're lucky, one will be celebrating a win or spending his signing-on fee.'

'I'm only doing this for short-term gain,' I told her. 'So I'm aiming to target one of those big spenders every night.'

'Well, good luck, darling – all the girls want that so you'll have plenty of competition,' she said, raising an arched eyebrow. 'But you'll have novelty value on your side to start with, so take advantage of it.'

'Thanks for the advice, Suzy, I really appreciate it.'

'No worries.'

After that, I decided to investigate the main stage. After all, that's where I would be getting the biggest audience and therefore the biggest pool of potential 'investors'.

I began doing some practise swings and dips. I needed

to get used to the shoes, apart from anything else. I was used to wearing high heels in the office, but not these kinds of 'fuck-me' vertiginous heels. I didn't want to fall over, Naomi Campbell-style, the minute I tried to execute a slightly tricky move.

In a few days' time I would begin my first shift. I had butterflies in my stomach at the idea of everyone looking at me up there, but it was excited anticipation as much as nerves. With my costume and wig on I already felt like another person, and she was a million miles away from the Geraldine Carson that went to work every morning at Sloane Brothers.

Suzy watched me as I practised a short routine on the pole. I'd do half with the suit on, half with it off, then finish by doing a burlesque turn and removing my stockings, corset and thong.

'How long do I have to stand here naked at the end?' I asked.

'As long as it takes to loosen their wallets,' she said. 'It's best that you have a robe at the side of the stage so you can put something on straight away to collect tips. A sexy silky one would do, and try to keep a garter on. Guys still like putting notes in them.'

'Yes, I'll make sure I do that,' I said. 'God, there's so much to remember . . .'

'You're a bright girl,' said Suzy. 'You'll get the hang of it pretty quickly.'

I joined Suzy back on the floor as Irena was finishing her routine on the table. She'd transformed herself from a wishy-washy wimp into a coltish leather-clad sex goddess.

'Does it feel good?' I asked her.

'A bit strange, I think,' she said. 'But I hope they'll like me.'

'I'm sure they will,' I told her. 'Don't worry.'

Suzy grabbed my arm. It seems she had decided to take me under her wing.

'Let me tell you something, Geri,' she said. 'You've got to be tough to do this, and I'm not sure Irena will be able to hack it. I can see you will, though.'

'Thanks,' I said, pulling off my wig. 'I hope you're right.'

'You don't have to worry about the dirty mac brigade any more,' she continued. 'All kinds of men come to clubs like this now, it's seen as normal guy stuff. When they start out, a lot of the girls swear they'll never go out with a customer but a lot of them do. Some even have long-term relationships – romantic and otherwise.'

I smiled and nodded but thought God, the last thing I'd do would be to get it on with a guy in a strip club. Suzy carried on with her lecture.

'You'll learn to suss out the good ones and also the bad ones. Don't be fooled by the expensive clothes, it doesn't make the man. Some will look loaded but be tight-fisted. Others might be verbally abusive. But on the whole you'll enjoy yourself more if you give customers the benefit of the doubt. Develop friendships with the regulars and you'll always be in demand . . .'

'It's really good of you to give me tips, Suzy,' I said, trying to get away. It was getting late and I had a date with my sofa. 'I'll try to remember everything you've told me.'

'Well, I'll be here to remind you if you don't, honey,'

she said. 'Do you want to have a little heart-starter with me to cement our beautiful new friendship?'

'I'd love to but I really have to get going now,' I said, hoping not to appear rude. 'I've got so much to do before I start training. Maybe when I've finished my first shift?'

'Oh, you little spoilsport,' she said. 'You're no fun. Mine's a double vodka and Coke then, as soon as you get your tips.'

'No worries, it will be my pleasure. I'll see you later,' I said, winking at Irena.

When I took off my costume in the backstage dressing room and wiped away my heavy make-up I suddenly felt quite vulnerable. For the first time, I felt a gnawing fear. 'Oh my God, Geraldine,' I said to my reflection. 'This is for real . . .'

Chapter Nine

My debut shift at the Pearl had been set for Wednesday night, the designated night for new girls to perform for the first time. I'd faked a dentist's appointment to get out of work early and give me a bit of breathing space before the 8pm kick-off but I'd spent most of the day trying not to think about what lay in store that night. Jackie, who was running the club in Declan's absence, had given me permission to arrive as early as 6.30pm to start my final preparation.

As soon as I walked in the door, Suzy came bowling up to greet me.

'Hello sunshine,' she said, a vodka and Coke already in her hand. 'Welcome to Dante's inferno!'

'Hi Suzy, can you show me where to go and get changed?'

'Sure thing – don't expect five-star accommodation, but it's not too bad,' she said. 'You'll have to share a mirror, but only with a couple of girls.'

She took me round the back of the main stage to a dressing-room area that was like a glorified ladies' loo but at least the lighting was good and it was reasonably clean.

One girl sat in the corner in jogging bottoms and a fleece, reading a celebrity magazine.

'Geri, this is Danuta,' said Suzy. 'She doesn't speak much English so just wave and smile.' I followed her instructions and the girl smiled wanly back at me.

'How come you're here so early?' I asked Suzy.

'I like to be here to welcome new victims,' she said. 'It appeals to my inner vampire. And I don't make a habit of disobeying Jackie's orders.'

We laughed, and I guessed Jackie had also told Suzy to put the rookies at ease. Well, it was working so far.

'Now, since you've got loads of time to kill,' she said, 'come and have a drink with me at the bar.'

'OK, but just the one – I want to be completely on the ball tonight.'

'Well darling, if you're lucky, you will definitely be on the balls,' she said, sashaying towards the bar in a Fifties-style blue satin prom frock.

'What's your poison?'

'Just a small white wine spritzer for me,' I said. 'To steady the nerves.'

'As the bar's not officially open yet, I shall be your bartender,' she said, pouring a large measure of vodka into her glass and tipping half a bottle of wine into a tumbler topped up with a tiny splash of soda for me. *This girl could drink.* 'Get that down you.'

I sipped it slowly, having no intention of drinking the whole thing.

'Are you working tonight?' I asked.

'I don't want to do a whole shift but I might trundle my sorry ass out there for a couple of hours,' she told me, taking a swig. 'One of my regulars will probably be in later. If you see a dark-haired, weaselly guy who looks a bit like Sinatra, leave him alone, he's mine.'

Sometimes I wondered if Suzy thought she was living in a wise-cracking 1950s movie. I guess the subterranean, nocturnal life suited her, though.

'I need a cigarette,' she announced. 'Do you smoke, Geri?'

'No, but please, don't mind me,' I said.

'Come and keep a poor girl company out the back in the freezing cold,' she said, taking a Chesterfield out of the pack. I wondered where she got the American cigarettes, and if she really liked the taste or if it was all part of the Marilyn Monroe act.

It was rapidly becoming clear that you did what Suzy said or risked being frozen out, so I dutifully followed her out of the fire exit, where she stood puffing away in an alleyway behind the club.

'You seem like a good kid, Geri,' she told me, waving the smoke away from me. 'Everyone has a different reason to be here and I don't want to know yours. Just do what you've got to do and get out of it as soon as you can. It's not good for the soul, although excellent for the spirits . . .' she added, winking.

'I'm not planning to make a career out of it,' I said. 'No disrespect to you or Jackie.'

'None taken. It's just that this world has a habit of sucking you in and not spitting you out.'

'Advice taken,' I said, shivering slightly. 'Anything else I need to know before I go to get changed?'

'Not really,' she said, a faraway look in her eyes. 'As

I've said before, just enjoy it. Because if you don't enjoy it, the customers will notice, and you won't get the tips. But at the end of the day you've got to do it for yourself, not them . . .'

'Thanks. Now I really must go and get changed.'

'OK sweetie, off you go,' she said, sounding like my mother – even though she was no more than five years older than me. 'I'll see you before your first dance . . .'

I scampered back to the changing room before she changed her mind and dragged me back to the bar.

When I returned, Irena was there, pale as a ghost.

'Hi Irena, how are you feeling?' I asked.

'Oh, hello Geri. I'm nervous. What about you?'

'My stomach's doing a bit of a dance but hopefully I'll settle down soon,' I told her. 'Give me a shout if you want any help with your costume.'

'Thank you, that is very kind,' she said, as if no one had ever offered her any help before.

It was coming up to 7.15 and I wanted to get into my costume and ready in plenty of time in case I had any teething problems.

Thankfully I'd chosen a front-fastening corset with lacing up the back so I didn't need any help with that. The suspenders seemed solid enough not to pop open unbidden and I'd bought some professional dancers' fishnets from a ballet shop one lunchtime.

The wig was easy enough to secure, given that my own hair was short, and I'd bought proper stage make-up that wouldn't melt under the lights.

As I prepared myself I felt like an actor psyching

themselves up for a role. I'd read that the costume was often a major part of the transition from actor to character.

That's certainly how it was for me as I began to transform myself into my alter ego.

With my 'suit' on over my corset and suspenders and the wig firmly anchored on to my head, I started to feel strong and sexy.

I smiled as I realised it was a parody of the outfit I wore to work every day – my armour. But this was armour of a different kind – one that celebrated my sexuality rather than kept it hidden.

Once I painted my face, the look was complete. I looked pretty good and felt fantastic.

At that moment, Suzy came into the dressing room, pushing her way past the other girls in the room to come and speak to me.

'Well, darling, just look at you!' she said, and I knew she'd had several more drinks since I last saw her. 'You look glorious . . . I think we need to give you a stage name for good luck. How about Ginger? Yes, I think that would suit you . . .'

I knew I would need a stage name for anonymity and agreed to Ginger, although I couldn't help thinking about the Spice Girls.

It was ten minutes before show time and the changing room was full of half-naked girls. Suzy was swaying slightly as Jackie popped her head around the door.

'Hi girls,' she shouted. 'Everything OK back here? Geri, Irena, how are you feeling?'

'Well, it's now or never,' I said, my stomach fluttering.

'Good luck. Just remember what I told you, relax and enjoy it. Suzy, can I have a word please?'

Suzy gave her a 'Who, me?' look and left us to our own devices. I hoped she wouldn't get into trouble with the house mother.

'OK, Geri – I'll give you the choice of main stage or table for your first dance,' said Jackie. 'What's it to be?'

'Oh God . . . I'll go for it – main stage, please,' I said, hoping I wouldn't regret it.

'The club has just opened,' announced Jackie. 'The first dancer is on in ten minutes. It'll be you after that, Geri.'

'No problem, I'll be ready,' I said, but the first-night nerves were beginning to kick in. I just hoped they wouldn't turn into stage fright.

I felt like a teenage model about to do her first catwalk show. Was my wig on straight? Had I smudged my lipstick? Would the suit come off at first tug? Would my ankles hold out in those heels?

I'd watched plenty of documentaries in which frenzied designers could be seen putting their finishing touches to a model's outfit before literally pushing her down the runway. Jackie didn't quite do that to me – in fact, in her role as house mother she put on a much more sympathetic face than when she was breaking us in on the pole.

'Your cue is the first few bars of "Thieves in the Temple".'

I hoped my musical hero Prince would inspire me to give as lovesexy a show as he did. My thoughts were of him as I entered the corridor that connected the dressing room to the main stage.

I watched from the wings as the girl before me finished her routine. She was obviously one of the more experienced dancers as she had an enviable fluidity to her moves.

When the music came to an end she walked to the front of the stage and out of my sight, presumably to pick up her tips from the audience.

The DJ would be cueing up my song now. I'd be out there any minute . . .

I peered around the curtain.

God, the place was packed. There must have been around two hundred guys in there.

'Good luck, Geri,' said Jackie, her hand gently guiding me along.

Was I tempted to run about a mile? Hell yes. But for all my faults, I'm not one to back down from a challenge.

I heard those familiar first few bars and made my way towards the lights.

Chapter Ten

I strode on stage with as much attitude as I could muster and stood behind the pole with one hand holding it and the other on my hip.

The temperature seemed to have skyrocketed about a hundred degrees and with a spotlight right in my eyes, it took me a moment to get my bearings.

I peered out into the audience, terrified I might see someone I knew. For a moment I froze. Yes, there was a familiar face – but it was only Declan, smiling at me and applauding. Inside, I smiled back.

I couldn't pole dance with the suit on, so I used some of Jackie's lap-dancing moves to kick off the routine.

I thought of Liza Minnelli as Sally Bowles in *Cabaret* and asked one of the guys at the front to pass me a chair. I used it to simulate a lap dance, grinding my hips over the seat, then sitting in it back-to-front, doing dips and kicking my legs up, then holding the back of the chair to stick out my ass and slap it with my spare hand.

I heard a few whoops so guessed I must be heading along the right lines. Next came the tricky bit – ripping off the suit.

I tossed away the chair and stood centre-stage.

The weird part was that was the moment I felt most exposed – most vulnerable. In that moment deciding whether I really dare do this. Whether I really did have the balls for this?

If it hadn't been for Declan, I might have backed out, but I just held his gaze the whole time. If I was just performing this for him, then I could do this.

Slowly I unbuttoned my jacket, shrugged it off one shoulder, turned my back on them and let it slip down my back and arms before spinning around, and throwing it into the crowd.

With a row of grinning men at my feet, I felt like the queen of fucking everything. I milked the moment for all it was worth, ramping up the tension.

Then, when I heard Prince singing the first line of 'Thieves in the Temple' I grabbed my 'ripcord' and pulled it hard and straight.

The suit came off with one tug as planned and I felt triumphant, standing there in my corset and stockings.

'Nice trick, babe!' shouted a small, dark-haired man, and I hoped it wasn't Suzy's Sinatra lookalike.

'Nice tits!' piped up another as I made my way back to the pole, giving them the first flash of cheek. 'Great arse!'

Ignoring them, I looked back over my shoulder coquettishly, zoned in on Declan, smiled and licked my lips, just like Jackie had taught us.

The crowd whistled and whooped again and I was loving the effect I was having. I draped myself around the pole, did my first wrap-around and felt so energised that even doing a cradle spin seemed like child's play. The fishnets were exposing just enough flesh to give me traction for the harder moves.

I was really in the zone now, feeling physically invincible.

I didn't notice any strain, pain or discomfort and finished the routine with an ambitious carousel spin, all the way down to the ground. Now all I had to do was strip . . .

All?

I scanned the crowd for Declan's face once more, but he was lost in the swelling crowd.

But I didn't need him anymore. I was on too much of a high. And unlike Ryan I wasn't going to leave this crowd feeling deflated.

'Dita Von Teese, eat your heart out,' I thought as I cupped my breasts then ran my hands over my curves and ass cheeks.

My blood was really pumping now. This is how I felt when I was on horseback, waiting to go into the paddock. But this time I had only *my* body to discipline.

I gently kicked off my shoes before bending and undoing my suspenders, lingering over each one.

I had the front row in the palm of my hand as I slowly, sensually rolled each stocking down in time to the music. Squeezing the corset I undid each hook one by one, turned around and peeled it off before throwing it to the side of the stage.

Standing there in nothing but a wispy thong and a garter, I did a few more grinding circles to the music, waiting for the song to come to its climax before gently wiggling the thong down to the ground and turning round to face the audience in my birthday suit.

Despite this being the moment of maximum exposure, I felt totally liberated. The buzz was indescribable – my naked body had every man in that room under its spell. Every inch of my skin was sensitised, tingling with sexual energy.

And in that moment, I'd never felt more alive. For the first time in as long as I could remember, I didn't feel put down, or angry, or frustrated, just incredibly *vital*.

I think I was starkers longer than strictly necessary but the endorphins were whizzing round my brain.

And suddenly Declan was back. He gave me the 'jug' in which the minimum £1 tip would be collected, although customers had the option of paying more, or putting money in my garter. Then he handed me my suit jacket and a £20 note. He was the first, slotting £20 in my garter. The guys next to him followed suit – £10 here, £5 there, until there was a wad pressed against my thigh.

I'd ignored Suzy's suggestion to wear a silky robe and put on the suit jacket, which just about covered my modesty, and slipped the thong back on to cover my trimmed bush.

Grabbing the notes and stuffing them in my inside pocket, it was a whole different ballgame being eye to eye with the guys in the audience. I was on their level now and had to be on my guard more.

Some guys just smiled sweetly and put a few pound coins in the jug. Others were more vocal, shouting, 'Hey baby, want to give me a free ride?' but dropping their shrapnel like good boys and allowing me to move on.

Unfortunately some were not so easy to deal with. One fat, balding guy came far too close for comfort and whispered in my ear, 'Do I turn you on? Do you think I'm hot?'

Resisting the temptation to shout, 'No, you disgusting, deluded pig!' I forced a smile and moved on.

Another, younger bloke with over-groomed hair and lashings of aftershave looked charming but only put the minimum tip in the jug and tried to cop a sly feel of my breast by making me push past him.

But these were the small fry and now I was no longer a pole-dancing virgin, I wanted to catch the *bigger* fish . . .

Chapter Eleven

Suzy had told me that once I'd done my duty with the jug, I should go and check out the customers at the tables and in the booths, because that's where the real money was.

Another girl had started her routine on the main stage so the punters were otherwise occupied, giving me the chance to explore.

I'd nearly given up hope when I noticed an attractive, Mediterranean-looking man sitting quietly at a table in the corner. I could tell by the cut of his suit and the expensive bottle of cognac on his table that he was the type who appreciated the finer things in life.

Zoning in on him, I even allowed a few hands to paw me as they placed notes in my garter. I finally locked on to his eyes – and they were incredible. Deep brown, heavy-lidded and enigmatic. He held my gaze without blinking for a good twenty seconds. He was gorgeous. What was a man like him doing in a place like this? Then again, what was a girl like me doing here? Note to self: must not pre-judge, must not pre-judge.

He made a discreet gesture to beckon me over and

as I approached him he plucked a beautiful tan leather wallet from his inside pocket and pulled out a £50 note.

'Thank you. That was a classy act.'

I put one leg up on the banquette next to him so he wouldn't have to move to reach my garter.

When he slid the currency inside the elastic, his little finger gently brushed the inside of my thigh. It wasn't deliberate but neither was it strictly accidental. But, my God, it was sexy. *He* was sexy. I blushed.

'Please, do join me later,' he said in a heavily accented voice.

I nodded and covered myself again before heading back towards the stage.

'Wow,' I thought. 'This guy has class. What a gentleman . . .'

I quickly gathered up my discarded items from the side of the stage and disappeared back into the sanctuary of the dressing room. Thankfully, all the other girls were out on the tables and on the floor so I was able to spend a few moments alone, collecting my thoughts and, more importantly, counting my money.

With my earnings topped up by my very generous benefactor, even after deducting the house fee and money for tipping out it looked like I would make £200 just from this one dance. Not bad for less than ten minutes' work.

I stuffed the cash into the pouch Jackie had given me and headed for the bathroom to splash my face with some cooling water.

One of the three cubicles was occupied, which surprised

me as I thought all the girls were working. I was about to enter an empty one when I heard someone whimpering.

There was enough space at the bottom of the door for me to glimpse a pair of familiar shoes – Irena's.

I wasn't sure whether to leave her to it or try to help. She was trying to muffle her sobs but they were getting deeper and more distressing.

'Irena?' I said. 'Are you OK?'

She didn't reply so I tried passing some loo roll underneath the door.

'Oh, is it Geri?' she asked, accepting my offering.

'Yes it is. Anything I can do?'

'No, I will be OK. I am just a little nervous.'

I didn't believe her but there was no time for me to provide a free counselling service.

'Right, as long as you're sure . . . I'll see you later then . . .'

I left her to it and changed into a black satin pencil skirt split to the thigh, which I slipped on over my corset and fishnets. A little fake fur shrug completed the look. The wig stayed firmly in place, though. I couldn't afford to be recognised.

All I wanted to do was get back out there before any of the other girls got their hands on my cognac man. I was ready to leave when Suzy came stumbling in.

'Hi, gorgeous,' she said, clearly the worse for wear. 'I was watching you out there. You did good. Room for improvement, of course, but not a bad start.'

'Thanks, Suzy, I'll work on it,' I said, hoping this would be a short conversation.

'No need to stand there displaying your wares for quite so long,' she continued. 'Always leave them wanting more.'

'Yes, it's OK, I'll do that next time,' I told her, moving away. 'I was aware of that. It was just such an amazing feeling I wanted to savour it.'

'Oh, you got it, baby,' she slurred. 'That's what girl power is all about. Never mind the bloody Spice Girls . . .'

'Yeah, I felt really . . . empowered out there,' I said.

'Empowered? Oh yes, my pretty. Using something as basic, as animal, as female sex appeal to manipulate men is fucking empowering. Oh, and raw cash is pretty empowering too. Knowing I can leave tonight with a big, fat wad of cash in my pocket does it for me, I can tell you . . .'

I laughed knowingly. 'Yep, I've already felt a bit of that thrill. I think I'm going to have a bumper night tonight . . .'

'I'm sure you will, darling,' said Suzy. 'Beginner's luck. Just try doing it night after night . . .'

'Anyway,' I interrupted. 'You need to change now, don't you, so I'd better let you get on.'

She was too tipsy to answer and I was already halfway out the door. Poor Suzy. I hoped she didn't get on the wrong side of Jackie twice in one night. God knows how she danced while three sheets to the wind but she could obviously look after herself.

I made a beeline back to the corner table, where my biggest fan was waiting patiently.

'You are back, at last,' he said as I approached.

'Yes, I'm sorry about the delay,' I said in my sweetest voice.

'Never mind, you're here now. Please, come and sit with me. Now, what is your name?'

'It's Ginger,' I told him. As tempted as I was to be Geri, to be 'me', I had to remain in character for this encounter.

'Pleased to meet you, Ginger. My name is Aramis.'

'What nationality is that? Turkish?'

'In part, yes,' he said. 'I've not seen you dance here before.'

Feeling a fake, I decided to be more honest. Well, up to a point.

'It's my first night,' I told him. 'I'm a rookie.'

'I see. Well then, I consider myself privileged to have witnessed your debut,' he said, flashing a gorgeous smile. 'You are fresh. And there is something intriguing about you.'

'Thanks, Aramis. I really appreciate your compliments, and your very generous tip,' I said, courteously. 'I must say you have excellent taste. In cognac, as well as women, of course . . .'

'I like to believe I am discerning,' he said. 'Can I get you a drink?'

I decided to up the ante. If this guy was for real I'd have to get him spending money like there was no tomorrow.

'Yes, that would be wonderful,' I purred. 'How about a bottle of vintage Krug?'

'Ah, a woman of good taste,' he said, completely unruffled by my extravagant request.

He clicked his fingers and a waiter came rushing over. This guy was clearly known for spending serious money. Bullseye . . .

Within moments I was sipping a perfectly chilled glass of liquid nectar. It could almost have been an after-dinner tipple with a rich client from the bank. Only, of course, they hadn't seen me naked as the main course.

'So, Ginger,' he continued. 'Are you going to reveal a little about yourself?'

'Aramis, I always feel a girl should retain more than a little mystery,' I said, lowering my eyelashes, which were heavy with mascara. 'Surely it's enough to know that I am a dancer, and I would love to dance just for you this evening.'

'I see,' he said quietly. 'Of course you are right. It is all about the mystery. But I am delighted you would like to dance for me. Perhaps we could retreat somewhere more private? I prefer not to share my dance with everyone in the room.'

'Of course, Aramis, it would be my pleasure,' I said, draining the last drop from my flute.

Now everything I'd been told so far had led me to believe I was as much in control in a private booth as I was out here in the open but still, for all my bravado, I must confess I was a little nervous. Shy even. In the glare of the lights, the faces all blurring into one, it was easier somehow. This seemed altogether more intimate, especially with a man like Aramis.

'Shall we go there now?'

'If you would like to go ahead to prepare, I will join

you in a few minutes,' he said, clearly knowing more about the etiquette of private dances than I did.

I drew back the heavy velvet drape separating the booth from the main floor. It was a sumptuous room, dimly-lit and draped with velvet, muslin and brocade in deep burgundy, with an upright padded leather Chesterfield at its centre.

The atmosphere was womb-like and sensual, like a sophisticated, but sexy boudoir. I couldn't quite believe I was getting a private dance on my first night. I just hoped those hours practising in front of the mirror would pay off.

I peeled off my pencil skirt and shrug so I could dance freely in my corset and suspenders.

Sitting down on the cool leather, I wished Ginger luck as Aramis entered, drawing the curtain behind him.

I smiled at him and announced: 'Welcome to my parlour . . .'

' . . . said the spider to the fly?' he laughed. 'Then you must now weave the most beautiful web for me . . .'

Aramis offered a well-manicured hand to help me up off the chair. It was then that I spotted his cuff links, which were gold, inlaid with diamonds. I knew luxury when I saw it and these babies looked as if they would cost more than my annual bonus.

The skin on his palm was soft, so I knew he'd never had to do a day's hard work in his life. I allowed him to swing me round so I was standing facing the chair.

He gently allowed my arm to fall and took up position on the Chesterfield.

'Whenever you're ready, Ginger,' he said, gently. 'Weave your magic.'

I stood a few feet in front of him with hands on the curves of my hips, legs apart, then started to sway, looking him straight in the eye.

The planets must have aligned at that moment because right on cue the DJ played Aretha Franklin's 'Respect'.

I started circling him, standing behind him, bending down to blow gently in his ear. The move, unexpected, caused him to shiver.

Working my way back to the front, I dipped down so the line of my cleavage had his full attention, then pulled away, turning round and bending over so he had a full view of my cheeks as I put one hand on each and swayed from side to side, gently slapping myself.

I moved back so I was right over his thighs and did some deep grinding circles, stopping just short of his crotch.

His hands stayed rooted to the arms of the chair; he knew the rules of this club and that he couldn't lay a finger on me no matter how turned on he might become.

I was allowed to make contact with him as part of the dance, but not his genitals. Even when I came close to his face, blowing gently, he showed admirable restraint. He just sat, fixing me with his intense eyes, his lips slightly parted.

I yearned to kiss those lips, just to know how it would feel, but Ginger knew he was the customer. He had an extraordinary presence, like a big cat eyeing its prey.

I wanted to pull out all the stops for him, give him a grand finale he'd never forget. I'd only seen Jackie do a body slide but thought what the hell, let's give it a go.

I gently parted his legs and put my left knee on his right thigh, then did the same with the other leg, pulling myself up to a kneeling position so I was looking down at him.

Slipping my knees down to nestle in the space between his thighs, I grabbed the back of the chair so that every part of my upper torso and face was within inches of his body. I could feel his heat and his breath but never made contact.

Then I slid slowly down to the floor, pressing myself against him briefly before coming back to a standing position and finishing the dance as I'd started it, with my hands on my hips.

My breasts heaved up and down yet he still sat silently, observing me. He allowed me to get my breath back before saying a word.

'Thank you, Ginger,' he said. 'That was truly exquisite. You have an extraordinary natural talent for this, did you know? Come here for a moment.' I moved closer. 'Let me tell you how much I wanted to touch you, to feel you, to . . .'

I pressed my fingers to his lips. Leave them wanting more – that was the golden rule.

'Aramis, I'm pleased you enjoyed the dance, but I have to go now.'

'Yes, of course . . .' he said. 'I understand.'

He fished out that finely-crafted wallet of his again and this time gave me two £50 notes.

'Here,' he said, 'because you were twice as good as the first time.'

'Thank you,' I said, slipping the notes into my garter. 'Hopefully next time I will be four times as good . . .'

We smiled at each other and I turned to leave, gliding out of the booth without a backwards glance even though I desperately wanted a last look at his handsome face.

With any luck I had him hooked and he'd be back for more.

I returned to the dressing room, satisfied that I'd done enough for one night.

Suzy was there, having just finished her shift, relaxing in her robe with another drink.

'Ah, it's the lucky rookie,' she said. Was she jealous? I didn't really care at that moment. 'I see you seduced the sheikh.'

'What do you mean?' I asked.

'Aramis, of course. That's what we call him,' she continued. 'His father is an Arab sheikh and his mother's a French/Turkish belly-dancer, so he comes from both sides of the tracks.'

'Really? That's interesting . . . I wasn't sure what nationality he was,' I said.

'I'm not sure where he was born, but he sure is exotic,' said Suzy. 'I've danced for him a few times and he's always generous. What did he give you?'

'Oh, £100 . . .'

'Not bad, could do better,' she told me. 'He gave me £200 once . . .'

I didn't want to compete with Suzy, but I couldn't help feeling a frisson of disappointment. What had happened in the private room had seemed special in some way. *Damn it, Geraldine, get a grip.*

'Oh, I'm sure you were worth it, Suzy,' I said. 'How long ago was that?'

'Erm . . . last year, I think,' she said. 'Anyway, he's got a few bob,' she continued. 'Stays in a rented house in Bishop's Avenue when he's in London.'

'What, Millionaires' Row?' I asked. Daryll had looked at several places there last year when he'd gotten his huge bonus.

'More like Billionaires' Row now,' she said. 'That's why he comes here rather than Mayfair – it's closer. He flits in and out of London on business. Make the most of him; he'll be gone in a few weeks.'

My heart sank a little. My big spender may not be around for long.

Tiredness suddenly overwhelmed me. I looked at the clock which said 1am and I felt like I was turning into a pumpkin. I took off my work clothes and put on my Juicy Couture tracksuit. It felt so good to be wearing comfy clothes and a pair of trainers.

Jackie came into the dressing room, raising her hands as if to call us to order.

'Ladies, can I have your attention please,' she said, a little too loudly. 'Thank you for making this another great night at the Pearl.'

She handed me my net earnings for the night, which amounted to a pretty cool £400.

I allowed myself to feel cocky about this – especially as no one had really taken advantage of me or touched me up.

I gathered up my belongings and wondered if I should take off my wig, it itched and made my scalp so hot. No, I thought I'd better keep it on, just in case.

Jackie had ordered me a mini-cab – a rookie's treat. Next time I'd have to find my own way home. I climbed the steps out of the club and the taxi driver flashed his lights at me.

Just as I was walking up to the door, I noticed the car parked behind the taxi. It was a Bentley. A uniformed chauffeur opened the passenger door and a tall, well-dressed man stepped on to the pavement. Aramis.

I stood stock still, the archetypal rabbit in the headlights. Thank God, I was still wearing the red wig . . .

'Ginger . . .' he said. 'Can I give you a lift anywhere?'

'That's very sweet of you, Aramis, but my carriage awaits,' I said, gesturing to the taxi.

'I see,' he said. 'Then I shall be back to see you tomorrow.'

I paused a moment to take in what he'd said. He'd be back. To see me . . .

'Are you coming, love?' asked the taxi driver.

Chapter Twelve

The next morning, there was a mound of paperwork to sift through on my desk but I couldn't concentrate on it. I found myself drifting off, staring into the middle distance, daydreaming. Once I even nodded off . . .

Scenes from my other life flashed through my mind. While I was being Geraldine Carson at Sloane Brothers, Ginger's nocturnal adventures seemed like a soft-porn movie in which someone else was starring.

I was still on the ball when circumstances required but when I was on my own, in the privacy of my office, sometimes my heart just wasn't in it. Worse still, Daryll had asked Luke and I to work on a project together, so I had to see even more of his arrogant face.

After my initial rage had subsided over Bonusgate, I'd had a brief chat with the HR manager, who told me nothing could be done unless I was prepared to lodge a formal complaint. I knew that would be frowned on and could potentially damage my career so I reluctantly decided to let it go without a fight.

Tania knew nothing about this, though, so I probably

should have been a little easier on her when she asked me if I was OK.

'Of course,' I replied. 'What made you think I wasn't all right before?'

'I thought you were upset about your bonus . . .'

'Tania, I told you, that's none of your business.'

She turned to go but stopped short of my door. I could see a few of the guys on the floor pointing and laughing at her.

'What's going on?'

'Oh, they're just behaving like idiots,' she said. 'It's because of what I did to Luke the other night – they're plotting against me now.'

'God, they're a pathetic bunch,' I said. 'Tania, I'm curious. Why did you dump him like that, in front of everyone?'

'Well, you quite rightly said your bonus was none of my business, Geri,' she said. 'And that is none of yours.'

'But it was so public, Tania, you can't expect me not to wonder,' I continued.

'Sure, but I'm not telling anyone why I did it,' she explained. 'That's between me and Luke. He knows, and that's all that matters.'

'OK, I won't ask again. I just hope you know what you're doing.' I was bursting to ask her about Declan, too, and where on earth she learned how to do a lap dance but that would have to wait.

I couldn't help but feel for Tania. She'd taken as big a risk as me in taking on the Brothers. Only Darryl had given me a life raft, congratulating me on how well I'd deflected an 'awkward' situation. It looked like Tania was barely holding her head above water.

'Can you call Daryll and see if he's ready for me yet?'

'Oh yes, he confirmed for 11am,' she replied.

'Great, I'll go over now then,' I said, picking up the client dossier I'd compiled.

As I walked into Daryll's office, Luke had already made himself at home in one of the leather recliners, his legs splayed in that way some men have when they want you to know exactly what they've got in their trousers.

I wasn't remotely interested in looking at his crotch so moved the other side of him and sat down opposite Daryll.

'Good morning, Geraldine,' said Daryll, looking immaculate in a blue pinstripe suit with lemon shirt, tie and pocket handkerchief. 'I trust you have recharged your batteries and are ready for action.'

'Of course, Daryll, I'm like the Duracell bunny,' I joked.

'I bet you are, Geri,' winked Luke.

I kicked myself that I'd walked straight into that one.

'Good to see you're both on form this morning,' interjected Daryll. 'Now, Geraldine, what have you got for me?'

'I think the analysts have come up with some excellent strategies and I've selected a couple I think the client will go for,' I told him. 'The figures add up so I think we have a really good chance of pulling this off.'

'Super. Luke, what's your take on it?'

'I've spoken to a few contacts and I'm not sure this is one we should back,' he said. 'This is risky, even for Sloane Brothers.'

I glanced over at Luke with a look of pure disgust on my face. Why had he not told me this before? We were supposed to be working together on this . . .

'Daryll, I have to disagree with Luke,' I continued, regardless. 'The information I have contradicts that view. If it comes off, the deal will be a good one for the client *and* Sloane Brothers.'

'I see,' said Daryll, picking up his Mont Blanc fountain pen and scribbling a few notes. 'As you are my top two people in M&A and you can't come to a consensus, I suggest you go away and work on the figures again and come back to me later.'

'No need for that,' said Luke, dismissively. 'I have to overrule Geri. This is not a goer.'

'Are you absolutely sure about this, Luke?' asked Daryll, perplexed. 'Do you not want to discuss it with Geri first?'

'I will if you deem it necessary,' he replied. 'But my conclusion will stay the same.'

I stared at Luke in disbelief. He was sidelining me completely.

'I suggest you have a quiet chat about it before you make your final decision,' said Daryll, as smooth as ever.

'If you insist,' said Luke, standing up and grabbing his papers. 'But I won't change my mind.'

Daryll threw me a supportive look and I decided to keep my counsel until Luke and I were in a closed office where no one else could hear us.

'Shall we meet in conference room two in half an hour?' I asked Luke, trying to stay as calm as possible.

'I don't see the point,' said Luke, 'but if you must.'

'Yes, I must, and Daryll has asked us to,' I reminded him.

'Whatever you say, Geri Boy,' he smirked. 'As ever, you wear the trousers.'

My head was absolutely thumping with sheer frustration. How dare he undermine me like that in front of Daryll!

I went back to my office and crawled all over the figures again. It all seemed perfectly viable to me. What information did Luke have that might blow this out of the water? Or was he doing this just to make me look like an idiot?

'Anything I can do to help, Geri?' asked Tania, walking in with a fax for me.

'No, Tania, leave me to it,' I said. 'Well, actually there is something . . . Can you check with the traders' PA to see if Luke had any client meetings last week? You'll have to be discreet about it.'

'Oh, it's fine, I've got to know Pam quite well now,' said Tania. 'Leave it with me.'

If Luke had been sneaking around behind my back, I'd soon find out. We were supposed to share information on this deal and I'd kept him up to speed on my side.

I could just about cope with his nasty little personal jibes but there's no way I was going to have him messing with my business reputation.

Tania returned with an answer within ten minutes. 'No, Geri, there haven't been any meetings that you don't know about.'

'Thanks, Tania.' I didn't think he'd be that stupid.

Whatever Luke was playing at, he had been careful not to leave any footprints. But then he didn't get where he was by being a fool.

He surprised me by arriving for our 'chat' before I did.

'OK, let's make this quick,' he said. 'You probably think I'm trying to shaft you but I'm not. I'm doing you a favour.'

'Really? How do you make that out?' I asked. 'I thought you were doing a pretty good job of making me look as if I was out of the loop.'

'Well in this case you are, but it's not your fault,' he continued. 'I got some cast-iron bona fide inside information on the client last week while I was in the sauna at the gym. And unless I'm mistaken, and you really do have a dick under that suit, there's no way you were going to be in on *that* conversation.'

'I see . . . so are you saying, in effect, that because I don't sit around in a towel in an overheated room sweating with a bunch of fat businessmen that I can't do my job?'

'No, Geri, you know I'm not saying that. I just mean that being a woman in this business has its disadvantages.'

'Well, it shouldn't mean that, Luke,' I replied. 'There's no way in this day and age that you should be having those sorts of conversations in a gym.'

'You know damn well, Carson, that deals are still done in places like this and many of those places are chick-free zones.'

'Then it's up to intelligent, educated guys like you to

128

make sure the deals come out of the locker room and into the board room,' I challenged him.

'Stop trying to change the culture single-handedly, Geri,' he said, stretching his legs out on to the chair next to him. 'It's not going to happen in your lifetime.'

'Yes, not if you can help it,' I sneered, walking across to the window, so he'd have to turn to face me. 'So what was this nugget of information, then, that bypassed our entire team of analysts?'

'It hardly matters, does it?' he said, standing too, and stretching his long arms to the ceiling, implying this whole conversation was too stiff for him. 'Suffice to say it came from a very good friend of mine. I am not prepared to compromise our relationship by revealing his identity.'

'How convenient. Well, your locker-room buddy better be spot-on. If another bank gets this deal after we passed on it, we'll both be in big trouble.'

'Are you doubting me, Carson? I'm saving your ass here as well as mine. It's solid gold, I'm telling you. Trust me.'

'That's the problem, Luke. How *can* I trust you?'

'You have no choice. You'll have to go with it.'

'You've got me over a barrel, haven't you?'

'Yep. And wouldn't I just love to have you like that . . .'

'Piss off, Luke. It's agreed, then. We tell Daryll we went over the figures again and came to the same conclusion – no deal.'

'Sure, if it puts the smile back on your pretty little face,' he laughed, knowing how much it would wind me up.

I gave him my widest Joker grin and left the room without reacting. Luke Cotterill had got one over on me again and this time there was absolutely nothing I could do about it other than have a sex change . . .

Biting my lip, I decided to get some fresh air but there was a cold wind whipping around the base of the building so I didn't stay out for long.

On my way back in I bumped into Tania. She looked about as happy as I felt.

'Tania?' I said. 'What's wrong?'

'Sorry, Geri, I know I should be upstairs but I had to get away for a moment.'

'Why, what do you need to get away from?' I asked, noticing a puffiness around her eyes.

'The Brothers, of course,' she said. 'They've taken to calling me names in the office. I try to ignore them but it's not always easy.'

I couldn't help thinking she'd brought this on herself but I knew how damned hard it was when you became the focus of the Brothers' little 'jokes'.

'I know they can be bastards,' I told her, 'but for God's sake don't let them see you've been crying, they'll move in for the kill. Sort yourself out and we'll both go up together.'

We were prepared to run the gauntlet but the usual suspects were strangely quiet when we returned to the office. I guessed they didn't want to take us both on – that would have made it easier for us to make a complaint.

In the safety of my office, she told me what had happened behind my back. 'Luke started asking me what my "pecking order" was going to be tonight, implying I was shagging around. It's so humiliating.'

'I hope you realise what a mistake it was to go out with him,' I said, not sure who I was most annoyed with, her or Luke. 'Office romances with male superiors are never a good idea. You've left yourself wide open to ridicule now. Just do your best not to react and he'll soon get bored. I'll try to take some of the heat off you.'

'I'm so sorry to put you in this position, Geri, really I am,' she sniffed. 'I do know the nature of the beast, though, so I'll get used to dealing with him.'

'You'll have to, Tania,' I told her. 'For both our sakes.'

I looked out of my glass box and saw Luke watching me talking to Tania and decided to go out and confront him.

He smiled at me in his self-satisfied way when he saw me approaching. 'Ah, Geri Boy!' he said. 'Sisters are doing it for themselves, eh?'

'Well, no one else is going to do it for us, Luke,' I said. 'Why don't you back off and pick on someone your own size?'

'Oh lighten up, Carson,' he sniggered. 'It's only a bit of banter. Tell Tania I'll give her a peck on the cheek later if she's got no takers!'

'It never ceases to amaze me how guys like you get so much amusement from such schoolboy jokes,' I said. 'Can we not get on with some work here?'

'Whenever you've finished discussing shoes and make-up, yes, of course,' he replied. 'By which time I will have read the *FT* cover to cover.'

'Good for you, Luke, I'll be testing you on it later,' I said, turning to walk away.

'Oh, just before you go,' he said, sounding almost conciliatory. 'You might like to know that you and Peckers have something in common.'

'What, that we're the only two people round here with any sense?' I asked.

'I was thinking more of a particular talent you both share,' he continued.

'And what would that be?' I enquired.

'It's pretty obvious, isn't it, Miss Pole Dance 2008?' he laughed. 'You both like making spectacles of yourselves. Only one of you does it for money . . .'

I felt a dagger of fear stabbing my guts. But how could he know? I decided to bluff my way out of it.

'Yeah, well I thought Tania was worth more than the £50 she took from you,' I countered shakily. 'And I was just doing it for the hell of it.'

'Sure you were,' he said. 'But why don't you ask Peckers where she learned to grind her hips like that?'

'It's none of my business, or yours.'

'Maybe, but you're desperate to know now, aren't you?' he teased. 'I'll leave it to you to do the girly detective work. See ya later!'

I returned to my desk wondering what the hell Luke was on about, but relieved he seemed to know nothing about my return to the Pearl.

Did he mean Tania used to be a professional dancer? Perhaps that's how she knew Declan . . . It was all falling into place now.

Tania wouldn't tell me herself, I knew that, but I had to get confirmation. There was one person who was sure to know because he was close to Luke and they probably discussed everything in the changing rooms at the gym or at the bar.

I emailed Ryan. *Do you know what companies Tania worked for before she came to Sloane Brothers? I'm sure Luke has spoken to you about it. I'll know if you blab to any of your mates out there about this and I wouldn't hesitate to tell them something very intimate about you if you did. Strictly between you and me, OK?*

I hesitated before I pressed send. Despite my physical intimacy with Ryan I wasn't one hundred per cent sure I could trust him. However, he knew I could make life difficult for him if I chose to so I figured the power balance was pretty equal.

A nervous few minutes passed before I got a reply.

Hi, Geri. Yeah, I know exactly who Tania worked for before Sloane Brothers. Surprised you hadn't worked it out yet. She was a pole dancer at the Pearl. Met Luke there, he's been a regular since before he started here. Helped her get the job. She paid the price, though, eh? I'll delete this if you will.

I sat back in my chair to digest this information. It made perfect sense, really – her relationship with Declan, her knowledge of lapdancing, the fact that security didn't stop her when she mounted Luke . . .

However, it made my situation even more precarious. I wondered if I should back out now. If Tania found out what I was doing in the evenings, the game would be up. On the other hand, if I got away with it without her knowing, I'd get even more of a kick out of doing it . . .

Chapter Thirteen

Of course, after a couple of weeks, the Pearl wasn't all Aramis and Krug, as Suzy was quick to point out one night when I saw her backstage. She could see I still had stars in my eyes about Aramis and was doing her best to bring me back down to earth.

'Darling, private dances are going to earn you the dosh but make sure you do your fair share of table dances too,' she told me before my shift. 'You don't want Jackie to see you wandering aimlessly around the club when there's a table pole empty.'

'I have to admit table work is my least favourite,' I said. 'The tips are never great and I don't like the customers gazing up at my ass like that.'

'Oh, get over yourself, Geri,' she said. 'We all have to put up with that. Be grateful that your ass is still worth paying to gaze at.'

'Fair point, Suzy,' I said. 'I'll bite the bullet. See you later.'

I changed into my Kylie-esque metallic hot pants and tight black vest top with a push-up Ultimo bra underneath and went to find a free pole. Most of them were occupied; the only one left was at a table with only a couple of guys sitting at it.

I climbed the steps to the top of the table and took up my starting position. There wasn't as much space to do fancy moves up there so I wasn't as ambitious with my spins and dips.

After a few minutes the table started filling up and eight men were leering at my tits and ass. This was a million miles from dancing for Aramis and I wasn't sure I liked it. I felt like a piece of meat.

I had no problem dancing for men whose faces were bleached out by the spotlights but from my vantage point I could see every nose hair, wrinkle and bald spot. I could even smell their body odour.

Trying to avoid eye contact, I focused on a point in the middle distance and carried on dancing. They were, at least, well-behaved and sat pretty much in silence, nursing their expensive bottled lager, smiling inanely.

Suzy had told me to stay up there for at least ten minutes but the time was dragging. I lazily circled the pole and scanned the room, looking for a distraction. Suzy had the men at her table on their feet practically clawing for her attention. A few well-placed high kicks and they were back in their places again. I smiled; another move I'd have to steal from Suzy.

I'm sure there was an art to sorting the winners from the losers, but I certainly hadn't mastered sexual profiling. Maybe the lone schoolboy with his paperback and Corona was actually an online tycoon with a heart of gold. Maybe the suburban hubby with his pressed plaid shirt had sexual fetishes concocted from long, lonely hours pruning the back garden. I kept searching.

That's when I saw him. No need for an in-depth psychiatric evaluation. I already knew this one was the genuine article. Aramis was leaning against the bar and staring at me. He was waiting for me to notice. I flipped myself around the pole and hoped he hadn't clocked my attention just yet.

I took my time and stretched my leg above my head then wrapped it around the pole. I dangled backward and tried to steal a glance in Aramis' direction to see if he was impressed by my acrobatics. But the space once occupied by my well-tailored olive-skinned saviour was vacant.

I released my leg from the pole, nearly kicking a man at my table on his balding head. I pressed my back against the pole and swivelled my hips, making a 360-degree turn, determined to find Aramis again. I finally spotted him at Suzy's table. Was it my imagination or did he glance in my direction and let his hand linger on Suzy's thigh when he slipped a bill in her garter?

Two can play at that game. I slowly shimmied down the pole and rewarded the balding man, who I'd nearly decapitated, with a nuzzle of my pert breasts. He wedged his nose between my breasts and then licked me. No, I was not good at spotting the nice from the nasty. The lingering feel of his saliva on my skin was not worth the £20 he tucked into my bra. And what was worst, I don't think Aramis even noticed.

About halfway through my slot, a younger guy came and sat at the table. At least he was something to look at, with chiselled features and dark, curly hair. Dressed in jeans and a polo shirt, he looked sporty with broad shoulders and good definition to his biceps. Unlike some of the other customers, he was wearing gorgeous after-shave that wafted up into my nostrils and cleared away the stale smell of beer. I tried to forget about Aramis and focused on the Mr Maybe right in front of me.

He observed me intently with a self-satisfied smile on his face and I found myself wondering if I had a chance of a bigger tip from him.

I went over in his direction, and gave him a spin to make sure he got an eyeful of my pert derrière, which he seemed to appreciate.

There was something about him, though, that reminded me of some of the guys I worked with. He undoubtedly thought he was God's gift to women, so I'd have to watch him.

I didn't mean to but I let my attention slip. I found myself checking out the corner table, Aramis' table. Sure enough he'd finished with Suzy and was sipping his cognac in private.

My confidence on the pole was increasing by the minute, and the shapes I was making surprised even me. I was in my element now, swinging into ecstasy.

This is how I was used to feeling after a few glasses of wine – light-headed, in a trance, uninhibited . . .

I glimpsed Suzy out of the corner of my eye. She was beckoning me over, and I felt like a kid who'd been told to get off the ride.

Finishing my final move, I smiled at my audience before climbing down from the table. Suzy winked at me and passed me a jug. 'Looks like you've got a live one and another one waiting in the wings,' Suzy said, indicating the over-eager boy and Aramis. All I wanted was to strut over to Aramis and continue where we left off, but men like Aramis didn't like to be chased. I had to play this one cool. I glanced at Aramis. He had his arm around another redhead. She was twirling a strawberry blonde curl around her finger. Did he expect me to believe he could trade one redhead for another?

The baldies and cheapskates popped a few coins and disappeared, leaving the curly-haired egotist.

I moved towards him with the jug, but he declined. I feigned a look of mock-horror. I ran a fingernail down his bare arm. I wanted Aramis to see that two could play his game.

'Sorry, you have to give me at least a pound coin,' I told him.

'Yeah, I know,' he said. 'Come over here and I'll give you a lot more than that.'

Oh shit, I thought. This one is going to be a handful.

'So, how much would you like to put in the jug?' I asked.

'Why don't we get away from these creeps?' he said. 'You're fucking gorgeous, I want you, and if you come with me you'll earn a lot more than a few quid.'

'Hey, steady on there,' I said, trying to stall him. 'Club rules dictate that you must tip me a minimum of a pound for this dance.'

'Fine, here's your quid,' he said, throwing a coin into the jug. 'Now let's talk *serious* money.'

'OK, big shot,' I said, trying to keep calm. I shot a

look at Aramis. The redhead was missing in action. He was watching me now and making no apologies for it. 'Let's go to the bar and talk business.'

I grabbed the boy's hand and I strode off towards the bar. This guy had pissed me off but maybe I could use him to my advantage – that is if I kept the situation under control.

Mustn't panic, I thought. If things get difficult I can just walk away and find security. But it would ruin the illusion I hoped to create for Aramis. I tried to think what Ginger would do. I smiled and said,

'I'd really like you to buy me a drink.'

'OK, sweetheart, what would you like?'

'White wine and soda, please.'

'Nothing stronger?' he asked.

'No, that will be fine.'

He then did a Suzy, buying me a large glass of Sauvignon with a merest dash of soda.

'So, what's your name?' he said, talking to my tits.

'Ginger,' I said, wanting to knee him in the balls. 'And what's yours?'

'Daniel,' he answered. 'Ginger, you are so fucking hot. I'll pay you £200 to come back to my place.'

I took in a deep breath to stop myself slapping him. For my sake and Aramis', I needed it to look as if Daniel and I were having a good time.

'Daniel, it's so kind of you to offer, but it's against club rules,' I said, hoping to fob him off.

'Oh come on, babe,' he said. 'Nothing to do with the club. It would be a little deal between you and me?'

'I'm sorry, Daniel, I can't do that,' I said, flipping my

hair and giving him what I hoped didn't look like the insincere smile that it was. 'Not on the premises,' I said through clenched teeth.

'Then come outside with me,' he insisted. 'Seriously, honey, you are so burning, I will pay you anything you want . . .'

I tried to compose myself as best I could. Dealing with the likes of Luke Cotterill was pretty good training for this situation.

'Daniel, I very much appreciate your offer, but I'm a lap dancer, not a hooker . . .'

As soon as I mentioned the magic 'H' word, his demeanour changed.

'Give me a break, honey. You're a commodity, didn't you know? If you don't wanna play, I'll find a slag who does . . .'

Calm, Geraldine, calm, I said to myself, my temper rising. God knows I didn't feel it.

'OK, Daniel, you do that,' I said. 'And the best of luck to you.' I took a deep breath in. Now I was ready to face Aramis. No, more than that. I needed to see Ginger through Aramis' eyes and erase how Daniel made me feel. A genuine smile crossed my lips as I turned towards the corner table.

Aramis was gone.

I'd blown it. What did I think I was doing? I already felt cheap and dirty from my interaction with Daniel and now I felt stupid as well.

I hastened back to the safe haven of the dressing room, where the other girls were changing out of their costumes.

I sat down, my heart beating fast, and tried to breathe easily. 'You OK?' said an Asian girl I'd seen around.

'Oh, yeah, I think so,' I replied, brushing out my hair.

'Looks as if you've got arsehole fatigue,' she continued.

'What?' I said, putting the brush down and powdering my skin.

'Fed up with wankers,' came the answer.

'Oh, right,' I said. 'Yeah, I just had a narrow escape with a guy who thought he could pay to fuck me.'

'Get used to it,' she said. 'It's gonna happen to you every night.'

I didn't have the energy to introduce myself.

Suzy barrelled back in and saw me sitting crumpled in a corner.

'Oh, you poor lamb!' she said, with no small degree of sarcasm. 'Did a nasty customer upset you?'

'Nothing I couldn't handle.'

'Not by the looks of it, doll,' she said, putting her arm round me. 'You're not as tough as you make out, are you? We'll soon have you like old boots, don't worry.'

I shuddered. Suzy always seemed so cynical and jaded – not only about the business we were in but also about life in general. I wondered what made her end up that way.

'You've not told me yet how you got into this game, Suzy.'

'Oh darling, surely you don't want the whole sob story?' she said, planting a big red kiss mark on the rim of her glass.

'Yes, I *really* want to know,' I told her, tucking my legs up on the chair ready for a good yarn.

142

She got up and walked over to the mirror, made a silly face at herself and fluffed up her blonde waves.

'You know how it is, Geri – you gotta have a dream,' she began. I swear, her accent was getting more American by the second. 'Mine was – no laughing at the back, now – to be a Vegas showgirl. That just seemed like the most glamorous thing on earth to a 19-year-old from Wembley Park.'

'Did you make it?' I asked.

'Hold your horses. Let me do the build-up . . . I was saying, I wanted to get me to the casino capital of the world, strut my stuff in spangles and fancy feather headdresses and land myself a high roller along the way . . .'

She stopped for a dramatic pause and a sip of gin and tonic, but I didn't interrupt.

'So I had a few ballet and modern jazz classes, practised in my bedroom with a push-up bra my mother had sewn sequins on to and started saving for the air fare. I had the legs, the tits and the ass, I thought I was on to a winner. Darling, I didn't have a clue . . .'

'Was that the end of that, then?'

'Oh no, you can't keep a good north London girl down, you know. I had a lucky break. Hooked up with this cool older guy who had always wanted to do the coast-to-coast drive across the States. We scraped together the money for a flight to LA and hired a car. He dropped me in Nevada and carried on. It was just like a road movie . . .'

'Wow, that's so cool,' I said. 'So you just pitched up there with a suitcase and hope in your heart?'

'Pretty much floated in on a candyfloss castle. I booked

into a cheap motel and found a waitressing job while I took dance classes. I was a tough kid. Stupid, but tough.'

She came and sat down next to me and fixed me with her big blue eyes. I noticed a sadness I hadn't seen before.

'Anyway, when I thought I was good enough, I started begging for auditions at the casinos. There was always an excuse: no vacancies, you're too young, you're not a US citizen, you need a permit, you're too inexperienced ... After six months I realised I was living in cloud cuckoo land.'

'God, that must've been so disappointing,' I said, as I watched her take a bigger swig of her drink.

'Anyway, I'd made friends at the restaurant and one of the other waitresses said I might as well check out the strip joints. Taking *all* my kit off hadn't been part of the plan but I was running out of money and I was damned if I was going back to London with my tail between my legs.'

'No, I'm guessing that's not your style,' I said.

'Funny you should mention that,' she said, gazing into space. 'I used to play the slot machines at the casinos in case a dime might make me a million dollars. One hired movie-star look-alikes to encourage punters to spend more. That's where I met Marilyn Monroe.'

'Not the real one, obviously,' I joked.

'Not unless she went to live on Mars with Elvis. No, this Marilyn was a shit-hot impersonator. There are hundreds of them in Vegas but she was the best. She told me I could get the look without major surgery, took me to a salon where they did the Marilyn hair, showed me how to do the make-up, the pout, the works.'

'She taught you well, Suzy, it suits you,' I said.

'Thanks, sweetie, I can still just about pull it off. Not sure what will happen when I pass 36, though. I'll have to do the "dead Marilyn" look then.' She laughed long and hard until she broke into a hacking cough.

'Too many fags last night . . . Anyway, I thought that bearing a passing resemblance to the sexiest woman in history might give me a slight advantage with the bookers. And I was right. I auditioned at this club on the outskirts of town and they loved me. Waived their usual rules, got me a sheriff's card, bingo.'

'So you did a Marilyn-themed strip?'

'Sure did, honey. I had a copy made of the famous white halter-neck dress she wore in *The Seven-Year Itch*, with zippers put in at all the right places. Some guys acted as if I really was Marilyn, it was crazy. The tips I earned . . .'

'It turned out all right in the end, then?'

'Well, I earned a living, but it wasn't exactly a classy joint and I had to do nasties.'

'Such as?'

'Use your imagination, love. Stuff like stick-shifting, polishing the zipper . . .'

'What the hell is that?'

'Grabbing the guy's dick through his pants and playing with it like a gearstick. The other one's obvious – grinding your ass so close to his fly that you might as well use Mr Sheen on his crotch.'

'Oh right, I see. That's what I call customer interaction . . .'

'Didn't they tell you lap dancing was a contact sport?

145

It isn't much fun if the guy underneath you is sweaty, balding and with a gut like a giant watermelon. Mind you, he probably hasn't seen his dick in years so you'll be doing him a public service by finding it for him.'

'That's one part of the job I don't want to think about,' I said, wincing.

'You get used to it, doll. Soon you won't even think they're ugly. They'll start looking like currency to you. Just make sure you get a good exchange rate.'

'So how long did you stay in Vegas?'

'A couple of years. I had some adventures . . .' she tailed off, waiting for me to beg her to continue.

'Go on, then, tell me the best . . .'

'Oh, if you insist,' she said.

'This guy came in the club one day. He was different – smartly dressed, not a sleazeball. I danced for him and he didn't ask for extras. I liked that. He told me he was looking for girls to audition for a movie. So I said to him, "Oh sure, and I guess that means you want a free dance. Do you think I was born yesterday?" He said, "No, I'm serious, here's my card, call me."'

'So did you?'

'God, you're an impatient girl. Yes, I bloody well did call. And he checked out, he was for real. I asked him where the audition was and he just said he'd be sending a limo to pick me up on the day. It was crazy but I thought, what the hell . . . Anything goes in Sin City. I'd found a share in a cute little apartment by then, and my housemates told me I was out of my mind, but I got in the stretch that day with four other girls who had stars in their eyes. We were so excited, going on this Magical Mystery Tour . . .'

'At least you weren't alone. *Then* I'd have said you were mad . . .'

'I'd been certifiable for years, darling. Anyway, we ended up on an airstrip in the middle of the Nevada desert. We got out of the limo and there was the guy I met in the club. He told us he was a casting director and the audition was being held on a private jet. How insane was that? I asked if it was staying on the ground. "No, ladies, you'll be dancing for me at 26,000 feet." What a blast . . .'

Suzy suddenly stopped talking and looked towards the door. Jackie was standing there.

'Getting nostalgic again, are we, Suzy?' she laughed nastily.

'Oh Jackie, you know me,' she said. 'I always like to entertain rookies with tales of my youthful stupidity.'

Jackie gave her a reproachful look and said, 'There are customers out there waiting for the benefit of your experience. Why not give it to them?' before leaving the dressing room.

'She Who Must Be Obeyed has spoken,' Suzy told me. 'I'd better carry on this story another time. Bear with me, it's worth waiting for.'

I had to hand it to Suzy, she knew how to cheer me up. I'd already almost forgotten about the incident at the table.

However, it didn't take a genius to work out that it might be a good idea for me to tip the bouncers and the barmen a little over the odds. After my experience with a potential john, I needed more than a few eyes watching my back . . .

Chapter Fourteen

Women sometimes came into the club with their partners or as part of larger, mixed groups but only to observe from the shadows. They would occasionally tip dancers if egged on by the men but generally knew their place.

One Friday evening, a few weeks into the job, a couple stood out from the rest. He looked savvy, perhaps in advertising or the media, dressed in Paul Smith with black, slicked-back hair and trendy black horn-rimmed glasses. She was equally well-groomed, raven-haired in a black Fifties-style skirt suit. Her face was angular, her eyes dark and penetrating. There was something predatory about her that unsettled me.

She watched me like a hawk while I was doing my stage show, nodding every time her partner whispered in her ear, as if they were filling in some kind of imaginary score card.

When I passed the jug around, he dropped in a few coins but she insisted on putting money in my garter.

'I like your style,' she said in a surprisingly deep voice.

'Thanks,' I replied. 'I like your generosity.'

I noticed she'd tipped me £20. But I didn't realise until

I got back to the dressing room that she'd slipped in a note with it.

Apologies for approaching you like this. I would like to pay you to dance for my husband, whatever your going rate. If you are amenable please meet me in the ladies in ten minutes.

I wasn't sure why she was being so coy, she didn't look the type. But I was intrigued so I went to meet her.

'Hi, I'm Ginger,' I said. 'I can dance for your husband, no problem. You could have asked me after my show.'

'Yes I know,' she answered. 'But I prefer to be discreet. And I wanted to ask you in person if you would mind me sitting in while you dance?'

'Oh, I see,' I said, as she doused herself in a fine rain of Chanel No.5. 'Well, that's unusual but I'm sure it won't be a problem. Are you concerned about what might happen?'

'No, not at all,' she answered, looking me straight in the eye. 'I'm happy with whatever you choose to do, please don't hold back. That's my point, Ginger. I very much enjoy watching my husband being turned on by other women.'

'Ah, I understand,' I said. 'As long as you don't mind paying – there's no such thing as a free show.'

'Of course not. Shall we say in fifteen minutes?'

'I'll be waiting for you in the booth,' I told her. 'Does your husband want a full strip or just a lap dance?'

'Full contact. And eventual nudity,' she said.

I thought that was an odd way of putting it, but nodded and left her to it. What a strange woman – she was behaving as if we were spies exchanging state secrets.

There was an intensity to her that made me wary; she seemed to take everything very seriously indeed. Still, I had to take into consideration that they might never have done anything like this before – but then again neither had I.

They were probably paying me to fulfil one of their fantasies. Would I live up to their expectations?

No time to worry about that, Ginger. I just had to get on with it.

I went back to the dressing room and put on my satin coat-dress – I thought the wife would appreciate that – and went to prepare the booth.

I peeked round the curtain but Suzy was finishing off a dance so I went to wait at the bar. Mr and Mrs Black, as I'd decided to call them, were sitting on stools at the opposite end, gazing intently into each other's eyes. Perhaps the spark had gone out of their marriage and they were trying to inject a little spice? Their body language suggested otherwise; my money was on them being an experimental pair who were on a rollercoaster sexual journey together.

I rather liked that idea. It was a dream of mine to find a man who was on my wavelength in that way, who desired me enough to want to include me in all of his adventures rather than doing what most normal men do, namely have affairs or go to clubs like the Pearl while their women remain in blissful ignorance.

Suzy and her client emerged five minutes later and she winked at me. I winked back and went to prepare myself for the Blacks.

Mrs Black arrived first, sitting silently on a chair near the entrance with her legs demurely crossed, as if waiting for a job interview. She was wearing nylons and perfectly matching black patent handbag and shoes.

Then Mr Black drew back the curtain – a little uncertainly. I beckoned for him to come in and sit down on the Chesterfield. There was an interesting dynamic going on between them. I wondered if it had been her idea rather than his?

He took up his place and looked over at his wife. She beamed at him and nodded. Oh yes, she was in charge of this scenario, there was no doubt about that.

He planted his hands on the arms of the chair as if he was afraid it would take off, then crossed his legs.

I started slowly, breathing deeply so he could see my ribcage rise and fall, arched my back and circled my hands over my hips as I swayed from side to side.

I saw his fingers tense so I smiled softly and began unbuttoning my dress, letting it glide down to the floor.

Beads of sweat began to form on his forehead. It was sultry in the club that night, and my own perspiration was mixing with my vanilla scent and his wife's Chanel to create a heady, musky atmosphere in the confines of the booth.

My exposed flesh, above my corset and below my panties to the tops of my stockings, glistened with a layer of moisture so I started massaging it into my thighs, cleavage and arms while doing deep dips and grinds.

I turned round so he could see my rear view, which gave me a chance to check out the wife. She'd removed her scarf and suit jacket to reveal a demure silk blouse that hinted at expensive lingerie underneath.

Her eyes were locked on to him, monitoring his responses to my every move.

He shifted in the chair and adjusted his trousers; she carefully circled her tongue around her lips and did the same with an index finger on her upper thigh – a concealed suspender was my guess.

I felt as if they were using me as a toy in their fore-play and it was turning me on. Another female presence was triggering my imagination.

Reversing towards the husband I pointed to the wife's chiffon scarf and she passed it to me.

I spun round, gently parting his legs and inserting myself in the space between them.

The scarf became a symbol of her as I draped it round his neck and coaxed his head close to my breasts so he could inhale my aroma.

Then I took both of his hands and wound the scarf around them, tying a loose knot and lifting his arms so they rested behind his head.

I straddled him and grabbed hold of the chair back and started thrusting my pelvis in and out, then up and down as if riding a breaker.

He was breathing heavily through his mouth and thrusting to match my movements.

She had asked for contact so I performed a full body slide, pressing my breasts into his body, rolling down over his erection and even lightly trailing my tongue over his fly.

I turned to the wife and caught her unbuttoning her blouse and stroking the top of her breasts.

She used small, teasing movements where mine were big and bold.

I untied her hubby's hands and used the scarf for a dance of the seven veils.

Then it was time for me to remove *all* items of clothing.

The heels came first, closely followed by the stockings, then the heels went back on.

At half speed, I peeled the corset off. I threw it at his feet. Then the panties. I tossed them on his lap.

I took the scarf and tied it in a bow around my naked waist.

'This was a gift, for you both . . .'

The husband looked exhausted. He took a handkerchief out of his pocket and mopped his brow, then gestured to his wife. She stood up and walked towards me, then languorously untied the bow. 'Thank you, Ginger, my husband and I are most grateful,' she said, her crystal accent making her sound like royalty. She handed me £100 – the price for an audience of two, plus a £20 tip for me. They left the booth as they arrived, in silence, as I put my dress back on. It was so hot I went to get a long, cool drink before heading back to the changing rooms. I couldn't wait to tell Suzy about the Blacks.

I found her outside again, lighting up another Chesterfield. I stood next to her but she waited for me to speak while taking a deep draw.

'Did you see that couple dressed in black that I just danced for?' I asked, excitedly. It had given me such a buzz. I even wondered if Ryan was free later.

'Oh yes, darling, they looked like a bundle of fun,' she said. 'She's uptight and he's a wuss. Not a great combination. And she obviously has his balls in the fridge.'

I laughed at her description. 'Yeah, she might as well

have been wearing white gloves she was so formal. Until I started dancing, that is.'

'It's always fascinating to watch buttoned-up women letting themselves go,' she said. 'It's one of my favourite pastimes.'

'You can't keep me in suspense any longer,' I said, putting up the hood of my tracksuit top to shield myself against the cool breeze. 'So what happened when you got on the private jet in Vegas?'

'Oh yes, that's right, I left you on the tarmac in the middle of the Nevada desert,' she said, blowing smoke rings.

Chapter Fifteen

SUZY'S STORY

Well, we boarded this aircraft and I swear, it was as big as Airforce One, with a lounge in the middle and a double bedroom at the back. Of course, my first thought was *Ah, there's the casting couch*. I was prepared for that one and my answer was going to be, *No, I'm not that desperate to get my name in lights*.

Anyway, the guy tells us he wants us each to do a striptease for him, and that we'd be doing it after take-off. It didn't occur to me to ask why or where we were going. I was along for the ride, after all. I just wanted to be sure no one would be riding me . . .

So I strapped myself in. I had several routines in those days but he wanted the Marilyn one, of course. My name came out of the hat first so as soon as the seatbelt sign was off, I was on. They let us dance to our own music, and mine was 'Diamonds are a Girl's Best Friend'. I had all the period details correct – the frilly Fifties knickers, the conical satin bra, the works. I had even perfected her bum wiggle, the one she did in *Some Like It Hot*.

He had a big fat smile on his face after I pushed my curvy ass in it. But the other girls were good too. You have to raise your game in Vegas, there's so much competition. Anyway, when we'd all done our turn, he brings us all a glass of champagne, thanks us for the show, and picks out two girls. Then the three of them disappear to the bedroom at the back of the plane. I thought, Great, I'm glad I haven't got the job if that's what I would have had to do. I don't come that cheap.

Honey, to this day I've no idea what went on in that room. By that time me and the other girls were stuck into the champagne, which the co-pilot kept delivering to us. I wasn't sure at first whether this was meant to make us so drunk that we'd all follow the other girls into the private room but I knew that if anyone tried to make me do something I didn't wanna do, I would be straight over to the emergency exit trying to open the door.

But it didn't come to that. Fizz always turbo-charges my libido and I was already in orbit after my routine. So go on, Geri, guess what Suzy did next?

Did I join the other girls for an orgy in the back room?

No, darling. I was *much* more inventive than that. While the co-pilot was busy chatting up the champagne floozies, I went up front to say a Marilyn Monroe hello to the pilot. God, was he cute – slim, muscular, dark-haired, perfect teeth, charming . . . You know, there's not a single red-blooded male on this planet who doesn't find Marilyn a turn-on. Soon we were cruising at maximum altitude, and so was the jet . . .

I acted dumb and started asking him what all the knobs and levers did; oohing and aahing on cue, making him feel all masculine and important. That one works every time, by the way – act like a bimbo and you'll get most customers to buy a dance.

Anyway, after five minutes of me cooing at him and flashing my cleavage in his face, I asked if he wanted a dance. So he switched on the autopilot and Marilyn did what she was built to do. I don't think the guy had ever had a lap dance before, he was so sweet. He also had the most magnificent joystick nestling under his belt.

I said to him, 'Sweetheart, let me help you with that, you look so uncomfortable.' He was mesmerised by me and sat there without a word as I unfastened his belt and unzipped his fly. I tell you, that thing gave new meaning to the word cockpit. I stroked his shaft as I sang Happy Birthday, Mr Pilot in my Marilyn voice and then gave him his present.

The best Billy Joel he'd had in his life. Strip club slang, darling. I'm sure you can work it out.

But I didn't let him shoot his load – Marilyn had to satisfy herself first. Did you know she was addicted to sex?

I turned round, pulled up my frock and slowly pulled down my panties. The captain was mumbling by this point, deranged with desire. He just kept saying, 'Marilyn, baby, come to me, come to me . . .'

So I obliged with my best reverse cowgirl, bouncing up and down on his lovely slice of beef like a bucking bronco while he pressed Marilyn's little pink button.

And with a dashboard like that in front of him he knew exactly how to hit the right switch. I even squealed like Marilyn when I climaxed, I'm such a pro. I tell you Geri, it was the smoothest landing I ever had.

Stick with me, kid – I'm the honorary president of the Mile High Club, you know.

After that, I went back out to the lounge, innocent as anything. The others were so pissed by that point they hadn't really noticed I'd been gone for a while. I asked the co-pilot where the hell we were going and he said we were just doing big loops over Vegas until the fuel ran out.

The director finally emerged with the two girls. Like me, he had a big smile on his face. I can't say the same for the girls. He thanked us all for auditioning and told us that the two bedroom divas were going to be in the movie – hey, what a surprise. That brightened up their faces.

The rest of us weren't bothered really. How many strippers get to drink champagne on a private jet? And I'd had my little bonus as well . . .

But then there's always the bump down to earth.

Being Marilyn was such a meal ticket at first but after a few months it started to get harder to switch off. I didn't know where she ended and I began. I was doing pretty well earning my dollars every night – some of it was dancing but most of it was hostess work, which means you have to drink alcohol with the punters. And everyone wanted to buy Marilyn a drink. Sometimes I knocked back twenty shots a night, which isn't good for the liver, let alone the soul. That's when the girls started calling me Boozy Suzy, and it stuck . . . Sorry, darling, I'll need another fag if you want to hear the rest of this one.

Oh what the hell, I've started, so I'll finish, as they say on *Mastermind*.

Anyway, I realised I was using the customers as an excuse to drink, that it just helped to numb me out and stop me feeling any pain. It wasn't fun anymore, Geri, and I started to miss home. I had pretty much made up my mind to go back to London at the end of that year when it happened . . .

I was in the club one night and I'd had one too many. I should've gone home but I thought I'd try for one more private dance. This guy looked OK; he was a kind of smart cowboy, dressed in denim with the boots, Stetson and everything. We'd had a few drinks so he was half-cut as well. I thought I had him sussed; we had a good rapport so it was pretty easy to get him to hire the VIP booth. So I'm in there, ready to go into my Marilyn routine, and I ask him to empty his pockets of anything sharp, which we all had to do to protect ourselves even though there were bouncers around every corner.

Then he suddenly yells at me that it's an invasion of his privacy. Jesus, there was no such thing as privacy in those clubs. So I asked him nicely, again, in my best dumb blonde voice, can he please empty his pockets. Next thing I know, he's pulled a gun on me.

So there I am, almost too drunk to stand up, and I didn't really react; I just stood there like an idiot, wondering what to do next. Then he said, 'You're not afraid of my gun, are you?' This seemed like the most stupid question I'd ever heard in my life. I tried to keep calm, so I said, 'No sir, of course not, you have every right to bear arms . . . just not in this club.'

Funnily enough this seemed to register in his addled brain and he put it away again, so I carried on and did my dance as if nothing had happened, but I was terrified. I mean, I like guys who pack a pistol, but not the gunmetal variety. This was in a back room without CCTV. I thought he might actually have fired a shot if the bouncers had stormed in, anything could have happened.

God, at least we don't have to deal with that kind of thing over here.

Oh yes, give me twenty lippy perverts any day, but hardware is another matter. It scared the shit out of me, Geri. It's all very well chasing the American Dream but not if you risk getting your head blown off in the process. It was the last straw, so I sorted out my affairs and booked a flight home as soon as I could. My mum met me at Heathrow and I cried like a baby . . .

God, Geri, I could murder a vodka and Coke. Let's hit the bar and find some nice juicy men with big fat wallets.

Chapter Sixteen

It took Suzy less than fifteen seconds to find that fat wallet.

I, on the other hand, was more in need of a drink after Suzy's story. Bloody hell, here I was thinking I was taking a huge risk working here. But what did I know? There was a whole other world out there, and I was still playing it safe.

'Hi Geri, how's tricks? Oh – sorry, my mistake – Ginger, what can I get you?'

'Well done, Wayne, you remembered.' I was glad I'd got Wayne serving me. He was decent to the girls. Always with a smile and a quip. There was another bartender, farther down the bar, younger and leaner and harder. I didn't like the way he looked at me sometimes – or at any of the girls. I made a point to stay away from him. 'When you see this red wig, Geri is in hiding. I'll have a whisky and Coke and light on the Coke, please. Oh, and tricks are really interesting.'

'Yeah? Pray tell, Miss Ginger.'

'I've just done a dance for a husband whose wife was paying. And she wanted to watch.'

'A truly liberated lady, indeed. I'll have to have a word with my girlfriend and see if she's up for something like that . . .'

'She really was calling the shots, though. I don't know who was more turned on, her or him.'

'And how about you? Did it float your boat?'

'Ah, that would be telling tales, Wayne.'

'Well, you can't say working at the Pearl hasn't broadened your horizons.'

'Absolutely. It's been a revelation.'

'More ice, Miss Ginger?'

'Yes please, I'm just too hot to handle . . .'

He dumped the whole bucket in front of me and we laughed.

'If you'll excuse me, Ginger, the hordes beckon.'

Sitting there, nursing my drink, I could see Irena at the end of the bar talking heatedly with Viktor, the other barman. Now what was that about? I wanted to warn her to stay away from him, but surely his kind of attitude transcended any language barriers?

But right then, I had my own worries as a greasy guy sidled over. Every club has its fair share of these. For the most part I'd managed to avoid them, and that night was no exception.

Excusing myself, I headed to the customers' bathroom. You could usually be guaranteed that the ladies would be empty.

I felt a welcome rush of cool air on my face as I opened the bathroom door and quickly closed it behind me. Then I realised I was not alone . . .

Beyond the door was a short corridor leading to the right, plastered with adverts for events around the capital that had happened months ago. But that wasn't what caught my attention now. A series of soft moans escaped around the wall. Someone was having some fun in here.

I thought about turning back around and walking straight out, but the sounds of pleasure made my skin tingle. 'That's it,' said a familiar woman's voice. 'Right there. Don't stop.'

I tiptoed along the wall and peered around the edge. Mrs Black was propped up on the basin in the corner of the room, her knees pushed up towards her shoulders. Her skirt was up around her waist, exposing her fully-fashioned nylon stockings and lace suspender belt. Her blouse was open to the waist, exposing her balconette bra and chest almost the colour of ivory.

Mr Black knelt on the floor in front of her, his head between her legs.

Mrs Black gave a delicious moan and ran her fingers through his hair, pulling his face harder into her pussy.

He withdrew his head for a second. 'You're so wet,' he said. 'You liked seeing me with that stripper, didn't you?'

'Shut up,' she said. 'Fuck me with your tongue.'

As he began bobbing his head back and forth, I tried to slowly edge my way back out without being seen.

But when I looked up again, I saw that Mrs Black's intense black eyes were right on mine. I froze with embarrassment, expecting her to order me to get out and leave them to it.

But no.

A smile formed on Mrs Black's face, and then her

165

mouth opened to form an 'O' shape, and her eyelids fluttered a little. She moaned again. 'I'm nearly there,' she said. 'Don't stop.'

This wasn't right – I beat a hasty retreat back to the door. I was reaching for the handle when I heard a moan.

'Don't go.'

'I'm not going anywhere,' mumbled Mr Black.

What is this? I asked myself. *Is she talking to her husband or to me?*

She wants me to watch? Now I understood. *Why else would they have left the door unlocked?*

What harm could it do? And after all Suzy's exploits, maybe I was due some of my own.

Next thing I knew I was locking the door from the inside, and walked back into the washroom.

The least I could do was oblige this part of her fantasy – the performer becomes the voyeur.

Mrs Black looked like the cat who got the cream when she saw I was back. She flicked her eyes towards the toilet cubicle, as she pushed her husband away.

This was getting very interesting indeed. I pointed to the cubicle, and Mrs Black gave a curt nod, biting her lower lip.

I could have turned around and left then and there, but I didn't. Mrs Black pulled her husband's head again, crushing his nose against the tip of pussy. Her other hand went to her bra, and pulled one cup down. She fondled her breast, taking her erect nipple between forefinger and thumb and tugging it sharply.

I took my chance and crept into the cubicle opposite and pulled the door to. Through the crack I could see that Mrs Black was starting to buck back and forth, her spine arching, nipples pointed towards the ceiling.

'That's it,' she gasped. 'I'm gonna cum, baby.'

Abruptly Mr Black stopped and looked up at his wife's face.

'Don't stop!' she said. 'I was so close.'

'Not till I say, slut.'

Provoking him, Mrs Black lowered her hand and started to stroke herself, but her husband took hold of her hand and pushed it above her head. With the other, he unbuckled his belt and trousers, which fell around his knees. His arse, almost completely hairless, was shapely and pale. A faint tan line began halfway down his well-muscled thighs. I could see his balls hanging below, as Mrs Black's hand suddenly appeared, cupping them roughly before disappearing again.

I let the door swing open fully and sat on the closed toilet seat. There was something intoxicating about watching such a controlled, well-heeled woman being taken in such a place. Now I knew what Suzy meant.

Mr Black moaned as she played with his balls, and bent his head towards her chest.

'Harder,' she said. 'Suck them harder . . .'

I saw the white of his teeth as they closed over the milky flesh of her breast and teased her nipple with his tongue. She sucked a breath through her teeth. I could almost feel her pleasure, on the cusp of pain. Mr Black drew back and turned slightly to the side, and his eyes met mine. I understood, he wanted me to see his cock, the part of him I'd teased so cruelly during our dance. It lay, thick and veined along his wife's thigh, the head twitching by the opening of her pussy. At that, he repositioned his feet slightly and pushed himself inside his wife. She gasped, and her hand clawed across the tiled wall and slammed on the button of the hand-dryer.

Mr Black pushed his wife's legs further back and started pumping slowly back and forth, the muscles of his butt contracting in a steady powerful rhythm.

'You love my dick, don't you, you slut . . .'

'I'm such a whore,' she panted. Her eyes were boring right into me. There was something intense, almost pleading about her gaze.

I was still naked under my dress and starting to feel really horny. I pulled up my skirt, and licked my finger for effect. There wasn't any need for more moisture – I was already damp from the show so far. I slid my finger over my lips, then slowly into my pussy. The hand-dryer suddenly cut out and the room was silent again, save for the couple's heavy breathing and the rattle of his belt buckle against the floor.

'You dirty little whore, I'm going to fuck you good and proper now,' he said, as he pumped into her faster.

'Whores deserve it,' she said, looking at me with a fiery expression. 'They ask for it . . .'

I noticed she had stacked her jacket, shoes, and bag neatly in a dry corner, and put his glasses and suit jacket on top – the reminder of her orderliness next to the chaotic scene of passion brought a smile to my lips. Who'd have thought this groomed and disciplined woman was turned on by being called a whore?

I pulled my finger out and stroked upwards to my clit, rubbing it gently so Mrs Black could see. Her hand fell back on the tap, which came on with a gush, soaking the back of her rumpled skirt. Her hand fumbled frantically around the sink, then she ran it up along her chest, up her cheek and through her hair, leaving a glistening slick of water.

'Mmm,' she moaned, 'your slut wants to cum soon . . . Can she cum soon?'

I wondered for a moment if she meant me.

'Not until I've finished with you,' he answered. 'You'd like that, wouldn't you?'

'Yes, yes, please, give it to me now.'

'I'll do it when I'm good and ready, bitch.'

I started rubbing my clit quicker, sliding the length of my finger up and down, lingering on the tip at the top of my stroke, then repeating the action in time to their fucking. It wouldn't be long now before I came too. There was a delicious warmth pulsing from between my legs, spreading across to my pelvis and up through my belly to the peaks of my tits.

'I can't hold it,' she murmured. 'I can't stop.' Her voice was nothing like the one she'd used in the club. The pitch was higher, panicked, submissive.

He pounded away for a few more moments and I saw her fingers tighten on his shoulders, her nails tearing at the fabric of his shirt. She was fighting to keep her eyes on my hand which ran frantically over my pussy, then her face twisted and she bared her teeth as her breath become laboured, her chest plunging up and down.

'Mmm . . . fuck me . . . fuck . . . me . . . mmm . . .'

I felt the hot rush explode through me, right to my

scalp and toes. My knees trembled, and one foot shot out against the wall of the cubicle door.

The noise was swallowed by that of Mr Black. He let out a growl somewhere from deep in his belly, and gave a single hard thrust. The sound of his orgasm ebbed slowly as his buttocks remained taut, and then slowly relaxed, involuntarily flexing as he emptied the last of his seed inside her. His breath turned to pants and Mrs Black broke eye contact with me, letting her head fall back against the wall, and her legs drop to the side of her husband's waist. She looked a total mess, her hair wet and matted down one side.

It was the first time I'd ever shared an orgasm with two other people. Their pleasure magnified my own, and it was half a minute before I felt able to stand. I let my dress fall back down.

Their veneer of respectability, their privacy, had been totally stripped away, and they leant close together, panting like two exhausted fighters in the centre of the ring, oblivious to the crowd watching on. The spell was broken. It was time for me to go.

I felt like I was leaving the bed of a one-night stand in the middle of the night. The post-coital routines, the rearranging of clothes, and the slow realisation of what they'd just done in front of a total stranger would be ruined by words and explanations.

I straightened my dress quickly in the mirror and made my way out. Neither Mr or Mrs Black even looked up.

I would never have chosen to watch a couple having sex but Mr and Mrs Black had seduced me into being a peeping tom. Being a voyeur in someone else's fantasy had been unexpectedly arousing. Now my juices were really flowing . . .

I thought about telling Suzy. What would she make of it? *No, keep it private.*

As I made my way back to the floor with a mischievous smile on my face, I saw my Middle Eastern admirer at his usual table, regular as clockwork. He'd been true to his word and been back to see me every night. Only this time he'd missed my real performance.

Chapter Seventeen

I wandered over to him, letting my hips swing seductively.

'How about a private dance?'

I wondered if he could smell the musk of desire on me. Could he see from the flush of my cheeks what I'd just been doing?

'Not tonight,' he said.

His answer sent a wave of frustration through me. I wanted him to lose control, to take me in the washroom and fuck me without a care.

'But I would like to take you out later.'

I arched an eyebrow and ran my finger across his shoulder.

'Where to?'

'Just for a drive. Would you like that?'

I imagined Jackie waving her finger at me. *Are you crazy, girl? Do you know how stupid it is to get in a car with a punter?*

'I don't know, Aramis,' I told him. 'I'm not sure that's a good idea, but I'll think about it.'

'It's your decision, of course. I will wait outside. If you come, you come . . .'

Hmm . . . Aramis and me in the back of a Bentley. That was full of intriguing possibilities . . . but perhaps he really did just want the company. His games, the constant cat and mouse, were beginning to grate. Who was in charge here?

'If you're lucky,' I said, and headed backstage to change. I pulled off my dress, freshened up, and changed into what I had nicknamed the 'Spinning Around' outfit – in honour of the legendary hot pants Kylie wore in the video – ready for my last table dance.

Wanting no further incident, I performed without putting in any special effort, thinking of Aramis the whole time. His was a quiet, persuasive self-assurance, nothing like the crack-a-minute arrogance that Luke Cotterill spouted in the office. At the end of two songs I dismounted and passed the jug around, eager to get dressed and leave.

Thankfully, unlike last time, I had no trouble with the customers and disappeared out the back as soon as possible. God, I felt so horny – I always did when it was warm but the Blacks had got me positively steaming. I longed to feel a man's body pressing against me, using me. The anticipation was worth hanging on to. When the release came, on my terms, it would be all the more powerful.

As I showered, I thought about Aramis' offer. I wasn't sure whether I wanted to go driving with him. Another plan was forming in my mind, one that would test him to the limit.

The club was almost empty when I came back out, dressed in my civvies, and Aramis' table was empty. Let him wait. As the bar staff wiped down the surfaces, I sipped a glass of mineral water, going over my options. He would still be out there, I knew that, waiting patiently in the back of his car like he had all the time in the world.

I downed the rest of my drink, said goodnight, and made my way to the door. The outside air was blissfully cool, and raised goose bumps along my skin. Aramis' car stood across the street, but he wasn't sitting in it. Suddenly there was a movement behind me, and I smelled his exotic scent, as he placed his hands lightly over my eyes.

'Guess who, Ginger?' he said. At the rich sound of his voice, and the softness of his skin against my face, I knew exactly what I wanted to do.

'Aramis, come with me,' I said, taking his hand and leading him down the side of the club.

'Where are we going?' he asked.

'Never you mind,' I said. 'Just follow me.'

I took him round the back of the club to one of Suzy's favourite smoking areas. It wasn't overlooked and, now that the club was shut, completely private.

'What are you doing, Ginger, my car is waiting . . .'

Before he'd had a chance to finish his sentence, I caught him unawares and pushed him up against the wall, feeling for his zipper and pulling it down.

My hand was soon inside his pants, my fingers tenderly pulsing his erect cock.

'Oh, Ginger . . . Ginger.'

'Shhhhh,' I said, putting my hand over his mouth.

I sunk to my knees and teased his erection with my tongue, my lips, even my nose, just enough to hint at what might be to come, without giving him the satisfaction of a blow job.

His skin was warm and aromatic, with a scent of cinnamon that reminded me of apple pie. His penis was smooth, long and pleasingly sculpted. I ached to have it inside me but now was not the time.

I stood up, fastened his fly and cautioned him to stay silent.

'Right, we are going to your Bentley now, and you will instruct your driver to take us to the Park Lane Hotel. I don't want a peep out of you until we get there. Understood?'

He nodded in acceptance and allowed me to take his hand. He'd agreed to play my game and he knew I was in control.

He did exactly as I asked and told his driver where to drop us. We slid into the back seat but I left space between us.

'You are not to touch me unless I tell you otherwise,' I told him.

The fact that we were travelling without a word heightened the erotic tension between us. Aramis said so much with his eyes, though. By the time we swung around Marble Arch he had already mentally undressed me.

We pulled up outside the hotel. 'Now, go and book us a room,' I said.

He had a word in the driver's ear and followed my instructions. I knew a man of his standing and discretion would have no problem getting a room at this hour.

Indeed, it was less than ten minutes before he returned to the car and nodded his head.

I stepped out of the vehicle and followed Aramis into the hotel lobby and then the lift. I watched the floor numbers increase until the doors slid open. Still keeping his lips sealed, he turned the room key and ushered me in.

It was the penthouse suite, with floor-to-ceiling windows overlooking the park and a huge chandelier hanging above a set of stairs that led down to the bedroom.

I couldn't help but let out an involuntary gasp. Tall windows gave a view out on to the city beyond. It was absolutely breathtaking.

'Pour me some champagne and sit down over there,' I said, indicating a large buttermilk leather sofa.

Once more he did exactly what he was told and I was feeling lightheaded with power.

I let him settle before approaching him, peeling off my coat to reveal my satin coat-dress underneath.

How far could I push him? Was he man enough to allow me to play him all the way?

I took a long, lingering sip, swilled the chilled bubbles around my mouth and let it slip down my throat. Then I moved close to him, planting soft kisses on his forehead, his right cheek, left cheek, and both eyelids.

I felt his breath tickle my face and was surprised it was so calm and even. He didn't attempt to touch me and seemed totally unfazed by the situation.

I took another mouthful of champagne and pressed my lips against his, working them open with the tip of my tongue until the liquid seeped through into his mouth, first a trickle then a gush.

He jerked slightly but swallowed and I withdrew, without permitting him the pleasure of kissing me.

'You must not touch me,' I said, 'unless I touch you.'

I took his right hand and slid each soft, smooth brown finger in and out of my mouth, not sucking but kissing and licking, every move designed to tease him and tempt him into disobedience.

But still he did not make a move, his dark eyes regarding me with interest, his face almost impassive, his body disciplined.

How was he containing himself? I was accustomed to boys like Ryan, who would by this stage have allowed his animal instinct to take over and be pawing at me. But not Aramis. He was impeccable in every respect; there was not even a bead of sweat on his forehead or a sign that he was uncomfortable.

Without realising it, he had thrown down the gauntlet. What could I do that would make him lose his cool?

I wanted to be subtle and surprising – and jumping on him would have been neither of those. Should I tease him more? Should I make him think I was going to give myself to him and then stop short?

My body ached to feel him inside me but the words 'keep them wanting more' kept ringing in my head. Even though this was my game, would he come back for more if I gave everything to him on a plate?

Taking his hand in mine, I guided him downstairs to the king-size bed and sat him down.

I switched on the pre-loaded iPod in a Bose sound

dock and put on some fuck-me R&B. He played voyeur as I danced for him – as Geri, not as Ginger.

This wasn't lapdancing, it was the slow, sensual movement of a potential lover, and he knew that. I was demonstrating my intention without words, woman to man.

Without further performance, I took off my clothes and stood before him naked. But I did not remove my wig – I wasn't ready for that.

I walked over to him, took his face in my hands and placed it gently between my breasts.

'You can kiss them now,' I whispered.

And he did so, with the utmost delicacy – so unlike the feeding frenzy I had witnessed earlier in the bathroom at the Pearl.

I stroked his head and ran my fingers through his thick, dark hair. It felt exquisite, so much more intimate than anything I had experienced for a long time.

Lifting his head, I kissed him again on the forehead and lifted his hands, placing them around my waist. Even then he didn't pull my body towards him – he left the reins firmly in my grasp.

I guided both palms to my buttocks, circling them over my cheeks and up to my hips. I wanted him to feel my shape, my womanliness.

Now I knew what I would do. I unfastened his tie and removed it, followed by his suit jacket, placing both carefully on a hanger. Then I removed his shoes – very expensive, hand-made tan leather brogues.

I stood him up, unbuttoned his shirt and pulled it out of his trousers, and threw it on the bed.

Just like I'd done earlier, outside the club, I fell to my knees, unbuckled his belt and unzipped his fly. Only this time I left it at that.

'Now remove your trousers and socks.'

He did so, calmly putting them tidily away, until he was standing in front of me in just his boxers.

His body was manly but not muscular, with dense, curly chest hair that started just below his chin and stopped, abruptly, just beneath his nipples, save for a strip that continued down past his navel.

I traced my finger down that strip from his sternum then hooked my finger in the top of his boxers and tugged them down over his swollen cock. Not even he could stop himself from having an erection. I loved that element of helplessness in men. A woman can be turned on without anyone knowing, which gives her more power; a man cannot conceal his arousal.

We made direct eye contact as I put my arms around him and our bodies touched, my breasts pressed against his chest, his penis against my abdomen.

'Dance with me,' I said, as we swayed to the music, flesh on flesh, his hardness against my softness as I allowed him to embrace me.

It was like the last dance at the end of a long evening. After a couple of songs, I broke away and drew back the bedcovers.

'Now get into bed,' I said, and he complied.

I joined him and resumed our embrace, entwining my body in his, inhaling his aroma, kissing his temples, his neck, his chest – everywhere but his member.

He let out the faintest of moans but silenced himself

again so that all we could hear was the swish of sheets and flesh gliding against flesh.

What we had remained unconsummated but still full of potential. I gently lifted his arms and legs and moved away.

'It is late, and we must sleep . . . Goodnight, Aramis . . .'

I turned over and left him there with his flaming desire. It was exquisite torture, being so near him yet not allowing him to satisfy himself, or allow him to satisfy me.

I was, however, satisfied that I had played a good game. So much so that I swiftly sank into a heavy sleep.

The blinds hadn't been drawn so I was woken by the early morning sun shining through the crystals in the chandelier.

Aramis was on his side, facing away from me, but appeared to be dead to the world.

I didn't want to be there when he woke up, that would have broken the spell, so I crept into the bathroom and quickly dressed.

Dear Aramis, I wrote on the hotel notepaper. *Thank you for following my instructions last night. Your reward will come tomorrow.*

Chapter Eighteen

As I sat in my office looking at Tania at her desk, with her ramrod posture and long, lean limbs, I had to admit to a new-found respect for the girl.

She had already been down the path I was treading and had managed to reverse off it to come and work in the City.

God knows she'd had to make sacrifices, though – not least of which was relying on Luke Cotterill to get her a job interview. I hope she knew what she was doing, burning her bridges with him by humiliating him at the club.

Now I'd seen the world she'd come from I understood more why she flaunted herself the way she did. That's just what she was used to – women using their bodies to earn money.

I remembered what my management training consultant had told me: 'Don't criticise a man until you've walked a mile in his moccasins.'

Or, in this case, a few yards in a pair of her six-inch platform heels . . .

My reverie was punctured by the arrival of a brief

email from Daryll. *Geraldine, would you drop by my office this morning? Many thanks.*

How odd. He'd usually call Tania, not send me a message. I finished my coffee and made my way over, wondering if Daryll intended to quiz Luke and me about our recent contretemps.

But there was no sign of my sparring partner in Daryll's office.

'Geraldine, how good of you to visit,' he said, as if I had any choice in the matter. 'Do take a seat. Can I get you a tea or coffee?'

'No thanks, Daryll, I've just had one. Is there a problem?'

'Absolutely not, my dear,' he said. 'I merely wanted to say that the decision you and Mr Cotterill came to, after your second meeting, was absolutely the correct one for Sloane Brothers.'

'Oh, I see, that's a relief,' I said, feeling slightly sick that Luke had got it right all along. 'Some new information had come to light that put a different slant on the figures, so I felt I should revise my position.'

'Of course,' said Daryll, but did he believe me?

'There is one more thing I wanted to say, though, Geraldine.'

I didn't like his tone. I braced myself for bad news.

'You and Mr Cotterill are my top people,' he said, emphasising the word 'top'. 'And the reason you both hold that position is because you are superb at your job, but you operate in very different ways. Luke is a charming chap, I'm sure you'll agree, and he has excellent contacts in many areas of the financial world. You, Geraldine, have exceptional talents also, but in contrasting areas. I rely on you to use your feminine instinct, to complement Mr Cotterill's modus operandi.'

'I see, so you are happy for us to continue working together?' I asked. So that was what this was all about.

'Absolutely. In fact, I'm delighted with the partnership,' he said. 'I believe it will be of great benefit to Sloane Brothers.'

'Great, Daryll. Well, I'm fine with that arrangement if you are,' I told him. What else could I say? 'Thanks for the vote of confidence.'

'The pleasure is mine, Geraldine. Now don't let me keep you.'

I had to hold my horses in front of Daryll. I'd wanted to say, 'Great, thanks for the compliment, but you obviously reward locker-room gossip more than feminine instinct otherwise I'd have been given the same size bonus as Luke.' Only I couldn't say it; bonuses were supposed to be confidential and I couldn't admit to knowing about the discrepancy.

Sometimes I felt as if I was trying to do my job while wearing a straitjacket. Luke was trying to drive me mad – and it was working. And now it seemed I'd have to continue my unholy alliance with him. Reading between the lines, I guessed Daryll actually enjoyed playing us off against each other if it got him what he wanted. 'Oh, Mr Sidebottom, if only you knew,' I thought. 'I will certainly be using my feminine instincts in the very near future, but not in the way you think . . .'

What got me about this whole sorry business was that it seemed all Luke had to do was go to the golf club or the gym and tap up a few contacts – probably on the promise of a night out at the Pearl – while I had to work much harder to gather good information and all the thanks I got from my boss was that I had 'womanly instincts'.

In fact, I was about to take a much bigger risk than any of these guys. They rarely stepped outside their comfort zone, more than happy to play poker with other people's money but not with their own lives.

In less than twenty-four hours I would be taking off my clothes for a bunch of men who would most likely be fantasising about what they'd like to do to me. Men like Luke, who probably felt very much in control of their world. But were they really? Surely if I was the one on stage making their cocks hard, I would be the one with the whip hand?

Luke had given me a slightly wider berth of late so I guessed he must also have had the benefit of Sidebottom's wisdom.

Tania hadn't been so lucky, though. The 'Peckers' jibes had become routine and relentless, and he was clever enough to keep them short of sexual harassment so there was little she could do.

Her way of coping was to tone down her body language, tie her hair back in a ponytail and start wearing clothes that covered her up a little more.

It was a pretty obvious tactic and one that I'd been forced to adopt straight out of university.

However, since Ginger had entered my life, I had decided to head in the opposite direction. Sick of sacrificing my femininity in the office, I'd decided to start wearing skirts, which puzzled some my colleagues and pleased others.

Ryan had been the first to notice, of course, when I showed up in a trim, tapered pin-striped skirt with matching suit jacket. The skirt was calf-length, modest enough to leave plenty to the imagination yet tight enough to get that imagination running.

I noticed a new email alert on my computer when I returned from my meeting with Daryll. It was from Ryan.

I kept telling the guys you did have legs even though they never saw them – apart from that night at the Pearl, of course! Anyway, well done – you're looking hot!

I sighed in frustration. Why did men like him always think a woman dressed for them, rather than for herself?

The fact that I have chosen to show my legs is of no consequence to you or anyone else. And I've certainly not worn a skirt to look 'hot'. You're half-Scottish, aren't you? Can't wait to see you in a kilt so I can tell you how damn sexy your hairy knees are.

And he hadn't even seen the ruffled blouse I had on underneath the jacket. While it wasn't exactly low-cut, it was more neck than I'd ever shown in the office. I liked the outfit because it reminded me of Mrs Black: prim and proper on the outside, wild on the inside. But Ryan's email had done nothing but piss me off.

God knows what I'd ever seen in Ryan. Now I'd encountered a seriously sophisticated guy like Aramis, he seemed like a boy playing at being a man.

I had no desire to shag him again so it was easy, almost fun, to bat him away whenever he tried to worm his way back into my affections.

My internal phone rang as I was about to tell Ryan to leave me alone for good.

'Geraldine,' said the familiar baritone, 'would you mind returning to my office?'

'Sure, Daryll,' I replied. 'I'll be right there.'

I was surprised. Another chat with the boss so soon after the last one? Maybe he'd suddenly developed a conscience and seen the error of his ways. I'd heard on the grapevine that Daryll had made as much as £2 million for his bonus – and since I was one of his 'top' people, perhaps he was planning to top up my bonus, to redress the balance a little? Reward me for my brilliant feminine instincts?

It wouldn't have taken that much to keep me sweet and motivated. I'd more than helped him make that money, for God's sake. All those brownie points I thought I'd racked up over the years, learning how to ride so I could mix in his circles . . . What had it all been for?

I tried to put it all out of my mind otherwise Daryll would see the resentment in my eyes. He didn't miss a trick, of course, that's why he'd made it to his current position. That and being an Old Harrovian.

'Geraldine, do come in, please join us,' he said, charm incarnate. Luke was already in his office – looking less cocky than usual and glowering slightly. If he was here under sufferance, that suited me fine.

'Now, as you know, I consider you two to be my star operators,' he said. 'And I am about to entrust you with a project that has the potential to be one of the biggest ever opportunities in Sloane Brothers' history. There is a very good chance that we will be able to acquire a company for a client that will enable them to create a global superbrand. Confidentiality and secrecy is of the utmost importance so no one outside this room will know the identity of the client. I will brief you both personally and you will report directly to me. You will be notified of a project name that will conceal the identity of the parties involved. Are there any questions?'

'Yes,' piped up Luke immediately. 'How are we dividing this up? Are we expected to attend client meetings together?'

'That will be at my discretion,' said Daryll. 'The division of labour will be along the lines of your individual strengths.'

That shut Luke up for a moment. I could see he hated this; the idea of working with a woman on equal terms was extremely uncomfortable for him.

'Geraldine, any worries from your side?' Daryll asked.

'Not at the moment,' I said, coolly. 'I'm sure your confidence in us as a team is well placed. I'm ready to get started. How about you, Luke?'

'Yes, of course,' he said, running his hands through his hair in an irritated manner. 'I'll clear the decks so we're ready to rock.'

I relished seeing him squirm. At least I could get satisfaction from that. Once upon a time I would have been aroused by the prospect of such a big deal but these days Daryll's praise was ringing rather hollow. However special he tried to make me feel I knew, at the end of the day, that Luke would be earning more than me.

'Good show,' said Daryll, standing up to indicate the

meeting was over. 'We'll get started on this one immediately. Now go forth and multiply – our profits.'

Luke and I laughed politely with him at his little joke and got up to leave Daryll's office. I was gobsmacked when Luke held the door open for me and said, 'After you . . .'

I thanked him and walked through, but knew he was only doing it for the boss's benefit. As soon as we were out of Daryll's earshot, he started up with the old tricks again.

'Guess you're looking to make up that bonus a different way, then?'

I didn't bother to turn round. 'What the hell do you mean?'

'Come on, Carson, a pencil skirt and a blouse that almost shows your cleavage?'

This time I swivelled to look him in the eye. 'Yes, and what of it? What are you suggesting?' I wanted him to spell it out.

'That you're finally learning how things work around here,' he said, chuckling to himself and disappearing off to his desk.

As he did so I was left with a clear view back towards Daryll's office. My boss was standing in his doorway, looking in my direction. Was he really eyeing up my legs?

'Jesus,' I thought. 'I'm surrounded by little boys who want to look up their mummies' skirts. Where the hell are the real men?'

I could have answered my own question: there were no real men at Sloane Brothers, only unreconstructed public schoolboys and male chauvinist pigs – pathetic, one and all. I had more time for the £1-in-the-jug regulars at the Pearl; at least there was an honesty about them.

Oh, I'd do what Daryll wanted me to: I'd keep pace with Luke every step of the way, but I didn't have quite the same emotional investment in the career outcome. Since I'd started working at the Pearl, my priorities had shifted.

It amused me no end to imagine performing for the Brothers on a night out, without them realising it was me. Winding them up, teasing them, and then extracting large amounts of cash out of them at the end of the night . . . Yes, that would be extremely satisfying . . .

Making up my bonus a different way, indeed.

I called in Tania to get her up to speed on the latest developments.

'Right, this is just to let you know that I've been asked to work with Luke on a highly sensitive project – and he obviously doesn't like it. We both know what that means – he's going to make life difficult, probably for both of us. He's already started making comments about me wearing a skirt, and I'm sure that's just the beginning.'

'What do you suggest I do then, Geri?' She looked curious, as though she had detected my change in attitude towards her. I'd begun to realise that Tania was far from the brain-dead bimbo I'd initially taken her for, and had come to rely on her as an ally in the testosterone-fuelled office.

'I know it's hard, but try not to react to the playground comments. And if he gets more personal, or it

191

becomes blatantly sexual, make a note of it with the date and time.'

'OK, I'll do my best. Are you going to do the same?'

'Trust me; I'm going to become the elephant that never forgets. Luke is clever, but sometimes he gets carried away, especially when he thinks he's on a roll, and that's when he sails close to the wind.'

She looked thoughtful and paused before continuing.

'Even though it's quite stressful, sometimes I think it's better if I do react to his taunts because then I might trap him into saying something really offensive.'

'God, Tania, don't put yourself through the mill like that, you'll start dreading coming into the office . . .'

'I'm not trying to be masochistic; it's just that I don't want him getting away with it.'

'No, I understand, and I'm with you on that one. But we have to play a long game. The fact that he now has to work so closely with me is going to provide plenty of opportunity for him to lose it. With any luck he'll end up hanging himself . . .'

'I hope so. I'd love to see that happen,' she said, with the determination of a woman motivated by revenge.

'OK, I'd better get cracking on this job. Do you have the pitch book?'

'Yes, the junior analysts have their initial findings ready but it can't be easy for them working in the dark.'

'No, but they're used to that. Now it's up to me and Luke to make sense of the figures. That should be fun. He hates detailed work – thinks that's for the "little people".'

I sunk myself into the research papers for Project X.

We still didn't know the identity of the client or the company, only that it was in pharmaceuticals.

I made sure I had a wealth of material to take to my first meeting with Luke the next day, just to annoy him, and arrived early, to annoy him even more.

Five minutes later, Luke stumbled in. 'Late night?' I asked without looking up, fanning my papers out on the table.

'Yeah, doing your job for you while you were getting your beauty sleep,' he said, groggily.

'In an all-night drinking den, by the look of it,' I said.

'That's where the deals are done, Carson, I told you,' he answered.

'No, Luke, that's just what macho throwbacks like you want to believe.'

'Spiky as your bog brush hair,' he said. 'Get your inner bitch back in the box and let's do some work.'

I tried to look smug. 'Absolutely. I'm ready when you are.'

'Look, Geri, we've gotta do this together,' he said, shifting anxiously in his seat. 'I don't like it any more than you do but if that's what the boss wants . . .'

' . . . that's what the boss gets, I know. He wants my feminine instincts and your masculine ability to sniff out the best boys' club gossip.'

'Yeah, whatever. What have you got, anyway?'

'Lots of background, lots of figures, lots of research – all the stuff you don't like.'

'Well, if you've crawled all over it I don't need to,' he grunted.

'I think you'll find the devil is in the detail, Luke, so I'd advise you to give this stuff a cursory glance if nothing else.'

'Do me a summary, then,' he said.

'OK, I'll do it this time but I'm not letting you get away with doing all the interesting stuff while I do all the donkey work.'

'Don't worry, I'll be dragging you along to meetings. I'll tell them you're my PA, obviously . . .'

'Oh, comedy gold, Cotterill; I don't know how you come up with them.'

He forced a smile and, surprisingly, didn't come back with more abuse.

'Right, let's get this show on the road; I need the hair of the dog . . .'

I surprised even myself. I'd stood up to Luke and thrown a few barbs back at him without behaving like a screaming fishwife and it had worked a treat. Beyond that, I was actually enjoying it. Was I beginning to get the measure of Luke Cotterill? I wondered if I had Ginger to thank for that . . .

Chapter Nineteen

I pulled on my khaki mini mac, wrinkled from being stuffed in the back of my car, and slipped on my pink Adidas baseball cap, usually reserved for hungover Saturdays in the office. I looked at myself in the rear-view mirror. Some disguise, but it would have to do. I was already late.

I nodded to Tony, the Pearl's bouncer, as I rushed by. His biceps were the size of my thighs. I felt safer with those arms barring entry to any big-time weirdos. 'Better not let Jackie see you,' he called after me. 'She's in a foul mood today.'

'Thanks!' I waved and kept moving. The talent was not supposed to come in the front entrance but I couldn't be bothered to walk all the way around to the back, not after the day I'd had in the office. I already felt as if I was a second-class citizen at Sloane Brothers. I didn't intend to be treated the same or worse at the Pearl. I slipped into the main room and looked around. So far so good. No Jackie.

Declan's voice rang out over the crackly sound system. 'Please join me in welcoming our foreign beauty Marlena to the stage.' The music started – a rattling, insistent tambourine – followed by the unmistakable piano intro of Robbie Williams' 'Let Me Entertain You'. Why is it that almost all Robbie Williams songs are perfect for stripping? Some encourage the slow removal of clothes in private while many beg for public nudity. Maybe it's just me. He was my bad-boy crush growing up. Suzy said she gave him a lap dance once, but if you believed Suzy she had given everyone a lap dance at least once, including Margaret Thatcher.

Irena stumbled on to the stage, glancing backwards as if someone had pushed her. She smiled that weak apologetic smile of hers, as if she was sorry she ever came to England; she was sorry to inconvenience us with her presence. She straightened up and shook off her nerves. As Robbie started to sing, Irena strutted centre stage, wearing nothing but matching bra and thong in an electric green and blue that made her body glow white in the hot spotlight. She didn't bother with costumes anymore. According to Suzy, she had problems a few nights ago with buttons and almost didn't get her kit off. Irena seemed to be getting worse, not better.

She surveyed the room as if she was memorising each client. It was early and the Pearl wasn't very full. A few of our regulars had settled in for the night. Tom, who sat at the same table at the back, only wanted to *talk* to the girls. Some of the girls wouldn't give him the time of day, but I always let him buy me a glass and chatted until Jackie spotted me. The Mac Brigade was sprinkled like perverted parmesan in the Pearl's saucy red surroundings. They thought we didn't know that they were wanting to wank under those coats. A piece of advice: Never give a lap dance to a man in a mac. There's the smell, the lack of undergarments and the creepy movement under the coat. Safer to target the businessmen. It was early for the City boys but a few clusters of businessmen in their dark suits and loosened ties were already pasty with sweat and sipping Jack Daniel's on the rocks. Better for me if they got nice and drunk so it was much easier to part them with their money.

Irena locked eyes with a curly-haired man, a boy really, sitting with his work buddies at a table near the stage. He looked away but then Irena started her pole work. She slowly lowered herself to squatting right in front of the boy. He couldn't resist a peek. She swivelled her knees together and wound herself back up the pole, never taking her eyes off him.

I didn't know who picked Irena's music, certainly not Irena. She didn't know much about British pop culture. She thought S Club 7 was a rival lapdancing joint and if you mentioned Take That, she always responded, 'Take what?' I was not convinced that she knew what song she would dance to before she stepped on stage. She could move and she knew the basics, but she didn't anticipate the music. She acted surprised when the music changed tempo and it always took her a moment to recover.

'Decided to join us, did you, princess?' It was Jackie.

'Sorry, Jackie, I got stuck at work.'

'I don't care. Get backstage and get changed and don't let it happen again. Next time I'll dock you £100.'

The crowd gasped. Jackie and I turned in time to see Irena trip on thin air and nearly take a header into the audience. The boy she had enticed earlier rushed to the stage and helped Irena steady herself. The guys he was with shouted taunts: 'Who's your new girlfriend?' 'Think you'll get a free blow job for that?' 'Hey, you're going to poke someone's eye out with that thing,' one guy yelled and pointed to the boy's crotch. He was rude but right, the boy might have been young but he was well endowed. Irena knew how to pick them. Maybe she wasn't so stupid after all. The boy slumped back down in his seat.

'I've got to have a talk with that girl,' Jackie said, her lips thinning.

I nodded. We watched Irena regain her composure and whip off her bra to reveal sparkly tassels attached to each nipple. Her tits weren't great but she was the only Pearl girl who knew how to twirl tassels. She whipped the metallic streamers one direction then the other.

'Taught her that myself,' Jackie said, proudly now. 'She's got problems, but she's also got talent, you know.'

I nodded, mesmerised by her hypnotic spinning.

'You could learn a thing or two from her,' Jackie said.

I looked at her in surprise. She kept her eyes on Irena. 'I've tried, Jackie,' I said. 'But the adhesive on the tassels gives me a rash. Red, raw tits are not the most attractive.'

'Not the tassels,' Jackie corrected. 'Look how she connects with the customers. You can move, Geri, I'll give you that, but Irena's got something else.' Jackie took a laboured breath. 'I just hope she doesn't lose it. She's got all the signs of a girl headed for disaster. I've seen it before and it isn't pretty.'

'What do you . . .' I started but Jackie cut me off.

198

'What are you yapping with me for? You need to get changed and get to work. If you see Suzy, tell her to get her ass out here. She's up next.'

In the changing room, I undressed quickly, not bothering to fold my suit. It needed dry cleaning anyway. Suzy popped her head in. I was completely naked and completely comfortable. A few weeks ago I might have reflexively grabbed for my robe but now I continued getting ready at a slow and steady pace.

'Hey, Ginger. Ready to rock 'n' roll.' She downed the last of her San Miguel and tossed the bottle in the overflowing rubbish bin.

'You better get out there,' I said. 'Jackie gave me an earful for being late. She says you're up after Irena.'

'What's crawled up her bum tonight?' Suzy slurred.

'I don't know and I don't want to find out. I think Irena may be her next victim.'

''Bout time that foreign cow got what's coming to her.'

'What does that mean?' I ripped the cellophane packaging from the new fishnet body stocking I bought in Jubilee Place over lunch. I'd come to believe there was something sexy about being nearly naked rather than completely. I think men like a little left to their imagination.

'Haven't you noticed? She's got those glassy eyes, walking around here on some sort of synthetic high.' That was rich coming from Boozy Suzy.

'What's her story?' I bent over, leaning my ass against the cold metal lockers, and squeezed one leg and then the other into the fishnet.

'God, how the hell should I know? I try not to mix

with her type. She's one of those girls who thinks some white knight is coming to rescue her.'

'Like a sugar daddy?'

'No, like some guy she met on holiday. Do you believe it? Well, I told her last week that she needs to just wake up and smell the morning after. She was just a holiday piece of arse. She's an idiot if she thinks this guy is coming for her. I told her no one wants some crusty foreign piece of rubbish when they can have grade A British.' She walked over and smacked me on the bum. 'Isn't that right, sweet cheeks?'

I rubbed the stinging red handprint on my behind. 'God, Suzy. Take it easy.'

'Suzy, one minute,' Declan called down.

'Gotta go!' and Suzy was gone.

I finished getting ready. I considered my normal pull-away business suit, but I'd had enough of the business world for one day. I opted for a bit of fun tonight and pulled on the maid's costume. I tested the Velcro and practised how to disrobe. I dug around in the prop box and found the feather duster and French maid's hat. I watched myself in the mirror and tried out a few moves with the feather duster. I decided the outfit called for new music. Janet Jackson's 'Nasty' should do the trick – a song with attitude. I had to remember to tell Declan my new song selection before I took the stage. Besides, I wouldn't mind a little alone time with Declan in the top booth.

I was halfway up the spiral staircase when I heard the yelling. Undeniably Jackie. Because of what Jackie had said earlier, I figured she had ambushed Irena as soon as she got off the stage. I took a seat on the stairs. No need to get caught in the cross-fire. Jackie's tirade mingled with Suzy's Hall and Oates' 'Rich Girl'. Jackie was talking fast and I couldn't understand exactly what she was saying, but I knew it wasn't good. That was probably all that Irena could figure out too, with her marginal comprehension of the English language.

I waited for a few moments after the yelling had subsided to finish climbing upstairs. Irena was slumped against the wall. She took something out of her pocket and popped it in her mouth. She swallowed whatever it was without water, throwing her head back to help it down. She closed her eyes like she was going to cry.

I closed the distance between us, and I don't know why, but I took her hand. She looked at our clasped hands and then squeezed my hand so tightly my fingers turned red. 'No one touch me like that in long time,' she said, tears pooling in her eyes. She sniffed and wiped her eyes. 'You are nice.' She cleared her throat.

I led her back downstairs to the dressing room. I had to help her down the staircase. I sure hoped Jackie didn't see her like this. She flopped like a rag doll on the nearest chair. 'Are you OK?' I asked, pouring her a cup of what passed for coffee in this place.

'Fine,' she paused, 'no problem.' She sometimes sounded like she learned English from the telly, repeating pat phrases.

I handed her the cup. She looked up at me with big milky blue eyes. 'Jackie say I could learn from you. Jackie say I shit.' She sat the coffee up on the vanity a little too forcefully and the coffee sloshed out on her hand. It must have been hot but she didn't flinch, as if she was used to physical pain.

'Jackie's just in a rotten mood. She yelled at me too. Don't worry about it.'

'No worries.' She picked up a make-up brush from the vanity and twirled it in her hands. She brushed it on her thighs and across her chest. 'That tickles.' She was somewhere else now, staring at the brush as if she'd never seen one before.

'You are pretty with red hair.' Now she stared at me, tilting her head as if the world was out of focus. I didn't doubt that her world was.

'Thanks,' I said. The make-up brush fell from her hands as if she'd forgotten she was holding it. I picked it up and handed it back to her. 'Jackie said I should get some advice from you.'

'Ad-vice.' She pronounced it as if it's two words. 'I not understand.'

'I want you to tell me something. Teach me something. I need to learn from you.'

'Advice,' she repeated. 'My English is no good.'

'You have very good English. It's getting better.'

'No. It's no good. Suzy laugh at me.'

'That is Suzy's problem. Not your problem,' I said.

'So many things to say,' she sighed. 'I sometimes think I will never understand this strange language, this strange place.'

'You and me both,' I muttered.

'What you want to know?' She stood up, swayed and then sat back down. 'I teach you anything.'

'It's your bond with the audience,' I said. She gave me

a confused look. 'You dance for them.' I point to the front of the house. 'The men. I dance but I don't have that connection.'

'Connection?'

I tilted her face up towards mine and looked her directly in the eyes. I pointed to my eyes and then to hers, back and forth. 'Connection.'

She squinted and smiled. 'I see you. You take home big money. You not need my,' she paused and smiled wider, 'advice.'

'OK.' I patted her arm.

'No. No. No.' She grabbed my hand. 'Don't go. I tell you. I tell you.'

I pulled up a chair and sat across from her.

'It is simple really. You dance for room,' she said, sweeping her arm wide towards a pretend audience. 'I dance for Simon.'

Chapter Twenty

IRENA'S STORY

Every summer growing up, I spend in Mierzeja Helska, on Hel Peninsula in Poland, with my aunt and uncle. They run hotel. I first start cleaning rooms. Then I wait tables. Summer when I met Simon, I sing Polish songs in café. My voice is not so good, but my aunt say it give place character. My uncle say boys come to watch pretty girl in nice dress. Starting, I close my eyes when I sing. All those people staring at me make me nervous and I forget words. My voice start all shaky and then I get warmed up and they cannot make me leave.

For Simon, I open my eyes. He come two days in a row. I see him sitting at back of café, hiding behind a book on first day. By time café closes, his book is in rucksack. On second day he sit closer and he have no book. He stare so much that I look away. When I finish for day, he come up and speak to me. I do not know English then. I say few English words to make tourist think I understand: yes, no, please, I no understand and thankyouverymuch. He speak and I smile and shake my head.

'I no understand,' I say. He point to me and then to centre of his chest, then he walk his fingers over imaginary beach. I nod.

He is beautiful. Tall. How do you say? Wavy hair that flop and cover his eyes.

We walk on beach. At first we try to talk with mess of hand and two- or three-word sentences. Then we start holding hands and gently tug each other in direction we want to go.

We walk for long time in the moonlight. He stop to show me how stars make patterns in sky. He connect the sparkly dots with his finger and I smile up at him, not really understanding. Maybe it is sound of his voice or moonlight on water, but stillness come over me. I reach up on my tiptoes and kiss him. And he kiss me back. He smell different than Polish boys I kiss before. They smell salty and sweet, like sand. Simon smell fresh with daily showers and British soaps and shampoos.

We are shy at first, kissing quickly and looking at each other's eyes. Then he wrap his strong arms around me and kiss me properly. At first I do not know how to respond, my body seem to fall away. I am not sure if I am standing or floating. I grab on to him and hold him to me. Our kisses and hands explore each other. He take my hand and we race for cover of sand dune.

He scoop me in his arms and gently lay me in the sand. He kneel beside me and take off his shirt. He fold it carefully and tuck it under my head. He place his hands on my thighs and I shiver, not with cold but something else. He glide his hands under my skirt. I am breathing so fast. As much as I want him to go on, I also want him to stop. Feeling is full of power. He run his fingers under elastic of my knickers at top of each leg, his fingers brushing my hair between. I try to smile but I tremble. He speak softly to me with his beautiful voice and words I do not understand. I know he is asking of me questions. I nod and say yes, then close my eyes.

He slip off my knickers and part my legs. I hear sound of his zipper. He nudge me, to get me to open my eyes. He want to show me his penis, but I do not want to see it. I seen my brothers' before and I think they are wrinkly ugly things. I am afraid that seeing it dampen tingly feeling that make my body ache. He stop touching me and sigh. I find his hand and pull him on top of me. 'Yes,' I whisper. 'Yes.'

He wiggle out of his jeans and use his fingers to find right place. I feel tip of his penis gently poke me, urging me to open. I spread my legs wider. I am wet everywhere. He begin to slowly slip inside. My eyes pop open when I realise how big and hard he is. He take his time and ease himself deeper and deeper. I breathe again when at last I feel our bodies together fully. I not expect the sensation of being filled up, complete. I grab his behind and show him rhythm to match feeling that grow inside me. Simon and I do not need words when we make love that night. I read rise and fall of his body and he understand heat of my skin.

Slowly I feel sensation build. I tense and hold my breath as feeling like tidal wave crash over me. Simon feel it too. Our voices and bodies rise until we collapse in each other's arms and fall asleep in fuzzy glow.

Simon is travelling on his gap year. He tell me later

that he only plan to stay a week. But one day become another. Every morning we meet and he teach me English and I teach him Polish. I sing and he watch in afternoon. In café, I begin to sing him English songs I learn from CDs tourists sometimes give me. But when I sing those songs I do not sing words, I sing sounds and Simon tell me later that I speak no language he heard before, but he understand every word. We make love whenever and wherever we can. My body burn with a fire that I never feel again.

We know our time together come to an end, but we never speak of it. I overhear him making phone calls and by then I understand enough to know that he need to return to England because he start college soon.

We not talk about our homes because it remind us that we have to leave this paradise we create together. Now I know I should have ask questions. Write down every name and location. But I never doubt for one second that we will be together again.

He give me his email address and set up email for me at Internet café. He show me how to send messages to him. He do not know his phone number or address at new college. He promise he come back when he save up more money. I promise I save money too and come and see him.

I want our last day to be special. I make us dinner. My aunt let me use kitchen and eat alone in special room in hotel. I collect all candles I find. The room glow and we eat in silence. I not speak, afraid if I open my mouth I cry. I promise myself I not spend last moments to cry. I see by his eyes he is sad too. I know we want to beg each other. I want to ask him stay. He want to beg me go with him. We open our mouths but we do not say things we want to say and do not want to say things we do say, words that mean goodbye.

After sad dinner, coffee go cold and nalensniki z sernikiem cytrynowym get cold and – how you say? – gross on our plates, then I lead him to beach. We stop to watch kites and parasailers in wind. Sky is alive colourful, with many clouds. I lead him to lighthouse. It is pretty red colour and high over other buildings, between Bay of Puck and Baltic Sea. Lighthouse keeper know my uncle and he agree to let me take Simon to top. Steps to top are hard metal. My high shoes click and his sandals clank behind me as we climb. Our steps slow as we get to top because we are tired and very sad.

When we reach top, sun start to go down. Sky is mix of purple and pink. View of sea take my breath. On one side you see lights and life on land. On other you see dark, wild ocean. We look out on ocean. Simon stand behind me and he wrap his arms around me very close. I lean onto him. He kiss back of my neck.

'Now I show you something,' he whisper in my ear. He take my hand and sit me on top step. He is on his knees in front of me and smile a sweet smile. He look very shy. He kiss me slowly and with fire as if he try to learn by heart this moment.

'Lie down,' he say after he kiss me a very long time. I lie on hard metal floor. I feel the points of the metal from floor on my naked back. Metal is cold and begin to feel through my dress. Simon take off my knickers. I wait for sound of his zipper and part my legs to wait for him. He take end of my sundress and pull it up. I close my eyes.

I feel his breathing warm on my pussy lips. His mouth? I tense.

'Just relax,' he tell me. He put his hand on my stomach.

And he kiss me. He kiss me down there. I start to sit up, but his hand he kept me down. 'Just trust me,' he say, his voice from down there. He kiss me there again, he play with my pussy lips between his mouth lips. I feel wetness, then I panic.

'Irena, it is OK.' Simon sit up and I see his face. 'I think you would like this. Just relax and enjoy, my darling.'

'What are you doing down there?' I ask. I was confused. My girlfriends not talk about anything like this.

'I'm going to make you feel really, really good.' He smile and disappear.

I take deep breath and relax. He kiss me again. He tease my lips open with his tongue. He circle his tongue, and make shapes on my clitoris. He hum a Polish song I teach him about sea. Sensation make small wave of pleasure, again and again. I whimper but I not afraid anymore. I love what he do to me.

Then he put my heels on his shoulders and open me wider. He begin to touch me. His fingers tickle and explore me. He touch. His tongue. My pussy is buzzing. It almost too much. It almost hurt. I feel the sense building. I repeat his name. I reach for something to hold. I feel as if I jump out of my skin. My hands find cold metal bars of rails from stairs on side of me. I hold tightly. Then I cum with explosion both inside and outside me. As my body shake, Simon is up next to me and hold me.

'Wow,' I say, and I laugh. 'Is this what you do in London?'

He laughed. 'I never done that before.'

I glad he said that. He is my first everything and I want to be his first something.

'Now for my surprise,' I say, when the sweet hum of orgasm had pass. I stand and take off my sundress. He look up at me. We never been all the way naked to each other. Making love on beach, in his hostel room, bathroom stalls and empty cabanas do not let us to be naked. I want him to see all of me. He stare at me for long time then he stand. He take my breasts in his hands and kiss each nipple. I unbutton his shirt and take it off. I run my hands down his bare chest. I unbutton and unzip his jeans. I like sound of his zip. He take off rest of clothes. Finally I let me to look at his penis. It is beautiful, it stand so erect and straight, it press against his stomach. I cup his balls with one hand and stroke his penis with other hand. Now it is his turn holding on to railing.

'I want you inside me,' I say. He turn me around and lean me over railing. I pressed my palms against glass as if I reach out for sea.

He slip inside with one thrust. I make wide my legs and let him in deeper. He grab my hips and ram himself inside of me, again and again. Pain both with pleasure shoot from my pussy to my throat. I scream, but he not stop. Always he know what I desire. I want it to be rough.

I want to feel something more than numbness that grow inside me.

'More,' I pant.

As our bodies tense in waiting for orgasm, light behind us flash on. Lighthouse explode in light. Our bodies stop, we are so surprise. Then light begin to spin and we continue, we rock with every sweep of light. Every burst of light that come over us make more our passion and our hunger for each other. I imagine light make shadow of our naked, joined bodies onto sea. We cum together, and we shout into light.

He slip out and I turn and hug him close. We stand in flashing light, we cry and say our final goodbyes.

All girls talk about summer boys who come and steal their virginity and hearts but not always in that order. My mom tell me not let any foreign man touch me. 'They touch you, they take you,' she say. She is right, but not in way that I want. Simon touch me and take me but he leave my body behind.

I go back home at end of summer. My family do not have computer and little village do not have Internet café. My friend let me use her father's computer sometimes. Simon and I send emails, but my English is not so good. I spend hours to translate his long messages. He is sweet and make poem but that make it harder for me to understand what he say. I send back message in broken sentence which match my breaking heart.

I leave school so I get money. I take three jobs. I work hard. I save up, buy ticket and come to London. I being stupid. I not make plan. When I get money for one-way ticket, I leave. I do not know London is so big. I think it is city like other city. I think I ask around and find Simon. It take me a while but I find where he go to school. I get job as cleaner at college so I look for him. I find someone who finally check college records. He drop out. No forwarding address. He vanish.

Sometimes I walk in London and look for him, even after all this time is pass. I see him everywhere – his hazel eyes, his wavy hair, his smile. When I dance, I imagine every man who look at me is Simon. When men touch me, put money in my garter, it his hands I feel. When I dance, I make love to Simon again and again. It is how I hold on to him, how I survive.

Chapter Twenty-One

When I worked my next shift, I wondered if I should tell Suzy about what had happened between me and Aramis. I needed to talk to someone and she was the nearest thing I had to a friend at the Pearl. I stepped outside with the smokers to see if she was there, but instead I saw Irena talking to the barman Viktor in what sounded like her native tongue.

They started to gesticulate and raise their voices; I guessed they were having a bit of a domestic. Maybe he was her new boyfriend – which was not a good idea and almost certainly breaking one of Jackie's cardinal rules.

I had no desire to get drawn into the argument, but when I was about to walk back indoors, I bumped into Suzy on her way out. She started talking at me in a loud voice.

'Geri, sweetheart, I've got to tell you, you've been lucky so far,' she boomed. She was always telling me how lucky I was. 'Wait till a DJ hits on you or one of the bouncers or the barmen . . .'

Just at that moment, Viktor walked right past us.

'Oh, good timing, Suzy,' I said. 'He probably thought you meant him.'

'I doubt he understood what I was saying,' she continued, pausing to swig from her glass. 'Another one who can hardly speak the lingo. Anyway, you'll see. That poor girl over there will get it worse, though, especially if she doesn't have a proper work permit. If they find out they're illegal, it's a nightmare. They'll expect sex for nothing then.'

'Surely that doesn't happen here, though?' I asked.

'Over my dead body – I'd kill the guy first. I don't know anywhere in London where the girls are expected to sleep with the customers but a few girls will do it on a freelance basis. In my opinion it's OK to do it with rich customers outside the club but not poor bar staff and certainly not bouncers who live on council estates.'

She laughed until she spluttered, then lit up another cigarette.

The 'poor girl', as Suzy always called her, was looking paler and more distressed than usual. She was wearing a thick cardigan but still shaking, and I wasn't sure if it was because of the cold weather or because she was upset.

She brushed past us without a word.

I wondered if I could risk confiding in Suzy about Aramis. If she thought it was acceptable to sleep with rich customers, perhaps she'd tell me go for it. On the other hand, she might even be a bit jealous, because she had once danced for him and now I was his favourite.

'Suzy, have you ever had sex with a customer?'

She gave me a withering look.

'Of course, darling. But only the ones who could afford

to keep me in mink and diamonds. And if you're entertaining the idea yourself, be sure you're discreet, don't get emotionally involved, and be prepared to walk away. Especially if it's with dusky businessmen who don't live in London . . .'

She pursed her lips and I grinned. 'Don't worry about me, Suzy; I know what I'm doing.'

'I hope so, Geri. Don't ask me to pick up the pieces.'

'There won't be any pieces, trust me.'

'Don't let me stop you then,' she said, in an arch manner.

I'd had enough of Suzy's advice, however well meaning. It was time to get going. I didn't usually work the floor before I hit the stage but that night I needed to know if he was there.

I made my way around the club, smiling at harmless regulars and ignoring potential trouble-makers. Was it just me, or did the atmosphere seem flat? Could I only get myself pumped up if Aramis was there?

I changed into the 'business suit' for my stage dance. I would not let this man get to me. I had a job to do.

When I walked out on stage I scanned the crowd again, but still no sign. I looked down at the men in the front row and did not see a single face I found appealing.

This was my biggest challenge – dancing for an audience I despised. I didn't feel like turning it on for these dopes; they did nothing for me so why should I do anything for them?

Now I realised what Suzy meant by going through the motions. I could understand now why it was easier for her to do this after a few vodka and tonics.

I dipped, I spun, I wiggled, I pouted, I stripped . . . I hated it.

My favourite corner table was still empty.

The customers must have thought I was on drugs when I passed the jug around looking like a zombie.

Then I saw him. But I didn't go straight to him; that would have been too obvious. I finally meandered over, as nonchalantly as possible.

'So, where have you been?'

'I told you that I would be here every night to see you, if I could. I have missed you on only two occasions.'

'True, but you left it very late tonight. The club is closing in five minutes.'

'Circumstances were beyond my control. Now, we have no time to waste. Will you dance for me?'

'Of course,' I said, gritting my teeth. 'Let's go.'

I took a few deep breaths to try and calm myself down. I hated that he could affect me like this. I drew back the curtain, adjusted my corset and suspenders, crossed my legs and waited for him to arrive.

He seemed to take forever, which wound me up even more. Was he trying to punish me?

Soon a familiar dark hand appeared around the side of the curtain. Aramis stood there with a wry smile on his face. He glided across the room and sat in the Chesterfield.

When I began my dance every move became more pointed, more aggressive. Usually I would look him in the eye but I just couldn't bring myself to do it.

I felt dead, unable to flirt, to connect.

My routine began – the dipping, the grinding, and the slapping. I didn't want to do it.

I spun round, pushed my face towards him. Then he grabbed my chin and tugged it towards him, an invasion that made me yelp.

I might as well have pulled the emergency cord. Within thirty seconds security were in the booth, ready to escort Aramis from the premises.

My eyes said it all but in case they didn't understand me, I put up my hands and told them to back off, which they did.

'What the hell are you playing at?' I hissed. 'Surely you know by now that you can't touch me in here?'

He didn't react. The bastard didn't react. He bided his time, and then spoke.

'Ginger, be calm and listen to me. Are you ready to stop playing games?'

I didn't reply. I couldn't speak. All my pent-up frustration welled up inside me.

I wanted to strike out at him, stop him making me feel this way.

He seized upon my indecision, lifted me up and deposited me on a couch in the corner of the room.

'Are you coming with me now?' he demanded, looming over me so I could feel his breath on my face.

I was blindsided by his dominance. I had been the one in control, until now.

'I won't come with you if you treat me like an object. Speak to me as an equal.'

'I respect you, Ginger, but you're like a skittish pony that needs to be reined in,' he said, moving away to give me some space. 'You're not ready to ride with the wild horses yet.'

It amused me that he was using equestrian metaphors. He had no idea I was an experienced horsewoman and I wasn't about to tell him.

'I know what you desire, Ginger. You act like a woman who wants control but you need the opposite.'

'How have you worked this out, Aramis? You know nothing about me.'

'I know enough,' he said. 'Here, take this.'

He handed me £100.

'What is this? A down payment for services that might be rendered?'

He glared at me. 'Don't insult me. This is for you, for your dance.'

My face reddened.

'Of course. I just thought . . .'

'That I was trying to buy you?'

He picked up his cashmere coat and slipped it on.

'As I have said before, I will wait outside. If you come, you come . . .'

And he drew back the drape and left.

I was shaken by his treatment of me, how physical he had been after holding himself back for so long.

I had no idea what to do. He had read me like a book and now I had no more plot lines to reveal.

I stood up and looked in the gilt-edged mirror on the wall of the private booth. I looked dishevelled – my wig was slightly askew, my lipstick smudged and one of my suspenders had sprung open.

Straightening myself out and putting my satin dress back on, I went out in search of Suzy. This time I needed her advice. She was at the bar, of course.

'What have you done to the sheikh?' she asked. 'I just saw him leave in a huff.'

'Let's just say it was an eventful dance. He has asked me to go with him in his Bentley but I'm not sure I should.'

'Oh, live a little, why don't you?' she said. 'He'll show you a good time, and he's pretty harmless.'

'It's just ... that he was different tonight, more assertive.'

'Thought that's how you liked them, Geri? Oh, and you might like to know that he paid a grand to come into the club after the doors had shut, just to see you ...'

'Are you serious?'

'Look at my face.'

'My God, he's crazy about me ...'

'That's the way it looks from where I'm sitting. Go on, girl, roll with it and see where it takes you. That's what got me to Vegas. Just make sure you book a return ticket.'

'Yes I will, Suzy. But I'm sure as hell going to make the most of the journey.'

She gave me one of her winks and I went off to collect my belongings and my thoughts.

I checked my make-up again and adjusted my wig. No, I didn't want to disguise myself anymore, not for him. I wanted him to see me as I really was.

I took off the wig and spiked up my hair again. How would he react?

I left the club and walked towards the waiting Bentley. The chauffeur stepped out and opened the rear door for me. I slid in beside Aramis, who just beamed at me.

'This is the real me,' I said. 'And my name's not Ginger, it's Geri.'

'I would have recognised that stride anywhere ... Geri.'

'So where are you taking me?'

'You will see soon enough. Allow me to take charge here, like I did when you took me to the hotel.'

I had no choice but to submit. It was a strange feeling, but once I allowed myself to let go of any responsibility, I began to feel a sense of liberation, as Aramis poured me a glass of champagne.

After another ten minutes heading west the Bentley glided to a stop outside a department store. The chauffeur opened my door and pointed to a door at the side of the building. Aramis offered me his arm and we walked up the steps and rang a bell.

We were buzzed in and entered a lobby area, where an elevator was waiting with its door open. I said nothing and neither did Aramis. He ushered me into the lift and pushed the button for the twelfth floor.

This wasn't a hotel. Perhaps a private members' club? The doors opened on to a front desk with what looked like a waiter standing behind it.

'Sir, madam, welcome. Shall I show you to your table?'

Aramis nodded and we followed the waiter past a sunken bar area and into a chic, minimalist restaurant with floor-to-ceiling windows. The view was spectacular, a whole panorama of city lights twinkling right across London.

There was just one table laid out, with a wonderful display of pink roses and aromatic vanilla candles.

Aramis pulled out a chair and helped me sit down, then sat opposite. The waiter brought over an ice bucket carrying another bottle of pink champagne.

'I hope you like my choice of restaurant,' said Aramis.

'It's stunning . . . I never knew it was here,' I said. 'But how come it's open, at this late hour?'

'A private arrangement. There are four kitchen staff waiting to cook you whatever you wish.'

'My God, Aramis, I'm so flattered. No one has ever done anything like this for me.'

'Then please, enjoy every moment.'

I was fully intending to. In fact, I was already wondering what to have for dessert . . .

Chapter Twenty-Two

My heart was in my mouth, which made it difficult to think about gourmet food. As grand gestures go, Aramis had surpassed all expectations.

He must have paid thousands to keep such a high-profile establishment open through the night. Everyone and everything has its price, though. That's something I learned early on in my banking career.

I wondered if I might be on the menu. Aramis looked as if he wanted to consume me.

'Geri, you are so beautiful.'

I couldn't help blushing. There was something so old-fashioned about Aramis, but he managed to make clichés sound spontaneous.

'I don't have much make-up on . . .'

'I prefer you with a natural look. You don't need any help.'

'I do, trust me . . .'

'No, you don't. You're a beauty, you just don't realise it.'

'I've never thought of myself as beautiful,' I told him. 'Attractive, yes, with an interesting face, but never beautiful.'

'You cannot judge yourself, nor can a mirror. You have a radiant smile that lights up your face.'

I looked away. 'You're making me feel bashful now . . .'

'Then perhaps you have never met a true admirer before.'

'Perhaps I have never met a true gentleman.'

He put his hand on the table, palm up, inviting me to place mine in his. Clasping it tenderly, he asked, 'Would you like to order now?'

'You've gone to all this trouble, which I appreciate so much, but I'm really not that hungry.'

'I understand,' he said, stroking my fingers. 'Perhaps just some oysters? They are the best in London.'

'That would be lovely.'

'And maybe some caviar too?'

'Mmm . . .'

The waiter nodded and disappeared into the kitchen. It was surreal, sitting in a boutique restaurant in the early hours with a man who appeared to worship me.

'Aramis, you have asked me nothing about myself or my life outside the Pearl. Aren't you intrigued?'

'I have no need for such information,' he said. 'It is enough that you are here with me now.'

'So you like to be spontaneous?'

'It is the only way to live. The present moment is all we have.'

I wanted to ask how much longer he would be in London but asking him about the future seemed inappropriate.

The waiter returned with a silver salver full of Whitstable oysters and a dish of Beluga caviar.

Aramis picked up an oyster shell. 'Tip your head back and let it just slip down, don't chew.'

It tasted sweet and buttery, the texture moist and delicate.

'Then let me feed you caviar,' I said, piling the black eggs on a blini with some sour cream and guiding it between his lips.

We savoured the food together, in an almost ritualistic way. Feeding each other with our hands became a sensual game, an elaborate foreplay. I wanted to slow it down, to milk every sensation, but at the same time, I couldn't help wondering where it was all leading?

'So what are we having for main course?' I asked.

'You will soon see,' he said, summoning the waiter, who promptly cleared the table and took away the flowers and candles.

'If you need anything else, sir, I will be in the kitchen,' said the waiter.

Aramis stood up. 'Geri, will you join me on the terrace?'

I felt a delicious thrill at him saying my real name.

One of the windows was actually a sliding door that led to a garden. The rain had stopped and a crescent moon was peeping out from behind a dramatic cloud, illuminating the sky.

'Do you think it's an omen?' I asked.

He didn't answer, just stood behind me and put his arms around my waist, gently kissing the nape of my neck. I felt the tiny hairs rise and the blood rush luxuriously to my throat.

I responded by arching my back. He ran his hands up

and round, stroking the contours of my corset, letting his fingers linger on my straining breasts.

His mahogany hands made my flesh look luminously pale. Then he slowly spun me round and pressed his lips against my bare shoulder, tracing his tongue along my collarbone.

A moan escaped my lips.

'You have beautiful skin,' he said. 'It's like cream.'

He ran his tongue across my top lip and gently prised open my mouth, searching inside, slowly at first then more fervently.

We kissed passionately for several minutes before the chill air sent us back inside.

He lifted me up so I was sitting on our table. I wrapped my legs around him and pulled him towards me.

Aramis responded by biting my neck and breasts – small nips somewhere on the cusp of pain.

He unzipped my dress, and eased it off my shoulders, then forced the links of my corset apart with his fingers. I was exposed at last.

Pushing me down so I was lying flat on the table, he planted delicate kisses from the top of my chest to my navel, returning to form a cross with his saliva by licking and sucking from nipple to nipple.

'Now I have my mark on you,' he whispered. 'You are mine . . .'

A delicious tremor ran through my body, like a shiver but warm, not cold.

Usually I would have thought of something clever or cocky to say to him, but words seemed superfluous. I felt myself giving way to abandon, relinquishing control.

He used those beautiful, soft hands of his to glide up and down my chest and belly, deftly slipping my thong to my knees on the way down.

As I lay there with legs apart, offering myself to him, he nestled his face between my thighs and stroked his tongue up and down my inner lips with a lightness of touch that had me writhing within seconds.

The table underneath me was hard and unyielding but curiously this only served to heighten my pleasure. My head was dangling back over the far edge, my mouth open in silent rapture, my eyes catching the odd glimpse of sparkling skyline.

The city lights seemed to blur as did my boundaries. When I started dancing at the Pearl, I had etched lines in the sand. Now Aramis, like the tide, was erasing them inch by glorious inch. I could not see him, just feel his hands, his tongue, his body . . . I focused on the sensation and tried to forget that I was on the rooftop with a man I barely knew. I wanted to live in the moment like Aramis.

Time seemed to suspend itself as I existed only in my senses. Then he paused. I held my breath. He cupped a hand behind each knee and slowly pulled my buttocks to the table's edge. My skyline view was replaced by the sparse collection of stars in the London sky. He spread my legs wider. I tensed and resisted him, but only for a moment. I looked at him. He was staring at me, not the parts that brought him pleasure but at me. I wrapped my fingers around the table's edge to brace myself. He held my gaze as he entered me – with care at first, allowing his flesh to expand within me, and then gaining momentum, in and out, achieving a comfortable rhythm, on and on. My hands relaxed. I let them wander. I showed him where to touch me. His hand was on my hand complementing the rhythm from within.

Soon our bodies shuddered. I wrapped my legs around his waist and he held tightly to my hips as we struggled to control the torrent of passion that swept over us. He emitted a low rumble of satisfaction. I gasped for air.

My mind reconnected after a moment of pure, transcendent sensation and I remembered the waiter, and the kitchen staff . . . Did they catch a glimpse? I thought back to the Blacks and realised that like them, I didn't care.

Aramis composed himself and lifted me down from the table, carefully helping me to dress.

I was on the early shift at the Pearl the following evening. I guessed Suzy would be in her usual place, propping up the bar and chatting to customers, and I was right.

Coming up from behind to catch her unawares, I slid on to the bar stool next to her, and ordered a white wine spritzer.

She swung round with a big grin on her face.

'Ah, the return of the prodigal daughter!'

'Cheers, Suzy,' I said. 'I propose a toast to you and your excellent guidance.'

We chinked glasses.

'So, what news from the front line?' she asked.

'Well, he took me . . . in every sense of the word,' I said. 'He took me to an amazing rooftop restaurant I didn't even know existed, and hired the whole place just for the two of us. He took me out on the terrace and showed me the city skyline. He took me back inside . . . and then he took me on a table . . .'

'And don't tell me, you were the dish of the day,' she laughed.

'Yes, you could say that,' I said, grinning at the thought. 'And I was exactly what he ordered.'

'And what about you? Did you get stuck into the meat and two veg?'

'Oh Suzy, you're so vulgar sometimes. It wasn't like that at all . . .' My mind wandered back to the night before. 'He was very . . . tender.'

'What, like a rare steak?' she said, stifling a giggle.

'No, you know very well what I mean. He was sweet, considerate and a skilled lover.'

'Sorry, darling, I couldn't resist. You seem quite taken with the sheikh.'

'Well, he made me feel very special. And made me realise I don't always have to be totally in control in the bedroom department.'

'That's good, well done. You have to let a man be a man from time to time, if he's capable of it, that is.'

'Oh, he's very much capable of it. Very masculine but still . . .'

She looked at me and furrowed her brow.

'OK, sunshine, I can see where you're going with this one.'

'And where do you think that is?'

'Candyfloss castle. You remember – the one I drifted into Vegas on.'

'No, Suzy, I really haven't got my head in the clouds.'

'Darling, I've seen that look in girls' eyes so many times. You might not be thinking of marriage and babies but you *are* considering the possibility of a mad, passionate affair.'

'And what's wrong with that?' I said.

'Because, my dear little friend, you are incapable of doing that without him really getting under your skin.'

'But I've got this one in perspective, Suzy, honestly I have,' I said.

'Ah, but if you did, you wouldn't have to be so defensive about it. Geri, I've been there, done it, got the T-shirt. He's unavailable.'

'How do you know he's unavailable?'

'Sweetie, he's an international businessman, he's never in one place longer than a month or so; he's a no-strings-attached merchant, however rich and charming. He can buy whatever he likes wherever he goes, and he just happened to look in this shop window and fancied you.'

'That's just not fair – he didn't pay me to go out with him.'

'You miss the point, Geri – he did buy you, really. He seduced you with his money.'

She was really pissing me off now, and she knew it.

'Look, love, I'm not criticising you and I don't want to spoil your fun but you'll thank me for this in a few weeks' time. Enjoy his attention but don't get hooked on it. He'll be moving on soon and we don't want you going cold turkey.'

'Listen, Suzy, I know the nature of the beast. He probably has a girl like me in every port. Please, just let me enjoy it while I can.'

I put down my drink, half-finished, and picked up my bag.

'I'll see you later, I'm going to get changed.'

'You're not upset with me, are you?' she said, pouting her bottom lip like a little girl.

'No, but sometimes I think you treat me as if I'm a teenager. I'm nearly 30, for God's sake.'

'I know, darling, but you're not as hard-bitten as me, and I do know the business better than you.'

'So you keep telling me,' I said, a little too harshly perhaps, 'but I'm learning fast.'

I had to bite my lip hard. I wanted to tell Suzy about what I had to deal with at work every day but I couldn't. As far as she was aware, my other job was something menial in admin. She had no idea that when my six weeks were up, and I'd made my ten grand, I was planning to leave. 'Honestly, Suzy, when Aramis comes in the club again I will be as cool as a cucumber.'

'Well I'll be there to throw a bucket of water over you if you're not. Are we still friends?'

'Yes, of course we're still friends. I'll catch you later . . .'

I left Suzy to her cocktail and went to the dressing room. I was still bloody annoyed with her for talking to me like that but I knew she had my best interests at heart. What she'd said had rattled me. I didn't like the fact that Aramis would soon be gone but I wasn't going to tell her that.

I would soon be dancing again, looking over to the corner table to see if he was there . . .

Then I remembered – he had given me his card. I fished out my wallet, and there it was – with just his name, Aramis. No surname, no business name or address, just his mobile number. I wondered if this was the card he used for *all* the women he met.

I didn't kid myself that I was special to him; he was the kind of man who made you feel like the only woman in the world when he was with you but I guessed he was the out of sight, out of mind type.

Should I text him? What the hell, what harm could it do? Fingers trembling, I sent him a message: 'Hi Aramis, this is your rooftop beauty. See you for a dance some time? Gxx'

Almost immediately a reply flashed up. 'I can't make the Pearl tonight – will call you tomorrow. Don't dance for anyone else.'

I couldn't help the wave of disappointment which swept over me. I didn't even look at the corner table that night, and I didn't do a private dance. I was saving myself for another escapade . . .

But as it turns out, it never happened. He was called off on business and by the time he returned to the Pearl I was long gone.

Chapter Twenty-Three

The next day in the office, I was now more convinced than ever that the adult male population could be divided into men and boys. Aramis – cool, restrained, stylish, respectful – was most definitely a man. Luke – hot-headed, arrogant, tousled, abusive – was a boy.

Unfortunately Luke was also the most dangerous type of boy – a bully. I could imagine him at boarding school with his wild blond hair and sneering face, picking on the class geek or rugby-tackling beta males in the quad.

I thought that by attempting to understand the psychology of the man I might be able to deal with him more effectively, and help Tania to do the same.

'Look what it says on this website,' I told her that morning, standing by the coffee machine, when she was looking particularly tense. 'The way to stand up to a bully is to be assertive, not aggressive – tell them calmly you disagree with what they're saying and that their comments are unacceptable.'

'It's easy to do that in theory but not in practice, you know that as well as I do, Geri,' she said miserably. Ever since the Sloane Brothers idiots had started with their 'peckers' jibes, Tania had been looking withdrawn and defeated, unlike the confident goddess that had walked into the office weeks ago.

'How about making friends with them because they're insecure?'

'Yeah, right,' she scoffed. 'I tried that one, remember?'

'Good point. What the hell did you see in Luke in the first place?'

'You can't deny he can be charming,' she said, looking a little sheepish. 'And he switched it on full-beam when he met me. He was also very generous and took me to lovely restaurants.' I tried not to think about Aramis.

'And also said he'd help you get a job interview here?'

She screwed up her nose. 'Yes, but I don't see the problem with that – I got the job on merit.'

That wasn't exactly what she told me that first night at the Pearl but there was no point in starting an argument; after all, we were supposed to be presenting a united front.

'I hope you've been doing what I suggested and keeping a note of his jibes, however insignificant they might seem at the time.'

'Yes, Geri, I have. I'm not some kind of bimbo, you know.'

'I wasn't insinuating that you were. Just keep a record is all I'm saying.'

'Rest assured I'm doing so at every opportunity,' she said, dryly.

'Good. Now when is my next meeting with the offender?'

She allowed herself a wry smile. 'In half an hour.'

'Right, I have another load of background research to go through before I see him. I have to be totally on top of all this material. If he senses a gap in my knowledge he'll put his boot right in.'

I headed back to my office.

'As you say, that's what bullies do,' she said, leaving me to my number crunching.

The figures were stacking up nicely so I was hoping Daryll would let us meet the secret client soon. I was prepared and hoped Luke would be too.

He seemed in an uncharacteristically sober mood when we got together that morning. I wasn't sure if it was a good sign or not.

Even so, his body language still announced that he owned the place. He sat in a swivel chair with one leg crossed over the other, hands behind his head.

'So, how's it hanging, Carson?' he said, with that self-satisfied grin I hated so much.

'If you mean how is the Project X deal shaping up, I would say pretty well, and I'd prefer it if you used my first name.'

'No need to be snippy,' he said. 'Where's your sense of humour?'

'It left the building along with your common sense,' I said. 'Do you know when Daryll is going to come clean about the client?'

'The sly old dog will leave it until he has no option but to tell us,' he said.

'Doesn't he trust us with the information? I mean, he said we'd been specially selected . . .'

'Yeah, specially selected to take the rap if it fails. Don't get up yourself too much, Carson, it's not that much of an honour.'

'I'm not expecting a medal, *Cotterill* . . .'

'Ha ha, no, but you've got the chest to pin it on, haven't you?'

'I don't find comments like that very helpful, Luke. Where do we stand on the project from your side?'

'Looking good. I've done some sussing out with contacts – discreetly, of course – and they can't see any reason why it shouldn't be a goer.' I wondered how he'd managed to do that, seeing as we were both supposed to be in the dark about the details of the project. Had Daryll let him in on the client's identity?

'No skeletons in closets?'

'No nasty surprises so far, it's checking out.'

'Shall we go back to Daryll to take it to stage two?'

'No, not yet. I have a little bit more sniffing around to do on my patch.'

'You make yourself sound like a dog, Luke.'

'That's me, Carson – a Rottweiler . . .'

'Yes, a dangerous dog,' I said in my most sarcastic tone. 'I wouldn't mind putting a muzzle on you myself . . .'

'Ah, not bad, Geri Boy. I bet you look good with a gag on too.'

I didn't react to that remark, simply filed it away. This technique didn't make me feel any less animosity towards him but at least I wasn't giving him the satisfaction of seeing me react.

'Right, well if we don't have enough to report back

to Daryll I suggest we reconvene at the same time tomorrow and by then you might deign to share some of your contacts' information.'

'Yep, if you like,' he said, slapping his thigh and getting up to leave. 'I'll let you get back to your knitting.'

'Thanks, Luke; I was halfway through a jumbo scarf that I was going to strangle you with . . .'

Even he smirked at that one. I went back to my office, ready to commit Luke's latest misdemeanours to paper. I passed Tania's desk.

'More ammunition to report,' I said.

'It's mounting up now. What were you planning to do with it all?'

'I'm not quite sure yet . . . but let's keep writing it down so we've got it to use against him when the time is right.'

She flicked back her hair and looked uncertain.

'What's wrong?'

'Well, it's not exactly something Luke has said, just something I overheard Ryan talking about while you were in your meeting.'

'Come in my office, close the door and tell me all about it . . .'

She closed the door behind her. 'He was joking around with some of the other guys about going out for a night on the razz and Luke got really pissed. Apparently he was boasting about this big deal he's doing that's going to make him rich.'

'Did he give away any details?'

'Ryan said it was a big merger involving a pharmaceutical company.'

I smelled blood.

'Did he name the company, Tania?'

'Um . . . I think so, I can't remember now . . .'

'Think, Tania, this is really, really important . . .'

'It was Bio something . . .'

'Yes, there are lots of big pharma companies with "Bio" in their name.' I sighed with frustration. 'Think harder . . .'

'There were two other names, I think – like surnames . . . Oh, I know – one of them was Henderson.'

'Bingo,' I said excitedly. 'Elkhart Henderson Bio?'

'Yeah, that must be the one.'

'Well done, Tania, you have just handed me a torpedo with which to blow Luke Cotterill out of the water.'

'Why, what does it mean?'

'That is highly sensitive information which may wreck the Project X deal if it leaks out beyond these four walls, so for God's sake don't mention it to anyone else otherwise you might get yourself into deep trouble.'

'But obviously Ryan and some of the other guys know it too, now?'

'I'll be having a word with Ryan later,' I said. 'Just leave it to me.'

I couldn't believe Luke had been so reckless but I guessed it was only a matter of time before his hubris caught up with him, especially when he'd had too much alcohol.

My neurons were firing in all directions. First I had to talk to Ryan, and then decide what to do about Luke. Plus I also had to deal with the fact that someone – presumably Daryll – had revealed the client's name to Luke but withheld it from me.

Still, why should it be a surprise to me that I'd been stitched up by the boys' club once again?

I didn't want to raise Luke's suspicions by letting him see me talking to Ryan so I sent him a flirty email.

Hi Ryan – it's been a while since we've had a catch-up. Fancy lunch? Who knows, it might be breakfast next. Geri x

Even the vague possibility that he might be getting his leg over usually did it for Ryan, so I was pretty sure my tactic would work, even if I had been ignoring him recently. And it did.

Can't we skip lunch and move on to the next course?! Only joking! Yeah, why not – see you downstairs at one? Ryan xx

As the shit hadn't hit the fan yet I presumed news of Luke's indiscretion hadn't reached Daryll's ears so I still had time to do some damage limitation and make sure it was going to reflect well on me and badly on Cotterill.

Ryan was his usual guileless self when I sat down with him in Corney & Barrow over a sandwich and a glass of beer.

'Had another big night out with the Brothers recently?' I asked, as innocently as possible.

'Yeah, it was a blinder. We had a "last man standing" competition with tequila slammers, and you can guess who won.'

'Don't tell me . . . Luke?'

'Of course – I don't know where that guy puts it, he's got hollow legs.'

'That must have loosened his tongue a bit as well,' I said. 'Did he give you any juicy gossip?'

241

'Most of it unrepeatable in front of a young lady,' he joked.

'Not that type of gossip, Ryan – business gossip.'

'Yeah, he did tell us about this big deal he's in on . . . but I guess you already know about that.'

'Yes I do, and I'm supposed to be the only other person in on this big deal apart from Daryll.'

'Oh, right. Come to think of it, he probably told us to keep it to ourselves.'

'But you did talk about it, didn't you, Ryan?'

He looked mortified.

'Only to a couple of the guys on the team, strictly in-house. I thought that was safe enough.'

'No, Ryan, it wasn't safe. It's not your fault but take it from me, don't mention it again and tell your mates to zip it as well or we'll all be out of a job.'

'Shit. Is it that big a deal then?'

'Yes, it is. So don't discuss it with anyone else.'

'Who heard me talking about it in the office, then?'

'Never mind who it was, just thank me for saving your sorry arse. Frankly I'm amazed any of you could remember anything after a night on slammers.'

He scratched his head and looked awkward, as if I'd just put him in detention.

'I don't want to cause any trouble, Geri,' he said. 'I'll have a quiet word with the guys. What about Luke, though?'

'Don't worry about Luke, I'll speak to him. Now finish your beer and let's get back to the office so we can stop this getting any worse.'

'OK. I'm sorry, Geri. Do I still get that dinner date?'

'Oh shut up, Ryan. I've got more important things to think about than entertaining you.'

I left him nursing half a lager and a wounded pride. Served him right, I thought, for being so bloody spineless.

I sat by the waters of the wharf for a while, wondering whether to march straight in and rat on Luke to Daryll. I thought better of it, though. Luke and I were supposed to be working as a team. It wouldn't look good if I stabbed him in the back now so I decided to hold fire. After all, revenge is a dish best served cold.

I had to rely on having put the wind up Ryan to get him to stem the office gossip, and then try to get Luke to admit he knew the identity of the client.

Walking back across the office floor, I was greeted by the sight of Luke with a face like thunder.

'What the fuck are you playing at, Carson?' he shouted in front of everybody. It shook me but I dealt with it calmly.

'I have no idea what you're talking about. Come into my office and we can discuss it between ourselves.'

Thankfully he followed me without exploding again and I shut the door before he could do any more damage.

'You stupid bitch! You've been discussing the project with your little fuck buddy Buxton, haven't you?'

'What? Have you lost your mind? I was saving both our skins, telling Ryan to stop talking about the project because it might endanger the deal.'

'Fucking right it will,' said Luke, pacing the floor. 'I'll kill him . . .'

'Hang on a minute,' I shot back, 'you bloody well told him about it in the first place.'

'What do you take me for? I've kept this well under my hat, Carson.'

'You don't even remember, do you?'

'Remember what?'

'You told your little gang all about Project X when you went on your bender the other night, didn't you?'

'No, I fucking didn't.'

'Then how come Ryan knew all about it, including the name of the client? Not even *I* knew that. Daryll hadn't told me, neither had you.'

'No, you're wrong, I kept my mouth shut.'

He looked as if he believed it himself.

'Why the hell would Ryan say it was you? He wouldn't have the guts to stitch you up.'

'He's just covering his back. There must be another leak.'

'Another leak? That's not how I heard it.'

'And who the hell did you hear it from?'

'It doesn't matter who I heard it from, Luke, the fact is that the whole deal might be in jeopardy. So before you go on a manhunt, let's get our priorities straight and make sure we're watertight again.'

He was more flustered than I'd ever seen him, which made me think he knew damn well he'd shouted his mouth off but was too pig-headed to admit it.

'Right, I'll close this situation down and find out who the rat is. I have my suspicions.'

'Yeah, you go off and do your own investigation, Luke. I think we'll both come up with the same suspect in the end, though.'

He stormed off to find his imaginary 'grass' and walked

straight into Tania, who immediately averted her gaze and went to her desk. He followed her, towering over her as she sat down.

'It was you, wasn't it, you fucking bitch? Shagging Sidebottom now, are you? Or did Geri Boy tip you the wink?'

'Luke, I don't know what you're talking about and I'd ask you not to swear or speak to me like that, I find it both offensive and threatening.'

'If you've lost me this deal I'll make sure you never work in the City again,' he said, almost spitting in her face. 'I should never have got you in here in the first place. You're just a dirty little slapper. The only thing you know how to do is open your legs.'

'Just leave me alone. I haven't done anything wrong. *You're* the one who messed up.'

'Don't fucking talk back to me, you ungrateful little cow . . .'

For a moment it looked as if he was raising his hand to her; she cowered and put up her hands to shield her face as he struck his fist hard on to her desk.

'Luke, mate,' said Paul, one of the other Brothers, 'get a grip.'

But Luke was so out of control he didn't seem aware he had an audience. Once the show was over and he'd walked away, most people pretended they hadn't seen anything, like bystanders at a mugging.

Tania looked genuinely frightened and came straight into my office, her make-up streaked by tears.

'Jesus, Tania, are you OK?' I said, instinctively putting an arm round her.

'Just about,' she said, her voice quaking. 'He's gone too far this time though, Geri, you were a witness to all of that, weren't you? He threatened me and nearly assaulted me.'

'Oh yes, we've got more than enough to hang him with now, it's just a question of how and when.'

'What do you mean?' she said, looking horrified. 'I'm sorry, Geri, but I'm going to report him right now.'

'We might have to be cleverer than that, Tania. Let me think about how to handle this.'

'No, Geri, he's crossed the line and I'm making it official. You're going to back me up, aren't you?'

'Yes . . . yes, of course,' I said. 'You sort yourself out and we'll discuss it later. Tania, um, we've never talked about your previous career before this one. But it will come up if you proceed with this.'

'Geri, I've got nothing to be ashamed of.'

And the way she tilted her head and pulled her shoulders a little higher made me a little ashamed that I couldn't do likewise, or at least confide in her. But I was still looking out for my own back.

I also hoped she couldn't see the doubt in my eyes. If Tania went to HR now with all guns blazing and I was her official witness, it would put me in a difficult position. I was facing a stark choice: back Tania and shaft Luke immediately, or let Tania fend for herself and deal the fatal blow to Luke when I wouldn't be putting my own career at risk. I was so wound up in my own thoughts, I didn't notice the tears had started to flow down Tania's cheeks again.

'You poor thing,' I said, and guided her to a seat. 'Stay here while I get you a cup of tea.'

'I'm sorry,' she sniffed. 'I guess it's all getting on top of me.'

By the time I returned with a drink for her, Tania had dried her eyes, and gave me a little smile.

'Here you go,' I said.

'Thanks Geri,' she replied. 'You know, I always thought this would be a doddle compared to where I worked before, but I was wrong.'

I laughed nervously. *Tell me about it.*

'Tania, Luke's been gossiping about your former, erm . . .' I said, offering her a tissue.

'Profession?' Tania smiled through the tears and blew her nose loudly. 'Geri, I've got nothing to be ashamed off on that score. You want to know how I got into that. Well, like mother, like daughter.'

Chapter Twenty-Four

TANIA'S STORY

I spent the first half of my life wanting to be more like my mum and the second half trying desperately not to.

Mum was a dancer. Growing up in South London I bragged to everyone who would listen. Most of my friends' mums worked at Tesco or pubs or nail salons. They brought home stale sandwiches or dabs of nail polish. My mum came home with armfuls of flowers. Her jewellery box overflowed with sparkly trinkets. All gifts from admirers, she said.

Every night she kissed me on my forehead and told me to be good for Gladys – our next-door neighbour who wore a housecoat with pockets always full of Fruit Pastilles. She was as wrinkly as my mum was smooth. She sat up knitting and watching our telly while I was lulled to sleep by the click of her knitting needles.

When I was eight or nine, Gladys got sick and went to hospital. Mum called everyone she knew, trying to find someone to watch me, including creepy Mrs Leslie who lived down the hall and always smelled of cat pee.

'Please let me go with you,' I begged her. 'Please. Please. Please. I'll be good, I promise.'

Mum stood with phone in one hand and her address book in the other. She glanced at the clock on the microwave. 'Come here,' she said as she hung up the phone. I rushed over, sensing a victory. She rubbed at a spot of crusty peanut butter at the corner of my mouth. 'All right,' she sighed. I wrapped my arms around her and squeezed, drinking in her sweet perfumed fragrance.

'Thank you, Mummy,' I mumbled into her stomach. 'You won't even know I'm there.'

On the Tube she held my hand so tightly my fingers felt numb. She whispered her list of rules. One: I must stay in the dressing room. Two: I was forbidden to go out front or watch her dance. Three: I had to hide if any man showed up. Four: I was not to pester the girls with my questions, and Five: I was not allowed to call her Mummy.

I could tell we were getting closer when she pulled me close and wrapped me in her coat. She tried to cover my eyes, but I could see flashes of people laughing and drinking and clinging to each other. The night sky glowed with flashing neon. I was so excited to be out in London. I kept trying to wriggle free to get my first real taste of nightlife. I'd see all the neighbourhood teenage girls get dressed up for clubbing and I couldn't wait until I was old enough. Mum kept looking around and telling me keep still. We ran the last bit, down an alley and right up to a big man with his arms crossed, guarding the back door of a brick building. It didn't look special, but I knew it must be if someone had to guard the door.

'Wait here,' Mum whispered to me and walked over to the man. The alley seemed more full of shadows than light.

'Hey, Robby,' Mum greeted the man. 'I need a favour.' She batted her eyes and snuggled up to him. 'My sitter's in hospital and I had to bring the kid.'

'Ah, Jas, you know the rules, no one backstage but the girls.' He held his ground but uncrossed his arms.

'Come on, Robby,' she purred. 'She's a good girl.' She handed him £20 and gave him a kiss on the cheek.

'Oh, go on then.' He jerked his head towards the door.

Mum gestured me over. 'Robby, this is Tania.'

He looked me up and down. 'Must take after her father.' He laughed and waved us through. Back then I was a chubby tomboy with frizzy red hair. I never wore anything but jeans and a baggy T-shirt. But I still felt like kicking him right in the shins. All I knew about my dad was that he wasn't around. One way to get Mum in one of her icy moods was to ask her about my dad.

Mum's body stiffened. 'Just don't tell Jimmy, all right?'

'Secret's safe with me.' He winked and smacked Mum on the arse. She held on to me tighter when she felt me going for him.

She smiled one of her tight-lipped fake smiles. 'Give us a shout if Jimmy or one of the guys comes round.'

'Anything for you, Jas,' he said.

'Why does he call you Jas?' I asked when the door clanked behind us. 'That's not your name.'

She knelt down in front of me. 'Listen, darling, people at work call me Jasmine.'

'Why?'

'It's like when you and Jenny play make-believe. All the girls I work with have pretend names for work. It's just a little game we play.'

'Can I have a pretend name too?' I asked. I hated my name. It was so stupid.

'I don't see why not.'

'I want to be Alexandra,' I piped up. A name fit for a princess.

'OK, Alexandra,' she said. 'We need to get going. I've got to go on soon.'

We walked down a narrow stairway. The temperature was a few degrees colder on the lower ground floor and I wished I'd brought my jacket. We weaved through a maze of boxes and wooden crates. Mum pushed me behind her as she stepped into the only doorway at the end of the hall.

'Hello, my lovelies,' Mum said. The air was thick with perfume and hairspray. 'I've got a little surprise for you.' She tugged at my sleeve and I peeked around her, suddenly scared and shy. 'This is my daughter Tania.'

I elbowed her.

'Excuse me.' She cleared her throat. 'For tonight Tania wants to be known as Alexandra.' She coaxed me from behind her.

The long thin room flickered in the overhead fluorescent light. Two make-shift vanity cases lined one wall and a rack of clothes lined the other. A full-length mirror was propped at the back of the room and made the room seem to go on forever. Four women fluttered between the mirrors, tugging at costumes and touching up make-up. The women all paused. My brain snapped a picture.

In that moment, I changed from wanting to be the world's first female professional footballer to being one of those women.

'This is Chloe,' Mum said, and pointed to a brunette with bouncy curls flowing down her bare back. Her emerald green gown glimmered with sequins.

'Nice to meet you, Alexandra,' she said, extending her hand.

My mum nudged me forward. 'Nice to meet you too,' I muttered, taking her hand but forgetting to shake it when I felt the silky smoothness of her elbow-length glove.

'That's Annie and Layla.' Mom indicated the two women at the back of the room wearing only lacy underwear. The girls waved. 'And the tart hogging the mirror is Natasha.'

I'd never seen anything like Natasha in real life before. Her fine platinum blonde hair slanted in a straight line towards her jaw. She was clad in black leather. She looked like a superhero in her strapless corset and thigh-high boots. She didn't acknowledge me. 'Who bring child to strip club?' she asked her own reflection in a thick Russian accent.

'Bitch,' Mum muttered.

'What's a stripe club?' I whispered as Mum ushered me into a corner at the front of the room. I heard Annie and Layla snicker at my question. Mum ignored me and tucked me near the rack of clothes. They smelled both sweaty and sweet.

'I've got to get ready, darling,' Mum said, brushing the fringe out of my eyes. 'Stay out of the way and remember our rules. I'll come check on you between dances. Do not,' she paused and tilted my face towards her, 'leave this room.'

'Yes, Mum, er, um, I mean ma'am.'

The next few moments were magic. I watched my mum transform right in front of my eyes. Her skinny jeans and flip-flops were replaced by black fishnet stockings and glossy black stiletto heels. She slipped on a sheer candyfloss-coloured gown and freed her chocolate brown hair from the clip she always wore. She dabbed glitter on her body and glossed her lips in a fairytale shade of pink.

'It's show time, girls,' a male voice beckoned.

'I've got to go. Be a good girl and stay here with Annie.' Mum kissed me on the cheek, leaving a sticky smudge. Mum filed out of the room behind Natasha, Chloe and Layla.

I fingered the costumes and watched Annie fix her hair. She painstakingly looped and pinned her curls into a messy bun. Soft spiral tendrils framed her face. My fingers aimlessly wandered from feathers and silk to latex and leather. I pulled the red feather boa from the rack, inching it down slowly so Annie wouldn't notice. It was soft and tickly at the same time. I let it pool on my lap and imagined what strange and exotic bird had scarlet red feathers.

'You like the boa?' Annie asked as she reached above my head and tugged a baby pink silk robe from the rack and slipped it on.

I nodded.

'Aren't you a pretty little thing,' she said, ruffling my hair.

'Not like you,' I said, hugging the feathers to my chest and burying my face in them for a moment. 'Not like my mum.'

'Come here.' She sat down at one of the vanity chests and gestured me over. I looked around before I left my hiding place. 'It's OK,' she reassured me.

I sat on her lap. In our reflection, I could see even more clearly all my flaws; my mop of fuzzy red hair, my blotchy white skin, round, green eyes that seemed too big for my face.

'You are a natural beauty,' Annie said, rubbing Mum's pink lipstick off my face.

'You're just being nice,' I said, and tried to pull away.

'All right, I'll show you.' She plonked me down in the metal chair and stood up behind me. She squirted lotion in her palms from one of the bottles under the mirror. She smoothed it in my hair and then brushed my hair until it shined and bounced around my shoulders. She turned me to face her. 'Shut your eyes,' she said, then she tickled my face with make-up brushes. It made my nose itch. 'Keep your face still,' she laughed when I scrunched my nose.

When she turned me to face the mirror, I didn't recognise the girl beaming back at me. I looked like a fairy princess, except for my wrinkled T-shirt. Annie must have read my mind. 'Let's see.' She walked over to the rack of clothes. She pulled out a black dress with layer upon layer of lace. 'This should do the trick.' She carefully removed my T-shirt.

The cool damp air whooshed around me and I wrapped my arms around my flat chest. Glancing at her ample bosom, I wondered what feat of magic would turn the two bumps on my chest into breasts one day. She slipped the dress over my head. The material was stretchy and clung to my skin. I wriggled out of my jeans. She found a pair of heels nearly my size. I teetered to the full-length mirror. 'The final touch,' Annie said, snaking the boa around me. We surveyed her work in the mirror. I smiled again and saw hints of my mum in my reflection. It was the first time I ever believed that I could grow up to be anything but gawky and awkward.

'Stand up straight.' She ran her hand down my spine. 'Jut your hip out a little.' I bent one knee and copied her posture, hand on hip. 'You are beautiful,' she said.

And I was.

Annie finished her make-up and I stared at myself in the mirror.

'Maxie, you down there?' A male voice interrupted my fantasy. I was a great lady invited to tea with the queen. Heavy steps clomped down the hall. Annie and I exchanged panicked expressions.

'Hide,' Annie whispered, and shoved me towards the corner. I wiggled back among the costumes as she struck the same pose she'd showed me earlier. She loosened the sash around her waist and let the robe fall open, exposing her pink satin bra.

'Maxie, my love!' A big barrel of a man exploded into the room. He was balding and sweaty and cradled an armful of apricot roses.

'You are a naughty little boy, Harold,' Annie cooed, and gathered the offered roses. 'You know you aren't supposed to be down here. Jimmy will cut your bollocks off if he finds you.'

'I took care of Jimmy,' Harold said, rubbing the tips of his fingers together. 'I got a little something for you too, Max.' He sat her on the table, knocking bottles, cans and brushes to the floor. He wedged himself between her knees.

'That's not little,' Annie squealed, and tried to wiggle free, but he had her pinned against the mirror. 'Harold, not here. Not now.' Annie lost the baby talk. She glanced at me wide-eyed.

'Jimmy said if you don't mind, he don't mind. And I want to get you while you're still smelling fresh.' He buried his head in her hair.

Annie wrapped her arms around him. She waved me away, while she spoke sweetly into Harold's ear: 'Kiss me right there. That's it.'

I slipped out of my shoes and let the boa slide to the floor. I slowly inched from the room. I paused at the doorway for a moment, tucked in the shadows where Annie couldn't see, and watched, mesmerised, as the two bodies seemed to become one writhing mass. His body jolted and jerked as she arched her back against the mirror and shut her eyes, creating fans of wrinkles on her face. She purred and reassured him, like a teacher. 'That's a good boy. Oh, yes, Harold.' He grunted like a pig, as sweat gathered and dripped from his temples.

I tiptoed up the stairs. Robby had the door propped open and was smoking a cigarette. 'You shouldn't be up here,' he said when he finally spotted me. He flicked his cigarette in the alley and looked me up and down and whistled.

I realised I was still in the skimpy dress. I tugged the straps up higher and hugged it close to my body.

'You sure look different,' he said, closing the door and slipping inside. 'Aren't you gorgeous.'

I tried not to be scared at his compliment. For some reason I didn't want him looking at me. I hadn't dressed up for him.

'You shouldn't be up here, doll.' He leaned down and spoke softly, the gravelly edge of his voice smoothed. 'If Jimmy sees you, your mum will be in the shit.'

'It's just Annie . . .' I started but didn't want to get her in trouble.

'Oh, I see.' He stood up and looked down the stairs. 'Annie got a little business.'

I backed away.

'Want to watch your mum dance?' he asked. 'She should be up about now. I could use a little pick-me-up.'

I nodded.

'Give me a sec.' He walked down the corridor that led to front of house. He ducked in the open doors that were scattered along the hallway and then rushed back. 'I think the coast is clear,' he said, and pushed me forward. 'She's already started.'

Down the hall and up a short set of steps and I was backstage. I peeked around a beaded curtain and saw my mother shimmering in the spotlights. When she danced, she flowed like water pulled by some unknown current. I don't know where she went when she danced, but she always seemed to escape somewhere else. Her eyes had this faraway look as if she wasn't in an east London club but on stage at the Royal Opera House.

I watched her artfully remove every item of clothing until she was stripped bare. In the hot lights her body sparkled like a diamond. I had never seen her look more beautiful. Her body was curvy where mine was flat and flat where mine was curvy. The men in the audience reached for her and clapped. I wanted to stay and watch her like that forever but I knew she'd go mad if she saw me there.

I sneaked back into the dressing room. Annie was alone again, staring at herself in the mirror. Her once carefully coiffed hair was a mess. She had a faraway look like my mum had sometimes.

'Hey, Annie,' I said. 'Where did Harold go?'

'He just dropped by for a quickie.' She cleared her throat and blinked away her far-off stare. 'I mean he just wanted a quick word.' She glanced at me with an apologetic smile. I wasn't sure what she was sorry for. She smoothed her hair and pinned curls back into place.

Once she had fixed her hair and reapplied her lipgloss, she left. I found the boa and strutted up and down the room, swishing the feathers up and down my body. I stared at myself in the mirror and tried to move like my mum had on stage.

'What in the hell are you doing?' Mum jerked my arm and spun me around. She was wrapped in a full-length red silk robe.

'I was playing dress-up with Annie,' I said, jutting my hip out and swinging the boa over my shoulder.

'You look like a little whore,' my mum shouted. 'Don't

you ever let me catch you . . .' She grabbed a box of tissue. 'Don't you ever . . .' Her hands were shaking, she was so angry. 'I have worked too hard . . .' She grabbed fists full of tissue and smeared the make-up off my face. 'Get changed. Right now.' She yanked the dress over my head. The lace scratched my face.

'I was just trying to be pretty like you,' I said, pulling on my jeans and T-shirt. I glanced in the mirror. Black tears streamed down my face.

'Don't be like me.' She collapsed on the metal chair. 'Don't re-live my life, my mistakes, Tania.' She looked at me in the mirror. She was crying too. 'I've raised you to be so much better.'

'I'm sorry, Mummy.' I lunged for her and hugged her.

'Promise me you'll never dance for a living. Promise me you'll never work in a club. Promise me you'll use your mind not your body to get ahead.'

'I promise, Mummy. I will. I promise.' I would have said anything to stop my mum's tears. It was the first in a long line of promises I would make and break to her.

Chapter Twenty-Five

Some nights hit you completely unawares. This particular Saturday night I arrived at the Pearl, I could never have dreamed what was in store. There I was collecting tips after a table dance, pissed off when a smartly dressed customer who looked as if he would fit right in at Sloane Brothers dropped a fiver in the jug. A bit mean, I thought. It was almost an insult. But all that was about to change when I felt a gentle tap on my shoulder as I swayed towards my next table, tip jug in hand.

It was Jackie who guided me by the elbow towards the swankier end of the club, where the seriously high rollers hung out with Declan. She had a really husky voice that day, so that I had to lean close to hear what she was saying.

'A customer has made a request – and is willing to reward very, very generously.'

'How much?' I asked.

'There's £500 in it for you.'

Five hundred quid! Now that wasn't to be sniffed at, especially after looking down at that lousy fiver swimming in my jug, and it would lead me to that £10k target all the more quickly.

'What am I being asked to do?'

Not being able to hear her above the din, I leaned further in, only to pull back when I made out her response.

'Girl-on-girl?' I spluttered.

Now I know, early on, Jackie told us to be prepared for anything, but I'd been at the Pearl for a while now, and this was *my* first time.

'Isn't there someone else?'

'The customer specially requested you, Geri. Now don't worry, you'll be in safe hands.'

'Who's the other girl going to be then?'

'I think this one requires a woman, don't you?'

The way she said it I knew who she was suggesting.

'You?' *But you don't dance!* was my first thought, and I had to bite my tongue.

Jackie must have seen my reaction but she merely arched an eyebrow. 'Well?'

I was genuinely taken aback. 'Really? Are you sure?'

'I'm game if you are, Geri,' she said, stroking my arm. 'What the customer wants, the customer gets, if he has enough money. Isn't that true?' Actually, I didn't know that Jackie didn't dance now, it was just that I had never seen her dance. The fact that she was willing to do so now . . . Either the patron was paying enough to make it worth her while, or – or she actually *wanted* to.

Slightly unnerved by her willingness, I backed away.

Jackie started to laugh, a low chuckle, and there was a look on her face that clearly said, 'I knew you wouldn't do it.'

'OK, let's go for it.' The words were out of my mouth before I could stop them, but I didn't want to back down from the challenge.

Jackie smiled, in a way that said she knew she'd won. I was starting to feel like a pawn in a game to which I didn't know the rules. Not much had happened since I'd started working at the Pearl to make me feel like this. I didn't like it at all.

'Right, let's go and find our patron . . .' Jackie smiled again, a flirtatious smile this time, and weaved her fingers through mine. Oh God, this was really going to happen.

Approaching the top table, I was pleased to see Declan, who smiled warmly up at me. 'Hi. It's good to see you.' And I was reminded of why I'd found him so attractive the first time we met.

The boss was paying one of his occasional visits to his suburban outpost. He'd been quite the mystery man since I'd arrived at the club. Save for that first night.

He was sitting with a young group of guys and pouring the good stuff: Cristal. These must be real VIPs. For the life of me, I couldn't work out what line of business they were in though. There was something just a little too garish and studied about their fashion sense to be City traders.

'Premiership footballers,' Jackie whispered in my ear, before giving a throaty chuckle, the sound low and sensual in my ear. My God, she was really working this. Was she trying to make me feel uncomfortable? To goad me? Well, I'd show her.

The first to make eye contact was the one sitting in the middle, who had obviously spent a lot of time and money on his appearance. He was exquisitely groomed with dark, close-cropped hair, arched eyebrows featuring a single ring piercing, luscious lips and lovely mocha-coloured skin. His friend, sitting next to him, looked vaguely familiar. The third man was pale-skinned with reddish hair – hardly a heart-throb – and presumably there to make the other two look good.

'I'm Craig, by the way,' he began. 'And this is Si, and the carrot-top is Ray. We've just won a game, thanks to Si, and we wanted to give him a little thank you.'

Si didn't say anything, just nodded and ducked his head. Ray punched his friend's arm.

'Hey, you sure we can't get in on this?' he asked.

'You got another £1,000 each?'

That silenced him.

Si, Jackie and I walked towards the plushest back room, all red velvet drapes, and satin-laden cushioned seats. Jackie confidently led the way and the customer followed her, glancing over his shoulder occasionally to give me lingering looks. I trailed meekly behind, wondering what I was supposed to do next.

Jackie took off her top layer to reveal a black Lycra top and tight black knickers that accentuated her hour-glass figure.

'Sit down,' Jackie commanded. It took me a moment to realise she was addressing the customer. She took my hand and I turned to look at her. My heart was suddenly pounding. I knew what to do in a lap dance, sure, no problem. But now? I had absolutely no clue.

She must have seen how nervous I was because she leaned to whisper in my ear. 'OK, Geri, just relax and follow me . . .'

Her words were meant to be reassuring but Jackie whispering in my ear must have looked erotic to our customer, because I heard him let out a low growl of approval. I shot him a glance, trying my best to make it look sultry with my lashes lowered teasingly. Si was seated in the booth, hands folded over his lap and grinning like a schoolboy.

Then Jackie took hold of my hands and put them around her waist. I remembered what we were doing with a jolt, and all my nerves came flooding back to me.

'Follow my moves, Geri. *Relax*,' she hissed in my ear. She started slowly swaying and I copied her movement. Then she slipped her hands on to my hips, bare except for the thin strap of my knickers. I put my hands on her back, just above her hips. When Jackie began running her hands all over my body, I did the same to her.

Maybe if I just closed my eyes, I could pretend it was the best-looking guy I'd ever seen, instead of Jackie. But her hands were soft as they squeezed the curves of my side, adding a strange texture to the familiar routine, not a hint of callus or rough skin. I gripped her back with my hands as I slid them up and down, her muscles, strong yet subtle, covered by silky smooth skin.

Soon, Jackie began moving things up a notch, running her palms over my bum cheeks and grinding her hips against mine. I pulled her even closer.

Jackie smiled a slow, sensual smile, and leaned back, pressing her mound against mine. She was watching me closely. Was it my imagination or were her eyes darker than normal?

I did as she'd asked and followed her lead, mirroring

her movements. I arched my neck as I let my head fall back and I spared our customer a glance from the corner of my eye. I could see our game was having the desired effect on him. He was leaning forward, lips slightly parted.

Straightening my back and bringing my head back up, I allowed my eyes to roam over Jackie's body, following their path with my hands. She had an incredibly sensual way of holding herself. Her small waist gave way to perfectly curved hips and a tight but shapely bottom.

She stilled her hands for a moment and gazed back at me through half-closed eyes. She certainly looked like she was enjoying my ministrations. Then she opened her eyes, stopped me with a look, telling me with her hands as much as her eyes that it was now her turn on me.

I could feel her fingers on my back, her breath on my neck, and the softness of her silky brown hair, as she pulled my top over my head, and then her own.

Her upper body was close to mine, and the next move seemed to come naturally to me. As I leaned in to embrace her, our breasts pressed together. I gasped in surprise before I could stop myself, only hoping it sounded more like a moan. I always loved pressing my breasts against a hard, muscled chest, but this felt so different, so sensual.

Her skin smelled sweet and floral. Jackie's lips brushed against my jaw as she turned her head. I forgot about the customer in the booth watching us. I turned my head back to meet her lips with mine, pressing them gently together. It wasn't for him; this time it was for me.

I parted my lips as she teased me with her tongue before allowing me to gently probe her mouth. I forgot about everything else. She tasted so good. My hands gripped her hips again, instinctively pulling her lower body towards me.

And just as suddenly she was pulling away. A sensuous look smouldered in her eyes as she walked around me to stand behind, her hand dragging across my body as she did so. And she stood, close behind me, close enough that I could lean against her. She placed her hands on my upper thighs, swinging them from side to side, bringing me into the movement of her own body, following the rhythm of the music. Jackie moved her hands slowly up my sides until she was cupping and stroking my breasts. I let out a real moan this time, as her delicate fingers played over my nipples, teasing them, and all the while our hips swayed together. I let myself flow with her, higher and higher, until I was close to losing myself.

Then the music stopped.

Jackie released me and eyed the customer, checking to see if he was satisfied. I came down, back into reality so suddenly that I felt slightly drunk, my blood still throbbing with desire.

Footballer boy was sitting in the booth, with an expression as though Christmas and his birthday had both come early. It would have been funny, if I wasn't feeling so jarred by what I'd felt while dancing with Jackie.

Jackie walked calmly towards him and he stood up, took out his wallet and happily handed over a stack of notes.

'I hope you ladies will join us for a drink once you're, erm, done.'

He walked out, giving me a lingering stare as he went through the curtain.

It was like he really believed that there was going to be a second act – just the two of us.

Jackie turned to look at me, and I was shocked at the look of disdain on her face. I'd been expecting her to thank me for the great dance, for playing along so successfully, but instead she said sharply, 'Geri, this is your weakness,' her hand gesturing to the booth the customer had just vacated. 'People will always be able to play you.'

I could not have been more shocked if she'd slapped me. I was still tingling from the high of our dance, and she was completely unaffected. It had all been an act for her.

'What do you mean, play me?' I demanded.

'Look how easy it was for me to persuade you to do something you really weren't comfortable with.'

'I did want to do it . . .' But I knew that was a lie. Maybe I'd come out enjoying the dance in the end, but I'd been desperate to back out of it before I'd started. And Jackie knew it.

'No, you didn't, Geri, you were doing it almost as a dare. You have to be clear about your boundaries otherwise you'll get yourself into trouble.'

'You were just testing me?' Part of me wanted to scream in frustration, but mostly I was just humiliated.

'Yeah, I was. You know, I don't think you're as confident as you make out. I'm just asking you to be careful, to learn about yourself.'

'Being cruel to be kind, eh, Jackie?' I couldn't keep the bitterness out of my voice.

'I didn't mean to upset or embarrass you, but I've made my point.'

I could feel my cheeks flushing, which made it even worse. Jackie had treated me like a child, and not for the first time. Was I really that naïve? She clearly thought so.

'Anyway, here's your share of the fee,' she said, counting out half of the money that the customer had handed her. 'But you've still got a lot to learn, Geri.'

'I'm sure I have,' I said, feeling silly and deflated. 'I'll see you later . . .'

Jackie's reaction had left me hollow and off-balance, no longer the sexy, confident woman who could bring grown men to their knees. What right did she have to make me feel like this? I'd played her game well enough, hadn't I?

Perhaps not. I'd let my emotions get the better of me, and that made me angry. At myself, at Jackie. I was fuming, aroused, all wound up with nowhere to go.

Chapter Twenty-Six

Back in the club, I spotted Declan moving away from the VIPs.

'Hi Geri, how's it going?' he said in his lilting Irish burr. 'How about I buy you a drink? You look like you could do with one.'

'Nothing I can't handle,' I answered quickly. 'How do you think I made a success of a career in the City?'

I didn't mean to sound so defensive.

'Ah, talking about the day job, does anyone else here know about that yet?' he asked in a comradely fashion as we walked towards the bar.

'No, and you've kept your word? You haven't told anyone – not Suzy, and especially not Jackie . . .'

'For sure. I've kept my word. For an indecent place, you'll find I'm a fairly decent guy. Besides, you seemed to be getting along famously with Jackie there . . .'

And for the second time in the same night I was blushing.

'I understand. Your secret's safe with me,' he said, leaning in conspiratorially. God, he was gorgeous.

And suddenly I felt very, very flirtatious. 'Most men

271

get really turned on by girl-on-girl action. How about you, Declan?'

'Of course I like looking at two pretty ladies getting it on, I'm a red-blooded male . . .'

'So you enjoyed seeing me with Jackie, then?'

'That goes without saying, Geri. You are both very sexy women. Now, where are you going with this, madam?'

'Where do you want it to go, Declan?' I smiled. I knew I was pushing it. He was my boss, for God's sake.

'You have the cheek of the devil, make no mistake,' he laughed, turning to have a quick word with one of the bar staff.

He was obviously doing his best to keep the conversation light-hearted. Had I miscalculated? Did he not really fancy me? I was sure the chemistry between us was strong and had been since the day we met. I sensed he was holding back but at least he hadn't made his excuses and left.

When he'd finished talking to the barman, he turned back to me and rested his warm hand lightly on my shoulder.

'OK Geri, what do you want to drink?'

'Just a small white wine please,' I said. 'Even though I'm off duty now.'

'I'm not, you know. But I'll join you for one . . .'

He ordered a bottle of Sauvignon and put one hand on my back to guide me through the crowd to an alcove table. Every time he touched me I craved more.

I thought of Suzy and did my best Marilyn wiggle in the hope that he would feel my swaying hips.

He sat down opposite me and filled our glasses.

'So are you enjoying your work here, Geri?' he asked, as if I was being given a job interview. I wished he'd quit being so formal.

'I've learned a lot. But I'm curious how a guy like you ends up in a place like this?'

He laughed at that.

'Seriously, Declan, I'd like to know.' I leaned in, resting my hand on his arm. It was such an innocent gesture, especially when you consider the other moves I'd made in the club, but the way he looked back at me, I knew I'd hit my mark.

'Well, where to begin?' he started. 'My father worked here for years. He was a bouncer. He always had a soft spot for Jackie and she was always good to him. They got each other out of a few tight scrapes.'

I remembered Jackie's story.

'Oh my God, your dad was Dublin?'

'Yeah, that's right,' but he said it with gentle pride.

'When he died, his life insurance meant I came into a bit of money. Jackie always said I was a born entrepreneur, and so we discussed my ideas for turning the business around. In a little over four years, we've got a string of lapdancing clubs. One more year and we'll sell up. I'll move into another business and she'll retire with a nice little nest egg.'

There was something about the way Declan looked at me while he spoke that convinced me I was not imagining things.

'I admire that. I never do anything half-heartedly either,' I told him. 'I give it my all, like you. And when I want something I don't stop until I get it . . .'

I ran my fingers up and down the outside of my glass. Could I be any more obvious?

'Geri, I always said you had something different to offer and I stand by that,' he said. 'I've seen a lot of girls dance in my time but you have real class.'

'Thanks, Declan, that means a lot to me.'

We had a mutual admiration society going on but it wasn't getting me where I wanted to be. I needed to find a way of getting him on his own.

'So you've caught my act more than once then?'

'I have caught you in action once or twice, yes,' he laughed.

'And have you ever wished it was you in there with me?'

Before he had a chance to answer, I made my play.

'I could do one for you now,' I said, moving closer to him.

'No, Geri, not in here . . .'

I could tell he was weakening.

'Look, come outside for a moment,' he said, pulling me up and pulling open the door that led us to a corridor through a fire escape.

Without warning he pushed me against the wall and pulled off my wig.

'I wanted to see you as you really are,' he said. 'Christ, Geri, you're an incredibly exciting woman, you know that?'

He ran his hands through my hair, cupped my face and kissed me fiercely.

I surrendered to him as he took my hands in his and pinned them back so I couldn't move. His lips kissed my mouth, my jaw, then my throat.

The air was cold enough for me to see my breath but I was burning up inside. I felt fragile and vulnerable, dominated by his physical presence.

And just as suddenly it was over. He stood straight and released my hands.

'Shit . . . sorry, I'm so sorry,' he said, 'I shouldn't have done that . . . I mean, we can't do this, Geri. You know the rules . . .'

I put my hand around the back of his neck. 'Oh Declan, sod the bloody rules – we both want each other . . .'

I tried to pull him towards me, but he resisted and took a step backwards.

'I apologise, I should have had more self-control . . .'

'I'm glad you didn't. It was amazing. Can we carry on somewhere more private?'

'Look, I'm saying no, Geri. It's a really bad idea . . .'

Now I felt foolish and, worse, angry.

'Is that it then? Just a quick fumble in the corridor?'

'That's it, Geri. As your employer I'm asking you to return to the club floor.'

Oh God, that hurt.

'Right, fine, as your employee I am doing what you say.'

And with that I stomped off.

Bloody hell, what had I done to deserve being rejected by Jackie and Declan on the same night? Who was wearing the pants now? Any other night, I would have been out the door but spotting Suzy and Irena at the top table with the three footballers, I thought what the hell.

The guys were talking rather heatedly – replaying some on-field manoeuvre, no doubt – when I arrived but Si looked up to give me a cheeky smile and Suzy slid along to make room, and began to give Irena and me the lowdown.

'You might not know it, but Declan can be Mr Schmooze,' she told us. 'He likes to look after his high-spending clients and tonight he's giving them a treat.'

Irena sat there looking blank so I decided to join in.

'And what would that be, Suzy?'

'Ah, it's the lucky rookie . . . Welcome to the witches' coven. Well, tonight Declan and Jackie are taking their favourite wallets to a private members' club – but not just any private members' club. In fact, the members are anything but private in this place. The clue is in the name – it's a hedonist club called Philia . . .'

'I think I've heard of it,' I said. 'Anything goes there, right?'

'Pretty much, as long as it's by mutual consent,' she said. 'But you can also go along and have a good old gander at other people behaving badly.'

'But why would Declan take customers there? How does that benefit the Pearl?' I asked.

'Just think of it as a special bonus for his favourite clients. He pays for them to have a wild night out and they keep coming back for more. It's just good PR.'

'So are you going, Suzy?'

'Sure am.'

'I'm intrigued to know what it's like.'

'Trust me, it's a real eye-opener.'

Declan wandered over at that point, and joined the guys, but far away from me.

Despite what had passed between me and the boss, I decided to brazen it out.

'Hi, Declan,' I said, standing up and squeezing myself between him and Si. 'So is this man bothering you?' I asked Si.

'Absolutely not, you little minx,' he answered. 'I've been singing your praises; telling Declan how he should give you your own show.'

'Were you now? Well, thanks for the rave review,' I replied, hooking my arm round him.

'No problem, sweetheart. You're such a good mover we could do with you in midfield. Better looking than Craigy-boy too.'

'So, Declan,' I said, sidling closer to Si. 'I hear there's a group going on to Philia soon . . .'

'That's the case,' said Declan, looking slightly uncomfortable. 'Jackie and I are treating these fine young men here to a night of decadence.'

'So Ginger, do you fancy it?' Si asked eagerly.

'Count me in, sounds a right laugh. What do you reckon, ladies?'

Suzy raised her glass, and nudged Irena, who nodded sleepily and smiled, repeating Suzy's gesture.

'Well . . . that's decided then.' Declan smiled, and patted Si on the back, as smooth and charming as ever, but his eyes betrayed his true feelings.

I had absolutely no doubt that Declan was jealous.

Good.

Chapter Twenty-Seven

In the back of the tasteless stretch limo, Suzy immediately climbed on Craig's lap while Si grabbed me and forced me on his. I let it happen. Declan and Jackie sat in the seats running the length of the limo, facing Ray and a bored-looking Irena. Poor Ray. She certainly wasn't doing anything for his ego. But then Jackie slid across, and began flirting with him, leaving Declan all alone. Meanwhile, Si wrapped his arms around my waist. As he shifted in his seat, I felt his hard cock roll against my buttocks. His hands travelled upward, stroking my nipples through my pink silk blouse, while his other hand tried to inch up the hem of my short skirt. 'Come on, baby,' he kept whispering in my ear. He would have fucked me right then and there if I'd let him. I wondered what the men at work would think if they saw me now; getting fondled in a stretch limo by one of their sporting heroes.

I glanced at Suzy. She was straddling Craig. He was fumbling underneath her dress. Suzy appeared to be adding another trophy to her professional footballer collection. Irena stared hard at her watch as if willing supernatural powers to speed time. I wished her powers had worked. Between the speed humps and the lump in Si's trousers, the taxi ride through the back streets of Highgate and Camden I was feeling a bit battered. As I pushed away Si's ever agile hands, I locked eyes with Declan.

'We're here!' Jackie called from the front as the cab jerked to a stop sending me flying nearly face first into Declan's lap. He helped me up, no sign of remorse or sympathy in those unreadable brown eyes.

To an innocent passerby, the building might have appeared abandoned. There was no building number or sign marking the entrance and no windows or bouncer at the door. Declan led the way up the steps and gave one sharp rap on the door. The door opened a crack and Declan slid a plastic black credit card through. Irena seemed even more unsteady on her feet than usual. I was staggering too, but not thanks to any chemicals. Si continued to hold me from behind and practically hump me as we walked. I couldn't wait to pass him off to some kinky bimbo in the club. Jackie had made it perfectly clear before we left the Pearl that we were there as hosts, not entertainment.

The door opened into a plush, but tasteful, lobby. The oak and leather glowed in a soft white light. If not for the name – Philia – engraved into a silver plate above the bar, we could have been standing in any of a number of posh London hotels. The barman poured seven glasses of champagne and I downed mine, hoping to squash the anxiety that was steadily growing in my gut. Suzy and Craig entered with the tell-tale signs of sexual satisfaction on their newly rosy cheeks.

A tall, slim brunette entered from a hallway to our

left. She was not what I expected. With her tight bun, blue suit and flat shoes, she was better suited for Sloane Brothers than a hedonist club. 'Mr Meleady, so nice to see you again,' she said, extending her hand. 'Mr Smith was hoping he could have a word.'

'Of course,' Declan said as he shook her hand. He set his champagne flute on the bar and turned to us. 'Enjoy yourselves. Unfortunately I've got a bit of business to transact.' He gestured to the lifts at the other end of the lobby. 'I suggest starting at the top and working your way down, if you know what I mean.'

Declan and the brunette disappeared and I suddenly felt a pinprick of fear. Declan was my security blanket and he'd just been ripped away.

'Shall we?' Jackie said, strolling over to the lifts and pressing the up arrow. Craig, Si and Ray followed as if pulled by a leash. Irena glanced at her watch again. Suzy powdered her nose and then skipped to join them. I wasn't sure I could go through with it. Lap dancing was one thing, but I'd heard rumours of what went on in these clubs. I was open-minded. What happened between two or three or a dozen consenting adults behind closed doors was fine by me. I wasn't sure, however, if I was prepared to open those doors and peek in. Irena's tap on my shoulder made me jump.

'I going,' she stammered. I thought she had the right idea.

'Let me get you a taxi,' I said, steadying her on her feet when she faltered.

'No. No. I fine. No worries,' she said, staggered a few steps and gave me the thumbs up.

'Come on, Ginger!' Suzy called, holding the lift doors open. Jackie glared disapprovingly at Suzy. The lobby wasn't the place for yelling. I feared the same rules wouldn't apply on the upper floors.

I gave Irena an apologetic look and headed for the lift. As it ascended, I felt suddenly claustrophobic. Beads of sweat formed on my upper lip. I wiped them away and tried not to imagine what I'd see when the lift doors parted. I had an active imagination but I had a sinking feeling that Philia would surpass my wildest musings.

The doors opened to a long dark empty hallway with none of the lobby's ambiance. 'OK, boys,' Jackie said as we circled around her. 'Take your pick.'

Suzy and Craig ducked into the first door. Ray trailed after his hero, Craig. I had a feeling they intended to sample all that Philia had to offer. If he kept up such a pace, this bright football star might burn out quicker than expected. I'd have to remember to check tomorrow's sports pages. I glanced in. The room was patterned after a medieval dungeon with rough stone walls and shackles. One man followed a dominatrix on hands and knees. Another woman was stretched on a rack being slowly slapped with a leather paddle.

Si took my hand and thankfully pulled me further down the hall. The next room was bathed in the glow of candle light. Every surface was padded. Soft music drowned out the screams and moans from the previous room. Four king-sized beds separated by sheer curtains created a stage of sorts. Bodies morphed together in a kaleidoscope of flesh. It was almost impossible to tell where one person started and another ended. Naked shapes stroked and kissed each other as multiple partners pleasured multiple people.

Jackie watched with us for a second and then slipped into a room up ahead. I followed Si across the hall. We lingered in the doorway. One solitary light bulb dangling from a power cord shed dim light over a shower drain. I could hear water running. The room smelled like a pool in summer – a hint of chlorine, sweat, baby oil and an acidic smell that I couldn't quite identify. As my eyes adjusted, I noticed shadowy figures coupled along the bare walls. To my left a man lay on the floor in supplication to the woman squatted over him. As my eyes adjusted to the light the scene came into focus. She was urinating on him. I staggered from the room and down the hall, leaving Si behind to fend for himself. I'd seen enough. I punched the down button repeatedly until the lift arrived and held my breath until the lift doors closed.

I stomped out the front door trying to dislodge and erase what I'd just seen. I'd watched my fair share of pornography. I had one boyfriend with a massive DVD library and the inability to finish with his six-inch without something on his 42-inch. But seeing men's fantasies staged and acted out for a live audience made me feel as if I'd been wrapped in a bedspread from a seedy King's Cross hotel. I couldn't wait to get home and take a shower. I planned to wash, rinse and repeat.

I was so wrapped up in my self-loathing that I almost didn't see. I'd hate to think what would have happened if I hadn't noticed. Or worse, if I hadn't stopped . . . It happens in London all the time. You hear people yelling and your first instinct is to keep walking and quicken your pace. Your survival instinct kicks in. Don't get involved. But that night when I heard raised voices, I paused. The sound seemed to be coming from the alley behind the Philia. I thought about turning around and taking the long route to the Tube station, but I was in a hurry to get home. I desperately wanted to be Geri again, just Geri. So I told myself not to be such a scaredy-cat. I kept walking but then I heard a scream, a woman's scream. It wasn't someone out having a good time.

I don't know what came over me as I raced ahead. What if that was me? I'd want someone to come quickly. As I reached the alley I slowed down. Maybe I was over-reacting. It was probably some scene from the club which spilled out into the alley. Probably one of its wealthy clients paid for a simulated rape scene. I prayed it was only simulated. I glanced down the alley and kept walking. I needed to take in all the information. Long black stretch limousine. Two men in black suits. A blonde. One man held the woman by a fist full of blonde hair and appeared to be trying to force her in the car. I could have sworn it was Viktor, the creepy barman from back at the Pearl. What was he doing here? I was sure he wasn't invited along on our little escapade. The blonde screamed again, not a word but a long, high-pitched vowel that could have shattered crystal. She shouted something in another language that sounded Polish.

Irena.

I hadn't recognised her at first. The blonde hair threw me. She'd been wearing her black wig earlier.

Chapter Twenty-Eight

My legs went weak. Now I had to do something. Fight or Flight. So I ran. How had I gotten tangled up in this? All I wanted was to make some extra cash and make sure that Zeus had a nice roof over his head.

I couldn't desert Irena. She above all people didn't deserve this. And there I was running back into Philia. I could have called the police. Dialled three numbers. Easy and then walked away. But I was certain Irena didn't have a visa. With the way she'd been acting recently, I was afraid she was mixed up in something illegal. I thought the police would make it worse. I prayed my snap decision was the right one.

I dashed in the front door. The doorman grabbed at my arm, but my weeks of dancing, hoisting myself upside down on the pole, had given me arms of steel. He was no match for me with the added adrenalin. I zigzagged through the club to where I'd left Jackie and Suzy, screaming out their names until they came running. I grabbed them both by the arm. 'We've got to go.' I panted. 'Now!' Their initial looks of annoyance faded. 'It's Irena.'

They followed me without question. We tore through the club, pushing people out of our way. Jackie kicked off her shoes so she could keep up. Suzy followed with the bottle of champagne she was sipping still clutched in her fist. As we rounded the corner to the alley, the black limousine from earlier pulled to a stop.

'That's them,' I screamed. 'They've got Irena.'

Suzy didn't hesitate. She lunged for the limo and smashed the Laurent-Perrier Cuvée Rosé Brut into the windscreen. Shards of green glass and fizzy rosé exploded as the £50 champagne bottle smashed a hole in front of the driver. The car jerked to a halt, the driver sprang from the door and ripped Suzy off the bonnet.

Viktor and one of the black-suited men from earlier piled out the back door. Jackie was waiting for them.

'Jackie, what the hell?' Viktor exclaimed, holding the other man back.

'Where's Irena?' I demanded.

'Irena?' He was a horrible actor. His guilt was written all over his face.

'Stop playing games,' I shouted and gave him a shove. 'She was just here. I heard her screaming. What have you done with her?'

He looked to the other man for direction. The man pushed him aside and stepped closer to us. 'Listen, ladies, mind your own business,' he said. 'Run along like good girls.'

Now my blood was boiling and I wasn't the only one. Jackie's face flamed red. She pushed him aside and I dived in the open car door. What I saw caused bile to rise in my throat. My stomach convulsed and I held the nausea at bay. Irena was passed out on the limo's leather seat, her wrist flopping on the limo floor at an odd angle. She looked paler than normal, nearly blue. A man was arched over her in the process of pulling down his fly.

'Get off of her!' I crawled in the car further but the man didn't seem to notice me.

Jackie poked her head in the limo and then immediately turned on Viktor.

'You don't understand, Jackie,' I heard him explaining. 'Irena was having a bad trip and we were just helping her out.'

'You son of a bitch,' Jackie shouted. I heard the unmistakable sound of a slap. I had no doubt that Viktor was getting a taste of what he deserved.

I pulled myself to kneeling and punched the man's arm as hard as I could. Now he noticed me. 'Get off of her you bastard!' I shouted and slapped him hard across the face.

He caught my wrist and squeezed until I thought he might crush it. 'I paid Viktor good money for this one,' he said, pushing me back hard. I fell back on my arse, my legs sprawled out in front of me.

I flipped to all fours and grabbed the only weapon I had, a hot pink stiletto. 'Get off of her right now.'

He didn't even pause. He acted as if I wasn't even there flagging my shoe at him. I whipped my arm back and lashed out at him as hard as I could, aiming for his pudgy body to avoid accidentally striking Irena. I dug my heel deep and hard down his soft, fleshy forearm.

Irena's head bounced on the seat as the man recoiled in pain. 'You stupid bitch!' he screamed and clutched his bleeding arm. I threw the shoe and knocked him on the head. Now he had a gash over his left eye to match the one on his arm. While he lifted his hand to the wound, I wasted no time. I looped my arms around Irena's shoulders and dragged her out of the car. I could hear Jackie and Suzy's raised voices behind me. Irena was dead weight and it wasn't easy to manoeuvre her out of the limo. I was as careful and quick as I could be.

I made eye contact with Jackie as I backed out of the car. She walked right over to Viktor, who was still trying to persuade her that he was only trying to help, and punched him right on the nose. I heard a crack and saw the gush of blood. Suzy rushed to my side and helped lift Irena into my arms. 'Get a cab,' I said to Suzy. 'Come on, Jackie, we've got to get Irena to hospital.'

'You stay back or I swear to God I will kill you,' Jackie shouted and waved her arms wildly at the four battered men. 'Viktor, if I ever see your face around the Pearl again, I will have you arrested for assault. I'm telling Declan about your side business and I won't be surprised if he pays you a little visit.'

'This way!' Suzy yelled. She was standing in the middle of the street with a black cab stopped inches from her. At first he wasn't keen to get involved, but Jackie waved a fistful of notes, and promised him double the fare if he could get us to A&E quickly.

Jackie and I cradled Irena in our laps, while Suzy urged the cab driver to go faster. Jackie kept slapping Irena's face, pleading with her to wake up, but she was like a corpse. After a while, I leaned back in my seat and cried.

The duty nurse had taken one look at Irena and called

for a stretcher, and then told us to sit tight. Despite the taut professionalism written in her features, I could see she was worried. The waiting room was the worst. All those wretched faces around us, no sounds apart from the occasional squeak of shoes on the lino floor, or the distant moan of someone in pain.

Finally, a West Indian nurse came out and asked for Jackie. We turned as one.

'How is she?' asked Jackie.

'She's going to be fine.' We collectively exhaled and reached for each other's hands. 'We pumped her stomach,' the nurse continued. 'She'd mixed a lot of pills with alcohol. She has a concussion. She needs lots of rest but should be back on her feet in a few days. We will keep her overnight for observation but she should be released tomorrow. Someone will be out in a little while to tell you her room number and then you can go visit her. She's feeling pretty scared and alone at the moment.'

Jackie, Suzy and I hugged each other as the nurse walked away. 'I'm starving,' Suzy said. 'Why don't I go grab us a few sandwiches and some crisps from the vending machines and we'll have ourselves a little celebration picnic.'

'I've got to go,' I said, breaking free of their embrace. Everything felt as if it was crashing in. I looked at the clock over the nurses' station. It was after three in the morning and I had to be at work in less than five hours. Hell, I even *wanted* to be at work. I was desperate to get this wig and these clothes off and slip back into my Chanel suit.

They both stared at me. 'Aren't you even going to stay and see if Irena is all right?' Suzy asked.

'The nurse said she'll be fine.'

'She will need us now,' Jackie added.

'I can't stay here. I've got to go.'

'Piss off then,' Jackie said with new venom.

'It's just . . .' I tried to think of how to finish my sentence. It's just I'm a selfish bitch who should have never gotten mixed up in all this. It's just I want my old life back.

'Just go.' Jackie walked away pulling Suzy behind her.

I sat on the shower floor and let the water rush over me until it went cold. I still felt dirty. I crawled into bed and pulled the covers to my chin. When I shut my eyes all I could see was Irena's pale white face, her eye liner and lipstick smudged as if a child had applied it. What had I become?

When my alarm went off I tried to pretend it was any other day. I showered again and dressed in my favourite blue suit with a gold-coloured silk blouse. I spiked my hair and applied my usual dab of mascara and lipstick and I was ready for work. But after I slipped in the driving seat of my Roadster, I didn't take my normal route to work. I pulled into Tesco's to fill up my tank and checked my watch. I was already late for work. I sent a text to Tania: *Family emergency. Will be in as soon as I can.* Then I headed straight for the hospital.

Irena's white skin and blonde hair practically made her invisible in the harsh white hospital light. Suzy was passed out in an orange vinyl chair and Jackie was sitting next to Irena's bed asleep with her head resting on the bed railing.

The door whooshed shut behind me and Jackie and Suzy blinked sleepy eyes at me. 'Hi,' I said and handed them each a cup of hot black coffee and a small brown bag with a blueberry muffin. 'Why don't you get some rest? I'll wait with Irena for a while.'

They both nodded, too exhausted to speak. Suzy kissed me on the cheek and Jackie squeezed my arm. They had forgiven me already. The door whooshed open and shut again and this time, Irena stirred. She opened her eyes and stared at me, unblinking.

'I hear . . .' Irena started but a sob cut her sentence short. 'You . . .' she tried again.

'Just relax,' I said and laid the £4.99 bouquet from Tesco's on her bedside cabinet.

'Jackie say,' she caught her breath. 'Jackie say you the one who find me. You save me.'

Yeah, I thought, but who was going to save me? This secret of mine continued to spiral out of control. I deserved to be the one in the hospital bed, not Irena. She was just trying to survive and get back to the love of her life.

'I'm glad Simon never come. I don't want him to see me this way. What would he think of me now?' She buried her head in her hands and wept.

I waited until her sobs subsided. 'It's going to be OK, Irena.' I sat down next to her bed. I leaned in close and held her hand.

'It no matter now.' She looked at me with big sad, bloodshot eyes.

'Maybe relax and think about a happier time with Simon.'

'I so stupid,' she said. 'I thought I come to this country and I be Mrs Simon Robinson. But look at me. He no want me anymore.'

'You are a beautiful girl, Irena.'

She closed her eyes and shook her head. 'I no feel beautiful.'

'I know what you mean.' I looked away.

'What happened?' I asked, not just to her. 'How did we get here?'

Chapter Twenty-Nine

IRENA'S STORY PART TWO

How do you describe black hole? All I know is I was surrounded by darkness and can not find way out.

Simon is still somewhere but I have no way to find him. I do not understand language. I have no money. No job. No friends. My email address not work anymore. I do not send emails when I work in Poland. I do not know the company steal it back if you not use it. I have no computer and no way to find Simon. But I still hope which keep me going.

I call home. My father refuse to talk to me. He is ashamed. My mother listen. She miss me. She tell me she love me. I beg her to let me come home, but she have no money to spare. I ask her to call her sister, but she is embarrass to ask for money. To ask for money for daughter who chased British tourist who steal her womanhood. She tell me to find my self respect and come home. She give me some help – couple from my hometown who live in London – Pawel i Mela Kowalski. She promise to call them. They are almost family. Mela's cousin Leon is married to niece of my father's brother.

I stand outside their house. I watch them through lace curtains. They look friendly. I knock on door. Everything I own is in two Sainsbury's bags. My body is shake from hunger, I am tired and desperate. If they slam door in my face, I do not know what I do. I have no more money for hostel and only £23.45 left in my pocket. I not look up when someone open door. I stare at woman's worn, brown shoes with laces.

'*Witaj*,' I said. 'I am Olga and Aron's daughter Irena.'

Mela do not speak. She only hug me with big fleshy arms. She smell of warm bread and honey, like my mother. I stand there with my arms pinned to my side and cry.

'You will stay with us.' She talk loudly so I hear her over my sobs. 'You can sleep on settee. You will work for Pawel, my husband. He can always use a girl to clean up after messy men on his construction sites. I will feed you so you get meat on your bones and then when you are ready you will go back out into the world.' Mela yank me from black hole. That is Mela. Life is simple to her. You work hard. You earn money. You find man. You get married and have kids. You teach them to work hard, earn money so they find spouse and start over again. At that moment, I never love anyone more than I love Mela Kowalski.

'*Dziekuje*,' I say. 'Thank you.'

She make me cup of strong black tea. She feed me scrambled eggs and *Twarog* cheese on fresh made bread. I am in heaven. She tell me news from village and share stories of her family. She have two strong sons who work in their father's construction business. Sons are happy married and give her six grandchildren. I sit at kitchen table and listened to her stories. I spend past months struggling to speak English and begging to be understand. To hear and speak Polish is relief.

Warm and relax, I lie down on settee while Mela go out to shops. I wake many hours later with warm fuzzy blanket around me. I think for moment I am back home. I rub my eyes from sleep and try to bring back reality. I remember breakfast and talk with Mela when I notice a big man watch me from doorway. I gasp and pull covers to my chin. He linger there for moment even after my scared reaction. There is something about how he watch me that make me feel naked. I become so used to being on guard that maybe I do not know how to trust anymore.

'Get dressed,' he say. 'You are going to work with me.' Then he disappear into kitchen.

I roll off settee. I was already dress. I wear my only clean clothes. They have to do. Mela hand me cheese roll as I leave. 'Pawel, you take care of Irena,' she say as she kiss her husband on cheek. 'You make sure she has lunch. I will see you for supper.' She hug me again. 'You have a good day.'

Pawel wipe his cheek as he let me into his truck. We ride in silence. I see him stare at me. I try to keep my eyes from him and not to think. We arrive at council estate with crumbling walls and graffiti all over. 'We are renovating the flats. You follow us and clean up. There are rags, broom and mop in the back. Be quick and don't steal anything from the flats.'

I nod and hide my offence. What he think? Single Polish girl chasing an English boy. 'Thank you for your kindness,' I say in best English. 'You can trust me to do you proud.'

'It was Mela's idea,' he say and make the words sound hard. He leave truck, and make slam the door behind him. I grab my supplies and run after him. He do not introduce me to his construction crew. He instruct them in Polish that they do not bother me. I follow them around all day, like mouse cleaning up crumbs. At least when boys whistle and shout at me, I understand what they want. Pawel seem to know when boys are talk to me. He yell for us to go back to work or come into room and stand and stare.

In beginning I think he is protective and I appreciate fatherly feeling. But it take me not long to know that his attention was more like the dog mark his territory. For first days, he barely speak to me. Mela say to him at dinner and tell him to be friendly. He grunt some questions at me and then ignore when I answer.

'He's shy,' Mela explain when we are alone. 'We raised boys. He's not used to young girls.' Pawel watch football, Mela and I chat with cups of tea. I mostly listen but I feel as if I am re-entering world. In those moments, I think everything maybe be all right someday.

And for the few weeks, my life seem to become normal. Then one touch change it all. One morning Pawel stop his truck in front of construction site like always. But instead of he leave his truck with only grunt in my direction, he turn off engine and sit there, he stare out front windscreen. So I sat like he, stare out front windscreen.

Then he reach over and put one hand on my breast. He did not caress it or cup it. He only rest his hand there. I do not look at him. I just keep my eyes look straight ahead. When my body begin to tremble, he move his hand and leave. I sit in truck for moment, try to think what happen. I decide to believe that I imagine it all. Kowalskis give me food and shelter. I think of Mela like friend. I have nowhere else to go. That night I come home and go straight to bed. I tell Mela I not feel well. She bring me soup that only make me feel worse.

Slowly Pawel's attention happen more. He touch me same way every morning but he again find me during day and he put his hands on me. At first it is only fascination with my breasts. I look away and pretend it is not happen. What I suppose to do? I stay with him and work for him. Maybe he consider this part of his rent. Then he start to come up behind me, reach around to cup my breasts, and then he rub his hardness against my buttocks. I want to be out of my skin.

Nothing change between us except these moment. I start leaving house every night after work. I tell Mela I make some friends. She is happy for me. Truth is I borrow one of Mela's Polish books and find pub few streets away. I buy one pint and read until I know Pawel and Mela be in bed. I wait outside house until I see bedroom light go off before I go in their house.

Pawel start keeping me at work site after all workers leave. He reach his rough, dirty hands under my shirt and bra and caress my breasts. He sometimes ask me to stand topless in front of him. He never touch me or himself down below so I tell myself it OK. It just become

297

as part of my life like scratchy woollen blanket I sleep under or *kielbasa* Mela cook on Sundays.

I am living with Mela and Pawel during almost four months. After dinner one night, I whisper to Mela that I move out soon. I meet a woman at pub who work for cleaning agency. I go to live with her and four other girls in flat near Tottenham Court Road. My room and job start in one week. She hug me and tell me she miss me.

That night I wake up as Pawel pulled back my woollen blanket. I have start to sleep in jeans and T-shirt to prevent this from happening. He lean over settee and whisper in my ear, 'Take off your clothes.' I shake my head and reach for blanket. He repeat this command and begin pull at button on my jeans. He going to wake up Mela. I have to protect her so I stand and slip off my clothes as silently as I can. He stare at my body, then he touch my private places. I beg him in Polish whispers to stop, to think of Mela, but he clamp his meaty hand over my mouth and tell me to be quiet. The knowing of what he going to do next was overwhelming. My body begin to shake and I start to cry. He hug me. 'No crying, please, no crying.' But I not able to stop. His cotton vest and underwear press against my bare flesh only make me cry louder.

'Pawel!' Mela shout. She appear from nowhere. I was so relief. 'Upstairs. Now.' She step into lounge. 'You. Get out.' Pawel scamper up stairs and not look back. 'He is a man. I expect him to be weak. We help you and this is how you repay us? By tempting my husband with your body? We were friends. I expected you to be strong.'

Her arms wave in air as she slap my naked flesh. I

dress as quickly as I can and put my belongings into my arms. My skin is hot from her hands. She do not stop shouting at me. She call me names as I run down street barefoot. I know by next morning my parents and village will know all about Irena ungrateful whore who try to steal Pawel away.

I lose everything again and now I also lose my family. I am saving to go home but now have no home where to go. I try to explain to my mother when I write home, but she tell me I am no longer welcome in her house. I am disgrace myself and my family.

Again I have to re-create my life. I work from seven in morning to ten at night to clean house. I take something is dirty and make it clean again. I enjoy work and to live with women. I tell my flatmates about Simon. They say me to hire private detective. They say on British TV, you hire detective and he find person for you. No big deal. Now I need big money to find my Simon. It is my flatmate Dita who tell me about auditions at the Pearl. I know what it is to perform on stage and to pretending to be something I am not. She say there is big money to be make.

I enjoy dancing but not touching so much. Viktor, barman, is really only one nice to me. I not know why other girls act as if I done something wrong. No one speak to me, all laughing at me behind my back. He point out good customers. He also help me with my money – how much to gave Declan and others at the Pearl. He take some for himself. He say he was my manager. That was OK. I need help with money. He know when I was down and give me free drinks sometimes. Once he give me little pill with smiley face on it. 'This will help you be happy,' he say. The pill make rough bits go away and leave me with a glow. I like the glow. It is better than blackness that slowly creep back in. 'The first one's free,' Viktor say. But every night he give me another.

I tell Viktor I need private detective so he set me up with friend of his. This guy want £2,000. He say he have ways of tracking people down. He say he will find Simon if I give him money. I save every penny. He come in once during every week and give me report and I give him free dance. He track Simon down to Oxford then he say the trail went cold. He need £100 train fare to check out a lead in Norwich, wherever that was. Every time he was so close and every time he come back with bad news. I wonder if Simon is run away from me. Last time I see detective, he ask for £500 more. He need money for travel and hotel to check out a lead in Wales. I give him everything I have and I never see him again.

I was one month behind with rent. My roommates are threaten to throw me out. Viktor say I owe him £700 for smiley pills he give to me. 'You didn't think you were getting those for free, did you?' I shrug. I thought I pay enough for those pills already.

'I know a way you can earn more money,' he speak really slowly as if I was stupid and deaf instead of Polish.

'How?' I say, but the twist in my gut tell me I do not want to know.

'You meet me tomorrow night. I will arrange for a private limo ride. A man will pay to be with you.'

I knew what he mean. I tell him no.

I tell him no. Please believe me.

He say I could not say no. I had take the pills. I need rent money. When we leave for Philia Club he say he meet me out back at 1am. I tell him no. He tell me to be there.

I meet him. But I only go to tell him no again. I do not want to make a scene. I do not need Jackie and others to think badly of me. I do not sell my sex. My Simon was only one who would ever have me. I do not agree but he hit me and my world go black.

I do not want to talk anymore. I want to sleep now.

Chapter Thirty

The next day Irena was released from hospital, and that could have been the last we heard of her, if it weren't for Jackie. I heard from Suzy that Jackie had been around several times to check up on Irena, and assured her that, if she were to come back, this time we'd all watch her back. Who knew Jackie would possess the maternal instinct? Even Suzy, who confessed to feeling rotten for all the times she snubbed Irena, went around with a bottle of Rioja to cheer her up.

A few days later I got the call from Jackie to head to the embassy. By that point, I'd already decided that my time at the Pearl had come to an end. But if I was going to go out, for God's sake, I was going to go out in style, and with an extra grand buoying up my bank balance.

After spotting that red light blinking, Suzy, Jackie and I went back to mine to work out our next move. Of course, there were dozens of cameras at the Pearl, but that was different. They were to make the girls, and the punters, feel safer. The ambassador's little scam was a violation, and not one we were taking lightly. Around midnight, we were heading back to the hotel.

Jackie was silent as the taxi turned into Park Lane. There was no champagne this time, no slinky black dresses. We were all in jeans, and tight tops. I'd even put on a pair of battered trainers that hadn't seen the light of day since the last time I went running the year before. This was about efficient execution, not titillation – three strippers in mini-skirts and stilettos wouldn't have cut it.

The taxi drove slowly past the front of the building, and I caught a glimpse, through the canopied porch, of the front desk. A security guard sat there reading a magazine – top-shelf no doubt. Once we were thirty yards away, Suzy knocked on the driver's partition. 'This will be fine.'

We pulled up to the pavement.

'I feel like James Bond,' said the cabbie, an old acquaintance of Suzy's who could be called on in a pinch.

'You look a bit like him too,' I said, though it was stretching the truth. Last time I checked 007 didn't have a comb-over and weigh sixteen stone. Suzy stifled her snigger as a cough.

Jackie and I climbed out, and Jackie went over the details of the plan one more time. It was bitterly cold and I rubbed my hands together. The riding gloves would prevent prints once we were inside, but were getting threadbare with age.

The taxi had dropped us at the side of the embassy building. Up lighters illuminated the second and third storeys of the classical façade, but all the lights inside seemed to be off – I could not see anything inside the windows as all the curtains were drawn.

The taxi threaded slowly around the corner towards the front of the building and I peered around the tarred black railings to watch its course. Would he keep his part of the bargain? For an awful moment, it looked as though he'd drive off, but then the red glow of the brake-lights came on and he swung a U-turn in the middle of the street, pulling up outside the front steps of the building.

'You're sure this is going to work?' I asked Jackie. 'There's a lot that could go wrong.'

'Live a little. This is nothing compared with the old days.' She checked her watch. 'Anyway, it's still five to. Mickey said two o'clock exactly.'

'What if the tape's not there? The ambassador might have taken it home.'

'The guy's got a wife and kids,' said Jackie. 'Why take the risk? No – it'll be safely stashed in his office.'

'And we can trust this guy, can we?' I asked.

'How do you think we got the gig?'

Jackie led me around the side of the building, where there was a double gate, electrically operated, with a door in one. A stationary camera above stared down with its glass eye. Arm in arm, we walked right underneath it as though we were strolling home from a party. The security guard wouldn't suspect a thing – let alone that these two respectable-looking ladies were about to break in right under his nose.

Jackie took out her phone, and hit the speed dial to Suzy. 'Now,' she said, and then hung up.

At the front of the building, our taxi driver with a taste for espionage would be climbing out of his taxi and entering the lobby, armed with a defunct London A-Z.

Suddenly my stomach was light with that mixture of extreme anxiety and adrenalin, just the way it was when we were closing a deal at work. This was the crunch time.

We stopped twenty yards past the side entrance, out of range of the CCTV, our breath misting in the cold night air. From Jackie's pocket, the music to *Cabaret* kicked off. Jackie killed the ring.

'That's our signal,' she said. 'Let's go.'

We walked quickly back up the street, and under the camera again. But this time I was confident no one was watching the live feed. In fact, Suzy would be watching from the taxi window as the cabbie was distracting the front desk security guard from his monitors, with his fabricated search for Cotterill Street; my own little embellishment on the plan.

At the gates, Jackie laid her hand on the door and pushed. It didn't open.

'Shit!'

'What? It's locked?' Fallen at the first hurdle.

'Shit, shit, shit!'

'Try again,' I said.

Jackie pushed at the door again, but still it held on the electronic latch. It looked like the down-payment to the kitchen staff wasn't enough. She held her head down. We had what? – a minute, tops – before our front-of-house ruse ran out of steam and the security guard took his seat again.

Jackie was standing with her arms akimbo and sucking in a deep breath when there was a soft click, and the door swung open. An oriental man, wearing stained chef's whites and a checked apron, stood on the other side.

'Sorry,' he said, his eyes travelling over Jackie's curves. 'Crisis in the kitchen. Fridge broken.' He gave me a pervy smile.

Jackie shook her head and together we crossed inside. There was a white van parked on one side of a small court-yard. I looked up but couldn't see any cameras in here.

'I thought you'd let us down, Mickey boy,' said Jackie. 'Which way, Mick?'

He wiped his hands nervously on the apron then pointed to an open door, which threw out a slanted oblong of light into the courtyard.

We followed him inside into a brightly lit utility area, on to a lino floor, and past a set of three identical Laundromat washing machines, two sloshing their contents and a third with its door ajar. This was evidently the behind-the-scenes part of the embassy.

Next we were in the kitchens, passing large sinks and a gigantic grill, where the heavy chemical smell of deter-gent dominated over a lingering scent of smoked fish.

I felt something touch my arse, and flashed round to see Mick holding out a clawed hand and grinning inanely. I slapped it away.

'How dare you!'

'Not yet,' said Jackie. 'Patience, grasshopper. Which way is the ambassador's office?'

Mick looked a little disappointed, but gestured with his head towards a glass-panelled door by the food heaters.

'Go down the hall, across the main dining room, and up the second set of stairs. The office is straight ahead at the top.'

Jackie gave him a peck on the cheek, and then paced off towards the door.

'What exactly did you promise him?' I hissed, as we left him standing in the kitchen.

Jackie didn't answer, but her smile told me I probably wouldn't want to know the answer.

It was eerily quiet as we made our way along a corridor stacked with chairs. I pulled aside a thick velvet curtain, and entered a dining room. I remembered seeing it last time we were in the embassy, and the memory brought back the illicit thrill from dancing and it sent a fresh tingle over my skin. I had to remind myself this was a different kind of mischief, with potentially much more serious repercussions. If we were caught inside, and the police became involved, my desk at Sloane's would be emptied before the sun broke over Canary Wharf.

The room was completely transformed since our last visit.

'They must be entertaining tomorrow,' said Jackie.

The long table was set for service. Elaborate floral decorations burst from the table every few feet, and the silver cutlery glinted in the faint light. Still, there was no time to stop and admire. Our footfalls were silent as we covered the room and pushed through another door at the far end.

I gave the entrance hallway a cursory glance to make sure it was all clear then waved Jackie through. The stairs were laid in mahogany-coloured carpet, and I took them two at a time. Jackie came more cautiously behind.

'That's it, isn't it?' she said, pointing at the brass inlaid door dead ahead. With a gloved hand, I eased the handle down, then felt for the light switch. It was a dimmer, and I cranked it up, throwing light into the room.

The room where we'd danced was a large square, dominated at one side by a mahogany desk, covered in green leather and what looked like a Tiffany lamp. The opposite side of the room was given to a seating area. A two-seater leather sofa and two wingback chairs around a coffee table. A door at the far end led to what I guessed was a toilet. Shutters were drawn across both of the tall windows, and bookshelves lined the wall behind the desk. Mostly decorative, no doubt.

Jackie went straight to the desk, and looked through the papers that were stacked there. I went to the filing cabinet that was positioned to the left of the door. Every little noise seemed magnified against the silence.

'Anything?' said Jackie.

I leafed through the papers in the bottom drawer, fishing with my hand right to the bottom.

'Not here. Try the desk drawers.'

Jackie bent over and pulled open each of the drawers in turn, then slid each back in silently. But when she tried the top drawer, it stuck.

'Bingo!' she said. 'This one's locked.'

I joined her side. 'Great! And why is that a good thing?'

Jackie pulled off her handbag and unzipped it. Inside was a chisel.

'I've learnt a thing or two over the years,' she grinned.

She slid it into the gap at the top of the drawer and levered upwards. There was a snap.

'Holy shit – that's seriously illegal.'

'What, and trespassing on foreign sovereignty isn't?'

She wiggled the chisel from side to side, and the sound of crunching wood came from the desk drawer. Jackie slid it open.

A copy of *Men Only* lay at the top of a pile of other magazines. Leafing through were several other pornos and a video camera.

'Jackpot.'

Jackie pressed the eject button and the tape holder popped open.

There was no tape.

Jackie slapped her forehead. 'This is hopeless. It might not even be in the office.'

Her mobile rang, and she glanced at the screen and answered.

'What is it, Suze? . . . OK, we're coming.' She turned to me. 'It's time to go. Our cabbie is heading out.'

But that's when I spotted something out of place. Scanning the bookshelf behind the desk, most of the titles were embossed and ancient – political works of politics and British history. On the edges of the shelf was a thick layer of dust, confirming my suspicions that the ambassador wasn't a big reader. That's when my eyes caught a book on the middle shelf – Gibbon's *Decline and Fall of the Roman Empire*. But it wasn't the title that caught my eye – it was the fact that of all the books in the shelf, this one was upside-down.

'OK, bring the cab round to the side. We'll see you in a mo.' She hung up. 'You ready?' she said to me.

'Wait a minute,' I said, and pulled out the book. Immediately it felt the wrong weight. 'I have a feeling . . .'

I opened the book, and there it was – a tape no more

than two inches long, embedded in the centre of the book.

'Oh, you genius!' said Jackie, taking my head between her hands and planting a kiss bang on my lips. 'Let's check it.'

She passed me the recorder and I put the tape in and rewound to the start, then pressed the play button. With our heads pressed together, we watched the small screen.

The ambassador looked straight back at us, staring into the lens. As he drew back I recognised the room in the background. There was the faint sound of a knock and the ambassador's head twisted towards the door. He walked in that direction and opened it.

'Sneaky fucker, isn't he?' Jackie whispered in my ear.

I knew what would come next. The ambassador opened the door, and in walked a statuesque blonde.

What the hell? 'That's not us,' I said.

Jackie hit the fast forward button, and we watched the woman strip for the ambassador at super speed. Next they were fucking over the edge of the table, the ambassador's arse bouncing up and down like a jackhammer. I paused the tape.

'Quite a skinflick,' Jackie muttered. 'Go forward more.'

I did what she said. The scene with the hooker ended and the image skipped. It was almost identical, but the room had shifted slightly. 'This must be a different day,' I said.

And there we were. The three of us, streaming into the room in our glad rags. It had been a great night, no doubt, and I felt myself smiling as I recalled the way we'd worked the room. Suddenly all our recent squabbles seemed a bit

311

silly. I stopped the tape as Suzy was mid-flow, clawing her dress up her thighs provocatively.

'Mission accomplished,' I said. 'Let's split.'

Jackie led the way, and I switched off the light and closed the door. Just down the stairs, across the hall and through the kitchen. One minute and we'd be home and dry.

That's when we heard his voice. 'Is someone there?'

Jackie and I froze on the stairs. She looked back at me and I could see the whites of her eyes. 'You shouldn't be in here,' said the guard, with a slight quaver in his voice. 'I'm armed.'

Jackie gestured wildly with her open palm, telling me to go back up the stairs. I turned and trotted back into the upper hallway.

'What do we do now?' she whispered.

'I know there's someone here,' came the voice again. He was on the stairs.

I took Jackie's hand and pulled her further along the corridor and around the next corner. The portraits of past ambassadors glared down with stiff-backed approbation from the walls.

'There must be another way out,' I said. 'A fire escape or something.'

A high-pitched tune pierced the air again. This time it was '*Wilkommen*'. Jackie must have had the whole bloody *Cabaret* soundtrack on her phone.

She stabbed a button and put it to her ear.

'I *know*!' she hissed. 'He's here. *Do* something . . .'

The sound of quickening footsteps came from the stairs, so Jackie and I ran down the corridor. 'I'm coming now,' shouted the guard. 'I'm not scared.' He certainly sounded it.

'There!' said Jackie, pointing to a white door.

We pushed open the door into a cold stairwell and didn't look back. Once we hit the bottom we were through another door and back in the foyer. Home and dry. I ran to the door and yanked the handle. It was locked.

'No, no, no!' I shouted.

'Just hold it right there, ladies,' said the security guard. He was standing at the fire escape exit and in his hands was a plant-pot – some sort of bonsai by the looks of it. He was brandishing it half like a weapon, half like a shield. His chest rose and fell quickly. He couldn't have been more than 19. 'It's over.'

'Quick!' said Jackie. 'The back door.'

The security guard's face fell in exasperation as we sprinted back towards the dining hall. 'Don't do that!' he wailed.

As we passed the long banqueting table, Jackie picked up a silver dinner platter and slid the copy of *Men Only* underneath. She'd barely broken her stride.

'That'll make them choke on their soup,' she said.

I was laughing as we ran back through the kitchens. Mickey was smoking a fag by the back door as I flashed by.

'Hey!' he said. 'What about my dance?'

'Forget it,' yelled Jackie.

She pushed the button by the back door and pulled it open as the security guard burst out of the kitchens. 'Stop them!' he shouted to the chef. 'They're thieves!'

I was out on the street. The cab was parked just a few yards away, and the door swung open. Suzy's head peeped out. 'Get in,' she said.

Jackie ran past, her long dark hair shaken loose. I wasn't looking back anymore, and leapt into the taxi after her. 'Drive!' she said to the driver.

'Yes, Miss Moneypenny,' he said in an awful Scottish accent.

We were giggling like schoolgirls who had just got away with smoking behind the bike sheds. The scene of the crime was far behind us but the taxi was stuck in traffic and inching along. It was going to take ages to get back to my place, where we'd left all our stuff earlier.

'I can't believe he was going to apprehend us with a pot plant,' Jackie laughed.

'Do you think he'll report it?' I asked, suddenly imagining my grainy image all over the front of the *Evening Standard*.

'No – a jobsworth like that – he'll be shitting himself. As soon as the ambassador finds out what's missing, he'll keep the whole thing buttoned up too.'

'So are you two cool again?' said Suzy, giving us a mock stern stare.

I looked at Jackie and she at me. She held out a beautifully manicured hand.

'Friends?'

I pulled off my riding glove and took her hand. 'You bet,' I said.

'Bloody London traffic,' said Suzy, ignoring what I'd said. 'I hate this place sometimes. I yearn for the open spaces of Nevada.'

She huffed and puffed for effect, waiting for me to respond.

'Yes, but surely you're a London girl at heart,' I said.

'I guess so, for my sins,' she sighed. 'So is Jackie, of course.'

I sensed my chance to ask more about how they met.

'So do you two go back a long way?'

'Oh yes, right back to the good old, bad old days, right, Jackie?' Suzy winked.

'How exciting. What was it like?'

But for once it wasn't Suzy bombarding me with dazzling tales, but Jackie opening up.

Chapter Thirty-One

JACKIE'S STORY PART 2

After that night with Desmond and Dublin and Tony, Linda let me dance. I came out from my hiding place behind the bar. I'd do a session on the pole early on, then work the punters for a while. Aunt Linda wouldn't let me do a lap dance for anything less than £100, twice what the other girls got, and for a private dance in the back room I charged £300. She wanted to keep me separate from the other girls. I didn't realise why at the time but she and Tony had other plans for me. I thought the punters wouldn't pay so much at first – what was so special about me? But word had got out that I was a ballerina and could do the most amazing contortions, and they lapped it up. No pun intended.

Back then, just going into the back room didn't necessarily mean you were going to fuck the punters, though most of them asked. I decided what I was going to allow depending on what I thought I could get out of them and whether I was in the mood. Mostly I'd just show them my moves and my body, then when they were spring-loaded, I'd bring them off with some grinding, or a quick hand inside the pants. Occasionally though, when I was feeling horny and when they were decent enough guys, I'd let them fuck me. Though I made them pay. Some girls liked to talk to the guys, let them think they were friends or maybe more. They'd keep them in the room for hours; every time the half-hour was up, the hand would go back in the pocket and more cash would come out, just so the conversation would continue. I didn't work like that. I tried to stay honest and I liked to think I gave them what they wanted, gave them value for money. I built up some loyal clients. Maybe you'd say it was just prostitution or one step up from there at most. Maybe, but at least I was in control. And I made a *lot* of money. Money I needed.

Soon after Tony took over, Melinda left and Jen moved in with me. We became closer than ever and we often used to work together. The guys loved it when we'd make out with each other and I didn't mind so much myself. We occasionally slept together, but we weren't together in the full sense, just looking after one another. I came to understand that I wasn't a lesbian – I liked men too much for that – but sometimes a woman was what you needed. She gave me tenderness and love, which I wasn't getting from my occasional couplings with the customers.

Tony used to hang around the club occasionally. He wasn't flamboyant like Desmond, and was a reserved sort of character. From what Linda told me, he ran an efficient operation. More interested in making money and keeping his head down than getting into fist fights and drowning siblings. He'd always smile and say hello to me, but he didn't follow up his offer. I'd made my decision and he respected that.

Thing was, I wasn't at all sure I'd made the right decision. I had my reasons, which I'm not going to go into just yet, but now I'd seen the way he operated, the way he was. He was a crook, he'd had men killed, I knew, but in a way he was the straightest man I've ever known. He was an old-fashioned gentleman gangster, and he never hurt anyone without very good reason. Compare him to the lairy businessmen, the drunken, red-faced market traders, or the drugged-up, arrogant students and there was no comparison. Tony was a real man.

One night he came in just as I was closing up. He looked tired. Dublin waved goodbye, knowing I was safe with Tony and the old bouncer locked the door behind him.

'Don't mind me,' Tony said. 'Just pour me a large scotch and I'll be fine.' I gave him the drink and left him to it as I tidied up and turned off the lights. The lights to the stage were the last to be turned off and were situated right next to the stereo, playing Oasis – 'Don't Look Back in Anger' – at low volume. It must have been around 1995, I suppose. Funny how you remember things by what was on the radio, isn't it?

Anyway, Tony looked so tired, and so lonely, on the spur of the moment I decided I'd give him a surprise, you know, to cheer him up. So I grabbed the remote for the stereo, cued up the song I wanted and scuttled over to the stage. I started the song and turned up the volume. I played Pulp's 'Common People'. The rest of the room was in total darkness of course, so I had no idea what

Tony was thinking of my performance. Or whether he was even looking at all. So I just danced for myself. My God, I was hot. My hair was really long in those days, and I flipped it around in time with the music, almost making it a fifth limb. That was thirteen years ago and I can't move like that anymore. At the time I was so slim, so limber and still strong from my ballet training. I gave it everything. My clothes came off piece by piece and as the song ended I was totally naked, humping the pole, sweat dripping between my breasts. I stopped and waited there.

There was a long silence, then out of the darkness I heard steps coming towards me. I waited, hung back off the pole, one leg slightly behind the other to take my weight, tits heaving and pointing to the sky. I heard the steps come up the stairs to the stage behind me, out of view. Then approach across the stage. They stopped right behind me. I felt exposed, innocent and vulnerable. I also felt incredibly turned on. This man was a gangster, a hard man. He could chew me up and spit out the pieces. As I thought of the danger, I felt my loins tingle. The anticipation of his touch was like an electric current running through my taut body. I closed my eyes and waited.

Then I felt his hand on the back of my neck, supporting me, holding me steady. And then his rough lips, whisky-sweet on mine. I slumped in bliss, like some winsome English rose from an old romance, and then he was holding me, clutching my frame to his hard body. I could feel his muscles through the thin cotton shirt he wore and I slipped an arm around his waist, the other hand went straight for his crotch. I shocked myself how quickly I had his cock out of his trousers and between my lips but I guess I figured I'd already waited long enough. He slumped to his knees and I lowered my head, taking his entire shaft into my mouth and tonguing it the way Jen had showed me how to do on a dildo. He groaned. His cock was thick, and a good seven inches. Perfect.

Later, as 'Streets of Philadelphia' played on the stereo, I held on to the pole while he stood behind me, driving his cock into me from behind, slow but hard. He reached around and gently massaged my clit as he thrust until I came with a moan I could do nothing to stop. Then I took him up to my room, being careful not to wake Jen – I didn't want things getting complicated – and we made love all over again, sweetly, slowly, like a couple.

I went to sleep as blissful as I'd ever been, hopeful as ever, but this time, less sure of my future than I was as an innocent 16-year-old with my ballet teacher in the studio. I'd learnt my lesson. However perfect things seem, you just never know what's around the corner.

And when all's said and done, Tony was no banker or accountant. He was a criminal. He might be killed tomorrow or banged up for a twenty stretch. I had responsibilities, or at least, one responsibility. I dreamed that night I was making love to Tony on a boat, on the top deck, under a perfect sky but all the while I was worried about storm clouds on the horizon as well as something down below, some precious, unspecified cargo.

In the morning Tony woke me up carrying a breakfast tray.

'I'm serious if you are,' was all he said.

He knew the score. He'd known it ever since that night in the bar when he'd asked to buy me a drink. After I'd helped Linda sort the till out, I turned around to find him sitting forlornly at the bar. I'd decided I needed to show him why I didn't think we could be together. So I'd taken him upstairs, to the flat, where Jen was sitting waiting, and holding a six-month-old baby. My baby. I took the sleeping infant from her and held her tight against my breast.

'Plenty of reliable babysitters around here,' I'd joked, weakly.

'She's yours?' he'd asked.

I'd nodded.

'The father?'

'Ballet teacher.'

He raised an eyebrow.

'This is why it's not a good idea to get involved with me,' I said. 'I've got baggage.'

'Look . . .' he'd started to say, but my little girl woke just then, and cried out. I comforted her and he shifted, looking uncomfortable. I needed to give him an easy way out. 'Would you mind, Tony? I've got to breastfeed her now.'

He'd looked surprised, perhaps not expecting me to be the breastfeeding type, then nodded quickly and shuffled out.

So three months later as he sat on the bed, breakfast tray complete with red rose on his lap, and asked me if I was serious I didn't hesitate. I nodded, trying to keep the smile off my face. Then I kicked the tray aside and grabbed hold of him. He kissed me madly, passionately until I nearly blacked out, then I found three of his fingers deep inside my pussy and I began to thrust against him, urgent in my need to have him inside me. He brought me off with just his hand, flipping my clitoris from side to side with a deft movement I hadn't experienced before. It drove me wild. I kissed every inch of him in return, pushing my hands through the light hairs on his chest and biting his nipples until he slapped me on the bum, pinned me to the bed face-down and began giving me a thorough screwing from behind.

Later he found my vibrator and chased me round the flat with it. This woke Jen who came out of her room, took one look at her boss charging around the room, penis flapping about and waving a pink eight-inch vibrator, shrugged and went back to bed again. Thank heavens Linda was babysitting for me that night, I'm not sure what a nine-month-old would have thought of it.

Linda was nearing 50 then, and Tony pensioned her off. She still popped in from time to time, but effectively I was running the place. Tony confirmed this with a promotion and a very generous salary. He wasn't so keen on me dancing now and wanted someone he could trust looking after the books. He didn't forbid me from dancing altogether; I still worked the pole and sometimes would help out with private dances if we were busy or if the money was right. Sometimes I'd dance just for the hell of it, and to keep in practice.

Some of the girls were a bit sniffy about me being their new boss, but I'd been there much longer than most and I think they'd started to look up to me for the most part. Jen moved on eventually, which was sad. But I think that once Tony was on the scene, she inevitably felt a bit left out. It was probably the right thing. Tony generally stayed at my flat rather than me going to his. Though I didn't enquire, I assumed this was because there was generally dodgy stuff going on at his place. Stolen goods, kidnap victims tied up with parcel tape, dead bodies, that sort of thing. Nicer at mine, really. Jen liked Tony, and fancied him too, but the place was getting a little crowded, and she'd been offered a job at another club in the city, much more lucrative for her.

She told us in her own way, by walking into my room one morning. Tony was staying over and we were naked, as was Jen. She stood there, her tight Brazilian winking at us cheerily, a massive tit poking at each of us.

'I'm leavin', innit,' she said, hands on hips. Then she noticed Tony's cock was swelling as he watched her. She looked up at me, as did Tony, and I shrugged and nodded. What the hell?

'Gotta say a proper goodbye,' I suggested. And so she stepped up on to the bed, straddled Tony and knelt down so that her soft pussy rested on his chin. He began lapping at her while I sat up, kissed her other lips and traced lazy circles around her nipples with my fingertips. After a while, she shifted down so that she could impale herself on Tony's cock and began to ride him enthusiastically, groaning deeply, eyes half closed. I stroked my tongue across her rosy nipples, my finger against her clitoris.

I felt fine about sharing Tony with Jen, or sharing Jen with Tony for that matter. I loved them both, in different ways. I don't really like the idea of threesomes with strangers, but this felt right. Especially as we knew Jen was leaving so there couldn't be any awkward moments at the coffee machine the next day.

It felt even more right when Jen buried her head between my thighs. Her face was so smooth compared to Tony's stubbled chin which was rubbing against my cheek as he kissed me from the side and stroked my tits. Then Jen moved up my body, pushing Tony aside and kissed me on the lips. I could taste myself on her mouth, which was a bit weird, but also incredibly sexy. She flipped me around so I was on top, on my haunches and I soon felt Tony's cock slide into me from behind. He rode me to orgasm as Jen and I kissed passionately.

Then she got up, leaving us exhausted but happy, and left.

With Jen gone, Tony asked me if I'd like to move in with him. The flat was convenient, it was just over the club of course, but he'd been arranging to buy a huge house near the river, and he wanted me there. He looked so nervous asking, like he was some 17-year-old schoolboy asking his girlfriend out on a date, rather than the head of an East End crime family. The crew was doing very well since Tony had taken over, and the size of the house was testament to that. I didn't have many belongings, only one really important item. So it wasn't too big a job moving. I'd only ever lived in poky flats or terraces, and it took me a long time to adjust to having so much space. Imagine rooms you don't use, don't need! My daughter could have her own room, maybe a play-room too? Maybe we could fill the other rooms in time . . . but I was getting ahead of myself. Too many corners with too many things around them in this world to start thinking like that.

We were there together for nearly a year and I was entirely content. I could play the wife, but I also had the club to run, to keep me busy, and my brain working. Also Tony had asked me to keep an eye on some other businesses of his. He needed someone legit, he'd said, to look after the legit sides of the business. He kept them clean, or as clean as a lap-dancing club, a casino and a porn shop could be. There was never any suggestion of money-laundering. Tony was too smart for that.

Which was why I was surprised when he came home one day and told me to pack a bag.

'What?' I said, standing there all big-eyed like one of those Easter Island statues.

'We have to leave the country,' he said, rummaging through drawers and shoving papers into the fire.

'Why?' I asked, stupidly. He just looked at me. For as much as I loved him, Tony was still a hard man. It was, in part, why I found him so irresistible. There were some things you don't ask an East End gangster.

'Come on!' he said. 'We ain't got much time. There's a boat waiting to take us to France.'

'I can't leave,' I said. We were standing in the bedroom, with its glorious view out over the Thames. I didn't care about the house. There was another reason I couldn't go. A small but important one.

He stopped what he was doing, his back to me. 'Well I have to go, Jacks. There's no way around that,' he said quietly. 'And if you want to be with me, then you'll need to pack a bag and get moving.'

I fought back the tears. 'I do want to be with you, Tony. But I can't come with you.'

Still, he didn't turn around. 'Why not?' he asked, though he must have known the answer.

I grabbed the handle of the door immediately behind me and opened it, revealing my daughter's bedroom, with a My Little Pony bedspread and a tiny hump under it topped with a mass of red curls. The soft glow of a pink night light illuminated the cherubic face of my little girl, now five years old.

'I can't go with you because of her, Tony. You know that. I told you four years ago you wouldn't be interested in a girl like me.'

'When I did find out it made no difference,' he said, taking off his shoes and softly stepping into the nursery to gaze at my child. Tony loved her as if she were his own, I knew that. He'd never seemed to mind. He'd never judged me. He understood that I'd had to sacrifice so much for her and that she was everything to me. She was the real reason I never managed to get back into ballet. She took up so much of my time. But I didn't mind. She was my world, and Tony knew it.

'I can't let her lead the life of a runaway gangster,' I said. 'She's starting school in a few months. I want her to have a normal life. I want her to have the opportunities I couldn't have, and those I threw away.'

He nodded. Tony was no fool. He knew I loved him, but also that he'd always be second to another. To my Tania.

'You didn't throw anything away, Jacks,' he said softly. 'I think you always made the right decisions really. And

327

if that means you're looked down on by the rest of 'em, then it's them that are wrong.'

'Stop being so lovely,' I sniffled. 'You're not making this easier.'

'I'm keeping the legit businesses running,' Tony said. 'I'll transfer them all into your name. Hold on to the profits for me, you can keep half. If I haven't come back in ten years, you can have all of it.'

I nodded. We both knew it wasn't for me, but for the little girl in the bed. I watched her as she slept, so deeply, so contentedly. Now the tears were coming in earnest and I couldn't stop them. We stepped out of the room and closed the door. 'I'll need to sell the house though,' he said apologetically.

'I don't care about the fucking house!' I shouted.

He just held me. I was shaking, sobbing. This was so unfair. Why, when every time life seemed perfect, did things like this happen to me? I looked up at him through streaming eyes. 'How long have you got?' I asked.

He smiled wryly, reading my mind. 'Just enough time,' he replied. We kissed, urgently. My hand went to his flies and I reached in, extracting his stiffening cock. I fell to my knees and inspected it for what would probably be the last time. I planted a goodbye kiss on the end, causing him to flinch and laugh. Then I opened my mouth and took his entire length inside, feeling the tip twitch against the back of my throat. He grunted in pleasure as I mouthed him gently. Then he pulled out and pushed me to the floor – we didn't have time for foreplay. His rough hands tore my flimsy lace knickers aside and he lifted my legs to indicate what he wanted me to do.

He liked it when I put my ankles behind my ears. Even after childbirth I was still pretty supple. He hoisted himself up and thrust himself inside me roughly. I could see naked lust and desperation in his eyes as well as something else. Fear? He grabbed my breasts and squeezed them hard. He was a strong man and tonight he was almost frenzied in his love-making, as if he were trying to make this one last time resonate within me forever.

I didn't want to know what Tony was running from, but it must have been serious. As always the danger of being close to this man served to heighten my passion and I met his plunging pelvis with counter-thrusts of my own, clawing at his back to get more of him inside me. We came simultaneously, he felt so big as he fired into me that I felt I was splitting in two.

He left me lying on the carpet, sobbing gently, as he collected his things and departed. I staggered to the window and watched the boat pull away from the public dock down below. He didn't turn to look back, and it was then that I knew for certain I'd never see my Tony again.

And that's pretty much it. The end of my story. I ran the businesses well. I moved my little girl into a comfortable flat of our own, she started school and turned out to be bright as a button. The filth came around a few times, looking for information. The taxman came sniffing around too, trying to find a way to take the businesses. But it was all clean. All legit, as Tony would have said.

My life was settled, if lonely. I later heard Tony was running a new crew in Spain, but I never heard directly from him, so I took that as meaning I was better off not trying to contact him, though I was tempted a few times. Sometimes I think that now my girl's left home and is busy making her own way I could try and find him again. But I can't stand the idea of finding him married to someone else, with his own kids. And I'm not the pert little ballerina he left behind, I'd always have felt he was comparing me to the girl I used to be. If we'd grown older together, it wouldn't have been so bad. No, once he stepped on to that boat, it was over, and we both knew it.

Chapter Thirty-Two

Two days later I was still reeling from the revelation that Tania was Jackie's daughter. My mother always used to tell me, 'Geri, what goes around comes around.' I usually dismissed such trite little sayings but after all that had happened in the past few days, I thought maybe I should have listened to her.

Finding out was a shock, but it all seemed to make sense now. Tania had undoubtedly inherited her mother's self-assured sexuality and feistiness – until Luke Cotterill knocked her confidence, that is.

She had reported him to HR, as promised, but they were waiting for me to decide whether to corroborate her statement before taking it any further. My fear was that if the case ended up at a tribunal, the company's solicitors would make mincemeat of her.

She wasn't happy about this, understandably so, and the atmosphere between us had become tense. I kept trying to talk her round.

'Tania – and I'm not being overdramatic here – imagine you're in court on a rape charge. There are no witnesses, and the defence dredge up your past as a lap

331

dancer. Do you honestly think the rapist will be convicted?'

'That's why I want you to witness my statement, Geri – surely you can see that if you back me up then my case would be so much stronger?'

'I wish you'd waited,' I said, 'gathered more evidence. My involvement would be wasted if you had already been torn to shreds by expensive lawyers, Tania. Don't you see? Luke will have briefed them that he helped you get the job in the first place.'

'But he's behaved appallingly and you know it,' she said, her voice cracking again. 'Surely any tribunal would see that.'

'Not necessarily. Imagine going through all that grief and knowing Luke would be crowing about how he screwed you over after you'd left the company.'

She went very quiet after that so I carried on forcing the point home.

'All I'm saying is that Sloane Brothers is a powerful company. If you want to take them on you risk ruining your career in the City before it's even begun. I know you've been wronged – and so have I – but you won't necessarily get the justice you seek in this way.'

'So what do you suggest I do?' she said, pacing around my office. 'Forget it completely and carry on as if nothing has happened?'

'No, of course not. I have another plan. It's a high-risk strategy but if I can pull it off we'll both get what we want.'

'And if you don't?'

'Then we go down the official path. It will still be open to us.'

I emphasised the 'us' so that Tania realised she wasn't on her own in all of this. She sat down opposite me and looked at me with victim eyes.

'You're a brilliant investment banker, Geri. But this is different; this is personal.'

'Please, Tania, have faith in me.'

She looked hesitant, wounded even. If she behaved like this at a tribunal she'd have no chance.

Finally, Tania agreed to give me a copy of her submission to HR including every recorded incident of Luke's sexist behaviour. Added to my own notes, it was a damning indictment.

The unknown quantity in all this was Daryll.

An hour later, I smoothed down my pencil skirt and stood up from my desk, I put on my Fifties-style peplum jacket and made my way to Daryll's office armed with my evidence. Luke was already *in situ*, sitting in a chair, his back to me. He didn't even bother to turn around. I wafted in on a wave of The One by D&G which mingled with Daryll's Joop! Pour Homme.

'Geraldine, good to see you,' he said, all bespoke suit and unruffled charm. 'Please, sit down and join us and help yourself to a tea or coffee.'

Luke scowled across at me – there was a look in his eyes I hadn't seen before – pure malice. My hands were shaking.

'Thanks, Daryll,' I said, handing over my report and reaching for a porcelain cup to pour myself a cup of strong coffee.

'No need. No need,' he said, taking the report and thumping it down on the table.

My heart plummeted.

'I've asked you both here today to inform you that, most regretfully, the deal we have been referring to as Project X is off.'

We both sat up at that.

'I'm afraid there has been a leak within this company of sensitive information pertaining to the client. And unfortunately that leak must have sprung from within our group of three.'

I jumped straight in with my defence.

'Well, Daryll, it couldn't have been me because you know very well I was not privy to the identity of the client.'

'Indeed, Geraldine, that is the case,' he said, like a presiding judge.

Luke's reaction was swift and retaliatory.

'Oh that's sweet, isn't it?' he said, turning on Daryll. 'If you were so worried that your precious deal would be blown, why the hell did you tell me the name of the client after our game of squash last week?'

Daryll's brow furrowed but somehow he maintained his dignified reserve.

'Luke, my dear boy, you are well aware that information exchanged in the locker room is confidential and must of course go no further.'

'You can't get out of it that easily, Daryll, my old chap,' sneered Luke. 'If I'm in trouble over this then so are you. If you make anything more of this I'll drag you down with me.'

I didn't know where to put myself after Luke's outburst. A look passed over Daryll's face that I'd never seen before – one of shame and guilt mixed with suppressed fury.

'I am not dignifying that comment with a response, Mr Cotterill.'

When he had composed himself again, he ignored Luke and turned to me.

'So you see, Miss Carson, I owe you an apology that all your hard work will have come to naught. Through no fault of your own.'

'Oh I wouldn't say it was an entire waste of my time. Perhaps you should read my report first.'

Even Luke bothered to look up at that, forewarned by the raised note in my voice.

There were a few moments of uncomfortable silence as Daryll browsed through my papers.

'Well, Geraldine, this is certainly not the report I was expecting from you, but it seems you have been very diligent in compiling it. So Luke, what do you have to say to the accusation of sexual harassment by not one – but two – women in the office?'

And suddenly Luke was up and on his feet; for the first time sensing he was on shaky ground.

'Whatever she's said about me it's an exaggeration. Come on, Daryll, the girls should be prepared to put up with a bit of banter.'

'Banter, Mr Cotterill? Do you consider calling Miss Peck, and I quote, "a sly little slapper", an acceptable way to address a young lady?'

'Well, I don't know if I used those exact words . . .'

'I can assure you he did, Daryll,' I interjected. 'I witnessed the incident, which culminated in Mr

Cotterill thumping his fist menacingly on Miss Peck's desk.'

I could see Luke was on the ropes now, if not quite out for the count.

'Thank you, Geraldine, for bringing this information to my attention and for considering the unfortunate impact it may have had on Sloane Brothers' impeccable reputation.'

He turned slowly towards Luke, who was looking more like a chastised schoolboy by the minute.

'My dear boy, I'm most awfully sorry about this but I'm afraid I have no option but to ask for your resignation.'

Luke's face turned puce. 'You what? How dare you, you stupid old goat. I've had enough of you and your old school tie anyway. You can stuff your job – I can walk into a better one tomorrow.'

'Well in that case, Mr Cotterill, I suggest you leave the building immediately. Sloane Brothers will no longer be requiring your services. Geraldine, would you show your former colleague the door?'

Luke's eyes flitted from Daryll and rested on me for several seconds.

'Fuck the both of you,' he said, then stormed out of the door.

Daryll walked casually around from behind his desk and closed the door.

'Take a seat, Geraldine.'

I sat down, while Daryll proceeded to march up and down the room, hands clasped behind his back.

'Of course this means I have lost one of my top people,

but fortunately I still have you, Geraldine. As a gesture of goodwill I would like to offer you a promotion and pay increase to reflect the loyalty you have shown to Sloane Brothers. I trust, then, that this will draw a line under all matters discussed in this office today.'

I shifted forward in my chair and looked him straight in the eye. This looked like the best apology I was going to get.

'I accept your gesture, Daryll, and you can rest assured that the dossier will not see the light of day again. However, if I am to "forget" about the leak as well, I think it only fair that you also give a pay rise to my assistant Tania.' He stroked his chin but didn't interrupt. 'I would also imagine that a fair-minded man such as you would also like to set an example to the rest of the company by stamping down on any incidents of misogyny and male chauvinism in the future.'

He sat down in the chair Luke had recently vacated, removing the barrier between us.

'You drive a hard bargain, Miss Carson,' he said, with more than a hint of pride.

'Yes, Mr Sidebottom, I do – and that's why you need me.'

'Indeed, Geraldine. I think Sloane Brothers could do with more capable young women such as you. Perhaps you could assist in that process.'

'I would be more than happy to do so,' I said, taking my chance to push him all the way. 'Together we can work towards establishing a much more intuitive and emotionally intelligent workplace. No more locker-room deals, eh Daryll?'

I stood up feeling ten feet tall and floated back to my office on a cushion of air.

'Tania,' I said, with a straight face.

'What? What happened, Geri?'

I paused for dramatic effect, just like Suzy would have done, before putting Tania out of her misery.

'We won . . .'

I waited for Tania to stop dancing up and down on the spot, before suggesting we go out to lunch to celebrate.

'There's something you don't know yet,' I said. 'A little confession I want to share with you.'

Chapter Thirty-Three

I left work early and arrived at the Pearl with the sun still bright in the sky. I wanted to tender my resignation to Declan before the evening buzz began. The Pearl looked a little lacklustre in the sunlight, the once sparkling façade now dulled from years of London pollution. The iridescent Pearl, now more of a smoky grey. The dead neon tubes. The lingering smell of urine.

I found Declan in his office flipping on the dozens of security monitors. Black and white images flashed as the cameras cycled through surveying every inch of the Pearl. Each screen revealed empty rooms, gaping cavities waiting to be filled: the dingy hallways more in shadow than light; the lapdancing rooms with their plush furnishings; the bare stage with its three poles looking somehow sad and lonely.

'What are you doing here so early?' Declan said when he finally saw me hovering. He swivelled in his desk chair to face me.

'Had a little unfinished business,' I said, sauntered over and sat on his lap.

'Don't start,' he said, playfully shoving me off.

I pulled an envelope from my handbag and handed it to him.

'What's this? A little bonus,' he said in his charming Irish lilt and stared at the envelope.

'Declan, I'm resigning.' I'd kept it nice and formal with a splash of politeness – it's been a pleasure, blah, blah, blah, thanks for the opportunity and so on – but no forwarding address or contact information.

'Oh,' he said.

'I'm sorry. I don't want to leave you shorthanded but . . .'

'You will,' he said. 'Did Ginger find another place to dance?'

'No, Ginger is retiring her red wig and any outfit with Velcro.'

He laughed. Maybe I could pretend that we'd met at happy hour at a Canary Wharf bar over two-for-one shots or that he was the older brother of a friend. He was that unique blend of muscle and style that didn't come around very often. We had unfinished business.

'Can you finish the weekend?' he asked, all business again.

'If it's OK, I'd like for tonight to be my last,' I said. 'I need a clean break. It's too confusing switching between my two personas. I was beginning to forget who was who.'

'So,' he paused, standing up and walking towards me, 'who are you? Geri or Ginger?'

'I think I discovered I'm a little of both.' I cupped his face in my hands and kissed him.

He pulled away. 'That must be confusing for you.'

'Not anymore.' I leaned in and kissed him again.

Breathing heavily, we pulled apart each understanding now wasn't the time.

'Can we meet later?' Declan asked, stroking the curve of my jaw.

'I wouldn't miss it,' I said, spinning on my heels and heading out.

The dressing room was alive with activity when I walked in. Suzy was already dressed in a dominatrix costume. She gently slapped me on the arse with her riding crop as I passed. 'What'll it be tonight, Ginger?'

'I think I'll get back to basics,' I said. Suzy rummaged around in the hanging rack and handed me my pull-away business suit.

'Give 'em their office fantasy, huh? How many of 'em you reckon ever really fuck their secretaries?' Suzy plopped on a nearby chair.

'More than you think,' I said.

'But I don't recommend it.' That was Tania. It took me a second to recognise her voice in this setting. I turned to see her and Jackie standing in the doorway.

'I hear you've met my daughter,' Jackie said. 'Small world.'

I nodded.

Jackie leaned in and whispered, 'Thanks for what you did for Tania, sticking up for her. Taking her with you. I owe you one.'

'I think we're even, Jackie,' I said.

'You watch out for my little girl,' Jackie said, giving Tania's cheeks a pinch.

'Oh, I think Tania can look out for herself.' I stripped off my business suit.

'God, Mum, you're embarrassing me. She's my boss after all.' Tania sat down next to Suzy. I'd always dreaded anyone from my day-job finding out about the Pearl, and Ginger, but I knew I could trust Tania.

Jackie helped me into my costume. I slipped on my wig. Transformation complete. After everything that had happened in the last week, it felt strange to be Ginger again.

I'm not sure how long Irena was there before we noticed her.

'Hello,' she said and waved. Her cheeks were rosy and her eyes were bright, no longer dulled by drugs, drink or Viktor's advances. Rumour had it that Declan paid Viktor a visit in the wee morning hours. He'd not only fired him but explained that no other lapdancing club in the city would touch him. He delivered another message about what it means to hurt another human being and explained what would happen if he ever messed with any of his girls again.

'Should you be here so soon?' I asked, ushering Irena into the room.

'I fine. No worries.' She smiled the same smile I remembered from our first meeting. Somehow she was hopeful again. I'd significantly underestimated this girl's strength. We all had.

'I dance tonight?' she asked Jackie.

'If you like, or you could also just work the floor if you'd rather.'

'No, I want to dance. I dance first,' she declared.

342

We all fussed over her. Jackie picked out the most glamorous gown she could find – black satin with a halter that dipped low in the front and back. Tania brushed and styled her blonde hair and applied make-up. Suzy gave her a few tips. 'Try something slow and elegant tonight.' She spoke too loudly and too slowly but at least she was trying. 'You know, old school. Don't flip around the stage or swing on the pole. Tease them.'

Irena nodded.

When she was ready, we all went to the front of the house to lend a little moral support. I joined Jackie at the bar. She ordered me a glass of pink champagne. I sipped the bubbly and watched Irena strut on stage. The music started and Irena tried to follow Suzy's advice. At first Irena's movement was bumpy as she found the music's rhythm. Irena searched the crowd. I knew who she was looking for. My heart broke a little. She looked from one man to another. Then she froze.

I followed her gaze. A young man with floppy brown fringe had walked into the room. He looked like a first-timer, hands in his pockets, dressed like he was out for Sunday lunch with his in-laws. They stared at each other for a long moment.

'It *can't* be!' said Jackie, then turned to me. 'Can it? Not Simon?'

I grinned. 'It most certainly is.'

Irena broke away from the pole and leapt off the edge of the stage. The eyes of the room followed her as the threw herself into the man's arms. Tears streamed down her face and, as he lifted up her head, I could see her lips moving. I realised he was crying too.

Jackie nudged me again. 'Why don't you take over?'

I nodded. Irena and Simon had moved to a cushioned seating area. I definitely felt like dancing. 'If you'll change this Godawful music. I need something with a little more edge.'

'You got it.' And she was off.

I made my way to the stage. As I passed Irena, she turned to me and said, 'This is Simon. He came for me.'

'I know.' I smiled.

All it had taken was a few phone calls and a little electronic handiwork from a man Suzy was friendly with at the Pearl. A free lap dance later and he had agreed to run a credit check on Simon Robinson. He gave me Simon's last known addresses. Simon had dropped out of school. His parents gave me his email address. 'Silly boy,' his mother said, 'went chasing after some Polish girl he'd met on holiday. I told him he was crazy.' I'd sent him a message and a plane ticket and prayed he'd come.

I climbed on the stage. 'The Time of My Life' started over the speakers and I lost myself one last time in the music, the movement and the rapt attention of an all-male audience. I ripped away the business suit and soaked in their admiration. I stood for a moment, naked and proud in the flashing lights and the clinking glasses. I would miss this feeling, a brand of power I'd never have again no matter how high I climbed in the corporate world. But I had learned a lot. I admit the Pearl was a strange place for an education. But maybe I had to be stripped bare to learn a few important life lessons about business, friendship, and, believe it or not, love.

Epilogue

'I knew the moment I saw you that somehow, sometime, we'd end up like this,' Declan asserted as I pinned him up against the wall in the entry hall to his apartment.

'Even though you offered me a job in your club?' I asked.

'I wanted to see how you'd shape up,' was his saucy reply.

'More than you wanted *me*?' I teased. Declan smiled, but didn't answer.

'Well, I don't work at your club anymore.' My voice was low and I stepped closer to him again, sliding my hands up his chest.

'And it's not my club anymore,' Declan said, tugging me against him and resting his chin on my head.

I pulled back. 'What?'

'I've sold the Pearl,' he said quietly.

'Really? Why?' I pulled back to look at him.

'I felt it was time to move on to other things, and I got a really good offer. You'll never guess from whom.'

'Who, then?' I asked, humouring him.

'Believe it or not, he's the owner of a very successful

chain of clubs – and he has a *very* distinctive hairstyle. He was so impressed with mine he made me an offer. But don't worry,' he continued, 'all our friends will be in good hands. I wouldn't have it any other way.'

'I know that, Declan, I'm just really surprised. What about Jackie?'

'She's helped me out in the business a lot so I set her up with a nice retirement package.'

'That's very kind of you.'

'Not at all. You must know as well as anyone else what she's done. She was more than happy to call it quits. Like me, she's been ready for a change.'

'So what will you do?'

Declan smiled, the same devastating grin that had charmed me when I'd gone into the club to pick up my purse and come out with a new life. 'I'd rather not say. No, don't pout,' he said when I pulled away to protest. 'Call me superstitious, but I'd like to keep it to myself until I'm sure it will work out.'

'When will you be sure?'

'Within the next couple of weeks. Then, you'll be the first to know.' I smiled at the implications of that, as Declan drew a finger down my nose, then traced the outlines of my lip before I caught his finger in my mouth. This wasn't a one-night thing, for either of us.

'Good.' I bit down on his finger, and he chuckled before withdrawing it.

'I always took you for a wild one.' I liked that.

'Kiss me, handsome,' I demanded.

'As you wish.' But his actions belied his subservient words as he pulled me roughly against him, one hand fisted in my hair, and brought his mouth to mine. All our previous passion immediately rekindled, as though it had been lying dormant, waiting for an opportunity to resurface.

His kiss was urgent, all tongue and teeth, and I tried desperately to keep up.

'I want you,' he whispered huskily, his voice hot and damp in my ear as his hands slid down my back to my ass, cupping and squeezing and lifting until I was pressed against his erection. I moaned and let my head fall back. Declan moved his mouth to my neck. 'Oh my God, you're so sexy,' he murmured as his hands moved back to my chest, his fingers fumbling as he undid the buttons of my blouse, stopping to grope my breasts between each one, as though he could hardly stand to deny himself the contact in order to get my clothes off.

He wanted to be in control, but it pleased me to see he wasn't. I arched against his hands, encouraging him.

'I want you,' he said again.

'Then take me. You know I want you to . . .'

In spite of all the thrills I got from being in control, from knowing what I could do to men . . . this was different. Declan was different. It was just as thrilling to know that he could do this to me; that I hadn't lost the ability to be completely seduced, reduced to raw, throbbing need. Or rather – that I had gained it. I'd never felt so comfortable before. I knew I could let him take me, let him do whatever he wanted and I would enjoy it, knowing he would enjoy it, too.

'However you want me,' I whispered and he pulled my shirt down my arms. 'I'm yours however you want me.'

I gasped as he swept me up in his arms, leaving my shirt a crumpled pile on the floor. I couldn't remember anyone ever performing such a romantic gesture. 'What a generous offer, *Ginger*,' he said as he carried me towards the bedroom.

'Not Ginger,' I said earnestly, burying my face in his neck to inhale his musky scent. 'Geri. I don't want to be Ginger anymore.' I gasped again when he tossed me on the bed, the feeling of gravity and the buoyant softness momentarily taking my breath away. With a soft grunt Declan landed on me, his hard body pressing me into the bed.

'Oh, really?' His voice was curious as his hand trailed up my midriff to squeeze my breast through my bra.

'Yes, oh God, Declan, that feels amazing.' I arched into his hand, silently urging him for more. 'It was fun for a while, but I think I prefer to be Geri.'

'And what does Geri do that Ginger can't?' asked Declan, both hands on me now, reaching behind to unclasp my bra.

'This,' I said, meeting his eyes. 'Ginger always had to be in control. I never knew how much I could enjoy it until I became her. But now, I know how much I can enjoy losing control. With you in charge.'

Declan stepped back from the bed. His eyes were dark, his hair mussed, his shirt dishevelled from our embraces, his erection bulging in his trousers. 'I'm in charge?'

'I'll do whatever you say,' I whimpered, need burning in my centre.

'I want to blindfold you.'

'Whatever you want, Declan. I want to do whatever you want.'

I lay back on the bed, my hands clenching the covers as I restlessly watched him opening a dresser drawer and taking out a silk scarf. He walked back to me, that sexy smile on his face, and leaned over. My vision disappeared. I lifted my head to allow him to tie the scarf.

'Is this all right?' he whispered.

'I'm yours,' was my answer.

I clenched my hands again as I heard the whisper of cloth sliding against skin. Declan taking off his shirt? His hands slid up my waist again and he peeled my bra off. I was amazed at how much more I could *feel* without my sight. My skin jumped at Declan's touch, not knowing where it was going next. The feeling was incredibly erotic.

More whispers of movements, and his mouth, wet and warm, pressed against the underside of my breast. He traced it with his tongue, then dragged his tongue up towards my nipple, lightly circling in, flicking it, then taking it into his mouth and suckling. I fisted my hand in his hair, encouraging him. It was so different without my sight – all I could do was *feel*.

Suddenly he pulled away. His hands traced down my arms and he cradled my hands in his, tugging gently. 'Come here, Geri.' I followed the direction of his arms, into darkness but knowing precisely where he was standing, and found myself pulled against him. I ran my hands down the hard, smooth muscles of his bare chest. Amazingly, I was more aware of his presence than ever. I could hear his breath, feel him beneath my fingers, and *sense* him all around me. I trailed one hand up to his chin and then traced the outline of his lips with my thumb. I leaned up to press my lips against him, lightly at first, but lingering. I flicked my tongue against his lips and he parted them in invitation. I kissed him slowly and he returned the kiss, drawing me in deeper, while his hands moved down my back to my ass.

Then he drew out of the kiss and, wordlessly, with one hand on my shoulder, stopped me. He was still in charge. Missing the feel of him on my lips, I could only guess where he was in the darkness before me, but his hands were tracing the skin above my waistband.

My own breath sounded hard in my ears. His touch was still so light and I longed for something more, something harder and faster.

'Declan, please . . .'

'Not yet, Geri . . . not yet. You said I was in charge. I've wanted this for so long.' His voice was next to my ear. 'I can wait a little longer to make it right.' With that, he hooked his fingers under my waistband to unfasten my trousers. A small tug had them falling to the floor. His hands back on mine, Declan pulled me forward, guiding me out of them.

Standing with bare legs but still wearing my heels, I felt like Ginger again. Declan must have thought the same thing, because he chuckled and said, 'That won't do at all.'

I felt as much as heard him kneel before me, his fingertips tracing ever so lightly down my legs to my ankles. He unfastened one strap, and I lifted my foot so he could remove the shoe. I heard it land somewhere on the other side of the room.

'Oh! Be careful, Declan. Those are Prada.' He chuckled again, a deep sound that reverberated through my body.

'Clearly I am not distracting you well enough.' He moved to the other shoe, lifting my foot higher to remove it and placing it, I was relieved to hear, more gently on the floor. Then he pressed his lips to my ankle.

I moaned.

His lips travelled up my calf, then his tongue flicked behind my knee.

'You taste good,' Declan whispered, so softly and so far away I could barely make out his words. 'But I wonder . . .' he pressed a kiss against the inside of my thigh . . . 'if I can find somewhere that tastes even better.' I moaned again as he dragged his tongue up my thigh.

'Do you think I can?' I nodded, although I wasn't sure he would be able to see me, with his head nestled between my thighs. I was suddenly unable to speak.

With one hand I leaned against the bed post for support, and with the other I gripped his head, struggling not to drag him exactly where I wanted that hot, sexy mouth of his. Declan was still in control, I tried to remind myself, but *I* was about to lose control altogether. And, though I knew what I wanted him to do, I had no idea what he was about to next.

I exhaled a sharp, short pant when he traced the very top of my leg, where it met my centre, with his tongue. He made a noise, which I felt more than heard, and it was all I could do not to scream. Then he moved again, his tongue tracing my slit through the satin of my underwear.

'Uhh.' My voice was rough to my own ear and I felt it with my entire body when Declan pulled away.

'Do you like that, then?' I nodded again, quivering

351

with anticipation and need. He hooked two fingers under the strap of my thong as he had done with my trousers earlier, running them between the satin and my skin, and gently tugging, until it also fell at my ankles. With his hands to guide me I stepped out of them.

'Declan,' I whispered, reaching out my arms to him, afraid I would collapse entirely without his support. He stood to embrace me fully, and I welcomed the feel of his entire body pressed to mine, so much more than just his hands, just his lips had been – as fabulous as that had felt.

I tilted my head up blindly and he answered my silent plea for a kiss. I tasted the faint trace of myself in his mouth. I could feel his erection straining against his trousers and I leaned back, slinging my leg over his hip so I could press myself against him. Declan moaned into my mouth.

I couldn't remember the last time I had felt so turned on. I wanted him inside me, I wanted it now, and I ached, not knowing when he would finally plunge deep into me, knowing he was so calm and in control when I was ready to melt inside . . . I would have screamed in frustration if it hadn't felt so damn good.

'How does it feel?' Declan whispered roughly, his hands on my bare ass, grinding against me, letting me know just how badly he wanted to be inside me.

I smiled, relieved that I wasn't alone in my arousal. I let the smile play on my lips, knowing Declan's eyes were on them as well as if I could see them. 'Do you want to know?'

'Yes,' he whispered, his voice now straining and I felt

him pull back a little to struggle against his trousers. 'Tell me,' he practically begged.

'No,' I said sharply. He froze.

'I want to show you.'

His breathing was heavy, I could hear it as well as feel his chest, moving up and down as I put my hands on him, sliding down until I reached his trousers. He hadn't done a very good job at taking them off.

'Let me help you with these,' I purred, pulling the fly further apart and pushing them down his hips, freeing his erection at last from the confines of his trousers and letting them drop.

'I thought I was in charge,' Declan grunted, his voice rough with desire.

'It's more fun this way, don't you think?' I asked. 'We can take turns. Now it's my turn to drive you crazy.' I didn't tell him that I couldn't take any more of his commands – or I'd explode. But I probably didn't have to; he knew it already.

He stepped out of the trousers and I felt the fabric of his boxers, letting my fingers trace his muscular thighs and skin, over so lightly, over his member, smiling at his sharp intake of breath. 'What do you think?' I asked playfully. 'Should I take these off now, or should I wait?'

'Wait for what?'

'Do you have another scarf, Declan?' I slid my arms around his shoulders, moving closer and pressing my breasts against his chest.

'You want to blindfold me, too?'

'Are you afraid, Declan? Don't be. It feels so wonderful.'

'I'm not afraid, no.' I couldn't read his voice and,

not able to see his expression, I was lost to what he was thinking – but his erection still pressed hard against me.

'I want to give you everything you've given me.'

His hands rested on my hips, pressing gently. 'Sit down, Geri.' I did as he asked. I heard him move towards the dresser again, open the drawer, and close it. Then I felt him next to me, felt the soft silk brushing against my skin as he trailed the scarf over me.

I couldn't believe he would let me do this. No other man I'd ever known – no City man, that's for sure – would have been comfortable enough to agree to it. But Declan was different.

'Give me your hand, Geri.' I held out one hand before me, touching the other to his arm. I closed my palm over the silk of the scarf when he placed it in my hand and felt my way up to his face to tie the scarf around his eyes, as he had done to me. He was smiling, I discovered as my fingers played over his lips.

'Stand up,' I said, once I was sure the knot was secure.

He did as I asked and I tugged him forward, between my legs, and placed my hands on the waistband of his boxers. I leaned forward to kiss his navel, making sure to press my breasts against his erection. 'You're such a big boy,' I purred. 'Are you ready for me?'

'Geri.' My name came out as a moan. I loved the sound of it.

Blindly, I pulled his boxers down. I felt his erection spring free and captured it in my hands, sliding them up and down, lightly at first and gradually increasing the pressure. I longed to see his face, but the sounds escaping from his mouth let me imagine the look of pleasure that he must have had.

He gasped loudly as I took his cock in my mouth, flicking my tongue and savouring the salty taste of pre-cum. 'Oh, God, Geri.' I moved my mouth as I had done my hands, amazed at how much more I noticed, deprived of my sight. The ache was growing stronger inside me, I shifted, trying to relieve the pressure building up in me. I gasped with relief when Declan tugged at my hair.

'Geri, now, I need—'

'Me too.' The sound of my own voice took me by surprise; it was so low and throaty.

I scrambled back on the bed, the smooth sheets sliding beneath me and I felt Declan on top of me. This – finally – 'Oh yes . . .'

I nearly jumped with surprise when I felt his tongue on my breast, which quickly subsided into pleasure as he suckled, the pulling sensation of pleasure echoing itself between my legs. Declan's thighs pressed against mine and I spread myself further.

'Touch me, please.'

Somehow his hand – I had lost track of them, it was too much – found its way to my centre, and he slid a finger, then two, inside me.

'Mmm,' I moaned, arching in rhythm.

'Oh, you're so wet.' His voice was in my ear now, as he slowly thrust his fingers and began tracing my clit with his thumb. I thought I might explode. I'd never been so close, so quickly. Then his hand pulled away. 'Oh, Christ, Geri, I want more but I can't wait.'

'It *is* more,' I cried as my hands groped down to grasp his ass, trying to pull him towards my centre. 'Declan, please,' I begged.

He let out a sound, a cross between a groan and a sigh, and his lips blindly sought mine, pressing clumsily against my jaw and my cheek before finding them.

I felt his erection pressing against me. 'Yes,' I hissed, arching to welcome him.

He filled me up, slowly, building the ache and fulfilling it at the same time. When he was all the way inside me I hooked my legs around his hips to keep him close, sliding my hands up and down his back, slick with sweat.

'Geri.'

I turned his head to kiss him. He began to move. I arched to meet each thrust and it was as though my entire body, not just my eyes, had gone blind. All I could do was feel, clinging to Declan desperately as he took me higher. I could tell by the ragged breath in my ear that he was close, too. Then I was beyond thinking. The muscles of my pelvis tightened and I strained, against him, with him, desperate to feel more.

Finally, finally, I felt myself begin to climax. My back arched off the bed, my muscles squeezed and I threw my head back to let out a silent scream as wave after wave of pleasure, the result of this incredible build-up, washed over me.

My body still tingling with aftershocks, I reached to my face and pulled off my blindfold in time to watch Declan cum, his mouth screwed up in pleasure as he thrust one last time, then sighed as he sank, replete, on to me. I wrapped my arms around him, reaching up to untie his blindfold.

'That was awesome,' he said, his eyes meeting mine, before he rested his head against my breast, listening to my heartbeat as it gradually slowed.

'I'd say you have some potential,' I said, patting Declan on his sweaty back as he lay, sprawled between my legs and on top of me.

'Potential?'

He looked miffed. I smiled innocently.

'Perhaps I can help you develop it,' I said, echoing the words we'd exchanged when we first met. Declan relaxed, smiling.

'I'd be delighted.'

Read on for an exclusive extract from
The Secret Diary of a Sex Addict

Chapter One

'Every now and then you should sleep with someone considerably less attractive than you,' Briony said breezily, flicking through a magazine.

Shelley looked up at her across their cluttered, back-to-back desks. 'Er . . . what?' She hadn't really been properly listening to her friend – who also happened to be her flatmate – twittering on, but sometimes Briony said stuff you just couldn't let by. 'Why?'

'You've got to give a little bit back,' Briony said, flicking some wayward blonde extensions back over her shoulder, this week's haircut being the exact polar opposite of last week's black bob. 'Y'know, make someone's day. Haven't you heard about that Random Acts of Kindness movement?'

'Yes, but that means buying someone a cup of coffee, or helping an old lady across the road,' Shelley pointed out. 'Not yanking your pants down at a Warhammer Convention and shouting "Get it here, mingers!"'

Briony was about to say something else but Shelley held up a hand.

'Not now, Brie,' she said.

'What's up with you?'

'I'm totally bricking it, that's what.'

'About the announcement?'

'Of course. How come you're so chilled?'

Briony shrugged. '*Que sera, sera.*'

Shelley bit her lip. The office was wired tighter than Jordan's bra. That morning the Chief Operating Officer of West End Magazines, their parent company, had sent an e-mail asking them to remain in the office for an important announcement abut the future of *Female Intuition*, the magazine Shelley had been working on for nearly four years.

Shelley tucked her unruly brown hair behind her ears and picked up a Styrofoam coffee cup, clutching it in two hands as though she feared it might escape. 'Do you think Kate's sick or something? She's been so quiet lately,' she said.

'Don't be a div, Shell,' Briony said, rolling her eyes. 'She ain't coming back.'

'*Isn't* coming back,' Shelley corrected automatically. She could never let a grammatical slip go by. She knew it was sad. She was convinced she'd end up alone, with a dozen cats, writing letters to the *Guardian* admonishing them for typos and punctuation clangers.

'She's been given her P45,' Briony said.

'You don't know that,' Shelley replied.

'So why is there a padlock on her office door?'

Shelley looked over at the glass office Kate had been in for two and a half decades. The office must have been cutting edge décor then, glass and steel everywhere, midnight-blue carpets, pastel vertical blinds, open-brick walls. *Female Intuition* had been the first London magazine to give computers to all its editors.

Now the décor looked shabby, many of the vertical blinds were lying horizontally amongst the mouse droppings on the faded carpet, and Shelley sometimes wondered if her computer were one of the original ones handed out, it was so antiquated.

Shelley sort of knew it must have been over, but didn't want it to be true. Kate Hurley had given Shelley her first job in journalism, straight out of Uni, or at least her first job writing for magazines, which is not necessarily the same thing. Kate had been editor here at *Female Intuition* for as long as anyone could remember and was legendary in the business.

'I need a drink, fancy anything from the kitchen?' Shelley asked.

'Ooh yes,' Briony replied. 'I have a splitting headache; get me a strong coffee would you?'

'Coffee's not good for headaches,' Shelley replied.

'Who says?'

'Everyone says. It's a diuretic, isn't it?'

'Don't give me any of that Scientology crap; get me a double-strength Ibuprofen and a strong coffee.'

Shelley wandered off to the manky little kitchen to get the drinks. She passed Freya Wormwood's desk on the way back and the Fashion and Lifestyle editor looked up, catching her eye. Though pretty, and with a figure to die for, Freya made the mistake of going with whatever hairstyle was currently in vogue, regardless of its suitability for her, unlike Briony, who wore a bewildering variety of haircuts, none of which were in fashion, but all of which seemed to suit her perfectly. Freya currently sported an enormous fringe which made her look a little like the Dulux dog.

'Not nervous are you, Shelley?' Freya asked in that sly, slightly sardonic voice she used with people she felt threatened by. Other women, to be specific. Shelley glanced at the myriad photos of her perfect boyfriend Harry on her desk, so many it looked a little like a shrine.

'No,' she replied, trying not to sound defensive and failing. 'What would I have to be nervous about?'

Freya looked away, but not before Shelley caught the beginnings of a smirk on her face. Freya was one of those women who claim moral superiority simply because they have a boyfriend when you don't. Not that anyone in the office had ever been allowed to meet the saintly Harry. Briony suspected he didn't exist and the photos in the frames had already been there when she bought them: *Harry bought me a divine new coat the other day; far too good for work, though. Harry's whipping me off to Bruges on the weekend; first class on the Eurostar. Harry's such a sensitive lover; unless I ask him to treat me roughly, that is!*

'Have you heard something?' Shelley asked, immediately regretting it. If there was something Freya loved even more than Harry, it was knowing something that other people didn't.

'I've heard a few things, Shelley,' she said. 'But I've been asked not to share them with anyone else for now.'

Shelley didn't believe a word of it. But she knew no matter what happened, Freya would sit and nod gently as though it was no surprise to her. Shelley stormed off, infuriated by Freya's smug attitude, and slumped down back at her desk. Briony arched an eyebrow.

'I wonder who's going to take over?' Shelley wondered out loud. 'They might fire us all, or close us down altogether.'

'Oh don't worry about that,' Briony said, still looking at the magazine, which Shelley couldn't help but notice was a rival publication with considerably higher circulation than *Female Intuition*. 'They'll just get a new editor in who'll make a big fuss about "new beginnings" and a "radical new focus" before changing the logo slightly, adjusting the font size and putting the handbags section on page 240 instead of page 170. That's all that will happen.'

'Really?' Shelley asked hopefully. 'No redundancies?'

'Nooooo,' Briony said, shaking her well-made-up head vigorously. 'Apart from firing a couple of columnists, maybe.'

'Briony!' Shelley squawked.

'What?'

'I'm a columnist!'

Briony paused. 'Oh, yes. So you are. Oh don't worry; I think there's at least two columnists more likely to go than you.'

'Who?' Shelley asked, coolly.

'Oh erm, Robin . . . and, um . . . um,' Briony cast her eyes around the open plan office desperately, 'erm, and Toni.'

'Toni left three months ago.'

'Really? Oh . . .'

'Never mind,' Shelley said, saving her from further

embarrassment. 'Maybe redundancy is exactly what I need. Sometimes one needs a kick up the bum to make one sort one's life out.'

'Oh does one?' Briony asked in her posh voice. 'What needs to change in your life then?'

Shelley thought it over. She was 25 and had only ever had one job, this one. She wasn't at all sure she was any good at being a columnist. How could she have anything important to say to women when she'd done nothing with her life? She'd postponed her gap year until she had some money, and had never got around to going now that she had. She'd never really had a proper long-term boyfriend, unless you counted Rob at Uni who she went out with for six months before sleeping with him, only to discover the next day that he'd been having a string of affairs, including a quick shag with her best friend in the toilet while Shelley was in the kitchen studying for her final exams.

She rarely went out and had no romantic interests, apart from a crush on the fit South African behind the bar at the Crown where they drank after work. In two years she'd ordered 57 bottles of Pinot Grigio from him but never plucked up the courage to ask him his name. She was sure she wouldn't be his type anyway. Antipodeans were used to wildcat lovers with bodies as supple as springboks, according to Briony's magazine. Shelley was as timid as a springbok and the only thing wild about her was her tousled, shoulder-length hair.

'You just need a good shag,' Briony said, interrupting her reverie. 'You need to be fucked till you fart.'

Shelley went bright red. 'Briony!' she hissed.

'You're hung-up on sex. You need to face your fears.'

'I don't have a hang-up about sex,' Shelley said primly.

'Sure,' Briony said. 'Have you ever thought about therapy?'

Shelley looked up at her friend sharply. 'Read my lips, Briony. I. Do. Not. Need. Therapy! We've had this before.'

'Mmm, touched a raw nerve I think,' Briony said, tight-lipped.

She would have gone on but was interrupted by the arrival of Sonia Bailey. The Chief Operating Officer came bustling in, exuding a no-nonsense, bottom-line kind of attitude. She was slight and had been blonde at one point, but was now apparently too busy to bother with fripperies like colour, or style.

Bailey was the sort of person, and there's one in every large organisation, who was never happier than when delivering really bad news, and Shelley's heart sank as she saw a glint of joy in the COO's eye. Cutting out 'dead wood' and hiving off unsuccessful parts of the business were what she excelled in, having little knowledge of the actual business of publishing magazines. Briony had claimed she got off on it and could only gain sexual satisfaction when she was firing people.

'Don't be disgusting,' Shelley had replied. That kind of crudity made her uncomfortable.

Bailey cleared her throat to get everyone's attention, which was unnecessary as everyone was waiting, heart in mouth, wondering how much redundancy pay they might get. Shelley had looked up the employment terms last week when the latest circulation figures had come through. 'One week's pay for every year I've worked here, plus one month's notice period, plus unused holiday . . .'

'Now everyone,' Bailey began, 'I have some bad news. Kate Hurley has taken early retirement with immediate effect. The board of West End Magazines were saddened to hear of this . . .'

Briony snorted but Bailey ignored her.

' . . . but we have accepted her decision. Kate's contribution to this magazine and to West End has been immense over the last 25 years and she will be sorely missed, but,' and at this point the glint in Bailey's eye took on a new, menacing appearance, 'it has been evident for some time that *Female Intuition* has been haemorrhaging readers and making a net loss for the Group which is deepening month on month, year on year.'

As she spoke, Shelley noticed Bailey's breath getting heavier until she was almost panting.

'From a height of nearly one million in 1986, the circulation has dropped to less than 70,000, and many of those are giveaways. People just don't know what the magazine is trying to do anymore. It has lost focus and the numbers don't add up.'

She took a deep breath, taking her time, cheeks slightly flushed.

'This magazine is no longer sustainable and the Group cannot support it.' Her eyes were nearly closed as she reached the climax of her speech. 'And so it has been decided that . . .' but at this point she paused and came back from the brink. When she opened her eyes, Shelley saw with interest that the glint was suddenly gone. Bailey looked disappointed. Deflated. This is the part of the speech she hadn't wanted to make.

'The magazine will be re-branded, with a radical new

focus.' Briony was stifling giggles as the staff stared at the COO, amazed. '*Female Intuition* will be given one last chance to re-invent itself.'

Bailey picked up a phone on the desk next to her, dialled and spoke. 'Could you come down now please?' she asked and returned the receiver. 'We're going to discuss the new direction of the magazine. I wish you all the best and know you can make this work.'

Bailey made a gesture with her hand.

'Was that a *fist pump*?' hissed Briony.

There followed a couple of minutes of awkward silence, then the door opened and in walked Aidan Carter. Shelley frowned. Aidan was the Marketing Director for the Group. *Only fair to consult Marketing on the new direction, I suppose.*

Not that she was disappointed. Aidan was easy on the eye and so, well . . . big. The way he carried himself made him seem even taller then he was, and he must have been 6' 3". Carter was notorious for his brash management style and forceful opinions and had apparently had several stand-up rows with other board members, at the conference table. He was the sort of man who, when he came storming into a room, eyes flashing, you both feared and secretly hoped he was coming for you.

Shelley watched as he walked over to Sonia, confident and long-limbed. Freya just *happened* to be in his way and simpered sweetly at him as she moved aside. Carter took the COO's proffered hand and clasped it in both of his.

Briony kicked Shelley under the desk, trying to get her eye, but Shelley ignored her. Briony had been convinced Aidan fancied Shelley ever since the Group Christmas party last year. She had tried to explain that just because someone dances with you, didn't mean he fancied you. 'He's just about the only decent prospect in a company made up of 80 per cent women and could have his pick of the ladies. He was only being polite in trying to dance with as many women as he could. He did the Macarena with Sonia Bailey for God's sake,' Shelley had pointed out.

'So why did he come back later to dance with you again?' Briony asked, knowingly. 'When *Careless Whisper* was on?'

Shelley had just blushed and got on with her work, not wanting to think about it.

Now Aidan stood tall, next to the tiny Bailey, who Shelley couldn't help noticing, sneaked a look at his crotch, to her at eye-level. She spoke again.

'Ladies . . . er and gentlemen,' peering over at the post-room boys, the only other males on the floor. 'You probably all know Aidan Carter, Group Marketing Director. Aidan has taken a keen interest in the fortunes of *Female Intuition* over the past few months, and is personally determined to turn this magazine around. I give you your new Editor-in-Chief, Aidan Carter.'

A set of gasps escaped around the room like timed pistons. Aidan had no experience as an editor, he was abrasive and demanding, he already had another job and worst of all . . .

He was a man.

'Thank you, Sonia,' Aidan began. He put a hand on one hip, which had the effect of brushing his suit jacket open and offering a glimpse of his chest muscles through an ever-so-slightly too tight shirt. Another chorus of plosive breaths went around the room, this time more appreciative.

'Firstly a couple of words about Kate Hurley,' Aidan began. 'A hero of mine. One of this country's finest journalists, and a pioneering feminist.'

Shelley blinked in surprise at this unexpected praise for the woman who had driven the magazine into the ground in the first place.

'She had a mind like a razor, a heart like a lion, and balls of steel. She will be missed.'

Though unsure about the third simile, Shelley found herself muttering 'hear, hear' along with everyone else.

'Do you know? My mother used to read this magazine,' Aidan continued, lifting the latest issue and waving it at the team aggressively. 'She loved it. This magazine helped her through some difficult times.' Freya nodded sympathetically and put her head to one side, blinking those doe eyes. Bailey nodded sagely.

Aidan walked over to the windows and everyone swivelled to follow. 'She read this magazine in hospital when she had breast cancer,' he continued, gazing meditatively out over North London. 'She read this magazine at home after my father left her. She read this magazine in the nursing home as she watched over her own mother dying.'

He turned back to face the group, hands at his sides, looking comfortable and relaxed, his face simultaneously full of loss and warmth. Every woman in the room wanted to cuddle him, and much more besides.

Shelley felt a bit funny. She squeezed her legs together and glanced over at Briony who was staring at Carter, mouth open. Freya looked like she was about to have an orgasm.

'Unfortunately my mother doesn't read this magazine anymore,' he said. 'Do you want to know why?'

Shrugs, and a few nods.

'She thinks it's too boring,' he said.

Grumbling and shaking of heads.

'Things have changed. My mother has changed. The world has changed. She wants more from her magazines these days. More stories about having fun and not so many about illness, more stories about love and not so many about heartbreak, more stories about life and less about death.'

'Fewer,' Shelley said automatically.

'What's that?' he said.

'*F-fewer* stories about death,' Shelley stammered. 'Not *less* stories about death.' Why had she said that? Was she about to get herself fired just as the magazine was being saved?

He stared at her hard, a strange look on his face, then he snapped out of his trance and walked off towards the window again, his square-jawed, brooding face shadowed before the May sunlight pouring in.

'My mother is tired of sickness, sadness and saying goodbye,' he continued. 'That was the past. People choose life these days. People choose . . . happiness . . . and people choose *sex*.'

And he spun for the finale.

'Ladies and gentlemen, let me introduce you to your

new magazine.' And with that he stepped over to an old ad board lying against the wall and flipped it to reveal a blown-up magazine cover.

The gasps this time were universal.

Briony had been wrong. The new editor wasn't just going to faff about with fonts and page orders. He'd changed everything, including the name.

The cover was an almost naked Mimi Corvair, the model recently dropped by Burberry when she was filmed having a coke-snorting threesome with the boyfriends of two other models. She had been dropped by virtually every magazine on the stands, except in their name and shame pages. The lads' mags still wanted her, but for what her agent considered the wrong reasons.

If Aidan wanted her on the cover it meant he was trying to make a mark. He was trying to kill *Female Intuition* and get the revamped mag back in the press. That was shocking enough.

But it was the new title which hit Shelley hardest.

In hot pink, and crowding the raunchy image beneath with huge letters was the new, bold title.

VIXEN.

Aidan paused for a moment, and then continued. 'I can't let this magazine dic, I owe it to West End, I owe it to you and I owe it to my mother.'

A mumble of agreement went around the room and this slowly built into a rousing torrent of appreciation which in turn led to applause. The room stood and thundered its approval. Even the post-room boys looked energized.

But Shelley reckoned she wasn't the only one who

was totally terrified. If sex was the new direction this magazine was taking, then she wasn't at all sure it was the right place for her. Sex wasn't really her thing. She'd only done it a few times, and if we were talking, y'know, proper sex, she'd only done it with two different men.

As they stood and clapped, she wasn't thinking about the future of the magazine, or the fresh opportunities she was being presented with. She was trying to remember if she'd even had any sex at all in the last year.

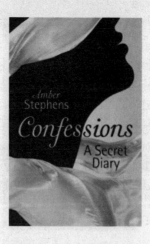

CONFESSIONS: A SECRET DIARY
AMBER STEPHENS

"My name is Shelley… and I'm a sex addict."

Shelley Matthews is married to her job. Which is just as well, as she hasn't had sex for over a year. But when her editor decides a re-vamp of the magazine is needed, Shelley is forced to go undercover – as a sex addict.

Attending therapy sessions, Shelley hears the intimate confessions of a whole host of extraordinary characters. Including Cian, a pop band pin-up who is enjoying all the trappings of fame.

Can Shelley keep her secret from the others as well as writing the story of the year? And most importantly can she keep her cool – and chastity – intact? And does she really want to?

Find out more at www.mischiefbooks.com

ISBN: 978-0-00747-971-9

GAME – JUSTINE ELYOT

The stakes are high, the game is on.

In this sequel to Justine Elyot's bestselling *On Demand*, Sophie discovers a whole new world of daring sexual exploits.

Sophie's sexual tastes have always been a bit on the wild side – something her boyfriend Lloyd has always loved about her.

But Sophie gives Lloyd every part of her body except her heart. To win all of her, Lloyd challenges Sophie to live out her secret fantasies.

As the game intensifies, she experiments with all kinds of kinks and fetishes in a bid to understand what she really wants. But Lloyd feature in her final decision? Or will the ultimate risk he takes drive her away from him?

Find out more at www.mischiefbooks.com

ISBN: 978-0-00-747775-3

POWER PLAY – CHARLOTTE STEIN

Now she's the boss, everything that once seemed forbidden is possible . . .

Meet Eleanor Harding, a woman who loves to be in control and who puts Anastasia Steele in the shade.

When Eleanor is promoted, she loses two very important things: the heated relationship she had with her boss, and control over her own desires.

She finds herself suddenly craving something very different – and office junior, Ben, seems like just the sort of man to fulfil her needs. He's willing to show her all of the things she's been missing – namely, what it's like to be the one in charge.

Now all Eleanor has to do is decide . . . is Ben calling the kinky shots, or is she?

Find out more at www.mischiefbooks.com

ISBN: 978-0-00-747769-2